The Bandamann Saga

Sigrun

Deilia Declares

Sigrun

The Bandamann Saga

Deidre Mapstone

Edited by Amelia Mapstone, Joshua Sweet
and Anne Chacchia

2015

Deilia Declares

Sigrun

The Bandamann Saga

Deidre Mapstone

Edited by Amelia Mapstone, Joshua Sweet
and Anne Chacchia

2015

For my family.

Thanks to my daughter, Amelia and my husband, William. This story would never have happened without you.

Thank you to my two boys, Morgan and Xander for being such great cheerleaders for me.

Thank you to my parents for letting me know anything I want to do is possible.

Sigrun

1

Sigrun Goes Live

The sun was setting on the village of Seal Harbor, Maine. Mixed into the bold, luscious colors of pink and orange sky, small, brighter lights popped on here and there, with more dark in between. There isn't much in the way of population here in Seal Harbor. On Mount Desert Island, there are villages and towns scattered around Acadia National Park. It was a cold, crisp night, even though summer had just begun. Being that far north kept things cool well into July.

As the sun dropped and dusk took hold, there was stirring in one of the brighter lights just on the edge of the village.

"C'mon, everybody! Take a look! I've just finished!"

Everyone rushed into the boys' room to see what Adrian had done.

"Ooh, I like the homepage," giggled Tillie.

Celebrating 35 years! It said on the front. There was a photograph of Sigrun, their family restaurant, looking its best. All of the faces were now lit with computer lighting, looking quite blue-green in tones, like they were underwater.

"Well, let's see it then. Show us what you've got," said Liam in his authoritative voice. Being the oldest son of four children, he was quite good at that. His light brown eyes became a funny, muddy color in the light and his dirty blonde hair went to brown. It had a careless look about it tonight. At work, Liam pulls it back neatly into a small pony tail, but afterward, it floats free and has a mind of its own. Much like the dichotomy of Liam himself.

A click or two later and all of the Lundgrens were into viewing their first website for Sigrun, their family owned and run restaurant.

Sigrun was a basic, family style restaurant. Right on the water, it was typical to the New England seaside. It was a two story building with the restaurant on the first floor and living quarters on the second floor. The entrance was located in the center front of the building, with large, picture windows on either side. There you could see patrons dining from morning 'til night. The faded, whitewashed siding led up to a group of smaller windows with their own little grey roof on the second story. It looked old and worn, but not run down. It was the most well-known restaurant in the area. Not only was it a hot spot for visitors during the tourist season, the locals were loyal to it year-round. The Lundgrens took care of and made repairs to Sigrun regularly. They worked 24/7 to keep their restaurant clean and in excellent condition. Here, being old did not mean it was time to get rid of it. There was pride among the Lundgrens, that gave the restaurant a level of comfort that was as close to being home as you could get, if not better. The food was simple, fresh and always the best. It was what kept them in business for over 35 years. That and the family that ran it: the Lundgrens.

Our History, was the heading on the next page of the website. It displayed an older picture of Sigrun, not looking much different, except for the faded coloring and boat styles in the background of the picture. It went on to describe how Sigrun had been a family business since the Lundgrens moved to town 35 years ago, how the owners, Heather and Cord Lundgren, once employed a few of the local kids to help them run the place, but now had kids of their own old enough to help them run the business. It had a list of the family with pictures to click on for a little description of each person.

Cord Lundgren --click-- *Owner and operator of Sigrun. Born and raised in Sweden, Cord came to the States when he* was 25 with Heather. They opened Sigrun and have been serving great food to the Cove ever since!

Heather Lundgren --click-- Co-owner of Sigrun with Cord, Heather came to the States with Cord and opened Sigrun. She has been helping on the inside and out since day one. Taking time off to have their children, she now works full time doing the books and mingling with the customers in only a way that she can.

Lyla Lundgren --click-- The oldest child in the Lundgren family, Lyla started working at Sigrun at 16. She took some years off to finish college and is now back to show us what she has learned!

Liam Lundgren --click-- The oldest son in the Lundgren family, Liam started working at Sigrun at 14, part time in the summers and on vacations. Finishing up his Associates degree in business at the end of this year, Liam is truly known for his talents in the kitchen and plans on putting them both to good use at Sigrun for a long time to come.

Tellulah Lundgren --click-- Finishing up her senior year this year, Tillie, as she is known to us around the restaurant, is learning the ropes here at Sigrun. We will be seeing much more of her around the restaurant in the years to come!

Adrian Lundgren --click-- The youngest of the Lundgren children, Adrian is in high school. He works at Sigrun as often as he can. We are sure we have yet to see the fullest potential in this Lundgren!

"Gee, we all sound so..."

"So weird?" Tillie chimed in, interrupting Lyla's comment.

"What do you mean, 'weird?'" asked Adrian back to Tillie. His porcelain white skin glowed an eerie green in the computer's glow and made him look a little sickly. His hazel eyes sparkled in the green hue, however and let his sister know he was ready to defend his creation.

"I mean, we all sound so stoic, like we're not real. We're robots working for this institution that is Sigrun." She said "Sigrun" like it was something scary.

"Well, I think it's really very good," responded Heather as she looked at Adrian with a mother's love.

"Yeah, son, really great! I sound so important. I love it." Cord said, chuckling and everyone else in the room responded with agreeing laughter. He was usually the one to persuade his family. Not only was he loud and boisterous when he spoke, his large size, but teddy bear appearance, made it nearly impossible to disagree with him. His face was covered in rusty scruff most of the time and his wavy blonde hair swooped this way and that. A jovial man, Cord Lundgren's light green eyes mimicked the ocean on a stormy summer day. His smile lit up a room and his personality put everyone at ease. He was easy going, but firm when he needed to be. He was the perfect head of both his restaurant and his family.

"Well, there's more too. Look, I put Anna, Danny and Marcus in here as well." Everyone peered down for a moment, reading quickly.

"So you did." said Cord, patting Adrian on the shoulder.

"Anna's going to love that picture, Ade," said Liam sniggering.

"I like it, actually," said Tillie. "Anna never likes any pictures of herself anyway."

"Let's see what the next page is," Liam said to Adrian.

Another click and they were looking at menus and schedules of specials and contact information. There were pictures of Seal Cove, the marina and some popular menu items. It was a simple, practical website, which was exactly what they were all looking for to best describe Sigrun.

"We'll see what this does for business," said Heather as she got up and headed back out to the kitchen. "I'm curious to know how many people around here actually pay attention to the internet." She smiled and turned out of the boys' room.

Claiming she was 57, Heather didn't look a day over 25. Her skin was smooth, not sun-kissed like her daughters', but porcelain with the blush of a new bride on her cheek. Her deep blue eyes were magical things, like the color of the sea at sundown. They tended to make people stop speaking when they took notice of them. Heather used this often to her advantage to quietly communicate with others.

"I bet most of them don't even know what a DSL connection is." Adrian smiled to himself feeling superior for a moment, a rarity in his life, so he savored it.

The family cleared out of the boys' room and went back to their usual business of getting ready for bed. The Lundgrens didn't just own the restaurant, they also lived there. Their living space was above the restaurant. They liked it because they had the best of both work and home in one place.

It was a studio style living area with the kitchen open to the living room. There were three smaller bedrooms, two on one side of the common area and one small master suite on the other side. Lyla and Tillie shared one bedroom and the boys the other. Over the years they'd learned to work out the kinks of limited space, mostly like how to keep the boys and their junk out of the girls' space. So everyone learned to keep track of their things and help others keep track of theirs. (The benefit of most meals coming from downstairs helped tremendously. Although Heather insisted on at least one dinner a week "at home". She said she had to "keep track of her family somehow.")

The next morning the town was abuzz. Cell phones and Blackberries were seen everywhere. You could hear the flips and clicks at nearly every table. The phone at the restaurant rang off the hook. There were several phone calls just in the morning alone.

"I've never noticed all this technology around here before," exclaimed Heather, surprised. "Funny..." she trailed off into her thoughts and went into the office.

"Of course not, Mom," Lyla replied, following her into the office. "Why would you notice that? The woman who still thinks it's risky having three computers in the house. Even though one is in the office!" She smiled at her mom and her mom smiled back. They both sat down at the desk. The two ladies continued to talk quietly, which meant only one thing: business.

If there was one thing Lyla excelled at, it was business. Not only did she go to college for it, she finished in three years instead of four. She took the most responsibility around the restaurant. Not because she was the oldest, but because it was just the type of person she was. She waited tables, she helped her mom with the books, even got them up to date with the computer. She always gave a hand in the kitchen if she could, mostly with criticism on taste and presentation. If looks could be deceiving, then she was the perfect example.

The two Lundgren sisters, actually, were like a breath of fresh air. When they walked into the room, they stood out with their blonde, sun-drenched curls. Lyla's light green eyes were always warm and friendly, much like her father's. Customers responded to the two girls with smiles all the time. Even the locals, known for their hermit crab ways, couldn't help but smile when Lyla and Tillie were working the tables. The two girls often worked the tables together, as the room was big enough for two waitresses, mostly during meal rush times. There was always something comfortable in the air when Tillie and Lyla worked the floor. They had such harmony and sync about them that it put people at ease in the room.

It was quite the opposite back in the kitchen, however. Liam was head chef, with Cord and Anna helping out during the rushes. Adrian would also put together a meal or two when he could. It was coordinated, but there was much more action going on in the kitchen than on the floor. The grill sizzling, the sound of chopping, stirring and plates hitting the counter. These were the background noises, the atmosphere of Sigrun.

The phone rang. Again. "Hello, Sigrun," Adrian answered. You could hear his smile as much as you could see it. "Hello? *Hello*? Humph. No answer," Adrian said as he looked at the phone as it went away from his ear and onto the hook. He seemed kind of dazed by it.

"Must be our daily call from no one," answered Liam, who continued to chop and prep food.

"Gee, I figured with all the business and calls we're getting this morning, we wouldn't bother getting *that* one," Adrian replied. He went out the kitchen door to bring in some fresh produce for the day.

This was the busy season. All the Lundgrens were on hand every day to help out in Sigrun. Adrian got the website up in time for Memorial Day weekend. This, being the unofficial start to summer, was the perfect time to get a site going for the tourist season. It was Adrian's suggestion, so he was the one who got to design the site. He was also the one who had the most computer knowledge and the time to do it. It was a proud day for Adrian. Being the youngest of so many talented siblings, Adrian had learned to take these moments in and enjoy them to the fullest.

"Ahhhh...listen to all that marvelous clicking!" he exclaimed as he came into the lunch crowded dining room. Some of the customers looked at him like he was an alien, but most just laughed or smiled, knowing Adrian.

"Well, you've done it. How does it feel to be so popular?" Liam asked as Adrian joined him back in the kitchen.

"Well bro, I'll let you know at the end of the day, when I get a tally on the numbers," Adrian replied with a huge grin on his face. "We've had almost three hundred hits already and it's not even noon." He went out the back door and brought in one last crate of fresh produce.

"I can hardly wait," Liam said quietly, dripping with sarcasm. He wanted to let his little brother live in the moment and enjoy it, but being the big brother at the same time, he didn't want him to enjoy it too much.

"You'll see," was all Adrian said in reply. He went to wash some lettuce at the sink.

"Leave him alone, Liam," said Anna sharply as she swatted at his large bicep. She was known for not mincing her words and never kept to herself. Anna was a small woman, just reaching five feet tall. Her hair was salt and pepper gray and was always coiffed nicely, albeit a tad old fashioned. Her face had many lines, indicating that she once loved to be tan. The lines gave her a friendly, grandmotherly look and her dark brown eyes lit up when she smiled. Liam shot her a grin and kept working.

Sigrun was abuzz. Both in lunchtime rush and in the new website. All throughout the afternoon, friends of Adrian's kept coming in and making comments.

"Hey, Ade! Nice site! I didn't even know you had an older sister!"

"Yo! Site is tight!"

"Adrian! Nice work! Can you do one of those for me?"

The word of Adrian's latest endeavor was all around the town by dinnertime. Even the tourists were making inquiries about Sigrun and some straggled in early for dinner. Most all positive, these comments made Adrian's head even bigger. By the end of the dinner rush he was like a parade balloon, he was floating so high. This boost was really good for Adrian. This website was just what he needed to feel like a contributing member of the business side of the family and not just a bus boy.

In the weeks that followed, the website proved to be the success they hoped for. Meal times were busier than usual, the restaurant overflowed, so the place was crowded most of the day. Adrian felt so good that even Liam's chiding couldn't bring him down. Every day you could see his gleaming smile from the kitchen. "When is that kid gonna come back from space?" Liam stood at the counter, chopping at a faster pace.

"Oh let him have his fun, it's adorable," replied Anna with a grin to Adrian. She really loved the Lundgrens and their children. Anna was a grandmother herself, but all of her children lived far from her now. She rarely got to see her family except for holidays and special occasions. Because she

14

was Italian, this left her looking for a family she could "adopt," one she could see every day. She found that when she found Sigrun. She'd worked there for over 20 years now and was more a member of the family than an employee.

Liam just turned his concentration back to the kitchen, as usual. Anna went out to the floor and squeezed past some customers to Tillie. "I'm gonna miss you soooooo much, Tillie! Who's gonna help me out here while you're gone?"

"Oh Anna, don't worry. Everyone said they would help cover for me, you know that." Tillie replied while she sat some people down at a booth. She flashed her gorgeous smile at Anna, then continued to talk to her new customers.

"Yes, don't worry, Anna, we'll all be here to cover. Now that Tillie is turning eighteen, she can do whatever she wants." Lyla said coyly to Anna as she passed with a tray.

"Oh," Anna exclaimed. "So, you think I just like Tillie for her 'work' help here, do you? Shows how much you know." Anna threw up an arm in her famous gesture of giving up and went back to work. The girls looked across the room at each other and couldn't help but smile.

2

Stupid Sunscreen

Tillie was about to take her first vacation ever. A *real* vacation. This was the first time she was leaving without her family tagging along. Even though they were very busy with summer starting and needed Tillie to help out, plans were made months ago. Tillie was turning eighteen and this was how she chose to celebrate. Everyone promised to work extra time to cover for Tillie.

Going away with her best friend Susan, Tillie was not only extremely grateful, she was uncontrollably excited. They'd be gone a whole ten days. She was a bit nervous, going to stay with Susan's at Susan's grandparents' house. She had not met them yet, but Susan's whole family was really nice to Tillie and they all got along, so she knew that meeting the grandparents should also be smooth sailing. Her favorite thought about the trip was leaving Maine. Not because she hated it or anything, but simply because she'd never been out of it before. They were going to New York to visit Canandaigua Lake in the Finger Lakes region. Even though it wasn't extremely far, she couldn't help feel a new adventure on the horizon.

She was very curious about what Finger Lakes were and what kind of name Canandaigua was, so she searched on the internet for them to see if she could find pictures or information. After a bit of searching, she found pictures on a

Finger Lakes website. The lakes were simply beautiful. She had no idea there were so many. They looked so tiny on a map, but the actual pictures of them put the map to shame. Water always excited Tillie anyway, she was fascinated with the fact that there were fresh water lakes in Upstate New York and she was going to get to stay near one. Fresh water. This simple detail was exciting to Tillie growing up near salt water all her life.

It turned out that Canandaigua Lake was one of the larger of the lakes. The word Canandaigua came from Seneca Native Americans and meant the Chosen Spot. Tillie thought that was beautiful. She was more eager than ever to see it in person.

After a long, uneventful drive, they arrived in New York. Tillie found herself unable to relax, too busy looking out at all the scenery, even if it was on the highway, with mostly trees. Susan's grandparents' home was not directly on the lake, but still had a beautiful distant view from the hillside it nestled into. A simple, yet elegant home, their landscaping was immaculate. Tillie was impressed with the different flower beds and the acres of cleanly mowed lawn. The home had gray-brown wooden shingles and white trimmed windows. Tillie felt at home right away, she thought it looked very much like an east coast cottage, only larger.

June third, a beautiful, sunny and not too warm day.

"Happy birthday, Tillie! We're going out to the lake today." Susan screeched so loud Tillie's eyes widened. They'd been hanging out mostly in one of the guest bedrooms since their arrival yesterday. Tillie sat up on the bed, fully attentive now and left her laptop suddenly abandoned. Susan's straight, blond hair was even brighter than Tillie's. Her green eyes always sparkled in the sunlight. She was tall and built like a ballerina. Tillie always thought Susan should model, but she wasn't interested.

"Oh! That should be some good sun and fun," Tillie said excitedly. Tillie loved the outdoors. She loved the sun. Above all, she loved water. All of those things in combination, to her were sheer bliss. Adding her birthday into the mix was pure bonus.

"So, let's make sure we have our suits, towels and sunscreen," Susan said. She grabbed a bag from her closet and tossed it toward Tillie on the bed. Then she grabbed another, larger, fancier bag for herself.

"Sunscreen?" Tillie asked almost childlike. "Oh, I don't really use sunscreen. I don't ever burn."

"Oh don't be daft, Till, everyone has to use sunscreen, especially out on the water. The lake amplifies the sun like a thousand times. Don't worry, you'll still get color, you just won't get severely burned." Susan laughed because she thought this was common knowledge for everyone she knew who grew up near a body of water.

"Well, ok, if you say so," Tillie replied and hoped she sounded convincing. She had no real intention of using sunscreen. She never seemed to have to touch the stuff. She just never burned. Really. She decided she would just make it seem as though she used it and hope no one noticed.

The girls piled their bags and other lake gear into the car. Then they climbed to the way back seats to make room for everyone else. Susan had a big family. She had two other siblings, but it was the cousins who created such a large flock. There were so many, Tillie could hardly keep up with who was who. She had cousins on her mom's side and cousins on her dad's. There were first cousins, second cousins and some removed; whatever that meant. There were cousins much older, all the way down to babies. It was all so confusing, Tillie was thankful she could just put them all into one "cousin" category.

Today the cousins weren't all present, but there were a few cars' worth. So, every car had every seat taken by somebody. The girls were in the way back of Susan's parents' minivan with Susan's little sister Jill. Jill adored Susan and any of her friends, because if they were friends with her sister, then they must be cool. Of course, this frequently made Tillie feel uncomfortable. As the third child in a family of four, Tillie rarely had anyone look up to her adoringly. But for the ride today, Tillie found herself smack dab next to Jill and felt the staring, much to Tillie's discomfort. Thankfully, Tillie thought, the ride wasn't going to be long.

"Over the river and through the woods," Susan's mom exclaimed as she got into the driver's seat and shut her door. The younger kids in the middle row clapped and smiles were broad all around. Tillie smiled politely, but felt awkward, like the outsider. She knew Susan's family well enough, but with the cousins around, she simply felt outnumbered and a little shy. She was used to a more nuclear family. Just herself, her parents and her siblings. She wondered how all of these people got along and got through a normal day. *I mean, just to feed them must be like a day at Sigrun,* she thought to herself as her thoughts drifted away and they pulled out of the driveway. A tiny hint of a smile came across her face in a dreamy fashion.

Even though the house had a view of the lake, once they got onto the road, the view was lost. A few minutes passed and Tillie noticed the trees and saw the hills a short way away. She knew that it was Canandaigua Lake. Was it the smell in the air that gave it away? Was it the lay of the land? Was it the sound of certain birds that she knew were always by water? Whether sight or sound, she never knew. But she always knew where the water was. She stayed quiet and wondered if that's how everyone was about water.

The multiple conversations in the car were chaotic. Tillie caught most of them, but it was hard to keep up with just one. But one thing was tied throughout all of them: the lake. She felt the butterflies make themselves known in her stomach. She knew them well and she liked them. This meant something new and exciting was going to happen and Tillie loved the new and exciting. She drifted to the leaves of the trees overhead. There were many, it was definitely woodsy. The car took a turn and a decline at the same time, rocking everyone left then right suddenly. This shook Tillie out of the woodsy canopy and she caught the words, "I'm gonna really do it this time." from one of the cousins in front of her.

Tillie wished she'd heard what it was he was planning on really doing, although she knew she'd find out, because she was sure it was something today, at the lake. She just hoped it had something to do with just himself and didn't involve taking anyone down with him. "Humph," Tillie muttered to herself for caring at all. The things you could involve yourself with when you were in close proximity to others for any length of time. *Silly*, she thought.

Then she saw it. The tent of trees above parted like a curtain to a stage. Tillie turned her head straight ahead and suddenly felt like she was home. Not home as in back in Maine, back at Sigrun. *Home*. Where she belonged. Always. The trees parted more still and the blue that was just a small triangle at first rose up like a great performance. Like a great, blue-green, majestic creation, unlike any other. And just when Tillie thought the water might actually do something marvelous, the car made a right turn and grabbed her attention away for just a moment. Back to reality. Until she took a deep breath through her nose. The smell of the lake filled her lungs up with such a passion and clarity, not completely unlike the ocean, but somehow a little different. She wondered if it was the fresh water rather than salt water that made this difference.

Tillie loved this feeling. This feeling that this was what it was all about. This was life. This was the Earth. This was everything. She was a part of it and she knew it. She looked past Susan out the window and took a deep breath of lake air. It was blue, well, mostly blue, with a little green, just a tint. The hills were lively green, deep and full of trees. She now saw the cottages on the edge and on both sides of the water. To be a part of something so majestic and beautiful was always such a thrill to her. It made her feel like she had a part in this world and was meant to be right here, right now.

"All set?" Susan asked, looking at Tillie like she was fragile.

"Uh...what?" Tillie blinked and focused onto Susan. "Oh. Are we here already?"

"Yep. C'mon silly, let's get going."

Tillie hadn't even realized the van had stopped, was already half emptied out and Susan was waiting for Tillie to move. She felt stupid. She hated when her imagination and feelings got the better of her in front of other people. She knew she wasn't stupid, but felt like from another's point of view, sometimes her behavior must have looked that way.

Tillie and Susan quickly gathered their things from the back of the van and also grabbed a cooler each, as there were lots of extras to help with. They made their way slowly toward the lakeside, down a gravel path, through some tall, shady trees.

Tillie followed Susan to the lake, the tall trees teasing and blocking the full lake view. Her stomach felt like butterflies rising and falling, mimicking the small boat waves that lapped at the shore. Even though they were small, Tillie heard them hit land and in her head, felt them as though she were the land. It felt good on her arms, the lapping of the fresh water. She blinked and again, came out of her daze. What was with her today? It's not like she'd never seen a lake before, or water. For heaven's sake, she lived on the ocean! *Get a grip girl*, she thought to herself. The trees came to an end and the girls arrived onto the patio area.

"Here's where we put our stuff," Susan motioned as she set down the cooler and hung her bag on a hook. She was inside an opened shelter. Tillie saw the shelter for the first time, she'd been so enthralled with the water. It was a glorious patio, really, with the instant and constant shade of the cover, as well as room outside for sunning. It was paved with large, flat stones colored grey, a light brick red and an almost sky blue. There was plenty of seating both inside and outside the shelter. It almost looked like a resort, but smaller scale. Tillie felt welcome and comfortable all at once. She went in and hung her things and freed her hands.

"This is really quite wonderful here," Tillie said dreamingly and turned back to the water like it was drawing her into its magic.

"Thanks. Yeah, we really love it here. It's so homey and naturey, don't ya think?" Susan tilted her head really campy, looked at Tillie and then felt silly for being so trite when she saw the look on Tillie's face.

"No, I mean, it's really wonderful." Tillie didn't notice Susan trying to be cute and silly, walked toward the water, toward the dock and looked around with the awe and wonder of a child. She looked at everything like it was new to her. Like the whole world just suddenly became some new place she'd never been to before.

There was a wall at the shore, going down into the water. That's where the dock started. There were those little waves Tillie felt were hitting her own arms, cool and refreshing to her. She took her first step onto the dock. She could have sworn she felt a little electricity here. A little zing into her lower legs. *Humph, that's weird*, she thought. *My imagination is really getting carried away in this place today.* She looked out onto the water and wondered just how fast she could get into it. As fast as the thought crossed her mind, there was a bump to her right arm that knocked her aside, as three of Susan's cousins dashed down the dock and right into the water. *Splash, splash, splash!*

"Idiots!" Susan called after the boys as she rubbed sunscreen onto her arms. "Here, Till, take some of this and put in on my shoulders and back please?" She handed Tillie the lotion. "Then I can put some on you."

"Umm, thanks, but I prefer to do it myself. I can reach all the spots, don't worry," she smiled convincingly to Susan as she looked back at Tillie in question. "Actually, do you guys have a bathroom out here? I forgot to, well, you know, go before we left the house and I didn't even think about it being here all day."

"Oh yes, there's one in the back of the patio. You see the door on the right side of the shelter? Yes, that one. That's the bathroom. You don't think we all just come out here for the day and use the lake, do you?" Susan laughed and finished rubbing sunscreen onto her face.

"Well, good, that's a relief," Tillie laughed back. It was a relief, literally. This thought made her laugh a little harder than she meant to. "I'll just take the sunscreen and do it in the bathroom, 'kay?"

"Suit yourself," Susan shrugged, turned and walked to the end of the dock. "See you in the water, babe." She giggled and skipped to the end of the dock, where she did a pirouette right off and into the water.

Tillie laughed and shook her head. Although she admired Susan bringing her dance techniques to the water, she couldn't help but laugh at the way Susan looked like she was almost a little kid again. She turned away from the lake and made her way to the bathroom, with the bottle of sunscreen in hand, which felt like a foreign object.

Once inside and the door locked, Tillie's smile vanished immediately. "Ahh!" She shook her hands like she burned them on something and dropped the sunscreen on the floor. She got to the sink as fast as she could, turned on the cold water and thrust her hands into the cool flow. She grabbed the soap on the side of the sink and started to scrub her hands quickly. But it wasn't fast enough. It hurt and hurt bad. *Stupid sunscreens! Why do they always do this to me?* The soap began to work, but she saw the red patches start to form all over her hands. *Damn! I thought I could handle it for just a minute. I mean, how long did I actually touch it?* It wasn't that long, but her sensitivity to it was getting worse as she got older. *What's going to be my excuse for this?* She had to come up with something and quick. *I won't be able to stay in the bathroom all day. Besides, I have to get into that lake, I just know it.* She let her hands sit in the cool water a bit longer, it felt so good. She closed her eyes and breathed deep, to calm herself and the air that filled her lungs made her eyes open wide. She smiled, turned the water off and finished changing into her suit.

Luckily, by the time she got out of the bathroom, she saw that most everyone was either in the water or on their way in. There was a short ladder going down the wall in the shallow side that the adults used most of the time. A lot of the kids came up the ladder at the end of the dock and jumped back into the water.

Her hands were red and only slightly throbbing now. The water cooled them nicely, but Tillie was still worried that someone would ask about them. She held her towel on them like a rabbit fur muff in the winter and carried it out onto the dock with her. She looked for a place to put her towel so she could jump in quickly. Even though the throbbing was better than when she was in the bathroom, being wrapped in the towel wasn't helping. Usually, in the past when this happened, keeping her hands covered was worse. She needed the fresh air and sun on them and of course, the water helped cool them. She was startled by the boat in the lift on the right side of the dock. *Phew! There is where my towel will go, practically as I jump in,* she thought as she approached it.

The end of the dock was already all wet from all the jumping from it. Tillie's feet touched the cool water and her heart jumped and started to dance. A smile crept on her face. She checked the end of the dock and the water just below to make sure it was clear and threw her towel into the boat. It was as if time stood still. It was as if no one was there but her. As if in slow motion, Tillie ran to the end of the dock and dove into the cool bliss.

3

Zigzag

The cool rush of water from the tip of her hands to the ends of her toes felt like heaven. Not just because it was so hot in the air, but this was where Tillie felt she belonged. Being in water always felt like perfection on Earth to her. She glided through the water, felt how every inch of her body was being cooled and the different temperatures inside her, evened out. She pulled her arms down to her side and pushing air out from her nose, tipped her head upward and broke the water's surface.

"C'mon, slowpoke!" Susan shouted out about ten yards. The water was deep here, over everyone's head. Tillie could barely see the bottom from the end of the dock and now, just a little out from it, couldn't see it at all.

Tillie saw Susan near a raft floating in the water. The water. It cooled parts of her that were hot from the weather. It felt so good. She just wanted to be still for a moment and enjoy it. She felt the kids behind her jumping in off the dock. The older cousins were already on and around the raft. Everything looked so perfect to Tillie. She was so happy she almost forgot about her hands. The perfect temperature of the water made them feel quite good. It occurred to her that she could just stay in the water for a while and no one would notice them. She grinned as her hands broke the surface. She looked at them. Her face went from smiling to puzzled and then relieved almost all at once. Her hands looked normal again. There wasn't an ounce of red to be seen. The throbbing felt more like a soft tingle now and it was dwindling. *Must've been how this water was colder than in the bathroom*, she thought. Anyway, she was relieved. Now she wouldn't have a care in the world. Today was lake day.

She swam out to the raft. Swimming felt good, it had been a while since she could just enjoy some carefree time away from Sigrun. She did not take it for granted. Her breathing was steadied by the water. It always seemed to be short on land, but would lengthen out and was strong and purposeful here. She made it to the raft in no time.

"Sorry I took so long. Had to get to all those hard-to-reach areas with the sunscreen." Tillie tilted her head to make light of the situation.

"I told you I'd help you, silly," Susan replied as she grabbed the ladder and stepped up onto the raft.

"I know. I'm just used to doing it myself."

Tillie grabbed the ladder next and hopped on board.

"Happy birthday, to you! Happy birthday, to you! Happy birthday, dear Tillie. Happy birthday, to you!" The raft sang in unison, then clapped. Tillie blushed.

Just then, two cousins went flying off the raft, sending it rocking back and forth. Some of the girls screamed and giggled, held on, or sat down so they wouldn't fall off. Tillie smiled, sat down and felt the warmth of the sun touching the water on her cooled skin. It was a wonderful combination of elements. She felt so one with the Earth.

The rest of the afternoon went on much in this way. People swam back and forth from the dock to the raft. The adults had floating toys and rafts that they hung out on and talked in the water. Susan's Uncle Roy got the boat out and took the younger dock jumpers skiing and tubing. They would zing by every few minutes hollering and whooping, bringing in boat waves that everyone seemed to just float right over. The time flew by. Tillie thought it was funny how perfection in the day was so still and perfect, then suddenly, it was over, as if time went slower and faster at the same time. So magical.

The boat came by for another pass. There was a shrieking scream and a bigger splash than they had seen yet. Tillie was in the water, having just dove off the raft and looked over to the boat. It pulled the tube but no one was on it. The boat immediately slowed and turned around. Someone must have fallen off. This wasn't the first time it happened. They liked to go back and forth to hit their own waves and rock the tubers. The waves surrounded the boat like they were going to attack it. Uncle Roy stopped the boat and looked into the water.

The other people in the boat started shouting, "Tim! Tim!" They looked over the edges of the boat and tried to see through the waves.

Tillie glanced back toward the dock. The adults that were on shore came out onto the dock, with their hands over their foreheads, to shield the sun. The ones that were still in the water started paddling toward the boat.

Tillie knew this was serious trouble. She caught Susan's eye and Susan looked horrified. She was on the raft and looked helpless for a moment. She stood up and dove in toward the boat.

Tillie didn't waste another second. She pulled herself under the water and swam hard. She could always swim better under the water than on top of it. She came up for a breath and found herself in the lead of the crowd now headed to the boat. Everyone from the boat except one of the older cousins, who stayed to spot, jumped into the water as well. Tillie went back under and stroked double-time. She felt the water rush past her furious strokes and kicks. She came up again, even more ahead of the rushing crowd, only a few strokes away from the boat.

"He's here somewhere! He's gotta be!" The cousin in the boat shouted and looked down over all the edges of the boat and tried to direct those who were in the water.

Everyone bobbed up and down and in and out of the water in a most crazy-looking fashion. The boat waves finally dwindled and the search took on a more determined tone.

Tillie took a quick scan of where everyone was looking. She felt she should scan where they weren't, just in case they were wrong about the location.

"TIMOTHY! TIM!" Tillie heard just as she submerged her head to search.

She opened her eyes in the water. All afternoon and she hadn't done that yet, so she didn't know if she'd be able to see anything under water. The water was fairly clear, so she was happy she saw her hands ahead of her as she stroked in the water. But there was nothing else to actually see, just water. So much water. What was sheer bliss two minutes ago was now the terrifying enemy. Stroke after stroke, Tillie looked and looked on all sides of her. Nothing. She saw nothing. Her face broke the surface and she took a huge breath of air. She saw that she'd gone almost ten yards from the boat search area. Maybe she went too far. She overestimated her swimming again. She turned around immediately and headed toward the boat. This time she tried a zigzag pattern back hoping to cover more area. She tried to keep better track of where she was in the water. Time was running short. Under the water she went, again.

This time she took about a stroke-and-a-half downward. She felt that if she went deeper she may be able to see better at the bottom. She frantically tried to remember what Tim was wearing. *Which cousin was he?* She thought as she stroked and then turned left to start her zigzag pattern. *Tim, Tim, Tim...so many cousins.* She remembered everyone that wasn't on the boat. Then quickly scanned her memory of who was on the boat. *Tim! He was the one who in the car said, "I'm gonna really do it this time!"*

Oh, God! What did he really do this time? Tillie's eyes opened wider and she broke the surface. Her control was better this time, she was halfway back to the boat. She looked over and saw everyone in full panic. Uncle Roy dove from the boat and went deep into the water. The older kids were doing the same and the younger kids headed back to shore. The other adults now scanned the water as well, creating a growing perimeter around the boat. Luckily it wasn't a windy day, so the boat wasn't drifting much from its original spot. Tillie dove down again.

This time, Tillie closed her eyes. She wasn't sure why, but she just had an overwhelming feeling to close her eyes. Three full strokes downward this time she swam, pulling strong but slower, more deliberately. She took quick note of how quiet and peaceful it was down under the water, when there was such chaos and panic above. This quiet gave her a clarity. It made sense down here. Like she could stay here and figure out where Tim was. She turned to the left.

Wasn't he wearing a life jacket? Tillie thought to herself. Stroke. Eyes closed.

How could he sink with a life jacket? Stroke. Eyes Closed.

Uncle Roy wouldn't let him go without one. Stroke. Eyes closed.

Tim, Tim...where are you? Stroke. Zig right.

Suddenly - *bump* - Tillie's face smushed into something. She scrunched up her arms and legs in front of her in defense. She had no idea what she hit, but it wasn't a rock, because it wasn't that hard. Eyes opened. *Tim. Oh my God! Tim.* Her underwater thoughts immediately relaxed her defensive stance and she grabbed Tim quickly. She had no idea how far down they were. It wasn't a matter of her having enough air; it was Tim she was worried about. He was limp in her arms and she was scared. *Stroke. Kick. Stroke. Kick. Hard. Hard. Harder!*

Finally, they broke the surface. Tillie held Tim's head up out of the water and brought him toward the boat. They weren't that far off, really, perhaps five or so yards. Everyone was doing the right thing in where they looked. They just hadn't gone deep enough. Tillie had been very deep. It took her more than five strokes to reach the surface with Tim.

"I'VE GOT HIM!" She yelled as loud as she could muster while still swimming toward the boat.

Uncle Roy was the closest, just having re-emerged from under water. "Roy! I've got Tim!" she shouted over to him, gasping for air.

Roy did not hesitate and reached Tillie in about a second and a half. "Oh, God! Oh, God! Tillie! Thank you! Thank you!" He went to take Tim from Tillie.

"No! I've got him. Get to the boat. You can take him into it when I get over there!" *Stroke. Kick.*

Roy swam with all his might to the boat. He climbed up the back and had arms ready to grab Tim as soon as Tillie reached him. Up Tim came like a day's catch in a fisherman's net, onto the boat floor. Roy immediately started CPR.

"Where's his jacket?" he demanded to know in between breaths and counting. He had a wild look about him and no one crowded him.

Everyone was still in the water, suddenly still and floating like buoys around the boat. The boat spotter was in the boat with Roy and Tim. He looked like he was burning up in his own skin. Like he should jump in the water any second to put it out. Then Tillie remembered that Tim was the boat spotter's little brother. As she floated there, she knew she had to get into the boat, for him. She slowly glided from the side to the back of the boat. As gently as she could, Tille got into the boat. Moving slowly to minimize her dripping water and not to disturb Roy's work, she moved over to his brother. *Crap. What's his name again?* she thought frantically. She couldn't remember. She went through the family list of names like a computer trying to decode a top secret file. *Aaron! Finally got it, thank goodness!*

"Aaron," she said quietly as she approached him. She put her hand on his shoulder.

Roy was counting and pumping on poor Tim's heart. Aaron jumped and looked at her as though she had just tried to kill him. Then, a second later, he just started to shake. He collapsed into her arms and wept. She was taken back a bit by this, as she didn't really know him that well, but she knew that didn't matter now.

Roy breathed into Tim's mouth. Tillie held Aaron, quietly, gently, still. Roy counted and pumped again.

"CALL 911! HE'S BREATHING!" Roy shouted as loud as he could to anyone that would hear.

"What? Tim? Tim! Can you hear me, bud?" Aaron broke free of Tillie, almost as if the situation never happened and collapsed to his knees at Tim's side. Tim coughed and sputtered out water. Breathing. You could hear the collective sigh of relief all around them.

"Stay with him, Aaron," Roy said and jumped up into the driver's seat. He sat on the back of the seat, started the boat and got it to the lift in what seemed like no time. There at the dock the other adults skittered about, trying to find the best place to be helpful. A couple of them caught the boat and stopped it in place. Another started the lift and it rose enough out of the water to be steady. Tillie went to the bow of the boat to stay out of the way, as she wasn't sure what was needed. Would they move him or just wait for help to arrive? She'd never seen anything like this in her life before. She hoped it would also be the last time.

Aaron was talking to Tim on the floor. Tim kept trying to sit up, but Aaron would just put him back down.

"I can sit up if I want to," said Tim trying to shove his brother's arm off himself with no real strength.

"Nah, bud, you gotta wait here. Please, Tim. Just stay here with me. Doctors are coming. They're coming." Aaron glanced around Tim, as if he were looking for treasures in a video game or something. He was still shaky and tried to busy himself to shake off the excess adrenaline.

Tillie suddenly felt herself in his shoes. Felt fully what it would be like taking care of Adrian if he had just almost drowned. Tears started to well up in her eyes. Drops fell free like a rainstorm starting. She just sat there silently, tears falling. She felt so helpless and full of dread. The scene in front of her seemed far away. Her sadness took over and made time stand still. Stand still but moving fast. Lake time.

Aaron's mother ran down the dock. "The paramedics are here! Get off the dock everyone!" She cleared the children off the dock to the shore. She got to the boat and jumped in wildly. "Timothy, baby! My baby!" She knelt down, grabbed Tim up into her arms and cried. Aaron hugged them both. Suddenly he was the calm one, there for his mother and brother.

"He's good, Mom. He's alright. He's going to be all right." He stroked the back of his mom's head.

"I *am* fine mom. Jeez!" Tim said between kisses all over his face.

"Oh, my sweetheart! What happened? What went wrong out there?" She backed off him and checked him much like Aaron had been doing just before.

"I dunno, Mom. I was in the tube," Tim answered. He coughed and both his mom and brother stiffened for a moment. "Then next thing I knew, I was hitting the water. I don't remember anything else."

"Oh sweetie, don't worry about it now. You're safe. You're wonderful. Thanks to..." she looked up toward Tillie. "Tillie, right?" She looked at her like a child unsure about her answer to the teacher in class.

"Umm," Tillie quickly brushed the tears from her cheeks and came out of her personal feelings, enough to answer, "Yes. Tillie. I'm Tillie." She sniffed.

The woman looked down at her son again. "Tillie saved your life, Tim," she said quietly and a bit full of awe.

At that moment, the paramedics got to the dock with a cot and everyone cleared the way for them. They went into their routine most professionally, as Roy gave them the rundown of what happened and tried to answer their questions. They hovered over Tim like magicians over their assistant in a magic trick. There was lots of equipment whipped out, a stethoscope, an oxygen mask, a blood pressure band and then some other things Tillie didn't recognize. All moving so fast around Tim, they looked as if they were floating in air.

"His blood pressure is a bit low," one said to another, as the other attended the oxygen mask.

Things were a bit of a blur after that. Everything happened as if watching a movie. Tillie could hear things, random things about the event.

"Where was his lifejacket?"

"Who found him?"

"What time did this happen?"

"Tillie. Tillie found him."

Tillie suddenly felt lightheaded. She tripped and almost fell over walking to the back of the boat. "Whoa there, Tillie," Aaron said as he grabbed her arm and helped her off the boat.

Being on the dock felt foreign. Tillie didn't know how long they were in the boat, but it was apparently long enough to get sea legs and the dock felt unsteady even though it was stable. She slowly made her way to land, in a very dreamlike state.

Tillie made it to the first lounge chair on the patio and sat down, looking wilted. She sat onto the lounger like she was going to sun herself and fell down onto it. She was exhausted and this was the first time she felt it fully.

"Here. Drink this." Aaron handed her a cold, frosty bottle of water. "You need to have some fluids. We were out there a long time." Tillie took the opened bottle and felt the cold in her hand.

"Thank you," she replied meekly as she gazed up to Aaron. He sat down next to her at the foot of the lounger. She sipped the cold water and felt it trickle down her throat past her lungs, into her stomach. She didn't realize how warm she had gotten out on the water.

"No. Really, Tillie. Thank *you*. *Thank you*. Thank you. You saved Tim. You did, you saved his life. There are no words my family and I could ever express to you about how grateful we are." The ambulance drove off down the road, with Tim and Uncle Roy in the back.

"Umm." Tillie sat up a bit more, feeling self-conscious. "You're welcome. Really, Aaron. I was doing no more than everyone else out in that water today. I just happened to be in the right place." She sipped more of her water. It felt good and gave her a little pep.

"Well, that may be, Tillie, but the fact is that it was you who did it. We'll never be able to thank you enough. You'll be our hero for life."

He held up his own bottle of water in a cheers gesture. Tillie met his bottle with hers and they both sipped. A car beeped from the driveway.

Aaron's mom shouted, "C'mon sweetheart, we've gotta get going! I don't want Tim to have to wait for us at the hospital! Thank you so much, Tillie! I am forever grateful to you!" She waved and held her arm up in triumph.

"Well, again Tillie, we'll never forget this day. And you." Aaron leaned in and hugged Tillie. At first it felt awkward, hugging this boy whom she hardly knew. But there was something comfortable about it. Something nice and sincere. She smiled as they pulled away from each other and Aaron stood up.

"You make sure you come back here often and see us, okay?" Aaron gave a look to reinforce what he was saying, to let Tillie know that he wasn't just saying that to be polite.

"Yeah. Okay. I will," Tillie replied and kept hold of her smile. The smile felt good. It was relieved and true. Aaron smiled back, then turned and ran to the car. They drove off with another wave and a beep.

"Oh my God, Till, how *are* you?" Susan plunked down onto the lounger and stared at Tillie like a doctor at a patient. She leaned in and gave Tillie a tight, long hug.

"I'm good, Sue, I'm good. I'm happy everything is going to be okay." Tillie took a nice, long drink of her water, feeling better every time she did that.

"You are the best, greatest best friend ever in the history of the world! I mean, how many people can say their best friend saved their cousin's life once?" Susan hugged her again, quicker this time, but still tightly. "This links you to our family for life, you know," she said and then giggled. "We're practically like sisters now."

"Oh Sue, we've always been practically sisters. That's what I like about you. You're like the sister without all the hassle." The two girls giggled and Tillie took a final drink of her water.

"You want me to get you another one of those? Oh and you must be starving! Let me find you something to eat, too. Stay right there and I'll be right back. Don't move." Susan went to the back of the patio where the coolers were and started to pull things out.

"Sue, I wasn't the one who fell into the water," Tillie cried back to her. "I'm fine. I can get my own stuff to eat." Tillie started to get up to join Susan.

"Don't you dare. You stay right there and enjoy your hero treatment for the rest of the day, miss." Susan returned momentarily with water and food.

"Thanks, Sue, but you really don't have to treat me like a hero. Like I told Aaron, I just happened to be the one in the right place out there."

"Like hell I don't, Till. Lucky or whatever, it was you who came up from the water with Tim." She opened another water bottle and handed it to Tillie. She then laid out some fresh fruit onto the lounge chair for her as well. "You're just going to have to accept that it was you, that's all. Some birthday, huh?."

"Wow, I guess I forgot, yeah. I won't be forgetting this one any time soon." Tillie munched on some fruit and smiled at her. "Now, go get me a sandwich, I'm starving." Both girls broke out into laughter. Susan stood up and headed back to get Tillie a sandwich. Tillie was glad the day ended on such a good note. It could have been so different...if it wasn't for her.

The rest of Tillie's vacation couldn't possibly top the first day on the lake. Although the rest of the time was spent mostly on the lake, the other days were very quiet, almost mundane. Tillie was sure getting her fill of attention for the rest of this vacation. It made her feel confident, because the praise was something she'd actually earned.

After a couple of days, though, she had time to play the recent events over and over in her mind. Not only was it the strangest birthday she could remember and she was now the "hero" to Susan's entire family, but she found herself going back to her first impressions of the lake itself. How beautiful she thought it was and how it took her breath away when she first touched the water. She could remember details she thought she'd forgotten in the rush of Tim's rescue. These details brought peace to her and helped her face the rest of the days on the lake with a simple happiness.

On the other side of her memories, there was all of the hard swimming she'd done and how much water she'd covered. The harshness of the rescue compared to all the other time they'd spent at the lake. How interesting that she did not prefer one over the other. The harsh swimming was just as enjoyable to her as the leisurely swimming out to the raft. Not that she preferred to be looking for a drowning person in the water, of course, but the sensations she had with both kinds of swimming were equally thrilling.

Why was she thinking so much about the water now? Was it because this was a whole new experience, going on vacation on her own, without her family? Was it the drama of the rescue? She knew it was normal to relive traumatic events over in your head, so she thought maybe that's why she was dwelling on the water so much. But why *just* the water? She shook these thoughts aside and chalked them up to an adventure of her own vacation.

After that couple of days of deep, watery thoughts, she decided that she was comfortable with her "hero" title because she'd worked hard and the outcome was very happy indeed. She was happy that she had been the one to find Tim. She wondered if anyone else could have done it. Although, maybe all of this constant hero praise was simply going to her head. Anyway, she thought of how much fun she'd have as soon as she got home with her new title. Oh, her siblings wouldn't live it down now, now that she was a "hero". This was definitely a birthday Tillie would remember.

4

Ah! My Eyes!

Back at home things were busy. The website did its job well. "We haven't been this busy in years," Heather said almost gleefully as she came out of the office. It was another lunch rush and she helped take tables in Tillie's absence. It was a pleasure to watch Heather work the floor. She seemed to glide around tables and her smile was contagious. "I wonder if it will quiet down by the fourth?" She said softly to Cord while picking up a sandwich dish in the kitchen.

"Probably, it does every year, doesn't it?" he replied. The Lundgrens loved the Fourth of July, the whole town did.

The Lundgrens were well used to the swell of people coming into the restaurant by now. They often compared it to the tides of the ocean. They liked the rhythm and flow of the comings and goings of their customers and knew how to interact at this speed. However, with the boom of business in June, there wasn't time to keep up with themselves much less each other. There hadn't even been time to go to Church this summer. Heather loved it when they went to Church.

"My hair hasn't seen sun since New York," Tillie complained to Lyla one afternoon. Working the lunch rush, both girls usually kept their personal lives outside their restaurant shifts. But because they'd been there, working almost constantly, they began sneaking in comments on their own lives.

"Oh, Til, I know. You're not used to all this shade when all of that sun is outside," Lyla replied sympathetically. "Don't worry, there will be lots of time to get out and steal some rays after the Fourth." Lyla flashed Tillie a caring smile and walked off to serve her next table.

Tillie went off to her next table with a little sigh.

On this particular lunch rush, things quieted down fairly quickly compared to the previous weeks. This was a sure sign that summer was in full swing and everyone wanted to be outside, not inside. Their takeout orders increased, while filling the tables decreased.

A car honked outside. Tillie looked out eagerly and saw her gang of friends piled in the convertible.

"Be right back," she said as she took her apron off and put it down behind the counter. She jogged outside and the girls flocked around Tillie.

Lyla looked out with a bit of nostalgia. It felt like yesterday that there was a car full of friends outside waiting for her. Now, most all of her friends were scattered to the wind, having found jobs all over the country. She kept in touch through emails and phone calls to the few that wrote and called back. Lyla shook herself out of her memory-filled daze and went back to wiping down the counter.

A few minutes later, Tillie came back in and brought the sea air in with her. It made Lyla look up toward Tillie. It smelled like there was more sea in the air today. Lyla wondered how and why. *Maybe it's my nostalgia*, she thought.

"Tanya and the girls want me to go with them to the bonfire tonight." Tillie came back around the counter, grabbing her apron. "I told them not 'til we close." The car was still right outside the door, full of life and laughter.

"Well, why put off 'til later what you can do now?" Lyla looked at her sister inquisitively.

"What'd ya mean, sis? I've got to be here for the dinner rush."

"Oh, bother with the dinner rush Till. We're on full staff tonight and I can feel that we probably aren't going to need it."

"Huh? Are you alright? You're not full of fever or something," Tillie said and gestured dramatically to her forehead. "Are you serious?"

"Yes, Till, I'm serious. I know you think I'm all work and no play, but I know there's a time for both. This is your time, Tils. I don't want Sigrun to be where you spend your time wishing you were someplace else."

"Wow," said Tillie, truly taken aback. "There is a woman in there after all. We were starting to think you were machine in there or something. Just kidding, you know me." Tillie put her apron and cloth back behind the counter.

"Oh, ha ha. Well, as I've gotten older, I'm realizing how you need to start taking chances where you can and have some fun along the way, ya know?"

Tillie came over to Lyla, trying not to rush as her excitement of a night off built inside her. "I always knew you were a secret party diva," she whispered into Lyla's ear and kissed her on the cheek. "Thanks, I owe ya one."

"Love you too, Til," replied Lyla. "Soak up some stray rays for me out there and have fun!"

Tillie was already skipping out the door toward the car. Lyla smiled as Tillie waved behind her without looking back. Lyla remembered the carefree days of teendom and went back to restaurant work.

The dinner crowd came in a little earlier than usual that night. Was there something going on in the town? Lyla couldn't remember. She sat a couple she hadn't seen before, tourists. Anna and Marcus strolled in from the back door, in deep conversation. Lyla wondered what it could be about this time. Those two were known for their crazy debates. Anna was gesturing like crazy, as usual and Lyla suddenly hoped that their conversation was rated PG, as they were now within earshot of customers.

The night roared on, in the ever flowing fashion to which it was accustomed. Everyone was in his or her place, doing his or her thing and the whole place was running smoothly. Adrian ran around the most, between the kitchen and waiting tables. He wasn't even phased by it, but instead looked charged from it.

"Ah, youth!" Anna exclaimed as she grabbed Adrian's face as he passed. "What I wouldn't do for a drop of your beautiful energy."

Adrian blushed a little and went on to the tables.

Cord and Liam were working the kitchen with Danny and the three of them worked as though they were performers on a stage. The counter stools were full and almost everyone on them was engaged with what was going on in the kitchen. It was like the entertainment act for the dinner hour. Knives were chopping, food was flying and smiles and laughter were exchanged. The men looked like the professionals they were; it was enjoyable to watch.

Cord was always at his happiest here. Here in the rush hour of mealtime. Here in the place where his family was altogether. Here where it was all perfect. His smile and rosy cheeks made you feel the warmth from the kitchen in a way that wasn't even too hot for the summer time. It warmed you from the inside out. It was always these picturesque moments that had people coming back to Sigrun. The ambiance was always so magical.

Right in the middle of a sauté, Cord thought he saw something sparkle out of the corner of his eye. It came through the window from the office. He glanced up in the direction of the spark and squinted, but didn't see anything and went right back to cooking. He saw it again. This time he looked up as he put the pan down onto the stove. He thought he saw something for sure this time, but it was gone now. *What was that?*

"I'll be right back," Cord said to Liam as he patted his shoulder and walked to the back door. "Get that sauté plated for me." He walked out the door.

"Oh sure, he gets to take breaks," Liam said to Danny. Plating the dish, he gave a strange, concentrated look. Then it occurred to him, "Hey! Dad never takes breaks. What's going on?" He looked to the back door and saw his dad turn the corner of the building. He stood at the door, staring.

"Oh, sweetie!" Anna yelled from the counter area beyond the kitchen. Liam looked at her.

"Huh? What?" he asked.

"I need a special for table seven, hon," Anna replied. This was a busy time in her shift, so she was in a hurry.

Liam came to, "Sure thing. And don't...with the sweetie thing. It's distracting." Shaking his head, as he's said that more times to Anna than he could count.

"Ok, hon!" Anna replied cheerfully walking back to the tables. Liam went on to make up the special for table seven.

Outside was a perfect summer evening. The sun came down to the point where the night cooled off the day. The sky was still bright and Cord was surprised that he saw a spark before, back in the restaurant. It must have been something very bright. He stood about a hundred yards from the restaurant, out on the beach. He placed his hand above his eyes to shade them from the lowering sun and saw it again: a spark. Big. Bright. Way out over the water, had to be miles away. It was so fast, if he hadn't seen it twice before, he would have doubted he saw it at all.

He slowly lowered his hand, squinting. *What was tha...*then it happened once more. This time it lasted a few seconds. Cord quickly looked around to see if anyone else was around to see it. It looked like maybe something blew up in the distance, but it was bluish green in color.

There were a group of kids playing their way down the beach. "Hey guys!" Cord yelled to them. "Did you see that explosion over there?" The giggling teens just smiled, waved and shook their heads.

"No way, Mr. Lundgren, where?" one of the boys asked and looked in the same direction as Cord.

"Well, it was over there," Cord replied, pointing in the direction of the spark across the water."

The boy looked out, squinting.

"Oh, that must just be the bonfire they're setting up, Mr L." he said as his girlfriend's hand grabbed his and he was dragged off down the beach.

"Oh jeez, right. The bonfire. I forgot all about it for a minute there," Cord said, trailing off, still gazing in the same direction. He sat there for a moment and thought, *What kind of bonfire*...then he started back toward the restaurant.

The night was busy until sunset, then time for bonfire fun and fireworks. All of Mt. Desert Island would be outside to enjoy the festivities. The Lundgrens even closed Sigrun early. So, just as Cord and Heather were on the way out the door, it was surprising that they should get a customer. Most everyone around the area knew how they closed for this evening. Also, there was a sign on the door that said, "Closed at 9:00 tonight for fireworks." But something about this night felt unusual, despite its routineness.

"Oh, oh, excuse me, are you closing?" the stranger asked the Lundgrens.

"Why yes, we close every year at this time. For the fireworks. You must be a tourist, not local?" Heather asked gently, as to not make the stranger feel stupid.

"Why yes...yes, that's what I am. Tourist!" the stranger answered a little too excitedly.

Cord furrowed his brow at the little, thin man.

"A little overdressed for mid-summer, aren't ya?" asked Cord.

The man looked older than Cord or Heather, with an unshaven face and shaggy, sandy colored hair. He wore jeans, a t-shirt and a flannel button down shirt with a hooded sweatshirt over that. He had leather boots on his feet, which made Cord sweat just thinking about them.

"What? Oh, am I?" the strange little man looked down at himself, then back at the two approvingly. "I just get cold way up here at night, so I thought I'd better have some layers."

"Way up here?" Cord repeated, "Where you from?"

"Oh!" the man nearly shouted, startled and flustered. "Oh...yes...well...I'm from...shall we just say that I'm from way south compared to this place! Yes," he answered with a large, friendly smile on his face. "So, can you spare a moment for a cup of coffee to keep me warm?" he asked looking childlike.

Cord was about to answer, "no", when Heather interjected, "Sure thing. I think I still have some nice and hot. Can I set you up with a cup to go?" she asked so sweetly, no one could have said no.

"Of course, my dear. That would be splendid, just splendid," he said following them over to the counter. He looked around, a little skittish and reached into his pockets, one after the other, looking for money for the coffee. His eyes darted from Heather and Cord to different points in the restaurant.

Cord stood at the door, while Heather went to the counter and poured the coffee into a paper cup.

"I don't know if I have exact change my dear," the stranger said, still darting his eyes around the place. "But I know I've got a couple of dollar bills somewhere in here." He kept searching pockets. He had many of them.

"You know what?" Heather replied, "It doesn't really matter. It's on the house." She handed the man the steaming cup of coffee.

"Oh no, no!" the man insisted, "That just won't do! I know I have the money and I insist you take it!"

"Well," replied Heather, as Cord crossed his arms, trying to be patient, "it *is* my restaurant and what I say goes, I'm afraid." She smiled her dazzling smile and even made Cord relax a little. "Now, you just take this cup as a 'welcome to Mt. Desert Island' and let's all go enjoy the fireworks. Happy Fourth of July!" She finished and guided the man toward the door.

"Fourth of July!" the man exclaimed, throwing his head back a little as if one of his hands had hit himself on the forehead, although both were gripping the coffee. "Of course. Yes. Happy Fourth of July!" He scurried out the door, looking behind him once more.

Cord and Heather followed him out the door and Cord locked up. "Bye now. Come on back when we're open and we'll show you what a real meal looks like." Heather called out to the man, who was already crossing the street.

"Thank you! Maybe I will!" The man waved without looking back. He walked in the opposite direction from where they were going.

"Strange. I thought he was going to enjoy the fireworks," said Heather.

"Humph," Cord mumbled. "Probably just wanted to scam the coffee."

"Oh don't be a grump. This is one of my favorite nights of the season. Let's just forget about the coffee. With all the business we've had this summer, we can afford lots of those." She took Cord by the arm and nuzzled into his big bicep. Then she leaned up and kissed his cheek. They looked like a new couple who just fell in love.

"Yeah, I know you're right. I just didn't like being interrupted with our schedule, that's all. My mind was already at the beach." Cord looked behind them to see if he could see the man. He was already gone.

5

Wait...Hello

The couple moved on down the street into the gathering crowds down on the beach, ready for fireworks. The bright golden yellow and orange bonfire could be seen in the distance.

As Cord and Heather approached the bonfire, they could see people of all ages being active, friendly and most of all, happy. There were groups of people playing music on boom boxes and a bandstand set up at one end of the crowd. A bunch of local kid bands were lined up to play. It was the island's venue for them each summer. Everyone waved at Cord and Heather as they walked through to find a spot for watching the fireworks.

Tillie was excited for this year's festivities, especially the bands. This year her friend Susan was playing in one of them. She couldn't be more anxious than if it were one of her very own siblings who were playing.

"Mom! Dad!" She yelled and waved over to them. "We saved you guys a seat!"

Cord and Heather grabbed each other's hands and headed over to their spot. The teens loved them for their youthful attitude at social events. They always had seats saved for them.

"Boy, we thought you two would never get here!" Liam said in his scolding tone and a smirk on his mouth. He loved doing that to his parents.

"Oh you know them, Liam. You'd think they were newlyweds the way they act." Lyla tilted her head in mocking. Then she smiled sincerely and laughed. As much as their children teased them about being in love, they really appreciated having parents who truly were in love.

"Umm...T-M-I guys! We don't want to know about the old folks' *looove* life!" One of Adrian's friends chided and the whole group went into their "sick" act. Swoons and fake vomiting was heard all around, amongst laughter and giggling as well.

"Ew! You're so gross!" Tillie yelled. "We *definitely* don't need to know about that!" She said, followed by more laughter.

Cord and Heather sat down, Heather feeling the heat of blush rising up her face. As much as she knew everyone was joking, she felt embarrassed when put on the spot.

Someone walked onto the bandstand. The bands were introduced for the night. It wasn't too formal, but the crowd settled down just the same in time for the first group to take their places on stage.

The night went on smoothly. It was a great night for the island to be together and the weather always cooperated, as if it knew what was happening. The night was three bands into the celebration when the fireworks started. The sights. The sounds. It all came together marvelously. These people knew how to mark the peak of summer!

The next band came on stage. Tillie wanted to make sure she saw Susan.

"Ooh! Ooh! Everybody look! Susan's up! She's on!" Tillie signaled to everyone to turn away from the fireworks and take note that someone important was now on stage.

The band started as fast as they could, as they didn't want too much silence between groups during the fireworks. Susan sang a duet with the lead singer. Tillie didn't know all of them personally, as they weren't from her school, but they looked familiar to her. She smiled widely and waved her arms over her head to try to get Susan's attention. Susan saw her and smiled back and even shot her a wave with her tambourine.

Just then someone grabbed the back of Tillie's shirt and she heard, "Hey, hero," close up in her ear, but loudly to get over the crowd's noise. Tillie's arms danced down to their normal position as she spun around to see who the voice belonged to.

"Oh my gosh! Aaron?" Tillie said, as she involuntarily hugged a tall, handsome young man. "Have you *grown*?" She said with a huge smile and realized the hug felt a bit awkward and stepped back a bit.

Aaron seemed a bit rigid. Tillie felt her cheeks flush with embarrassment. Aaron just stood there, looking a bit in shock.

"Susan didn't tell me you'd be here. It's so great to see you! How are you? How's Tim?" she said a bit more timidly than her previous questions.

"Uh, good. Great. I mean...he's real good, thanks. It's really great to see you again too." Aaron finally looked like he came to life.

"Gosh, it's been a whole, what, three weeks?" Tillie said smiling. She touched his arm and then again felt awkward. *Great, more cheek flushing.*

"Yeah. Yeah. Something like that. Two-and-a-half, or so," Aaron said, trying to hide the fact that he kept track at all. "Well, I've gotta run. I just wanted to say hi." He started to back away.

"Hey, wait! You just got here. Are you staying in town long? Come by Sigrun if you can tomorrow. Or whenever!" Tillie said, sounding surprisingly desperate. Was she? That was a weird feeling.

"Ok, yeah. I'll stop by tomorrow!" Aaron yelled as he quickly got swallowed up by a dancing crowd.

Tillie felt the excited rush of the moment dwindle slightly at his exit. *Hmmm,* she thought, *I didn't realize that Aaron brought excitement.*

Tillie finished watching the band on stage, going into her own little world for the next moments. It felt surreal seeing Aaron again and so suddenly. She wondered why Susan hadn't mentioned him coming into town. Her thoughts wandered to when she first met Aaron and his family.

Was it really two-and-a-half weeks since she saw Aaron last already? She saw Susan all the time. Almost every day. After all, they were "practically sisters". So in her mind, everything about saving Tim was still very fresh in her mind. Tillie came out of her reverie. She shivered a little as the night air touched her arms and she turned her attention back to the stage.

Susan and her band just finished and Tillie shouted and clapped. When she finished, she saw that the large group she was with was a bit more settled than she was. Most were seated and were enjoying some picnic goodies during the end of the fireworks. This was the style of the evening, no food tents, or people selling things. Everyone got to have a night off to enjoy in the middle of the summer. Tillie quickly settled down and rummaged through the picnic baskets.

"Who was that Till?" Adrian asked with a cheesy grin.

"Aaron," she replied and flashed a cheesy grin right back at him.

"Oh," he said, taken back a bit, but kept pushing like younger brothers do. "For a minute there, I thought you had a new admirer."

"Oh, please! Will you quit it?" Tillie said.

"Yeah, Adrian, quit it!" Adrian's friend Ben said in his most mocking girl voice.

"Ugh," Tillie said as she took a bite of sandwich. "Why are boys such...boys?"

"If we could answer that question, we'd be rich," answered Lyla with a laugh. "So, that really was Aaron, huh?"

Lyla asked trying to sound nonchalant. She took a swig of tea from a bottle.

"Um, yeah, it *really* was," answered Tillie, bracing herself for the oncoming questions.

There had been so many recounts of how she saved Tim's life. First, of course, her family wanted to hear every detail as soon as she got home. They all sat in the living room and listened intently, so she only had to tell it once in detail. In this family, once a story was told in full detail and all questions answered, it was as if it had happened to them all. So Tillie had lots of help recounting the story, but there were still random people who wanted to know about the town's heroine.

For all the details she told, all the questions from people at work and friends from school, she hadn't really said much to anyone about Aaron. Now she knew that was about to change. She knew her sister well. But at least this was Lyla she was dealing with and that was a comfort.

"Ok, Lyles, sock it to me," Tillie said.

"What?" Lyla said in her most innocent tone.

"Oh, come on!" Tillie said as if she were completely exacerbated.

"Okay, okay, like I can try to be coy and sly with you anyway," Lyla said in her matter-of-fact tone. "Is it so bad to want to know more about Aaron?"

"Nope," Tillie said. She took a bite of sandwich, so it was a mouthful at the same time as her answer. She chewed and swallowed her food. "I mean, no, it's not. It's just that I haven't really given him much thought, so I didn't really have much to say," she finished and grabbed a drink.

"Well, from what I just saw here tonight, you coulda fooled me," Lyla said with another swig on her tea.

"I know. It was weird, right? I mean, I was genuinely happy and even excited to see him. I mean, it was a surprise, Susan didn't even tell me he would be here. Do you think she even knows? Of course she knows, I mean and what was the deal with his attitude? *He* came up to *me* to say hello. So, why the awkward? Really, guys are so weird sometimes!" Tillie finally finished, took a big breath, realized she was completely babbling and took another bite of sandwich to stop herself.

"Gee and you said you didn't really have much to say," Lyla said with a reassuring smile. She loved these big sister moments. She loved feeling helpful to her siblings with their life struggles. They always came to her with their questions and she was good with answers. This time was no exception. "Look, Till, I'd chalk half of your excitement up to the whole evening. You were clearly enjoying the music and your friend in the band and so forth."

"Yea, that's right. That's true," Tillie interrupted and then seeing Lyla's I'm-not-done face, finished her sandwich quietly.

"And anyone who would sneak up on you is bound to be surprised back. I know, I've been there, done that."

Tillie nodded and wiped her mouth.

"So, really, it was just awkward circumstances, that's all. He was polite enough to come and say hi, but didn't expect such a warm reception. He even agreed to stop by Sigrun tomorrow, right?"

"Mmhmm," Tillie said finishing her last bite. "Yes, tomorrow or whenever," she trailed off for a second. "Gosh that sounded stupid. 'Whenever', like that was so clever. Ugh." She took another swig of drink.

Just then Susan approached the group.

"Hey everyone! Did you all hear the bands ok tonight?" The group clapped and cheered and she took an exaggerated bow. She giggled, found Tillie and sat down with her and Lyla. She waved at Heather and Cord "Hi, Mr. and Mrs. Lundgren!" Then, to the girls, "Oh that was great! I just love this night!" Susan finished with a huge smile on her face and went digging in the picnic basket. "I can only stay a minute, but I couldn't resist Anna's brownies over here, now could I?" She flashed a wink at the girls, finding her prize. Lyla gave Tillie a look of 'okay, now's your chance'. This didn't go unnoticed with Susan, so she looked to Tillie with question on her face.

"Oh. Umm...Susan, you were so great up there. You really are a natural! You'd better send me tickets to your first real concert." Tillie flashed her smile and the girls were enjoying the moment. "While you were playing, I ran into a mutual acquaintance," Tillie stammered a little at her last word and Susan interrupted.

"Oh, you saw Aaron! Great! I was hoping he'd be able to find you in this crowd!" Noticing the look on Tillie's face, she asked, "Didn't I tell you he would be here? He came in for the Fourth. His family thought it would be good to get away from home for a while. Truth be told, we think it's because he's been so possessive of Tim since, well, you know, that they thought getting away from him would be good for both of them. Help them get on with normal stuff, you know?" Susan took a bite of brownie and looked at the girls very matter-of-fact.

Well, that was a simple enough explanation for Tillie. It put her at ease a little and all of her previous questions washed out to sea. Maybe it was the cool summer night air that calmed her.

"I told him to stop by Sigrun tomorrow...or 'whenever'," she hand gestured little quotes around her word whenever and rolled her eyes a little bit at herself.

"Of course! I'll bring him by after the lunch rush, if that's okay. I mean, we'll eat there of course, but you know how us locals hate the tourist crowd." Susan laughed and got ready to stand up. "I'm sorry, I've gotta go already! I wish I could stay out all night with you all, but my fans await!" Susan stood up and took another overly fake bow and all three ladies laughed.

6

Crazy Champion

"Bye, Sue! Catch you tomorrow then!" Tillie finished, then reached in her bag for a sweatshirt. The night air had an unusual crispness to it for July, but sometimes the sea brought that crisp air in, almost a thank you for being patient with the hot sun all day. Tillie enjoyed it, but still had to cover up, just a little bit.

With the fireworks well over and the bonfire burned down to mere embers, the beach opened up like flour falling through a sieve. Little by little there was more sand than people and all that remained were a few of the younger crowd. This was the Lundgren children's favorite time of the summer, by far. It was quiet on the beach, despite the goofing off of some groups of kids and young adults, the sound of the ocean easily drowned them out.

The four Lundgren children said goodbye to their friends, found an isolated spot as near to the water as they could and just relaxed to gather their strength for the rest of summer. There were small conversations between them, but nothing too serious, no one teased anyone...much. Now that they were all older and more mature, they just sat and enjoyed life together. And of course, the water. The one thing they all loved equally.

"Man, I wish we could sit here every night like this," Adrian said with his eyes closed, deeply breathing in the sea air.

"I know. Isn't this the best?" Liam answered with a bit more energy than Adrian seemed to have this late in the night. Of course, Liam being older, he was a bit more used to nightlife than his younger siblings. "There's nothing like the sound of this shore, I tell you. Nothing." He pushed some sand around with his feet and enjoyed how warm it felt compared to the night air, as if it was a blanket. "Feels like God is right here with us in these moments, doesn't it?"

"Mmm," Tillie chimed in with her toes digging into the wet, cooler sand. "Yeah, I know what you mean, Li. The sights, sounds and smells are so unearthly, even though they are totally earthly," Tillie took a deep breath. "Yep. I could definitely get used to this every night." She faced the water and saw that the moon rose over the horizon. It wasn't quite full, maybe a three quarter, but it was bright enough to bask in its light.

"We really are so very lucky to have this. All of it. You know? I mean, think about it. Where we live, what we do for a living, who we have to do it with. It's all so very lucky! How many people can say they work with their families and like it?" Lyla contributed to the conversation with her ever words of wisdom. She too admired the partially full moon.

"Ye-ep," Liam said as he stretched his arms back behind him, "We are the lucky ones, that's for sure. Not everyone gets to enjoy a slice of heaven." He brought his arms forward and also turned and noticed the moon.

After Liam's statement, all of them were feeling relaxed, lucky and peaceful. Then there was a very bright green light on the horizon, under the moon. This light was *bright*. All four of them stood up at once, full of adrenaline and questions. Yet, no one said anything. They were dumbfounded. They watched the bright green light on the horizon get brighter, as if that were even possible and then disappear down into the water.

"What the..." Adrian trailed off, pointing out to the water.

"Yeah, exactly my words, bro!" Liam replied, still looking at the spot that held brightness in their eyes like a camera flash.

"I don't believe..." Lyla trailed off as well.

"Holy cow! Guys! What the hell was that?" Tillie had the words and was not afraid to use them.

All four looked around to see if anyone else noticed the light. There weren't many people left at all on the beach. In fact, it was almost completely empty. The four of them had enjoyed the night to its fullest and didn't notice anyone else. No one else noticed the very bright, green light.

"Well, we sure don't know. But there's one way to find out," Liam said as he stripped his shirt off and headed toward the waves.

"Whoa! Where do you think you're going?" Lyla demanded trying to grab hold of Liam's arm.

"I'm going to find out what the hell that was!" Liam walked on until he was waist deep in the waves.

"Oh my God! You *can't do that*! That thing, whatever it was, we don't even know what it was! And it was way too far to be trying to swim to!" Tillie yelled out to him, but to no avail.

Liam dove head first into the next wave. Adrian jumped forward, planning on joining him. But Lyla was faster with him this time and grabbed hold of his swim trunks.

"Oh no you don't *little* brother," she gave him her sternest of stern voices. "Not this time. Not again." She was serious and had a very good grip on the shorts.

"What do you mean, 'not again'?" Adrian looked at her like she was crazy. "Let go then! I won't go. He's too far out there now anyway. Look!"

He pointed to a dark shadow moving fast in the water. Was that Liam? Already out that far? How was he ever going to find the spot where that light disappeared in the dark? There wasn't a spot of it left to be seen. It appeared and disappeared so quickly.

They all knew Liam was an excellent swimmer. He had excelled in swimming in high school. He had broken records left and right in his junior year, when he suddenly up and quit the team. When everyone demanded why, he would shrug them off. He acted like he no longer cared about it. Most people forgot about his great skills altogether by the end of that year.

But Liam didn't forget. Liam loved to swim. He did it every free chance he had, when and where people wouldn't catch him. And he was *fast*. He was so very fast, he wished many times someone was with him to time his speed and distances. He swam this piece of beach dozens of times, out far, where the beachgoers wouldn't see and knew it by heart. If he couldn't find where that light went, then maybe it was just a figment of all their imaginations.

Liam swam hard. He knew he could get to that spot quickly. He handled it perfectly, eye on the prize, when a wave hit him out of nowhere. He was pummeled like a piece of seaweed, turned thrashing under the water for almost a minute. It wasn't a problem for him, holding his breath this long, he'd done it plenty of times. It was the tossing and being thrown around like a beach ball that made him lose his bearings.

"Where is he?" Tillie yelled, frantic and ready to jump in after him. "I can't see him anymore!"

"Look, don't worry, okay?" Adrian said, grabbing Tillie by both shoulders. The gentle touch of his hands on her helped calm her down and bring her back to reality. "I've seen Liam swim lots of times. He's good. *Real* good, Till." Tillie looked back at Adrian even more confused than she was before.

"What do you mean you've seen Liam swim?" Lyla chimed in and walked in front of both Tillie and Adrian, facing away from the ocean now.

"Well, I wasn't supposed to say anything. I mean, I've kind of caught him swimming. He doesn't even know I've seen him. I followed him one afternoon. I thought he was going for a hike and I was going to catch up with him and tag along. But he stopped and dove off a cliff. I almost had a heart attack, I swear!" Adrian said in agreement with the girls' faces. "When I caught up to the cliff edge, I looked down to the water to find him. I was ready to jump in after him if I had to. But he wasn't there."

"Why the hell have you never told us this!" Tillie demanded, freeing herself from Adrian's hold.

"Look, like I said, it freaked me out when it happened. But then I saw him. He wasn't at the bottom of the jump like most people would be. He was out in the water, *swimming*. And like I said, he was really, really good and fast. I'm talking fast, like...motorboat fast. No, I'm not kidding," Adrian answered Lyla's silent doubt.

The three stood there for a moment, thoughts and questions swirled like a hurricane over their heads. They all turned back toward the water.

"So, I learned to follow him on his little excursions and I've seen him swim lots of times. But he doesn't know it. And since he never says anything about it to us, I took that to mean that I shouldn't either," Adrian finished. They all sat perched on the sand, straining their night eyes to find their brother. They silently begged the moon to be fuller, just for a moment.

Before long, although it felt like all night to the three on the beach, they spotted splashing coming at them. Liam emerged from the water like it was just another day.

"If it weren't for that damn wave, I would have had it," he said shaking the water off himself, like a dog. All three siblings stood up and just stared at him. "What? Do I have seaweed in my hair or something?" Liam swished his hand through his hair just in case. He stopped when he got closer to everyone. Then he looked puzzled. "Really. What's the deal?"

"Well dear brother, the deal is, *you*. Swimming. Fast. And a lot." Lyla accused as graciously as she could so not to put him on the defense.

"Yeah, I know," Liam replied shrugging his shoulders. "I swim, okay? I love it. I can't *not* do it." He went over to their area on the beach and rummaged through bags, "Do one of you ladies have a towel in here somewhere?"

Lyla crossed over to him, passing Tillie and Adrian who shot her pleading looks. She shot them a look back, reassuring them. She got to her bag and handed a towel to Liam.

"Well," she said as lightly as she could muster, "It's not like we expect you to never swim, Liam. It's just that we've never actually *seen* you do it. Not lately, anyway."

"Not since high school," Tillie chimed in. Lyla turned her head to Tillie, then back to Liam and nodded in agreement.

"Well. It's not like I have to advertise when I go swimming! Jeez guys! What's with the interrogation?"

Lyla thought, *Oh great. Now we'll get nothing from him. He's defensive.*

"Hey, bro." Adrian cleared his throat and walked toward them with Tillie following behind. They all took a seat almost simultaneously. "We don't care if you decide to swim or not, right girls?" Tillie and Lyla nodded in agreement. Adrian always tried to be the peacekeeper.

"Yeah...we just wonder...well," Tillie hesitated. She didn't want to make Liam angry by bugging him too much about something they all knew he didn't want to talk about. "Why didn't you tell us that you swim? It's kind of weird that you would go swimming by yourself all the time."

"Who says I swim all alone?" Liam dried off his head and seemed very nonchalant.

"Umm...I did," Adrian answered like a naughty child in school who admitted he'd put tacks on the teacher's chair.

"Aw, jeez." Liam stopped himself, "Man! What kind of bro are you who can't keep a simple secret?" He looked at Adrian and waited.

"It's not that I wanted to tell them anything! But you just went running out there and...hey! What do you mean, 'keep a simple secret?' You *knew*? You knew that *I* knew?" Now it was Adrian who took on the master's voice, scolding his puppy.

"Course I knew, little brother. Most of the time I knew you were right behind me like always, following very loudly I might add. Don't ever go into detective work, you'd suck," Liam added.

Lyla decided to cut into the conversation before it got too heated. "Look, Liam. It's all very strange, don't you agree? I mean, it's not that you swim, you do it *alone* and you let your brother sneak around thinking it's all very hush-hush? And, as we all saw tonight, you are *wicked* fast! Which begs the question, among many, why? Why did you let Adrian think it was all a secret?" There was silence among everyone now. Silence as time ticked by.

Liam let out a long breath, which brought patience and calm to everyone. "Okay. Let me explain. I'll tell you everything, but you have to listen. No interrupting with a thousand questions before I'm finished," he stopped for a second and looked directly toward Tillie.

She knew he would and she just gave a short nod.

"Alright? Good," Liam didn't wait for an answer. "So, remember back when I was in high school? My junior year?" Everyone just sat and listened intently. Liam continued. "Well, I was on the swim team, as you know and I was breaking records like every time I swam an event. It came so easy to me. You guys have no idea." He ignored the puffs of air from Adrian and Tillie and went on with his glory days history. "Seriously. It was *too* easy. I mean, I wasn't even trying to break records and I was doing it all the time. And we're not talking breaking records by split seconds here. I was taking five to ten seconds off of records that were at the school since I could remember! I even *tried* to swim slow, but apparently I sucked at that. I would go out in the ocean in my free time to see how fast I could go. Guys," as if he didn't have their full attention at this point, "*I was passing motorboats.* I mean, they weren't going flat out or anything, but they were freaking motorboats!"

"C'mon," Tillie blurted out.

"I was just a kid. What did I know about how fast I was supposed to be able to swim? But swimming faster than boats? C'mon is right, Till! Swimming that fast isn't right, no matter what. And no, to answer the obvious question, I don't take steroids. Barely knew what the things were at that age." He rummaged around and found a bottle of water, opened it up and took a swig. "Once I realized that I was unnaturally fast, I quit the team. It's not natural to swim faster than boats. *I'm* not natural."

Everyone sat silent. Thinking. Waiting. "I quit the team, but I couldn't tell them why, could I? I mean, I couldn't let anyone know I could swim that fast! There would be questions, tests, who knows what! I decided that I really didn't want to know. If something is wrong with me, then so be it. I'm healthy. It doesn't hurt me to do it. So, I just go about my life. It's nobody's business whether I swim or not, or why or why not. Of course I keep it to myself, I don't want anyone to see, but I like to be able to swim all out if I want to. I love it. And it seems the more I do it, the more I want to do it, ya know? I've just been doing it this way for so long now, it didn't occur to me to share it with anyone, not even family.

"One afternoon, on one of my secret swims, I noticed Adrian behind me. At first I was going to just let him catch up to me and pretend I was hiking or something. I had this feeling that I should keep it a secret, what I was doing. Then suddenly I had this urge to just jump. Just jump right off the nearest cliff and see what Adrian would do." He couldn't help let out a little laugh at his young brother, the look on his face now and remembering the thrill he felt jumping off the cliff.

"Holy crap, Li! You scared the crud out of me that day!"

"Ha ha, yeah, I knew I would. Then I knew you'd follow to the cliff edge and see that I was fine. I thought maybe you'd even jump in and join me. But you never did. You never said anything to me about it." Taking his serious tone back, "I knew then that I'd let things go on as they were. I knew I didn't have to worry about you saying anything. I knew you had my back." He took a long swig of water.

"Okay, yeah. Yay, bro power," Tillie finally spoke up. She couldn't hold her tongue any longer. "So you two had this secret with the swimming thing. It's weird, but I strangely respect the fact that you bonded through this. I mean, you two know that you are close and you didn't even have to say anything to each other. That's cool. I guess. I'm just not so sure where that leaves us gals. You know what I mean? Not that you don't have our backs and whatever, but why wouldn't either one of you tell us about Liam's fantastic skills until tonight? When things were crazy and weird, you decide to let it all out!"

"Hey, there. Take it easy now. Things *are* crazy and weird here tonight. Did we just all forget about that crazy sh...tuff we saw out on the water? No, not me ya little freak." Liam grabbed Tillie around the neck and gave her a weak noogie on her head.

"You'll always be the crazy shiz out on the water to me now," she replied laughing. "That crazy champion!" She giggled and slinked away from Liam to avoid anymore noogies.

"But really, guys, Liam's right," added Lyla, which brought everyone back on track with the night's events. "What was that thing anyway?"

Everyone sat quietly for a moment. They all replayed the night in their heads quickly and tried to make sense of it. There were still so many questions.

"That light! Did you reach it, Liam?" Tillie asked as she rummaged through a large beach bag and brought out snacks and water for the rest of them. The night's activities were so crazy, everyone found themselves suddenly hungry.

"No. Like I said. That wave knocked me for a loop and I couldn't get my bearings after that." Liam replied.

"Well, I don't think I've ever seen anything so bright. It was a UFO. I know it!" Tillie exclaimed.

"Till, let's not jump to crazy conclusions. We really don't know what it could have been. It was probably one of those weather balloons. You know, fell from space kind of thing," Lyla trailed off, losing her sense of confidence with something so unfamiliar. She sat in thought and waited for others' ideas.

"Oh yeah right, Lyle, just a weather balloon. Weather balloons are known to light up the night sky and then disappear into the sea!" Tillie grabbed a bag of chips and crunched loudly.

"Yeah, Till's right! I saw this show once," Adrian started, "all about UFO's. Those things can move quick! Quick as that thing we saw tonight! And they *always* have lights on them! Oh, crap! Tillie was right guys! We saw an actual UFO tonight!"

Lyla spoke up, "Obviously what we saw was unidentified. And it was a flying object. That is, until it hit the water. But there is no need to think it had anything to do with aliens Adrian. That's just a bunch of bull. Not in this day and age, with the technologies the government has? There would be people all over this beach by now scoping it out. Do you see anyone here, little brother? No and you won't either. Because what we saw had nothing to do with aliens. So, calm down. We'll have to wait until morning. If it was anything important, we'll either see it wash up on the beach, or hear about it on the news. Everyone just keep their eyes and ears peeled tomorrow, 'kay?"

"Well, okay, but I'm keeping mine peeled for aaallllliieeeennnss," Adrian finished and everyone burst into laughter. It was late and with all the excitement of the night, everyone was pretty tired and giddy.

"Alright, alright," Lyla tried to finish on a serious note through her own laughter. "But seriously guys, let's pay attention tomorrow, okay? That's the only way we're going to figure this out. And *no more* secrets between us, got it?" She glanced a long while at all three of her siblings. Everyone agreed.

"Let's get home guys," Liam announced like a parent ending a fun day out for the family. "If we're going to be keeping an extra ear out for anything strange from tonight and working full shifts, we'd better get at least a little shut-eye." Everyone agreed again.

7

A Green UFO

The next morning was like many others. It was hustle and bustle at Sigrun, getting in the food for the day and starting prep work for lunch. However, today, the four young Lundgrens were worn out. They all felt a bit like they were moving under water. It was unusual for all four of them to come to work this way on the same day. Everyone assumed it was due to the late night before that the kids were running on empty today. No one talked about anything strange or odd happening last night. No one except the Lundgren children.

"Did you hear anything yet?" Tillie asked Lyla in passing.

"No such luck." Lyla replied quietly.

They all tried to keep a low profile about the night before. They didn't want to appear crazy to everyone else in Sigrun. They also didn't want to be questioned by their mother. There was no fooling that woman. She sensed when people made things up or hid things from her, especially her own children. She wouldn't let up on them until they gave in. All four of them knew this and made up their minds, without telling each other, just to avoid her as much as possible for the day, until they got some information, so they didn't sound like a bunch of nutty kids.

While Liam and Adrian worked in the kitchen, they missed any opportunity to overhear anything from customers. They listened, quite intently, to the news, rather than music on the radio that day. There was no typical banter between the boys that could be heard on any given day in Sigrun. They were quite solemn. So far, the boys heard nothing about the bright, green light over the ocean late the previous night. They said nothing about it to each other for fear of being overheard by someone else in the kitchen: Dad, Anna or Danny.

The boys discussed it quietly to each other that neither would react if they happened to hear something on the radio.

The lunch crowd filed in. It was a smooth tide of customers as usual. People came and went steadily and without problems. Most people that came in the day after the Fourth of July were fairly tired from the previous night's festivities and moved through the restaurant like quiet ghosts. This felt even more eerie to the children with the memory of the green light from last night still fresh in their minds.

The lunch crowd dwindled. The phone rang. It broke through the usual lunch crowd noise. Not that they hadn't had any calls yet that day, but it simply happened at a quiet moment in the restaurant.

"Hello, Sigrun. Liam speaking. How may I help you?"

Liam didn't usually answer the phone, as he was too busy in the kitchen. But he happened to be passing the kitchen phone when it rang, which made him jump on it to stop the ringing.

"Hello? Oh. It's you. The usual today then?" He hung up.

Everyone working at the restaurant went back to their business, as they knew that it was the daily call from no one.

The girls took their lunch break out back, as they frequently did in the summer, to soak up just a few rays of sunshine. Here they caught up on their thoughts of the day. Today's thoughts of course were all about the bright green light.

"So, anything new?" Tillie tried containing her impatience.

"I wish," Lyla replied defeated, hoping for some information soon. "I haven't heard a peep about last night from anyone. Darla and her friends came in here for lunch and I *know* they were on the beach when we were. I just don't get it. How could we be the only ones who saw that thing?" She took a bite of her sandwich wrap.

"I know, right?" Tillie finished her bite and continued, "I mean that thing was bright as, excuse me but, hell, you know? It lit up the whole beach! And *no one* seemed to notice but us? Glad I'm not the only one who thinks that's totally weird! Wonder if the boys heard anything about it on the radio? I'll ask Liam when I go back inside." She finished her bottle of juice.

"Yes. Let me know too, 'kay? No secrets anymore here, kiddies!" Lyla said in a mocking parent tone.

Tillie stood up, finished with her lunch. "I'll go ask him now. Be right back!" The door closed behind her before Lyla had a chance to say anything back.

Lyla was just finishing with her lunch when Tillie finally came back out. "Gee, you must have some news then. That took forever. I finished my sandwich already. So, what's up?"

"Actually, no. There's nothing. Liam and Adrian said they've been listening all day on the radio and there has been no mention of last night's 'light show'. Weird, right?" Tillie sat down across from Lyla.

"Right. Weird. What took you so long then?"

"Oh, I ran into Aaron! He said he was going to come in, remember? Luckily it was while I was on break, so...yeah," Tillie trailed off, realizing she sounded a bit enthusiastic.

"Ooh, Aaaaaron," Lyla mocked. "But wait, you don't have much to say about him. I forgot." She gave such a sweet, sickly smile it made Tillie swat at her.

"Oh stop it. He's nice okaaay? So I get excited when I see him, okaaay? So I *like* him, okaaay? Ugh. Oh crap. I like him? How did that happen? *When* did that happen? Oh man,

I've only known the boy for like a month, not even. What is wrong with me?" She put her head down on the table.

Lyla laughed. "It's okay, Till. These things happen. You and Aaron went through something most people never go through together. It was a life-altering experience. There are bound to be some feelings that come from that. I say go with it. You're young and beautiful I might add," she said as she petted her sister's golden locks. "And he is obviously interested." she smiled at Tillie, sincere and true.

"Really? He's interested too? How do you know that from seeing him, like, once?"

"Oh, boy. Youth is really wasted on the young. Thanks for making me feel like another generation today. But yeah. It's completely apparent that you both have something there between you. And also, apparently, you were the last to know. Now you know. What are you going to do with it?"

"Well, what *can* I do with it? I mean, he doesn't even live here and is only in town a few more days. What is there to do?"

"If you need a list, you are hopeless. Good luck to you, I say." Lyla stood up. "Time to go back to work, my dear. You can figure out what to do while we work dinner tonight. I have faith that you'll figure out what to do, you're a smart girl." Lyla finished, feeling very motherly by this point. She grabbed Tillie by the hand and led her into the restaurant. Tillie, feeling very needy, let her.

"Faith," Tillie mumbled. "Perhaps I should go to Church Sunday. That might help me figure it out."

"Yes. Church is always good to clear the head. I'll go with you if you like," Lyla replied full of genuine kindness.

"Thanks," Tillie breathed out as they entered the restaurant. She smiled, defeated, but happily so.

Dinner was a bit busier than lunch. The boys switched the radio back to music and figured that if there was news, they would have heard it first thing in the morning. The news came on about every hour on the music channel, just little updates and quips throughout the rest of that day and the boys listened carefully each time.

People that the four Lundgrens knew they saw on the beach the night before came into the restaurant for dinner, but no one talked about the bright, green light. None of them could understand how that was. They shot each other looks when they saw someone who they thought might talk about it, but nothing. Then there were a lot of shoulder shrugs back and forth.

The day came and went most uneventfully, much to the confusion of the Lundgren children. They were hoping for a report on the news, or another eye witness to the previous night's events. As the day came to a close, they all helped clean up, volunteering to do it all themselves to give the parents a night off. It really was because they wanted the place to themselves to be able to discuss the previous night without being overheard by their mom or dad.

"So, nothing. All day. Nothing?" Lyla repeated herself sounding almost crazy as she wiped down tables.

"Yep. Just that. Nothing. All day," Adrian agreed with her, not knowing what more to say. There was disbelief in his tone.

"I can't believe it either," said Liam from the kitchen. He was usually in charge of shutting that part down. "I listened all morning to the radio. All morning and not a word. I just don't get it," he finished as he went to the sink and turned it on, leaving just the sound of running water coming from the kitchen.

"What I don't get, is why I saw Darla, Jeff and Scott and all their friends here today and no one said anything about it!" Tillie closed up the cash register. "I mean, how could you be on the beach last night and miss that light?"

"Maybe it was all a dream," Lyla responded sounding tired, relenting. "Maybe we all fell asleep on the beach at the same time and some weather balloon thingy woke us up and we put more into it than what was really there. I mean, we've all done things like that before, where you get woken up by something and then you think something was happening, but then it isn't?" Lyla stopped talking and questioned herself if any of that sounded right. She kept wiping down tables.

"Are you serious? What kind of lamebrain reasoning is that?" Liam came out of the kitchen, shut off the lights and started mopping the floor. "Sis, you must be tired. Get some good sleep tonight, 'kay? You are clearly not yourself." He continued mopping around where Lyla had cleaned tables.

"I know, I know! I just can't seem to figure out why we are the only people who seemed to see anything last night!" She said, exasperated. She finished the last table and went into the office.

"Aw, don't feel bad," Adrian yelled back to Lyla. "None of us can!"

"We were the only people who saw a bright, green light over the ocean in the middle of the night," Tillie said sounding like a reporter on the nightly news. She was trying to sort the facts. "Four people saw a bright, green light appear over the water. Then just as suddenly, it disappeared into the water. It was the middle of the night." She paused, trying to think if she got all the facts right. Then said, "Is that everything? Did we miss something? None of these things seem to tie together. This is so frustrating!"

"I know. It *is* frustrating. Why us? Why did *we* see something and no one else? What makes us so special?" Liam repeated.

"We *are* special, I guess." Adrian replied and looked as though he was trying to figure something out.

"What is that supposed to mean?" Tillie finished with the cash register and wiped down the counter. Everything was close to clean now, which meant time downstairs was almost over. They couldn't linger down here too long or Heather and Cord would start to wonder where they were and come looking/snooping.

"I just mean, look at the facts. You saved someone's life *in the water*. Liam can swim faster than motorboats, *in the water*. We saw something happen together, *over the water*.

So, my question is, what is it with us and water?" Adrian puffed up a little and felt very proud of his deduction. They paused in their working and chewed on that idea for a minute.

Lyla re-emerged from the office. "You have a point Adrian," she said, startling the three out of their thoughts. "On all of those things, you are right. And then some. We *all* have some history with water."

"Wait, what? *I* do? What 'history'? I mean, I like to swim, I swim well. Well, not Liam speed, but I'm good. I like the water, but I don't remember anything ever happening to me with water that was special. Share, please."

"Share? What are we sharing tonight?" Cord entered silently from the kitchen and nearly scared everyone out of their shoes.

"Umm...sharing, dad? Us? Ha ha," Tillie exclaimed and laughed.

She looked at everyone else to get them to join in and kept laughing a little too long. Adrian looked over at Lyla with his look of "we'll talk later." She nodded once.

"Oh, don't try to con me, young lady," her father replied, but kept a light tone of fun.

"Oh, Dad, we were just sharing our thoughts and Adrian asked me about mine, of course." Lyla always knew how to save the day.

"Oh! And don't we all love your thoughts, my dear!" He waltzed up to Lyla and kissed her on the forehead like he had done since she was a little girl. "You kids were taking so long down here, your mother sent me to help out. Apparently she feels sorry for you down here all by yourselves. But I see you are just about wrapped up here, aren't you?" Cord finished and waited for everyone near the kitchen.

"All by ourselves? Dad, there are four of us." Adrian explained like he was teaching math to a first grader.

"Oh *I* know that son," Cord replied in a friendly tone, "But your mother just isn't used to you all being four able bodies and minds. Working together. Look at you all! The place looks great. Thanks kids!"

Everyone knew that meant the night was over. Another successful day at Sigrun came to a close. Albeit a peculiar one.

8

Wonder Baby

Days flowed by. The summer was hot, steamy and already at the end of July. Summer time felt as though it went by twice as fast as any ordinary time.

Adrian tried hard to get time alone to talk with Lyla. He even went too far when he tried to share the bathroom with her, but that ended, not surprisingly, with her throwing him out of the room with a "Later, moron!"

Days went by without time to talk. Every time Adrian shot Lyla a pleading look, they were interrupted with work, or worse, parents. By the time they got upstairs at night, they were exhausted and went off to bed. Tillie and Liam even tried to create situations for them to talk alone, as they knew any information shared would soon enough be shared with them as well.

Day after day, Adrian tried to join the girls for their break after the lunch rush in the restaurant. He went out back only to find they had company most days: Aaron. It was filled with a lot of awkward silences and Lyla trying to start conversations. Adrian ended up going back to work early most of the time.

One day, walking into the dining area from the kitchen, he heard, "Hey there young, man." Anna said a bit flustered, "Watch out! Old lady here!"

"Wha...," Adrian looked up from his thoughts and he and Anna collided. His face flushed immediately and he apologized. "Oh gee...oh! Gosh, so sorry Anna! Really! Let me get that for you," he bent down to pick up the tray of dirty glasses that was knocked to the floor.

He was so distracted, all of Anna's yelling in Italian put him back to reality.

"I really am sorry, Anna. No, don't worry. Nothing broke, see?" He had everything back on the tray, ready to carry it into the kitchen. "No, no, I'll do it," he said, "I'll clean it up. You just go and fix yourself up. And again, I really am sorry!"

"Oh!" Anna said among a lot of other things Adrian didn't understand. Then finally, she said in English, "Alright then, young man! Just remember that when you come in here, whatever was in your head is now *off* until you are off duty!" With that, she stormed herself off to the restroom.

"You're right, you're right, sorry!" Adrian yelled to her, but she simply waved her hand back at him in a shooing manor and kept walking. He unloaded the glasses and went to get a rag to clean the floor.

"Don't worry, bro, I've got it. You go and see if you can find Lyla. I know that's been your distraction this last couple of weeks." Liam was cleaning up the floor before Adrian had a chance to argue about it. "Can't say I blame you. So, go, see if you can talk." Liam nodded his head back outside toward where the girls were with Aaron.

"Man, thanks a lot, Liam. You're right, I know. I just hate upsetting Anna, for anything. She's sure one hot-blooded little lady! You think I ought to apologize again when she comes back?"

"No way. Leave it alone. She'll cool off, she always does. She just felt a bit embarrassed. She doesn't like to make mistakes in front of customers and she lost her cool in front of them, so that got her all flustered."

"Yeah, I see what you're saying." Adrian stepped out the back door, to see if he could talk to Lyla once again. He walked outside and this time thought he'd ask if he could talk with Lyla alone. Something about the business, he would say.

Yes, that had to work. Being five years apart in age, Adrian wasn't used to spending time with Lyla alone, outside of work.

"Yes, Adrian?" Lyla asked as he approached.

"Well, yeah, umm...I forgot to ask you...sorry if I'm interrupting," he looked over at Tillie and Aaron. Tillie shook her head and rolled her eyes. "Anyway, Lyla, can we take a walk? I have some questions...ideas for the website and I just wanted to run them past you to make sure I have all my information right."

"Yes, of course Adrian. I was finished with my lunch anyway." She picked up her napkins and went toward the restaurant to throw them away.

Everything sounded so formal, Adrian felt strange asking Lyla to talk.

Tillie was right on board, "Don't worry, sis, I'll get those for you." She grabbed Lyla's lunch things and set them on her empty ones. She knew why Adrian wanted to talk. Things were also more comfortable with Aaron. Spending lunchtime with him and Lyla was becoming routine. Tillie didn't mind being left alone with him for a change. She felt ready to see to see what it was like.

"Oh. Thanks," Lyla replied and sort of trailed off. She looked at Adrian. "Shall we walk, then?" Again, it sounded like they were in a different place in time. *Ugh. Let's walk already*, she thought.

The two walked out toward the beach. They kicked off their shoes by the bench before the sand. It was an unconscious decision on each of their part. Just felt right. Adrian waited. He knew that Lyla would be the first one to talk. Why they needed to be alone. Why they were here, now. He waited.

They were about a hundred yards from Sigrun by now. The waves were also on their side, roaring with the wind today. The other people on the beach wouldn't hear anything, even if they weren't listening. Adrian waited. The sun was shining and it was really a beautiful day. It gave them a taste of what they'd been missing while they were at work. They didn't really want a taste. As much as they enjoyed working at Sigrun, they didn't need to be teased with sand and sun. Adrian looked out over the waves. He waited.

Finally, when he felt he was going to burst out and yell at Lyla to speak, she answered his silence. "You were just a baby." She said, almost accusing.

"Huh? What? Oh," Adrian replied, feeling foolish and scolded.

It was so easy sometimes with Lyla to feel that way. It's not that she meant to be the parent and him the child being corrected, but this was the way things were between them. They were all used to responding to each other based on who was older. They were also all just starting to get use to the age where it wasn't necessary to do so anymore. They helped each other out, stood up for each other and took care of each other without worrying about who was older like they did when they were little. It seemed the older they got, the closer in age they became.

Adrian ignored his blush, "Sorry, I know what you're talking about. Go ahead."

"Thanks. You confused me there for a minute," she said with a smirk on her face. "Anyway, like I said, you were a baby, I think you were almost one-and-a-half, so that meant I was only seven. I remember I was seven because we just celebrated my birthday and I felt oh so much older. Just one day makes such a difference in your age then." Lyla kicked some seaweed out of her way. It splashed into the oncoming waves. The sand was warm on her feet and the water a cool refreshment for them.

"Heh, yeah, I remember those days," Adrian said, missing them a bit.

"So, Mom and Dad took you into the water. I sat on the beach and built a sandcastle near our towels. It was just the four of us, I can't remember why," Lyla trailed off for a moment, trying to remember. She continued her memory. "Anyway, Liam and Tillie must have been out with friends or something. So, all I can really remember is Mom and Dad swam with you out in the water. I wasn't really paying attention. I was into my sandcastle. So, next thing I knew and I didn't know how long it was, but I was putting the finishing touches on my castle, so I guess it had been a while that you were out there. Mom and dad were bringing you in, almost cheering for you. Congratulating you for something, I wasn't sure what."

"Okay, c'mon! You're killing me here. Get to it, would ya?" Adrian blurted out like he'd been holding his breath this whole time.

"Okay, okay. You're right. So, when I asked them what happened, they simply told me that you were a swimming champ."

"That's it? What the heck, Lyles, I thought you were going to tell me something important here! That could be any parent swimming with their child! How is that special?"

"Well, if you would let me finish," Lyla got all parental again for a second. "I went back to my castle and they thought I wasn't listening. The two of them couldn't stop talking about you and your skills! And I distinctly remember dad saying, 'It was well over a minute! He was swimming under that water like he was born to do!' Now, keep in mind, I was young, so I may have some of that wrong," she responded quickly because of the way Adrian was now looking at her. "But I just always remembered it that way. I never asked them about it. I didn't think there was anything to ask. I just thought that's what babies are supposed to do, like Dad said."

"Under for over a minute? Really." Adrian seemed too stunned to say any more. He just looked at Lyla, begging her to make sense of it all.

"That's how I remember it, yes," Lyla replied. "Like I said, I could be wrong, but over the years, whenever I have thought about it, it never changed or wavered. Those are the words Dad said. And it's not even the 'over the minute' part that surprised me. As I got older, the part that I question is the 'like he was born to do.' You were born to be under water for a long time, apparently. Yes, that's what I'm saying," Lyla replied to the, again, strange look she was getting from Adrian. The poor boy looked downright tortured. "Now that I think about it," she continued, "it's all very strange and I should be asking Mom and Dad about it right now!"

She turned and looked as if she were going to run back. Just then, Adrian grabbed her arm.

"Don't move, okay? Just don't move. Listen. It makes *perfect* sense, Lyles." Lyla now looked at him a bit flustered. Adrian continued, "I can always be underwater, shall we say, comfortably. I mean, *really comfortably*. When I'm under the water, it hardly feels as though I am in any different climate than when I'm in the air!"

"You know, we should really go get the others. They need to hear this too, Ade," Lyla said, her heart fluttering. She looked a little wild about the eyes. Adrian tried to calm her down.

"No, look. I am saying that they were right, don't you see? Being under water for me *is* as comfortable as being out here with you now. It just always has been. I thought it was just the way it was for everybody. Whenever I swam with friends, I could stay under the water for so much longer than they could! I never understood why they would come up gasping for air after what felt like just a few seconds to me. Then they started to question why I didn't do the same. I just told them I didn't know why I didn't and from then on, I learned to hide the fact that I was different. I thought they would think I was some sort of freak if I told them or showed them what I could do. So I never explored it after that. I just pretended that I was like everyone else I saw in the water. I never told anyone."

There was long silence after that. The two of them just looked at one another and silently tried to figure out what to do about it all.

They both started slowly back toward the restaurant. The day seemed somehow permanently changed. It was still a beautiful sunny day on the beach, yet there was something extra. Something indescribable, but both of them could feel it like electricity in the air. It made the day somehow less clear, despite the sun fully shining.

They were almost back to the restaurant. They had to settle things soon, before they got back. There had to be some sort of plan and a way to tell Tillie and Liam.

"Meeting tonight. My room. Make sure Mom and Dad are in their room first. Don't let them see or hear anything." Lyla put the plan down. They were all set. "Man, I'll have something to pray about Sunday as well," she said more to herself than to Adrian.

"I'll tell the others," Adrian replied. "Liam and I will meet you girls in your room. Don't worry, we'll make sure it's late enough, Mom and Dad won't hear a thing."

"Good. See you tonight. After tonight...heh," Lyla half laughed as they approached the restaurant.

"Where have you two been?" Cord asked his youngest and oldest children as they walked into the kitchen from the back door. "Seems awful mysterious, you two disappearing down the beach." He gave them a scolding look, but the one where they knew he was in a joking mood.

"Gee dad, what is this, the inquisition? A kid can't talk to his older sis about girl troubles? Aw great, now I've gone and spilled the beans. Thanks, Dad." Adrian covered his tracks like snow blowing over a mountain top.

"Aw, son, don't be shy about girl troubles! And besides, why would you go to your older sister when you have your great ole' dad to ask for advice?" Cord answered as he put his arm around Adrian's shoulder. Liam laughed as he prepped vegetables for the night's meals.

"Well, Dad, I wanted some advice that didn't originate in the cave days. No offense," Adrian added with his hand in the air toward Cord like a white flag of surrender.

"Ha! None taken son, none taken! You're probably right anyway. This old soul's advice would probably be too over-the-top for your young years!" He roughed Adrian's hair and gave a little push on his head. "Now wash up and get helping your brother. He's been prepping all by himself, thanks to your long walk on the beach. Huh, must be nice."

Adrian went over and did what he was told. Everyone knew that Cord was great to joke around with, but when he talked business, he was all business. His kids and employees knew this well.

"I'm gonna see if Mom needs me in the office," Lyla said, still laughing from Cord's not-quite advice to Adrian. "See you guys later." She looked at Adrian more seriously this time, then quickly turned around and headed out to the office.

"What was that?" Liam asked Adrian. Now the two were alone in the kitchen, as Cord had gone out to the dining room with Lyla.

"What was what?" Adrian asked back.

"Well, I mean Lyla. What was her look when she said 'see you guys later'?"

"Oh yeah. Almost forgot. Not really. Meeting. The girls' room. Tonight. After D and M are in for the night. You know what I mean?" Adrian gave Liam a look of *now you're in the club*. A smile crept upon his lips.

"Oh. Oh yeah. Sure. Right," Liam responded, still chopping veggies, speeding up a little as the thoughts raced. "Well, back to work. We'll have time for discussions later," he said in a lower voice this time, almost trying to convince himself as much as Adrian to concentrate on work.

Luckily the rest of the night was a busy one. Kept everyone's mind from wandering too far. Adrian was able to give Tillie the head's up about the meeting in passing during the evening. She was pleased to finally find out what is going on. She was such a busybody. All of the mad, golden curls on her head were a sign of the busyness inside her mind.

Heather told the children that she and Cord would do cleanup tonight. They were a bit surprised, but Heather told them it was to make up for the four of them doing it the last time, "all by themselves". She still couldn't bring herself to admit that all four of her children were growing up. They all laughed and teased her a bit, but Lyla and Tillie gave her a hug and Tillie kissed her on the cheek saying, "Thanks mom. You'll always be the best."

"So you all, go then. Go on upstairs and take the night to relax. I think you can all use some of that," Heather finished, shooing the children upstairs. Cord was already mopping the floors and most of the main things were done, so the children knew they weren't leaving their parents to do most of the work. It was more of a gesture on Heather's part, but one they accepted graciously.

"Gee, funny how tonight Mom and Dad decide to give us a night off, huh?" Adrian smiled at Tillie and Lyla as they went upstairs into the living room area.

"I know! I was thinking the same thing!" Tillie smiled right back and then added, "Let's go talk right now! I've been busting all day to find out what is going on!" She ran across to their bedrooms.

"Hold on there, lil' sis," Liam called after her. "Mom and Dad are still awake. I'm not sure we can chance..."

"Oh, it's fine, Li. It'll only take a minute," Lyla interrupted. Liam looked over, slightly surprised at Lyla's statement. She was usually the cautious one.

"Oh. Alright. Fine. Let's do this," Liam responded. The boys and Lyla crossed over the living room to the bedrooms and went into the girls' room. Adrian, being the last one in, looked back to make sure the coast was clear. The studio was empty and it was quiet. He closed the door most of the way and left it just ajar so they could hear when their time was up.

"Okay, so? What's going on already?" Tillie couldn't hold her excitement in any longer.

"Okay, okay, so, it's not really big or anything," Adrian started to say, but again, Lyla interrupted.

"Well, it's pretty significant Ade," she said. "I mean, it's not Liam swimming boat speed or anything, but it's right up there for sure." She smiled at him, reassuringly. She looked like their mother for a split second. Adrian smiled back and instantly felt comfortable with his situation.

"Well, yeah, I know, but it's not like some long story or anything," looking at Tillie, he remembered how he felt waiting for Lyla on the beach. He blurted out, "So I can hold my breath for a really long time under water. I mean, a *really, long* time. I haven't tested it lately, not since I was little, but being under water for me is really just like being here now, with you." He stopped there and waited for reactions from Tillie and Liam. Expecting Tillie to burst out with something first, he looked at her.

"Well, that's great, bro!" It was Liam who actually reacted first. Everyone turned their heads like they were watching a tennis match.

"Yeah, that's really neat!" Tillie added. Again, heads turned.

"I thought it was going to be something really weird. Like, I don't know, you grow a tail in the water or something!" Liam said with a smirk. "Well, cause, you know bro, you've always been the weird one," he added, then laughed.

The girls looked at Adrian and laughed too, but not quite as heartily as Liam did. Adrian started laughing too and did a mock of a hunched-over, crazy-looking fool.

Just then, they heard a door open across the house and then Cord. "Hey, kids! What's so funny in there?"

The children's laughter quieted down and they realized that their time alone was over for now. They also all looked at each other with relief because they knew that nothing was overheard and that the laughter could be about anything they wanted. The relief was sensed all at once.

The next second, Cord and Heather opened the door. Tillie was on her bed, sprawled out across it. Liam sat on Lyla's bed and leaned back on the pillows. Adrian was left standing, as Lyla sat in the only chair in the room. He looked like he'd just given a speech to all of them about something. Realizing this, Adrian suddenly found some room to sit on Lyla's bed.

"Well, what's all the fun about?" Heather asked as they came into the room. The room was completely full now, as it wasn't very big to begin with. "I'm sure glad you all are relaxing, I just didn't realize there would be a party when we got home!" She laughed and it sounded so wonderful that everyone else couldn't help but laugh with her.

Heather had such a hold on her family and they all just adored her for it. She didn't realize the power she possessed when it came to her family. But she knew that they were the most important things in her life, so she was always there for them. That was the best thing she thought she could do. Again, they loved her for it.

"Oh, mom." Tillie chimed in first. "Adrian just did a funny impression. We're all tired out, so we were laughing, maybe a bit more than necessary, but it just felt good! Hey, while everyone is in here, Lyles and I are going to Church Sunday. Any takers?" Tillie's smooth transition of topic was genius, as usual.

Everyone was in agreement as Heather looked around at her four children. It was in this most random moment that she really saw them. Not that she didn't see them every day or that she didn't pay attention to them, on the contrary.

Every so often there were stolen moments of perfect clarity when she looked upon her children. (Every parent has had that moment, so fleeting, sometimes they went unnoticed. Sometimes they didn't. They usually ended with the child saying, "What? What are you looking at?" or some such accusation. The parent then realized that they've been completely staring at their child.) She was so enveloped in them for just that moment that nothing else in the whole world mattered. Her heart filled so rapidly and fully just then that it pounded in her chest and forced a deep breath from her. Contentment. Happiness. Love. A large feeling, for just a slice of time. Heather just experienced that, times four.

She suddenly felt overwhelmed by her beautiful, practically adult, children. They were all so wonderful just then, so perfect. It was so clear. They were constantly changing. Even right in that moment, she knew they were changing. In that same moment she felt a lifetime of changes and growth from all of them and at the same time, felt as though it had all gone by in an instant. She felt the fullness of life all in that one moment. She was very content.

9

Real Power

Just as quickly as the moment came, the next thing Heather heard was, "Are you okay mom?" Liam stood up and put his arm around her and looked at her, slightly concerned. The moment was over.

Heather smiled and said, "Oh yes. Quite fine, actually. Quite fine." She drifted for a second, then finished, "You all look so great getting along and so happy. It warms a mother's heart and then...*church!*" She gestured dramatically to her chest and did a wonderfully fake swoon. She knew this would bring the moment to a close, but without being accused of being a weird, mushy mom. Sure enough, the girls laughed and the boys half laughed. "Now, I must bid you adieu and goodnight!" She exited the girls' room in her dramatic, silly fashion and grabbed Cord's arm on the way.

"Oh. Yeah, goodnight then kids. Love ya." Cord said as the door closed almost in his face. Heather pulled him with the door. She knew when it was time to exit any situation. Always the lady.

"Love you guys!" The children said almost in chorus. A mushy moment for sure to most, but in the Lundgren house it was a frequent one, so no one thought much of it. And Heather went to bed that night and felt as happy as if she won the lottery.

The "kids" waited a few moments until they heard their parents' bedroom door close. They knew it was for the night, so they breathed a collective sigh of relief.

"So, Ade, we should test your skills sometime soon," Liam started, right back into the conversation.

"Wha? Yeah, that would be pretty cool!" Adrian responded with a grin across his face.

"Ooh, yes!" Tillie exclaimed, "I want to be there when he does. I'll be the timer."

"Yes, we probably should." Lyla sounded like her authoritative self. "And yes, Til, it would be fun," Lyla finished as she drifted off in thought. A smile crept across her face as well.

"Okay, so when do we do this?" Adrian sounded almost anxious and looked from sibling to sibling.

"How about this weekend after closing? Saturday night, not too late. Remember, *church*," Tillie copied her mother's fake swoon.

"Well, Til, that might work. Do you mind doing this in the dark, Ade?" Lyla looked over to Adrian.

"Oh, c'mon! Do you think someone who doesn't consider holding their breath under water actually holding their breath would care if it's dark or not when they did? You don't care a lick, do ya, bro?" Liam clapped his hand onto Adrian's shoulder.

"Yeah, it's fine really," Adrian answered as his shoulder gave a bit under Liam's strength. Not letting on of course, Adrian continued, "Why don't we go out to the bluff after 10 and we'll see what I can do? The beach will be mostly empty by then and I'm sure that anyone left wouldn't be paying attention to us." Another smile in anticipation. He looked almost like an innocent child asking about why the sky is blue.

"The bluff. Is that necessary? I mean, the cliffs and all, how are we going to really see what is going on in the water?" Lyla listed her questions, always calculating, always figuring.

"Oh yeah, you're right. As usual," Adrian instantly answered.

"Okay, the beach then. Where we all saw what we know we saw, but no one else did. Seems to me that anyone out there is definitely not paying attention to anyone else," Liam announced.

"Yeah, okay. I say let's do it," Lyla finalized. That meant it was set.

"Great! Oh this is going to be awesome! I wish I could ask Susan and Aaron to join us," Tillie went from giddy to almost disappointed all in one sentence.

"Yeah, *no*." Liam sounded almost like a lion protecting its young. "We have to promise each other right here and now that these things about us all remain between us and only us. No telling anyone. Not even Mom and Dad. Not yet anyway. We're not even sure what is going on with all this stuff and we don't need to worry them about it. Not until we know more, at least."

"I agree." Lyla seconded his motion for secrecy. She stood up from her chair and looked very in charge. As beautiful and feminine as Lyla appeared, she filled a room with a presence of importance. Others knew she was all business when she spoke. She had no problem stepping up to the challenge. "We simply need to know more. About everyone. We need to figure out what exactly it is we do know, so we can approach Mom and Dad with what we don't know without freaking them out or worrying them."

"Yes. That's good." Tillie chimed in, "I mean, we don't even know if you have any special 'water abilities'." She finished with finger quotes around the last words. There was silence. Everyone turned their eyes to Lyla. "Do you?"

"Well, I wasn't sure I should mention anything," Lyla started, but was interrupted by multiple voices.

"What?"

"What do you mean?"

"You've been keeping secrets?"

"We weren't supposed to have any secrets anymore!"

"Well, what is going on?"

"You'd better spill it, sis!"

"Jeez guys, take it easy!" Lyla crossed over to the door, opened it enough for her face to stick out and listened across the room for any stirring. There was nothing. Luckily. "Now, everybody just chill out and let me explain."

"This better be good, we have to get up early tomorrow for deliveries." Tillie suddenly looked like a little kid at Christmastime. Eager to go to sleep, but really not able to at all.

"Okay. Well, like I was trying to say before I was so bombarded with everyone's thoughts, I wasn't even going to mention anything, not until Tillie brought it up."

"Me? What did I say?" Tillie gestured toward herself, acting completely innocent. A little melodramatic.

"Well, you just brought up the fact that we didn't know anything about me yet." Lyla answered her sister in a most gentle way and smiled at her. This put Tillie at ease. "I'm not even really sure this counts, but taking in everyone else's stories of late, I think it might. Okay," she started again as she sensed everyone's impatience. "Do any of you remember back when I was a junior in high school and on the softball team?"

"Ha! Yeah, if you want to call keeping score 'on the team'," Liam laughed as his finger quotes hung in the air.

"Well, yes, okay, but I was still on the team and still had to be at practices and games and got credit for it, so whatever. I was invited to Dawn's sweet sixteen birthday party. It was going to be the party of the year." Lyla looked very in the moment now, back to her younger days.

"Oh yeah, I remember Dawn," Tillie added and remembered her youth now. "She was always so nice. I remember you guys planned that party for months! I was so little, I used to think I was going to go with you guys, you were so cool!" Tillie grinned hugely and wrapped her arms up around her knees and looked like a sweet, little girl again. *Funny*, she thought, *that brings me back to feeling twelve again.*

"Ha ha, yeah. You always loved being the tagalong, Til," Lyla still said sweetly to her sister as she felt the vibe from her pose. She continued, this time determined not to be interrupted. "So, okay, Dawn's party. Huge. Party of the year. Etcetera. Then, the week of the party, I found out the softball team had a game added to the roster for that same day! I talked to the coach and there was nothing I could do short of faking illness to get out of it. Which wouldn't have worked, because then I wouldn't have been able to go to the party, either. I was so upset. I remember thinking it was the end of my year. It was as if the whole world was against me and I was mad at everyone that week! Heh." Lyla almost laughed at how trivial it all felt now, when she called up the feelings so readily. They just felt hollow now.

"Anyway, so, Saturday morning came and the game started at ten and the party was at two. It would have actually worked out well if it hadn't been an away game that was going to take three hours of driving time. Anyway, I keep getting caught up in the details, sorry." Lyla plunked down onto the bed with Tillie. The girls were on one bed, the boys on the other. They operated like this frequently without realizing it.

"So, as it happened, I was sitting in my room, about to get ready to go to school for the game and I was really upset. I remember just sitting there feeling my anger and just not even thinking, really, just feeling it. Every thought that came into my head was so negative, that I just chose to feel instead of think. My anger seemed to consume me. Like the more I gave into it, the more it took me over. I really don't remember ever being that mad before or since," she trailed off and tried to remember, then back on track. "Seems so silly now, all of it. So okay, so feeling all mad, I stood up and went to the closet to change. I looked out the window and I saw this huge mass of gray clouds coming across toward the house. I mean, this wasn't an ordinary storm coming across, in fact, it seemed to come out of nowhere. The sky had clouds in it that day, it wasn't particularly sunny, but these looked like gloom and doom all over the place. It startled me actually. Sort of brought be out of my mood for a second. Then I had a brief thought that maybe the game would be cancelled and I could go to the party. I remember feeling like this surge of energy through me all of a sudden." Lyla was quiet for a few seconds; no one interrupted the silence. "Yes. I can remember now. It was almost like a shock, like when you rub your feet on the floor and then touch something. But it was through my whole body and brought chills to me and made the hair on my arms stand on end."

"Lyles! You *are* special!" Tillie almost squealed. "This is fantastic! Isn't it? I mean...oh...sorry." She squirreled back to her pillow on the bed and let Lyla continue.

"I had never had a feeling like that before or since. Much like my angry feeling. I went to the window and opened it. Something just drove me to do it. Like I felt a connection to this coming storm. I wanted to *feel* it too. I stood there, in front of the window and opened my arms out toward the clouds. The breeze hit me. It felt cold and hard and just charged me even more. I felt so alive. I felt so one with this thing, whatever it was, coming on. The more it came across to the house, the more I wanted it to. It felt such a part of me, like something I'd been missing all my life. Like some part of me was coming home. And boy, did I want it to. My breathing was fast and the breeze turned to wind by then. The dark clouds sped across the sky and they no longer frightened me, but thrilled me. I remember I felt both this charge of energy and my anger at the same time. I saw and heard lightening flash, it seemed almost right in front of me. And I wasn't scared, no. It was amazing. It didn't occur to me that I could possibly be hurt by this storm. Didn't even occur to me."

Another moment of silence passed. The whole room felt charged somehow now. Everyone was fascinated into a daze by Lyla's recount of the storm.

"I remember," Liam said quietly. "I remember that storm." He came out of the daze to explain. "Wasn't that the day the school cancelled all its activities and you spent the day in your room?" Lyla nodded. "I thought you were just being a dramatic teenage girl, Lyles! I had no idea," he trailed off again and listened.

"Yeah, yeah, that was it, Liam. And yes, I spent the day in my room, but I wasn't really in the room. It felt like I became part of the storm. It was as if I left my body here and went out there to it and let it fill me and I filled it. I stood at the window and just let all the wind and all the rain and even the lightening surround me. I started to cry. The storm got worse. I cried harder and harder, it seemed I couldn't stop myself. And it also seemed the harder I cried, the more it rained and there was more lightning and thunder. It was all so amazing and beautiful and terrifying at the same time, I couldn't move. I didn't notice when Mom came into the room."

"Uh!" Tillie gasped and her hand came to her mouth.

"Yeah, Tils, Mom came in. 'What on Earth is going on here! Lyla, what are you doing?' She was suddenly right behind me and grabbed me back to Earth. She closed the window and looked at me. She looked so worried and scared it brought me right back to reality. It was like one second I was out there, with the storm and the next I was right there with Mom. Wet with rain and tears, I stood and looked at her for a second, then collapsed into her arms."

"That's the last I remember of the storm. The next thing I remember was waking up all snug in my bed and it was dark outside and still raining, although much calmer, but steady. Mom sat by the bed and was right there as soon as I opened my eyes. I was really out of it. I don't remember much of anything she said, or if she even said anything. I felt exhausted, like you do when you've been sick for a few days and then you're better, but weak? Yeah, like that, but really bad. Mom had a tray of food near the bed and I saw it and I didn't even have to ask her. She was on it and had it to me before I could speak."

"Holy crap, Lyles, I remember all of this. Mom said you'd gotten sick from being caught in the rain. She said you'd caught a chill or something. She seemed so calm about it, so I didn't think twice. And all this time," Liam drifted into his thoughts.

"The short end of this long story is that everything was cancelled that day due to the storm. The game. Dawn's birthday party. Everything. It was quite a doozy. Mom told me the party was cancelled and that they would reschedule everything for a later date. I remember feeling so foolish and childish. I felt like all that anger was for nothing. If only I'd checked the weather for that day, maybe I could have avoided all of this."

"I never really thought of my connection to the storm. Not until all of you and your stories started coming to the surface of late. Not until Tillie mentioned me and my 'special ability'. I'm not even really sure of it now, except I would like to learn more. I never really explored it because Mom never said anything about it after that day and I just thought it was all in my crazy, teenage head. So, over the years, I just put it in the same place you put any memory. And left it there. Until now. Now I want to know, along with the rest of you."

"Well, let's find out. Together." Adrian spoke up confidently. "Let's both put our 'powers' to the test this weekend. Why not?"

Liam gave his approval. "Seems like a good idea, Lyles. What do you say?"

"Oh, my gosh! This weekend is going to be awesome." Tillie approved, not surprisingly.

"Whoa, whoa. Let's not be hasty about this, now. Like I said, I'm not even sure I had anything to do with that storm and why would I want to cause another one like that if that's what I can do?" Lyla had a tinge of fright in her voice.

"Take it easy, sis," Liam got up and went over to Lyla on her bed. He put his hand on her shoulder, but gently, not like he did to Adrian earlier. It reassured her. "We can just test the waters, pun intended." He smiled, like only Liam could smile.

Lyla smiled and relaxed just a little bit.

"We don't know if this possible connection of yours was all or nothing. Let's at least test if it is. Your account of what happened sounded very intense, maybe that's why the storm was too. Let's see what might happen if you felt something more positive. We can just see what happens, okay, Lyles?" He patted her lap and held her hand.

"Yes. That doesn't sound too bad," Lyla replied and smiled back at him. "You guys will all be there to stop anything if it gets out of control, right?"

"Absolutely." Adrian agreed. "We wouldn't let anything bad happen. Promise." He sat up from the other bed and joined hands with Liam and Lyla.

Tillie slapped her hand on top of the pile and said, "Okay, it's a deal then, people. We are going to do this, this weekend." Lyla took her hand from the bottom of the pile and placed it to the top. Liam followed and so forth until all of them moved hands around and everyone laughed. It felt good to end on such a relaxing note and eased the tension from Lyla's story. There was real power there. They just needed to find out how much.

10

Testing the Waters

The weekend came more quickly than they could have imagined. Things at work were so busy, the kids didn't have much time to anticipate anything. The four of them found themselves closing up Saturday night with Heather and Cord. It was all pretty usual, everyone had their jobs and things went smoothly. They decided they had to tell their parents about going to the beach after work, but they made it sound like they were all meeting friends down there. So Heather and Cord wished them well and they were off to the beach.

"Wow, that seemed almost too easy." Tillie was the first to break the silent walk. She made sure they were all far enough out of earshot to talk.

"Yeah, I know. Almost too good to be true." Adrian stole a quick look behind him, just to be sure no one was back there.

Lyla and Liam just smiled, like they knew something the other two didn't.

"What's so funny?" Tillie looked like someone had just made fun of her.

"Oh nothing," Lyla answered, still sharing the smile with Liam.

"Oh yeah, cause that look is nothing," Adrian added. "Whatever, guys. C'mon, let's go." Adrian took a stride ahead of everyone. His way of pouting.

"It's just that you guys are being too paranoid. It's cute," Liam chimed in with his big smile.

"Yeah guys, relax. It's Saturday night and we just gave the house to our parents for a while. Do you really think they're going to want to come out with us?" This time Lyla let out a bit of a laugh and Adrian and Tillie both stopped in their tracks. They turned to face Liam and Lyla.

"Ok, that was just T-M-I, Lyles, really." Tillie swung back around and her long curls grazed Lyla's face.

It made Lyla laugh this time.

Adrian stepped forward to keep Tillie's pace. "Yeah, totally gross guys, thanks for the imagery. Now I'll need even more therapy when I grow up."

Liam and Lyla just laughed together. They couldn't help themselves.

They reached the beach, which was about a hundred feet from their back door, in what felt like no time. The air smelled so sweet and clean. There was something about night air on the ocean that made it a magical atmosphere. It transported you to another realm. They looked for the place they were in the last time they were here. There were a few bonfires going, people enjoying the night. Funny, that was what the children were supposed to be doing tonight. They hoped their story was believable. They didn't like hiding things from their parents, but they thought this was for the better, for now. Until they knew for themselves something more.

"Yes here. I think we were about here," Liam said. He spread his arms out indicating the general area.

"I think you're right," Adrian agreed. He looked around to be sure.

"This will do. Besides, it's remote from everyone else here tonight." Lyla sounded the most authoritative, as usual. Yet somehow she managed to not sound bossy. Her family loved her for that. Sometimes it even gave comfort. Tonight was no exception.

"I've got my timer ready to go," Tillie finished as she took her stopwatch from her pocket and put the string around her neck. Everyone looked at her puzzled for a minute. "What? Okay, so it's not mine. I borrowed it from the track team for tonight, alright? I know people!" She felt very put on the spot and determined to prove her innocence.

Everyone went back to setting blankets out on the sand. They wanted to look like everyone else, so as to not draw attention to themselves. Tillie relaxed and helped them.

"Okay, so who's first?" Adrian asked as he took his shirt off. He kicked his shoes off and was ready to take his pants off, bathing suit being underneath of course.

"Well, bro, we might as well go first, as you'll probably take the longest to test out and I know I could swim all night. Then, when we're done, we'll both be here for you, Lyles," Liam finished and looked at Lyla reassuringly. He also stripped off his outer clothes to his suit.

"Sounds solid guys. Thanks," Lyla added. She and Tillie sat on the blankets and finished getting settled.

"What if someone sees Liam?" Tillie actually sounded worried.

Liam laughed, "Oh, don't worry about that! I'm going straight out across the bay! No one will catch a glimpse of this." Liam made his best muscle pose and everyone laughed.

He loved doing that whenever he was in his suit and it still made them all laugh.

"Okay, but really guys, I'm going to go to the island across here and back. That's about a mile each way. I figured that would be easiest to calculate." He looked over at Tillie.

"Okay, I'm ready when you are, *bro*!" She answered his look and smiled.

"So, I figure if Ade and I start at the same time, you'll still be timing him when I get back. So then we'll just wait for him to come up. Ade, fifteen minutes, 'kay? We don't really want to take all night and if you can last that long, then we know it's something special and we can test a longer time later." The two brothers looked at each other and took a couple of cleansing breaths.

"All right. So we're going to swim out a hundred yards. We'll wave at you when we get there. I'll go down and Li will go out." Adrian gave a quick nod to the girls, then looked to Liam to take the lead. The natural order of things in their family.

"Got it," the girls said in unison. Tillie giggled, but composed herself quickly and held the stopwatch at the ready.

"Alright, let's do this, bro! WOO!" Liam ran to the water with Adrian close behind. Next thing the girls knew Liam was waving. Adrian was just a few seconds behind and then they saw him wave as well. Tillie waved back and with her wave, they were off and her watch clicked. The girls saw a splash, then nothing. Tillie looked busily at the stopwatch and Lyla kept an eye on the water.

Only 10 seconds or so passed before Tillie could hold it in no longer.

"Holy cow this is exciting!" Tillie beamed and glanced over at Lyla.

"I know, Til, I know. Holy ..." Lyla looked at the water, amazed.

This made Tillie look up as well. Out came Liam from the surf. He looked completely at ease and very happy. Tillie clicked the watch without even looking at it.

"Well, how'd I do?" Liam came to the blankets and grabbed a towel and wiped his face and head and settled the towel around his shoulders.

"Oh! Uh." Tillie looked down at the watch, but couldn't see it in the dark. "Oh crap, these things aren't made for night races," she said frustrated.

Lyla took a flashlight out of the bag and handed it to her sister. Tillie looked at her with surprise.

"Well, you never know! We were going to the beach, in the dark and yeah, so I wanted to be prepared!" Lyla shrugged her shoulders unapologetic for her thoroughness.

"Thanks," Tillie said sincerely as she checked the clock. "Holy cow, Li! It's just over two minutes. Look! That's a mile a minute, man! You are awesome!"

"Yeah well, not that I didn't know that already, but thanks, lil' sis," Liam said with a huge grin on his face. He felt great to see how well he could swim and he felt equally happy to be able to share it with his family. "Now, how is Ade doing?"

"Um, we haven't seen him yet," Lyla answered. She was suddenly filled with dread. "Li, what if he is in trouble under the water and we don't know it? We just sent him down there at night! What are we, crazy?"

"Take it easy, Lyles," Liam reassured Lyla once again. He sat beside her and dried himself off some more. "I, too, came prepared. I gave Ade my waterproof mini-light. I told him if he needed us, to light it and let it go. You see," answering her panicked look, "I put it on a floating keychain. All he has to do is light it and let go. I'll get to him within seconds or even less." He put his now dry arm around his sister and gave her a one-armed hug. "Don't worry."

"Okay, good. Thanks for thinking of that, Li. I can't believe I didn't think of it myself." Lyla patted him on the leg and asked Tillie, "How much longer, Til?"

"Oh, uh," she checked the watch. "Four more minutes. Man, he's been down there for eleven minutes, guys! This is so amazing!" Tillie was the one to share her amazement with everyone. They adored her for it, because sometimes they got too serious to see it themselves.

"You're right, Tils, it *is* amazing." Liam grabbed her with his free arm and hugged both girls, together. The girls let out a giggle, then he set them free.

"Okay," Tillie said checking the watch. "Just over two minutes left. Man, this is exciting! Does anyone see him yet?" Tillie squinted out over the water.

"Nope, nothing yet. Should I swim out there, then?" Liam stood up, ready to go.

"Not for another minute, Li," Lyla answered. She was being particularly quiet now. Her voice didn't have that same authority and confidence it usually had.

"Alright. One minute." Liam looked out over the water, concerned.

The next wave into shore brought more in than just the tide. They looked at a shadow that appeared in front of the waves and it was Adrian standing at the shore, smiling like Liam had done when he finished swimming. It was in the moonlight, that Adrian looked very much like Liam. Their silhouettes had become very similar. This light showed how much Adrian had grown over the summer. His body was noticeably lengthened and he was only a couple of inches shorter Liam's height of six feet, two inches.

"Fifteen minutes, on the dot I believe," Adrian said as he reached the blanket. Everyone was so pleased and at the same time astonished, they said nothing back right away. "Don't everybody congratulate me at once," Adrian looked from face to face. All congratulations came in unison:

"Sorry, man! That was fantastic!"

"Oh, Ade! That was amazing!"

"Yes, yes, really terrific, Adrian!"

Adrian sat on the blanket, mostly dried off now, gleaming from head to foot.

"Yeah, I'm telling you, I think I could sit down there indefinitely," he finished as he wrapped the towel around his shoulders like Liam had just minutes ago. "I mean, it's just another place for me. I don't feel like I'm holding my breath at all! I actually got kind of bored under there. Next time I'll have to bring something to do. I guess a book is out of the question."

"Who says there'll be a next time?" Lyla questioned quietly. She sat up a bit and cleared her throat. "I mean, what are we doing here, trying to break world records, or are we trying to find out *exactly* what we are?" She looked back and forth to each one of them. They knew she meant business. "These tests tonight don't really prove anything other than we all have some crazy abilities. It doesn't really answer any important questions." Looking at her siblings, she could tell she was about to get arguments. She cut them to the chase.

"*Why*? *Why* do we have these abilities? *Where* did they come from? Does anyone else know about them?" Answering their confused faces before they could speak, she said, "Look guys, I don't mean to rain on the parade here, but am I the only one who wants to know all this stuff? I feel like we are truly in the dark here and there is only one solution. We need to go to Mom and Dad. No, I mean it. We need to talk to them. When have we ever kept anything so important from them? We all know this leads to them. Somehow. We need to know. And I think they'll have the answers for us all." She sat back and stayed silent. She looked defeated.

"Hey, hey there, Lyla." Liam tried to be consoling. "We all agree with you, don't we guys?" The two youngest nodded their heads in silent agreement. "See? We're all with you on this. This was just a first step. A semi-test. We just needed to stretch it out and see what it could do, what *we* could do with what we've got. We, none of us except for Tillie here, have really had a chance to see what we're capable of in this department. This was just to see it in action. What is the trouble with that? Are you okay, Lyla? Lyla?" Liam grabbed her arm as she rose.

Lyla levitated. She suddenly straightened into a standing position and brought Liam up with her. She felt very powerful. Liam felt a surge of energy from her arm. He released her like he'd been shocked. Suddenly, the wind picked up coming off the ocean. The waves crashed into the shore and their blankets got soaked. The tide came in fast. Faster than they had ever seen it. Tillie scrambled around and tried to gather their things while she kept a worried eye on Lyla.

"Lyles! Lyla! What's wrong? What did we do? Stop it, please!" Tillie shouted as she and Adrian picked up the bag and blankets. She looked as though she was about to cry. Adrian put his arm around her and they took a step back from Lyla and Liam.

The tide rushed in around their feet. It was fast and strong. In and out and every time it came in, there was a bit more water. Tillie wanted to run. She was scared. Adrian sensed her fear and held her fast.

"It's going to be okay!" He had to shout over the wind.

The rest of the people on the beach cleared out fast. Fires were put out by the rushing tide and people scattered upward toward the town. The four of them were alone now on the beach.

Liam stood in front of Lyla, between her and the ocean. "Lyla! Stop this! It's okay! It's going to be alright!" He shouted at the top of his lungs, but it was as if no one was even in front of her at all. She threw her arms up and looked possessed. Tillie buried her head into Adrian's shoulder and wept. Adrian dragged her a few more steps back, away from shore.

Liam remembered just then what Lyla had said about Mom touching her arm and 'bringing her back to earth'. He grabbed both her arms in the air. There was a strike of lightning across the water and a loud crack of thunder just as Liam flew back and landed in the next incoming wave. Lyla also flew back and landed softly in the surf. She was sitting upright and her eyes grew big. Her arms fell by her side and she fell back into the water, unconscious.

Liam was the first to her side and picked her head up out of the water. Tillie screamed as Adrian ran over to help Liam. The surf calmed down and Liam picked Lyla up out of it and carried her away from the water.

As they walked away from the ocean, it receded to its normal level. The wind turned steadier and died down. Lyla hung in Liam's arms like a wet rag doll. Tillie had tears streaming down her face. Her hands over her mouth, she followed silently behind them.

As they reached dry sand, all they could hear was the soft surf and Tillie muttering, "Oh my God. Oh my God. Oh my God," over and over. Liam placed Lyla down in the sand as gently as he could. Adrian stood just behind him, to Liam's right.

"Is she alright? Is she conscious yet? Tillie, will you please stop?" Adrian turned around and grabbed Tillie's shoulders. He grabbed so hard she jumped, then was silent. He eased up on his grip looking at her apologetically.

"Oh, God! Oh, God! What happened? What did we do? Did we do this, Ade? Oh, God!" Tillie was properly hysterical now. She went back to her mumbling.

11

A Special Sight

Adrian looked back over his shoulder at Liam and Lyla. He saw just the slightest movement as Lyla's head turned. He let out a sigh of relief.

He turned back to Tillie and said, "She's going to be alright, Tills. Look. She's already waking up. It's alright, okay?"

He pulled her into a quick hug and turned them both around to show her Lyla. They both walked over to the other side of Lyla and fell to their knees. They looked at her and they looked at Liam and waited. Tillie let out a sniffle.

"Lyles. Lyla. Lyla, are you alright? Do you remember anything, Lyles? Sweetheart! Answer us, okay?" Liam did his best to plead his big sister into consciousness. He held her hand, lightly tapped on it and hoped she'd wake up. "She feels cold. Guys, give me a blanket. She's cold!" Liam reached out to Tillie and Adrian and they scrambled to answer his request.

"They're all wet, Li! Everything got wet! What do we do?" Tillie answered on the verge of hysteria again.

"It's okay. Just give me one that doesn't seem too wet. We'll make it work." Tillie handed over a mostly damp, sandy blanket. Liam shook it out quickly behind himself and threw it over Lyla. "Someone's got to go back to the house. Gotta get something dry for her. Oh crap. And don't let on!" He continued fumbling over Lyla.

"I'll go," Adrian volunteered quickly. "Til's too upset. She'll ruin everything. I'll go." He stood up ready to leave. "Don't worry, I'll be back as soon as I can and I'll be quiet. They won't know a thing," he said as he turned and ran. Luckily he was a good runner and was in shape enough to get home and back as quickly as possible.

"God, I hope so. I really hope so," Liam turned back to Lyla, held her hand under the blanket and pushed the wet hair off her face.

Tillie prayed under her breath. This was so frightening! She couldn't believe she was watching her own sister unconscious on the sand! She flashed back to Aaron and Tim and the boat, the whole thing came into her mind like a Technicolor movie. She felt so nervous now compared to then! Lyla better be alright. She wasn't sure she could take it if she wasn't. She kept praying. She wondered if they should be doing CPR on her.

"Li, should we be giving her mouth to mouth?"

"What? No. No. That's not her problem. Look. She's breathing. She's just not awake. It's alright, sis. It's going to be okay." He let out a large breath of relief and continued to try to talk to Lyla.

"She's breathing? Oh thank God! Thank you, God!" Tillie looked up into the pitch black sky as she said the last words. Then she quickly looked back to her sister. "Lyles? Lyla honey? Lyla, it's me, Tillie. Tils. Wake up, please, sis! Just wake up for us, okay?"

Finally it was quiet, as Tillie's praying went silent. Both of them just sat and looked at Lyla. They felt like they were stuck in time. Stuck in a moment of horror. Wishing it would end.

Thankfully, Adrian returned in less than ten minutes with an armful of blankets. "Here! Here they are! And Mom and Dad didn't hear a thing! I was good!" Adrian knelt down next to Lyla.

Liam took the wet blanket off Lyla while Adrian placed one blanket on the sand. They worked like synchronized swimmers and got Lyla onto the dry blanket and covered with another one in seconds. The whole while Tillie just kept saying Lyla's name to her.

"She's warming up. Thanks, Ade. You did great." Liam said toward Adrian, still holding Lyla's hand.

Tillie fixed Lyla's hair, as if how Lyla looked mattered and called her name. Tillie still appeared a bit frazzled, but not hysterical anymore. Her hands shook over her sister as she tried to smooth Lyla's hair and the blankets.

After five or ten minutes - it was hard to say, as time went by in such a weird way that night - it got silent all around. The wind disappeared completely and the surf was even quieter than just a few minutes before. Tillie settled down by Lyla's head and the boys were on either side of her. Waiting. They all just sat, waiting.

"Hey, what's going on? What happened?" A groggy, scratchy voice broke the late night silence and startled the three siblings. Lyla immediately tried to sit up.

"Whoa, whoa there now, Lyla." Liam stopped her and just took her hand again. "Do you remember anything? Do you remember what happened?"

Tillie clapped her hands together and smiled. It was just her nature to show her excitement and she was just too excited to see her sister wake up.

"Umm, am I supposed to know what's going on?" Lyla said with a wince. Everyone sat closer with concern. "I'm okay, I'm okay. I just want to sit up, all right? Give me a minute here." She tried to push up to her elbows. Liam and Adrian both had her hands and helped her sit upright. Slowly but steadily she came up. She lifted her head and opened her eyes and tried to focus on something, anything. She tried to remember.

"Oh, Lyles! Lyla!" Tillie couldn't help herself and hugged Lyla from behind. Lyla was startled at first, then sunk back a little into Tillie's hug. This gave Lyla a bit of strength. When Tillie let go, she felt good enough to sit up on her own.

"I'm fine guys, really," she insisted and the boys let go of her hands. She touched on the back of her head and rubbed a sore spot. "Ouch, what happened there?"

"Must've been when you fell back," Liam answered her and left it open for her to finish.

"Fell back?" Lyla drifted off for a few seconds. Then it hit her. "Oh, God! Oh, you guys! I'm sorry! I'm so sorry!" She put her hand up to her face, looking horrified. All three of them almost fell on her in an embrace.

"It's alright, Lyles!"

"Oh Lyles, we love you!"

"It's okay, sis! We know you didn't mean it! We love you!"

Lyla sobbed. With all that love just coming at her as she realized what had happened, she couldn't help it. Of course Tillie had to cry, too, because the two of them don't let each other cry alone. It was a sister pact and, well, they just happened to do it every time. This made the boys hold their sisters tight. They hated to see them upset. And this was actually a happy moment, so they should be relieved, not sad.

In all this jumble of emotion, someone started to laugh. It was muffled at first, so it was probably one of the girls, as they were in the middle of this massive hug-fest. The laughing became contagious and the hold on the hug released. They all laughed, with tears still on the girls' faces. No one spoke right away, they just laughed. It was such a great release and it really wasn't because of anything in particular.

Finally, when the laughter died down, Liam had to speak up, "Okay, Lyles, please tell us. What the hell was that?" They actually laughed again, but just for a moment.

"I know, I know. I'm so sorry! I really am! I can't believe I did that...again! I didn't even know I was feeling anything specific, so I'm not really sure how I did it."

"Maybe it was because you were right on the water," Adrian deduced. "We were all there and all our experimenting made your feelings really high...or something."

"That sounds like it might be a possibility," Lyla said thoughtfully. "I mean I wasn't that close to water before, so it stands to reason that being closer to it would make it easier to...*control* it? I don't really think that's what I did, as I didn't feel in control of anything. But I don't know what else to call it. Still so many questions." Lyla drifted off in thought and it was like everyone else was right there with her in her head.

"I know. You were right, Lyles," Liam interrupted everyone's thoughts. "We need to go to Mom and Dad. I think after tonight, it's time." No one argued. They all knew Liam was right.

Everyone helped Lyla start home when she said she felt up to standing. It was actually quite beautiful the way they pulled together and helped each other through it all. They didn't realize it themselves, but to an outsider watching, it would have been a special sight. Because they didn't realize it, they just acted on the love for each other.

The four of them arrived at the house, with Lyla just needing a little help to get up the stairs. She felt much better and Liam instructed her to grab something to eat before she went to sleep. Tillie got her a quick snack and brought it to their room.

The night was over. The night was late. All of the Lundgren children were exhausted; physically, emotionally, mentally and spiritually. They all hit their beds hard that night. Sleep was almost instant.

The next morning was very quiet in the Lundgren home. Heather and Cord woke up and enjoyed some coffee and the morning paper at the kitchen table. Cord whistled a quiet, but happy, tune between his sips of coffee. Heather felt particularly chipper, as they were all going to Church this morning. They were able to make arrangements with the restaurant staff for the morning to do it.

"I wonder if I should wake them, hon." Heather gave a semi-concerned glance toward the children's bedrooms.

"Now, now. Don't you think they're all big enough to wake on their own?"

"But no one is awake yet. I don't even know what time they got in last night. I never heard them. Which means it was late. Very late." Heather finished as she drifted off in a calculated thought.

"Well, you're probably right, there. Go ahead. Wake 'em up. Better safe than sorry, I guess." Cord sipped on some coffee and went back to reading.

Heather stood and walked slowly over to the bedrooms. She found herself trying to be quiet, as if she didn't want to wake them. She smiled at herself, then resumed a more natural walk. She was almost to the girls' door, when out popped Adrian from the hallway.

"Mornin', Mom." He gave her a big kiss on the cheek. "Do we have time for a bite before we leave? Or did I sleep in too late?" He had barely stopped for the kiss and continued into the kitchen.

She turned toward the kitchen to answer Adrian. "Umm, yes, you can have something if it's fast," Heather replied. Then slowly looked back at the doorway, then back to Adrian. "Ade, honey, is anyone else awake yet, or is it just you?" She wanted to know before she rendered herself useless yet again in the lives of her children. Every day she felt the pull of her children's growing independence.

"Umm, Li's up. Dunno about the girls. I knocked on their door as I passed," he answered as his head dove into the refrigerator.

Heather turned around and walked to the girls' door. She felt a slight ping of happiness that this trip across the floor had some use to it after all. She knocked on the door. At first it was a bit delicate. Then as she knocked, she reminded herself that it was a wake up knock and knocked louder. "Girls? Girls, it's time to get up if you still want to make it to church."

Liam came out of his room. When he reached his mother and the girls' bedroom door, he gave it a good smack and made Heather jump just a little. "C'mon lazy princesses! Time's a-ticking!" He laughed and continued into the kitchen.

Heather waited at the door for a moment. She listened for any sort of stirring, or noise of being awake, from the girls. She didn't hear anything at first. She wondered for a split second if she should go in and wake them. She felt almost an uncontrollable urge to do so.

Then suddenly Tillie opened the door. "Morning mom! Was that you knocking? I thought I heard Liam," she said looking past her mother.

"What? Oh, yes, it was me first, but then Liam came by and," she didn't even have time to finish.

"Okay, great then. Lyla will be out in a few. Just getting dressed." She also kissed her mother on the cheek and headed toward the kitchen.

"Oh. Okay, then. Wonderful." Heather replied and followed Tillie. "I'm so glad you all didn't get back in too late last night. I thought you were all going to oversleep." She sat back at the table to finish her coffee and enjoy her children.

"Well, Mom, surprise. We're all up and ready." Tillie smiled at her mother as she sat down with a glass of orange juice and a half a bagel.

"Yeah, Mom," Adrian laughed, "we knew we were getting up this morning. Do you think we're all irresponsible or something?" He forced a laugh.

Tillie shot him a quick glance of "knock it off". He settled down and sat at the table to eat breakfast. He got the food into his mouth as soon as he could. The reason for his shutting up.

"Well, I must say, this is truly lovely," Heather looked around at them. "Is Lyla going to join us for breakfast?"

"Probably not, Mom." Tillie blurted. "She did kind of oversleep, so she said that she would just meet us in the car." She took a bite of her bagel and tried to look nonchalant. She glanced quickly at Liam and Adrian. Liam didn't even seem to notice her. Adrian looked back at her, but just kept eating.

Heather started to get up to put her things away at the sink. "Oh. Okay then. Should we bring something for her to eat in the car then?"

"Yeah, sure. I'll grab her the other half of my bagel," Tillie said. She felt a bit more relaxed and a smile crept over her lips.

"Okay, then," Heather replied, "I'm going to get dressed. C'mon, Cord. You too." She practically drifted over to their bedroom with Cord following behind her.

"See you in the car in seven minutes kids," Cord said as their door closed.

"Oh, my gosh!" All three kids got up from the table as fast as they could, put their dishes away and made a lot of racket so they could talk. Water ran fast, dishes clanged around and conversation happened.

"I know, I know." Adrian spouted. "I really wasn't sure we were going to be able to pull it off."

"How is she?" Liam asked seriously, concerned. The boys hadn't seen Lyla yet today and they worried about her all night. "I hope I didn't scare her with my knock. I honestly thought mom was about to open your door. That's why I did it."

"Smooth thinking, big bro," Tillie answered. "I'm not sure what I would have done if she had!"

"So, how is she then?" Liam repeated the question.

"She's all right. She's much better, just weak like a baby foal. I had to wake her. I hated doing it! She said she was much better. She didn't look so hot. When she looked in the mirror at herself she almost gasped. Then muttered something about makeup. So I figured I'd try to buy her some extra time to put herself together."

"Smooth thinking on your part," Liam said. He dried his hands on a towel and patted Tillie on the back. "See you guys in four minutes in the car." Liam went downstairs.

"Yeah, see you," Adrian said. Then to Tillie, "Go get Lyla. Help her to the car if she needs it. We'll distract Mom and Dad if we need to. See you in three." Adrian patted Tillie on the arm and went to the car.

Tillie went back to her room to check on her sister.

"Lyles, Lyles, we're ready to go," she said as she opened the door.

She was a bit slow about it, because she didn't want Lyla to feel panicked. In fact, after last night, she wasn't sure she wanted Lyla to feel much of anything again. When the door was fully opened, she found Lyla putting on some earrings, headed toward the door. "Are you feeling okay?"

"Yes. Yes, sis, I'm much better, really," Lyla answered sounding very sincere, which made Tillie relieved. "Does my makeup look obvious? My eyes were such a mess this morning, I really had to go all or nothing and nothing wasn't an option." Lyla touched her cheek lightly and waited for her sister's opinion.

"Actually, sis, I was going to say you look beautiful. Incredibly beautiful." Tillie was also sincere and Lyla knew she wasn't being sarcastic, although she didn't feel beautiful this morning. "Just tell Mom and Dad you wanted to try out some new stuff. They won't think anything of it."

"Thanks a lot, Tils. I'm going to need the confidence boost if I'm gonna get past Mom this morning." The girls both walked, arms around each other, to the car. "Oh crap, my sunglasses. I think I lost them on the beach."

"Oops, nope you didn't. Hold on, I'll get them out of the room. I put them away last night when I was erasing evidence." Tillie ran back and returned quickly with the glasses.

"Thanks yet again, sis," Lyla said and she put the glasses on. Luckily the sun shone brightly in the morning sky so there would be no suspicions.

The girls made it to the car and Lyla didn't even need assistance, so there was nothing different looking about that simple event.

The rest of the morning went off without a hitch. All of their worries turned out to be overkill. The only thing that was different was Lyla wore makeup.

They all thought her makeup would raise suspicion, but all their mother said was, "Lyla, how lovely. So nice of you to dress for church." The sense of relief washed over them like the smell of the ocean. And just like the ocean, it felt really good.

12

Hello? Hello?

The Lundgrens made it back to Sigrun in time for the end of lunch hour. All the Lundgrens decided it was a nice break in their summer to be able to spend some time with God and each other, away from work for a change. They vowed to do it again before summer ended. For now, they all got back to work. There was no time for important conversation. They'd have to wait to decide what to do about telling their parents.

The rest of the day was mundane at Sigrun. All four children ran around busy with their jobs. The day went by without time to talk to one another about their next step, but they all knew they were on the same page. That made them all feel better, for they knew the plan would come together soon. Their parents would soon know everything.

The end of the day came quickly. Perhaps it was because they only worked part of the day, but it felt good to be out of routine for a change. Not that they didn't like it at Sigrun, but sometimes the routine got tiresome and getting away gave them all a new sense of appreciation for their jobs and even each other. It was good to get a broader perspective and life view from time to time.

August was flying by. It was their busiest time, full of tourists. Their island was invaded with hikers and campers trying to get a piece of nature to take home with them. The children couldn't find any time to get their plan together.

Several weeks after "Lyla's incident" or "the incident," as they all now referred to it, Liam passed the girls' room on the way to bed.

"Hey, there," he said quietly, checking behind him to make sure Heather and Cord had gone to bed. "I just wanted to say, Lyles, I never got a chance to tell you how great I thought you were the night after...well, you know, the incident. I thought you handled it all really well! I mean it, sis, if I hadn't been there, I wouldn't have known anything had happened. You really impressed me. You too, Till. You came through without tipping anyone off."

He went into the room and started to shut the door. It was almost shut when Adrian pushed it open and came in. Tillie moved onto Lyla's bed and the boys sat down on her bed. They all knew what they were here to talk about and no one wanted to waste time.

"Alright, so when are we doing this? The sooner the better if you ask me," Lyla got right to business.

"I was thinking sometime after work. I know mom and dad are always tired and well, we all are, but I was also thinking that that might be the right time to approach them. Kind of get them when defenses are low," Liam stated. He'd given this a lot of thought.

Adrian added, "That sounds good. What day, though? It's not like we know which day will end right on time, ya know? And August is always so busy. We barely ever get a night that ends on time."

"Well, why don't we just say whichever day does end on time?" Tillie perked up, proud of her idea. "School starts the week after next, so either way, things are going to be busy."

"That sounds good, sis. There's another good thing from you today." Liam gave Tillie a cheesy smile and Tillie cheesy smiled back at him. Then she sniggered.

"Yeah. That sounds good. There's bound to be a day *some* time that ends *on* time. If not, we'll see to it that one does, right?" Lyla spoke with her authoritative, business voice. It was good to hear her back to her full self.

"Ok. So, first night, on time. Even if that's tomorrow. Agreed?" Liam shot his hand out flat in front of the girls.

"Agreed!" Everyone said at once and hands piled into the center. They clasped their hands all together, then did a group handshake, then released.

A week went by and there were no on-time nights. All of the children agreed day in and day out that they would try to get things done on time, but it always ended up that someone or something lingered on in the restaurant and made it later and later. Usually this was considered the norm and none of the Lundgrens had a problem with it. They enjoyed their jobs and late nights were part of the territory. But with this hanging over their heads, the children felt eager and anxious to get things over with.

A few late nights were spent in the girls' room talking. Planning and reviewing how they could find time to talk to their parents. The anxiety really started to build.

"Well, if this goes on much longer, I'm going to just blurt something out by mistake," Tillie said very matter of fact.

"I know, sis, it's been really hard for all of us," Liam empathized.

"So what are we going to do?" Adrian bounced on the bed like a fidgety child.

"Look. We've got Labor Day coming up this weekend," Lyla announced. "After this weekend, things will calm down and I am sure we will find the time. We just have to hold in there a little bit longer. And with things being as busy as they have been, that shouldn't be too hard. Sis," she turned to Tillie, "you're just going to have to suck it up and hold it in. Just for a bit longer, 'kay?"

Tillie sat for a moment and looked thoughtful. "Well, okay. I know this is important. I was just hoping to get it out before school started. I get stressed enough as it is this time of year, you know!"

"How could we forget? 'Senior year this' and 'senior year that'. That's all we've heard all week." Adrian rolled his eyes and fell back on the bed.

"Well, I can't help it, I get excited, okay? It's not like you all don't already know that about me. So, well...yeah." Tillie tried to finish sounding confident, but failed.

"Alright, then," Lyla started, "next week. Guys," she directed herself toward Adrian and Tillie, "let us know which day is going to work into your school schedules and we'll try to make sure we get the job done at work."

"Okay, sounds good to me," Adrian replied happily.

"All right. I can let you know by the second day of school. That gives me time to meet with all my teachers, get my schedule down and find out if there is anything going on after school that week," Tillie finished as if reading off a list.

"Okay. Until next week then." Liam stood up. "Goodnight ladies. Sleep well." Liam was the first to get up, but Adrian beat him to the door. With a wave to the girls, he was out first.

Labor day marked the unofficial end to summer and brought a change of schedules for the Lundgrens. With holidays came more customers, one last time for the year at Sigrun. Tillie and Adrian would start school just after Labor Day. Marcus and Cord were scheduled to fill in for them. Everything was in place.

The last morning of summer vacation started just like any number of days at Sigrun. Liam got to work prepping in the kitchen with Cord and Adrian. The girls bustled in the dining room, readying tables and sweeping the floor. Heather went into the office where she got down to business making phone calls and working on the books.

The lunch time crowd soon arrived. This time of year, customers were about half tourists, half locals. A last hoorah for anyone who wanted to take in a few days of nature before the end of summer. The children shot each other looks all morning, just like they had for the past few weeks. It was a hidden language between all of them by this point.

Amidst the harried hurrying of lunchtime, the phone rang. It rang two more times before someone picked it up. Someone from the kitchen hollered out to the dining room, "Lyla! Phone for you!"

"Okay! Be there in just a sec," Lyla shouted back. She placed orders on her tables, wiped her hands on her apron and grabbed the phone hanging on the wall outside the office.

"Hello? Hello?" She inquired quickly into the phone. She heard two people already in conversation. "Hello? Can anyone hear me?" she said again as she ducked into the office and stood just inside the doorway.

She plugged her free ear and propped the phone to her other ear with her shoulder. About to close the door to the office, she stopped short. She grabbed the phone with her hand and let go of the door.

"Well, yes. Yes, that's true," Lyla heard on the line.

"Dad? Dad, who are you talking to? Can you hear me? *Hello*!" Lyla almost shouted into the phone. There was no response. She listened.

"What do you expect, anyway? She is two hundred years old," an unrecognizable voice said.

"Who is this?" demanded Lyla. There was no response. It was like she wasn't even there.

"So, you know it must be time for Lyla, at least," the voice said. "It is her time to learn about her mother and who she is. You knew this day would come."

Lyla leaned against the nearest wall. She was too confused and dumbfounded to do or say anything. She listened.

Back in the dining room, Tillie felt the lack of helping hands and looked around for Lyla. It was very unlike her to leave during a rush without saying anything. Tillie was busy, so she hadn't heard the phone call announcement for Lyla. She couldn't imagine where she'd gone off to. She glanced around the room in between setting plates down on tables and taking orders.

After about five or ten minutes, Tillie saw Lyla in the office doorway standing stock-still, mouth agape. Tillie's face looked inquisitive.

"Excuse me for just a minute," she said to the current table whose order she was taking. She scooted into the office, slightly pushed Lyla back and closed the door. "What's wrong?" she asked half concerned and half annoyed.

Lyla dropped the phone, not looking at or responding to her sister.

"Hey you!" Tillie said as she grabbed Lyla's shoulders and shook her. She then bent down to pick up the phone. She checked the phone and heard nothing, so she turned it off and set it on the desk. She waited for what seemed like a most painful few seconds for Lyla to respond. Nothing.

"Hey! Seriously, you're scaring me now! What is wrong?" All Tillie pictured in her mind was her sister's face the night of the incident. Her heart beat quicker for a few seconds.

"I...I...don't even know where to start," Lyla said breathlessly.

Tillie guided Lyla over to the desk and helped her sit down. She felt the worry building up inside her. She hated this feeling and to have it happen for her sister two times in a row may be just too much for her to handle.

"Stay right there. I'll be right back." Tillie scooted from the room and returned in what seemed like a flash, with a dripping glass of ice water. Lyla blindly took a sip from the glass, then just stared blankly again, looking like a machine processing information.

"C'mon, Lyles! What is it? You can tell me, can't you?" Tillie started to sound panicky. She tried to hold it in, as she didn't want to repeat the other night. But she couldn't help how she felt right now.

"I don't know," Lyla spurted, coming back to life. She blinked a few times and focused on her sister. "We'd better get back out there." She said as if nothing happened.

"Whoa. Whoa. What are you doing? Are you sure everything is okay?" Tillie asked and tried to make Lyla sit back down.

"Oh sweetie, I'm sorry. I didn't mean to scare you. Of course I'm fine." Lyla replied as she reassuringly grabbed her sister's shoulders and gently moved her back so she could get back on her feet.

"Well then, what the hell was that? You go all coma on me, then suddenly, everything is back to normal? I was expecting a storm to hit any second! You really freaked me out!" Tillie even looked out of the office window to make sure it was still sunny.

"Oh gosh, Till, I'm sorry. I was just trying to figure out what was going on. I think someone was playing a prank on me with Dad. He was talking to someone I didn't recognize. They were saying all of these weird things about Mom and me. About all of us, really..." she trailed off for a second, but then continued. "Dad acted like it was all real. Like he's known it all along...but it couldn't be real. It just couldn't!" Lyla smiled at Tillie and shook a little as if to shake water off her shoulders. "Someone was just trying to get me to laugh, I suppose," she said to herself as much as to Tillie. "I know I tend to take myself too seriously at times and I know how you all like to remind me to lighten up."

"Well that's a hell of a way to do it. It almost gave me a heart attack. The look on your face was anything but funny." Tillie shouted trying to get rid of the nerves that had built up inside in the last few seconds.

"Well then, I guess they got two of us for the price of one, huh?" Lyla jested, trying to downplay the worry in her voice. "C'mon, then! Either way it's wasted enough of our time. We've gotta get back to work." She patted Tillie on the shoulder and led her out of the office.

Even though they were only off the floor for five, maybe seven, minutes, they were definitely backed up with orders and tables. The girls took the rest of the lunch rush to catch up, even with Heather and Marcus pitching in to help.

After the lunch and dinner rushes, things quieted down quickly. Even though it was a weekday, things ended on a late note. No, tonight did not end on time. Tonight would not be the night. Lyla was grateful, actually. In light of what happened this afternoon, she wanted to discuss it with the boys, to see what they thought and how to include it in their tell-all to Mom and Dad.

The girls were once again tidying up in the dining area, while Cord and the boys scrubbed down the kitchen. Heather came into the dining room from the office. She grabbed a cleaning rag from the counter between the kitchen and dining area and went to wipe some tables down.

"So girls, another successful summer, wouldn't you say?"

"Sure, Mom." Tillie chirped. "We know how to rock it out in this town." She smiled tiredly and wiped a table.

Lyla looked up from mopping the floor and gave a smile. "Of course we did, Mom. When you give the best, you get the best. That's what I always say." Lyla went right back to mopping with a little extra spring in her step, following her own words.

"I see you ladies ran into a snag at lunch today," said Heather casually. "You didn't have any problems in the office, did you?"

Both girls' heads turned from their chores to their mother. Then they looked at each other for the answer.

"Umm...er...gosh, Mom, what trouble would there be in the office?" blurted Lyla very clumsily. She felt her cheeks go red almost instantly. She looked back down at her mopping and pretended it needed her full attention.

"Yeah, Mom, we're not little kids anymore," Tillie said with a snicker. "We can go into the office without finding any trouble," Tillie finished with a nervous giggle.

"Oh. Good, then," said Heather. The girls knew this conversation wasn't over yet. "It's just that we got quite backed up and I couldn't see you two, anywhere. Then I saw the office door closed. At first I didn't think anything of it.

Perhaps you needed a new tablet or something," Heather finished. The girls paused from their chores again. They kept their eyes from their mother this time. "But when I saw Tillie dash out of the room and then back in again with a glass of water, I thought something must be wrong. And then we were so busy the rest of the day, I didn't even get a chance to ask either of you. Is everything all right?" There was an uncomfortable silence and the girls weren't sure whether it was their turn to say something or wait. "You're all right though, Lyla dear, aren't you?" Before Lyla had a chance to answer, Heather continued, "Because you both came out of the office and finished the day nicely."

This time, Lyla knew it was her turn to speak. "Yes, well, Mom, umm…" she stuttered for a moment and tried to find her words and make sure they were convincing. "You were right. I went to look for an order tablet and I had bent down at the desk to get one. Till walked in as I stood up too fast and nearly fell over."

Tillie's eyes lit up and a smile of approval came over her face.

"So yeah, I sat her down and ran to get some water," Tillie chimed in. "By the time I got back to Lyles, she was laughing at herself for being so silly."

"Yeah, I'm always in such a hurry at work. You know me. Got to get it all done."

The girls, both satisfied with their story, looked to Heather for approval and acceptance.

"Oh. I see. So, there was nothing about a phone call or something? I thought I heard someone say Lyla had a phone call?" She looked innocently at her two girls.

The girls' faces both fell again, but Lyla was in control. "Oh yeah, there was. But when I got to it, there was no one there. You know, must have been one of the boys playing a prank on me," she stated as fact, worth forgetting for its mundaneness. "So that's when I figured while I was in there, I'd get another tablet."

"And that's when I found her. Yeah, well, you know the rest," Tillie interrupted, but was confident in her resolve.

"Well good." Heather finally sounded satisfied. "For a minute there, I was thinking maybe you girls were trying to keep something from your ole' mom."

All three ladies laughed, Tillie a bit overdone, but everyone was used to her doing that. Greatly relieved to have that conversation over with, the girls finished up for the night while Heather retired upstairs.

When the girls finally got into their room, with the door slightly ajar, Tillie spurted, "Jeez, that was a close one, huh?"

"What was a close one?" Adrian poked into the room sniffing for the latest news.

"Umm...ever hear of knocking?" screeched Tillie as she headed for the door.

"Oh. Yeah. Sorry," Adrian said as he knocked on the door while still holding it open. Tillie tried to shove him out with little success. "So, what was close?" he persisted.

"Man, you boys are so nosy!" Lyla laughed. "Anyone would think you were the girls with all the gossip you like to dig for!"

"Gossip? Did someone say gossip?" Liam asked as he barged in and pushed Adrian all the way into the room. Letting himself in, he closed the door, ready for the story. "Okay. Spill it. We want all the juicy details. Remember, we're going for no more secrets here, ladies." Liam flopped down onto Tillie's bed and Adrian bounced on the edge looking like a kid on Christmas morning.

"It's nothing really at all." Lyla attempted to blow them off. She crossed over from her vanity dresser to her brothers to shoo them out.

At the same time, Tillie blurted out, "Well, Lyles got some weird phone call, or prank, or whatever, during the lunch rush. You boys wouldn't happen to know something about it, would you?"

"Tellulah!" Lyla shouted to hush Tillie as soon as she could. It was too late. The boys were all over it.

"Sorry, sis. No more secrets." Tillie shrugged at her.

"What do you mean phone call or prank or whatever? Which one was it?" Adrian perked up, eager to hear the answer.

"Well, if you must know, I got a phone call that turned out to be a prank. That's all," stated Lyla.

"We think," chimed Tillie.

This time Lyla just shot her a look. The look all big sisters know how to give their little sisters.

"Gee, thanks, Till. Why don't you just go ahead and tell them the whole conversation?" Lyla directed Tillie irritably. "After all, you were there. I was only the one actually on the phone," Lyla spilled out more than she intended.

"Ooo," cooed Adrian in a mocking, girly voice.

"Dooo tell," Liam echoed in the same girly fashion. Both boys put their hands up under their chins, looking very silly. "So, it wasn't the daily call from no one?" Liam asked coyly.

All too familiar with this form of brotherly mockery, both girls got defensive immediately. They turned their backs to the boys and shared their sly smiles with each other, knowing that this worked every time.

"Aww, c'mon. You know we are dying over here," Liam said more sincerely. "Just tell us what happened, 'kay?"

As usual, Tillie was the first to give in to Liam's charms. Being the younger sister, she lacked the experience Lyla had at ignoring her brothers.

She turned slowly and said, "Well, as Lyla said, I wasn't even the one who got the call. But she said something about Dad and some voice she didn't recognize talking about all of us."

At this, Tillie remembered the panic that Lyla caused her with the comatose look on her face. The one Tillie would just as soon forget. She turned to Lyla then and asked the question that bugged her all day.

"Lyles, what exactly was said in this mysterious phone conversation?"

All three siblings turned their faces, bodies and attention toward Lyla. The room grew quiet and the atmosphere felt suddenly heavy.

"Mom and Dad are in bed already, right?" Lyla asked tentatively, signaling to the door.

Adrian leapt from his perch on the edge of Tillie's bed and did a quick check. "Yep. All clear. Man, this must be good. Now spill it," he said as he got into a more comfortable position on the bed.

The boys suddenly looked like two little kids waiting for their bedtime story. It made Lyla let out a nervous laugh before she said anything.

13

Moon Bathing

"Well, let's see. I came into the conversation somewhere in the middle." Lyla began slowly as she tried to recall the whole episode in detail. "It was definitely Dad...and someone else I didn't know."

"Wait, wait, wait," Adrian interrupted. "Why were you listening in on a phone call? I thought you said the call was for you?"

"Yes. Someone yelled out to me from the back that I had a phone call. I went into the office to take the call for some quiet." Lyla trailed off into her memory for a moment.

"Wait a sec. I don't remember anyone from the kitchen saying you had a phone call," Adrian interrupted again.

"Take it easy, bro," Liam interrupted Adrian. "How do you know? You might have stepped out for a few seconds or something."

"And miss the lunch rush? I don't think so, Liam," Adrian defended himself. "I was there, working my butt off the whole time! I don't remember anyone saying anything about a phone call during the lunch rush," he stated, finally.

"Well maybe you just had your head stuck in the freezer," teased Lyla. "But I heard what I heard. Anyway, like I said, it was a conversation already started between Dad and this stranger."

"Man or woman?" Adrian once again butted in.

"Man," replied Lyla. "And I remember that they couldn't hear me. I kept saying 'Hello?', but no one responded. So I just stood there. I almost hung up when I heard the strange man say, 'What do you expect anyway? She is two hundred years old.'"

This time it was Liam who interjected with the question, "Okay, two hundred years old? Who the hell is two hundred years old besides the turtle at the zoo?"

Tillie let out a giggle and Adrian chuckled. Liam grinned.

"Mom." Lyla said plainly, but the impact was anything but plain.

"*What*?" squealed Tillie as she turned toward Lyla and got serious again.

Adrian sat up straighter on the bed. "That's bull."

"Well, you know they must be joking then. What's Mom." Liam asked, gesturing to the rest of them for assistance. "She's what, like, fifty-eight?"

"Fifty-seven," Tillie corrected him.

"Yeah, so what is all this two hundred stuff about? They trying to play a practical joke or something?" Liam asked, then thought quietly to himself, trying to make sense of it.

Lyla, still and serious stated, "No. No they didn't sound like they were joking. Besides, what would be the joke? They didn't even know I was on the phone. They couldn't hear me, remember?"

"Maybe they just wanted you to think that, Lyles," Liam said. "Yeah, maybe that was the whole point. You thought they couldn't hear you, but they just pretended," he went on, trying to convince himself as much as the rest of them.

"What would be the point of that?" Tillie offered. Liam looked to Tillie to answer, but she went on, "It's not exactly funny to say your mom is two hundred. I mean nobody lives that long! So where's the laugh in that?"

Before anyone could answer, Lyla continued. "Nobody can live to two hundred…unless they are different. Not from here." Again, silence fell over the room.

"What are you talking about?" Adrian asked, almost angry now. "Are you saying Mom is freaking two hundred years old and that she's like an alien or something?"

"An Atlantean, actually," stated Lyla.

"A what?" Adrian and Tillie asked at once.

"She comes from..." started Lyla.

"Atlantis," finished Liam. "You're saying our mom is from a legendary city and is two centuries old?"

"Umm, no. I'm not saying it at all," answered Lyla. "I'm saying this is what I heard on the phone."

"So what else was said in this fascinating phone conversation?" asked Liam seriously. "No more questions, kids. Let's let Lyla get the whole story out. We need to hear all of this. So what else was said, Lyles?"

That was the last question before their lives changed forever.

They heard a creek from outside the bedroom. All four children panicked for a second. They sat as still as deer in the headlights. A few seconds passed and no sounds. Nothing. Lyla continued her report on the strange phone call.

"Okay, so this guy basically says to Dad that I am 'of age'. He said it's time to 'prepare for the ceremony'. He said that Dad 'knew this time would come,' and that I was just 'the first of four of these ceremonies.'"

All four of them took a collective breath. Adrian's mouth opened to speak, but then closed again quickly.

Lyla went on, "Dad wasn't saying much. Some 'mm hmms' and yeses. He agreed with and understood what this man said. There was no surprise in his voice. He knew all of it. It was like he was receiving instructions for a party downstairs. Just something you talk about every day; your daughter 'coming of age' in Atlantis!" Lyla let out a sigh. She tried to relax and believe and understand what she just said out loud.

"So, according to this bizarre phone call, I am due to be inducted into Atlantis. Atlantis is *real*. And our mother is from there. Oh yes and she is two hundred years old!"

Another breath to recover her almost hysterical voice back to a more normal tone.

Tillie took a peek out of the door, then shook her head and sat back on the bed next to Lyla. She took her big sister's hand. At the same time Adrian looked out the window. Since "the incident," the three siblings were careful to keep Lyla's emotions in check.

"There are so many questions to this story, Lyles," Tillie said reassuringly. "So many things about it that could be misinformation. Like, I mean, the whole thing could be made up!"

After a few moments of silence and confused, puzzled faces Liam said, "Well, I know how we can find out." He stood up looking authoritative. "We ask Dad. About the whole thing."

Back-to-school came quickly, like Lyla said it would, for Adrian and Tillie. As the two of them came down the next morning into the restaurant to grab a quick breakfast, the rest of the family were getting Sigrun ready for the day. Adrian poured himself a cup of coffee. "Want some, Till?" he asked Tillie sitting at the counter.

"Wha," Tillie shook her head. "Oh, coffee. No thanks. Nervous enough today as it is."

"You still get nervous after all these years, Tillie?" asked Cord. He carried a big crate of fresh produce into the kitchen for the day's menu.

"Umm...what, Dad?" asked Tillie distractedly. She realized then what he said and added quickly, "Oh yeah! Yeah, that's why I'm nervous, alright! Gotta make a terrific first impression on my final year of high school. Tons of pressure." She nodded to keep the charade looking real. She gave Adrian a look, then quickly went back to her bite of toast and juice.

All was fairly quiet about Sigrun this particular morning as everyone prepared for their day and most of the Lundgrens were lost in thought. It was decided during last night's bizarre conversation that Liam and Lyla would confront Cord together tonight after work when everyone was upstairs. This was partly why Tillie was so on edge this morning, as she knew she had to wait to get some answers. She also hated the thought of being one of the last to know anything about anything.

Adrian and Tillie were off to school in the hand-me-down family car, picking up a couple of their friends down the road on the way. Liam and Lyla kept to themselves most of the morning, staying very duty bound keeping to their jobs. It wasn't unusual for Lyla to be so into her work that she sometimes got lost there. But for Liam to be too busy to shoot the breeze with anyone who passed through the kitchen was a bit noticeable.

"Hey there, Mr. Mime," Marcus teased as he pretended to be a man-in-a-box. Marcus came in to take the day shift today for Tillie. "When you get out of your world and join us here I need a Number Four breakfast for table seven." Marcus hung the order slip on the order carousel.

"Huh?" Liam stammered, oblivious to all of Marcus' antics. "Yeah, right. Breakfast for seven."

Marcus chuckled. "Man, whatever you are smokin', I'll have two," followed by more chuckling. "That's *one* number *four* breakfast for *table seven*," he repeated even more slowly than before.

Liam grabbed the ticket. "Oh yeah, of course. Sorry man, I'm a little distracted. Umm...er...classes start this week and already my mind is in a dozen different directions." It wasn't a complete lie as much as an exaggeration. Liam went right to the breakfast preparation.

"These kids today," Marcus said to himself. "They take everything so seriously!" Marcus did a jazzy step to his next table and began charming table ten, some middle-aged women who loved to come into Sigrun and gush over Marcus and his Jamaican accent. "Ladies!"

Liam glanced toward Lyla. She was busy taking an order and pouring coffee at the counter, so he went back to business in the kitchen.

Hours passed. The lunch crowd started to roll in on schedule. Anna came into work and went back to the kitchen to help Liam.

"Hello, sweet cheeks," said Anna reaching to give Liam's cheeks their usual squeeze. The children were all used to this from Anna by now, so it was quite a shock when Liam jumped back.

"What the-" he stated, stepping backward. Anna looked at him very confused. "Oh! So sorry, Anna! I've been so distracted today," he said as he rushed forward awkwardly.

Anna caught his cheek and said, "Oh my little Liam! Work has made you all grown up! So fast, too! Don't forget my dear, that you will always be my little sweet cheeks!" She patted Liam's shoulder and went into the back to get ready for work.

At the same time as the cute exchange going on in the kitchen, Lyla and Marcus walked busily back and forth from the tables to the counter hanging their orders. Lyla was at the counter when Liam jumped back from Anna. This caused Lyla to twitch herself and her heart skipped a beat. She froze in her spot and watched the two in the kitchen. By the time Anna was pinching Liam's cheek again, Marcus was behind Lyla with another order. "Excuse me, hon, is this the line for the show?" asked Marcus in his most dashing way.

"Oh!" Lyla shouted and her order tablet shot up into the air and landed on the counter. It looked as though she was going to fall over.

"Gee, hon, so very sorry, Lyla," Marcus exclaimed as he grabbed her shoulders and held her in position. "You okay?"

"Oh my gosh, Marcus!" Lyla scrambled to right herself, picked up her tablet and tried to look orderly. "I'm the one who is so sorry," she said, gaining her composure to her usual level.

She glanced out the windows. No clouds forming. A little puff of breath released from her with relief.

"I'm so jumpy today! Must have been that extra coffee I had this morning. Guess I won't be doing that again!" She gave a quick laugh and walked back to the tables, hoping that was a convincing blow-off because she was feeling anything but convinced herself.

"Man! Maybe you should get whatever your brother has," Marcus said more to himself than anyone else. "These two surely must be up to somethin'." He trailed off, back to the tables with a shrug of his shoulders.

Lyla glanced over to the kitchen at Liam. His head was down and he was busy working. Then Lyla noticed Heather standing in the doorway to the office. Her mom was just leaning against the doorjamb looking around the room. In the same instant Lyla saw that, Heather went back into the kitchen and talked to Anna. *Phew!* Lyla thought to herself. She relaxed for a second and then remembered that she hadn't even noticed her mother in the room last week when she got the bizarre phone call. Yet her mom knew that it happened. So if her mom was standing there in the doorway, she saw everything happening just then, for sure.

If she hadn't seen her mom when she got the phone call, then how did her mom know about it?

Lyla spent most of the rest of the afternoon thinking about this question. Her mom wasn't a sneaky lady. It's not like she would purposely eavesdrop on her own daughters...would she? So, then, how did she know?

The lunch crowd wound down. Lyla was just setting an order down at its table when the answer she'd been searching for all afternoon came to her: Dad.

He must have told mom about the conversation, she thought.

The day ended out without any more surprise incidents. Lyla and Liam were able to catch a break with each other between the lunch and dinner crowds. Lyla shared her idea with Liam about their mom.

"That does make perfect sense," he said. His brain almost made a clicking noise as the idea sunk in.

This revelation helped the two oldest children relax enough to get through the rest of dinner. They now figured that they didn't have to keep this secret from their mother. They decided during their break that they, meaning all of the children, would confront both parents. Tonight.

"Tonight?" Tillie was checking a text message on her phone.

"Yes, Till, tonight," Lyla replied. They were cleaning up the dining area; Heather had already gone upstairs.

"Oh shoot." Tillie closed her phone. "I can't tonight. First meeting for homecoming committee and I can't miss it! Can't you guys just do it and then tell me about it later? As much as I hate that idea, I really can't miss this meeting if I want to be on the committee." Tillie scrunched her face like the whole idea hurt.

Lyla could see that Tillie's day back to school went better than her day at work. She embraced the back to school spirit with her usual gusto.

"Oh jeez, Tillie!" Lyla whined at her sister, being very tired from her stressful day. "Liam and I talked about it and decided this way would be best. That way there are no secrets in this house anymore. Besides, you were the one who was ready to burst."

"Well, can't we just do it tomorrow? I'm free then," Tillie finished in a most careless fashion.

"Till, this isn't your next doctor's appointment or something. You don't just reschedule something possibly, no, *probably* life-altering because of homecoming." Lyla snapped her cleaning rag a bit too hard. It knocked over the sugar dispenser on the table. She picked it up and wiped the table down for a second time.

"Lyles," Tillie said as she finished sweeping the sugar that made it to the floor. She stopped and looked at her big sister. "You really need to take some time off and get out of this place." Lyla guffawed. "No, I'm serious," Tillie said. "You guys are all taking this stuff like it's fact. We don't even really know exactly what is going on here."

Lyla went from looking insulted to being in thought. "I guess *someone* gave things some thought today," she said.

"Yes and...well...it helps to get out of this place for a little while. Why don't you take the morning off tomorrow and go hiking? Ask Anna if Julie can come in for you. The fresh air will do you good."

"That's easy for you to say," Lyla said in a defeated way. "You always think you can do anything with a little fresh air."

"Well, it never hurts," Tillie answered back. She headed upstairs with Lyla dragging behind her.

The girls were up in their room much like every other night getting ready for bed. Liam popped his head in the door.

"Knock, knock," he said before he opened the door all the way. Lyla was about to tell Liam that all plans were off when Liam said softly, "Tonight is a bust ladies. Adrian is M I A."

"What do you mean, M I A?" Lyla asked tiredly, but concerned.

Liam came into the room and closed the door. "I mean, I can't find him. I don't know where he went. And no one else seems to know where he is either. Till, did he have something going on for school tonight?"

"Well, no, not that I know of," Tillie answered.

"Well great. This is just a great end to my day," Lyla said sounding frustrated. "So, should we just do this without him, then? I mean, we shouldn't be worrying about him, he's not actually missing, is he? Man, I'm tired tonight, so I can't even think straight. Maybe it is a good idea to postpone."

"Don't worry, sis, I've got calls out to his buds and I'm sure we'll find him before it gets too late. Mom and dad didn't seem to recall him saying anything to them about being anywhere specific, though," Liam finished and trailed off into thought.

"Well, should we be sitting around here then?" asked Tillie in almost a panic. She stood up and looked ready to put out the search party.

"Take it easy. Man, you girls have a rough day, did you?" Liam said as he grabbed his phone from his pocket.

"Hold on. It's Todd." Liam looked at his phone and read the text. "Nope, the guys haven't seen him either." Liam looked off thinking.

A few moments passed. The girls felt anxious.

"Well are we going to go look for him or what?" Tillie demanded. "I can't just sit here not knowing," she finished as she headed toward Liam and the door.

"Hold on," Liam said and stopped Tillie. "I have a thought. I think I might know where he went. Can you girls get out of here without alerting the 'rents?"

"Heck yeah, we've been doing it all summer, haven't we?" Tillie answered still anxious. "Now let's go."

"No, no. I'll go first. You girls follow in about five or ten minutes. *Quietly.* I'll meet you at the beach where we tested," Liam was out the door before they could ask him any further questions.

"Tested? What does he mean," Tillie looked to Lyla for the answer.

"Where the incident happened. Where we were all tested," Lyla answered drearily. "C'mon, let's get ready. We'd better get our suits on, I have a feeling we'll be needing them. Do a check out there before we go out 'kay," Lyla indicated over to their parents' bedroom.

"Yeah, okay. Hey, do you think it's a coincidence that when we need mom and dad to be out of the way, they are?" Tillie looked back out of the room and back to Lyla.

"Umm, I dunno Till, I'm too tired to think of that kind of happenstance right now. Let's go." Lyla stood up and went to the closet.

Tillie went out, then came back in quickly. "We're good. Coast is clear," she said in an almost whisper. The girls changed quickly. They went out undetected.

About twenty minutes later, the girls caught up with Liam who was already on the beach. He stood in his swim trunks looking out toward the water. His clothes were in a pile a little ways behind him.

"Okay ladies, coast clear? Did you get out alright?"

"We're here aren't we," Tillie answered her big brother with a smile.

"Yes well true. So I was thinking of where Adrian might be tonight. It occurred to me that this might be the one place that he would be that no one else would know of," Liam gestured toward the water. "He could be down there and no one would know. So it's up to us to find him." Liam started for the water.

"Whoa, hold on there, Liam," Lyla insisted. "We don't know *if* he's down there, let alone *where* down there he may be!"

"I know sis," Liam sounded calm. "And I know this is going to sound nuts but...just listen okay?" Liam responded to Lyla rolling her eyes. "Our last time out here. Our tests. When I was in the water at the same time as Ade I could feel him there. I just knew he was there. And I swear, if I had to, I would have been able to swim right to his location. It was comforting at the time and I just thought it was because I already knew he was there. I just thought I was making myself feel better about the whole danger of what we were doing. Being at night and all, we were really a bit careless with the testing. I know, I know, we didn't have much choice. But I'm telling you, I could find him if he's in there." Liam waited for Lyla's response.

"Well I'm not letting you go alone, that's for sure," Tillie said as she stripped down to her suit as fast as she could. "I can cover under water like nobody's business. And if you can feel Ade, then I probably can too."

"Wait little sis," Liam started with his big brother act.

Tillie cut him off. "Not this time big brother. I am going with you. I found Tim. I found him fast and he was deep. I can find my own brother, I know it. I'm not taking no for an answer. In fact, I'm not even asking at all."

"Well," Liam said in surprise. "I guess you are growing up now, aren't you?"

"Hold on here!" Lyla finally spoke up. "What are we doing? Doesn't this feel just like a repeat of the last time? Are we going to take any precautions this time? Do we even have anything to take precautions with?" She sounded semi panicked and authoritative at the same time.

"You're right Lyles," Liam calmed at her words of reason. "But we really didn't bring anything for safety, did we? I mean, I know I didn't." He stood there looking a little like a lost puppy.

"Well, luckily for you all I think ahead," Lyla said as she placed a large beach bag down on the sand and started rummaging through it. She pulled out two flashlights. "Here. They're water proof up to 50 yards. Picked them up shortly after the incident. Just in case. There's one for each of us, so these are yours to keep. They work pretty well too, I tried just shining it in the water one night on my break. So keep hold of them and please be safe out there." She handed the lights to Liam and Tillie. "I feel so helpless here. With my 'special powers', I don't feel there is anything I can do from here. I can't even control it, whatever it is."

Tillie stepped forward and hugged her sister. "Oh Lyla, are you kidding? What would we ever do without you?" She held out the flashlight as proof. "And don't worry, we'll get answers soon. We will. And then we will all know what all this is about!" She spun around with her arms up in the air gesturing to the heavens.

"Thanks sis. I know you're right. I just feel very frustrated right now. Now get going and Godspeed!" Lyla grabbed Tillie's hand and Tillie smiled back.

"We'll be okay," Liam reassured his big sister. "This won't take long. Promise."

He went toward the first incoming wave and dove into it. Tillie followed just behind him.

Lyla took out a blanket and set it on the beach. She sat down and placed Liam's and Tillie's clothing on the blanket carefully. She took her time as she knew there was nothing else for her to do but wait. She occupied her time with the mundane things left here with her.

A few moments passed and Lyla looked out onto the water. She could see the lights in and out of the waves. They looked like little twinkling stars in the vast water. They comforted her. They made her feel safe. It was quite a windy night, although a clear one, you could feel the bite of the end of summer. The wind was a bit more crisp than even just last week.

Lyla stared out onto the water still. A sudden calm came over her. A feeling of sureness that her siblings would find their baby brother. She felt safe and secure, warm even. Her eyelids grew heavy. She didn't want to close them for she didn't want to fall asleep. She didn't want to be irresponsible. She wanted to be here for them in case they needed her for something, anything. She took a deep breath and tried to stay awake.

When she exhaled, she fell back softly onto the blanket, as if a magician put her into a trance for his next magic trick. Her eyes closed and her body was straight on the blanket. The wind around the beach died down. It grew very calm and the waves diminished to small, almost nothingness, just lapping the shore. Lyla's body looked like it floated over the blanket, just hovering there. She looked peaceful and her face was radiant. It was as if the moon found her there and gave its light to her to borrow. She looked stunning.

14

No More Secrets

Moments passed with no one else on the beach. It was getting late and no one in the water knew of Lyla's state, but it had the most amazing effect on the water. It was still, calm and clear. You could see the ocean floor in the shallow water just by the moonlight. It was an amazingly beautiful sight to behold. It was too bad that no one was there to see it.

The lights still flashed around and a while later three figures emerged from the water. They were still quite far out, but as it was so calm, you could see quite a distance. It was shallow enough for them to walk into shore. There was no panic, no emergency. Everyone was alright.

As the figures got closer to shore, you could hear them laughing and playing. They were clearly enjoying themselves, but also trying to get back to Lyla to let her know everything was fine.

"See, Lyles," Liam shouted, "I told you we'd be fine!"

"Yeah, sis," Tillie exclaimed, "We found him, just like Liam said!"

Adrian hollered, "Sorry, sis! I didn't mean to worry anyone," his voice dropped at the end as they reached the shore. They looked at Lyla lying there peacefully.

They looked at each other. They looked back at the water and noticed how calm it was. How clear and beautiful at the same time.

"Lyla? Lyla, honey? Lyla?" Tillie knelt down beside Lyla quietly. Everyone knew that there was nothing to worry about this time. She just looked too beautiful and tranquil for there to be anything wrong. Tillie took Lyla's hand in hers and rubbed it gently. It was as if she knew this would bring her back. There wasn't any need for anything drastic. Everything around them was so calm, it made them feel calm too. The boys searched the bag for towels. Of course, because Lyla was so amazing at organizing, there were some there for everyone.

"Is she okay?" Adrian dried himself off, ready to sit down next to Tillie.

She kept gently caressing her sister's hand. "I think so," Tillie said. "I don't know why I feel that way, but I'm pretty sure she is just fine."

Liam sat on the other side of them. He picked up Lyla's other hand and gave it a gentle touch as well. "Hey there, sis. That was amazing. You can wake up now, hon," he put her hand down and then touched her face, wiping some stray hairs off of it.

Lyla started to stir. She moved around and seemed to land back onto the ground. Her eyes fluttered then opened. She saw the three faces she'd just been dreaming about staring down at her. They all looked so wonderful she couldn't help but smile.

"I'm sorry guys, did I fall asleep? I was trying to stay awake in case you needed anything." Lyla stretched and tried to sit up. It was slow, but she managed it. "Crap, I did, didn't I? I'm sorry. What did I miss?"

She looked from one to the other for an answer, but they all just looked back at her, smiling. They started to look a bit creepy with no one talking.

"Well, what happened? I see you found Ade. So you went for a swim did you, Ade? Why couldn't you just tell someone?"

Lyla started to feel aggravated. The moonlight drifted away, a few wispy clouds in its path. The wind came up almost hitting them in the faces like it had to make up for lost time. The waves came up on shore again. The sounds of the ocean were back in place. Lyla was awake.

"I know, I know, I'm so sorry. I didn't think it was a big deal. Then I lost track of time." Adrian sat closer to Lyla, sucking up a bit. "It's so easy to forget about everything up here when I'm down there," his head gestured toward the water, but he didn't take his gaze off of Lyla.

"And you two are alright with this, I see?" Lyla looked from Liam to Tillie and waited.

"Well, yeah. Look, sis, we found him didn't we? And it's not like he was in any danger or anything. I mean, how long did you say you were down there tonight, Ade?" Tillie looked over to Adrian for a little help.

"Well, I think it was over two hours." Adrian answered looking bashful. "Not to brag," he added.

"Don't be mad Lyles," Liam added. "What helped us all was you."

"What are you talking about, the flashlights? That's no big deal, but I'm glad they came in handy."

"No Lyles, that's not what I'm talking about," Liam said softly to her. This took her off guard at first and her defensiveness fell a bit.

"Then what do you mean?" she asked more sincerely and quieter.

"It's what you did. Out here. For us. You don't even know, do you? You did it again, sis," Liam looked at her, then looked around, then back at her.

"Oh crap, I did *it* again? I'm sorry!!! Oh jeez, I didn't mean..." Lyla felt awful, a knot formed in her stomach.

"Oh gosh, no!" Tillie interrupted Lyla's unnecessary apology, "You did it, but it was brilliant! Tell her what happened, Liam."

"Well, Till and I were out there among the waves. It was kind of hard to keep in touch with each other and try to 'feel' Adrian too. The lights really were helpful for that, by the way. But then it got calm. Like, really calm. Tillie and I could see each other yards away suddenly. The moon shone down on us and I could see down into the water. It was really amazing." He paused, but Tillie couldn't wait.

"Yeah and then I looked at Liam. I was about to ask him what happened, when it hit us both. We suddenly could feel where Adrian was! It was incredible! We found him in a matter of minutes after that! It was just like Li said it would be!" Tillie was giddy.

"We didn't know what happened until we came up on shore and saw you here," Liam said. "You were so...well...peaceful. You looked amazing!" Lyla looked at him with a slight frown. "Not to say that you don't every day..."

"Oh please, get on with it," Lyla stopped him right there.

"But I mean the whole scene was so tranquil and peaceful! It was really beautiful." Liam finished. He felt as though he hadn't really done the scene justice with his words.

"Yes it was." came a voice a few yards away.

All four children looked up to see Heather and Cord walking toward them. The panic struck like lightening through all of them at the same time. They only had seconds to exchange looks of terror and freaking out before their parents were upon them.

Liam spoke first, trying to smooth it all over.

"Yeah, hey! What are you guys doing here? We were just enjoying a night swim together and Lyles fell asleep! We were just telling her that she missed a really great moonlight swim." Liam smiled broad, his handsome win the girls over smile, to keep it convincing.

"Yeah, I guess I had a really tiring day today." Lyla said and knew that was a true statement regardless of the circumstances. "We didn't worry you did we? I told you guys that we should have left a note." Lyla suddenly sounded more like her usual self.

"We were just too excited to get out here. You know, one last hoorah of summer." Tillie almost sang out with her best smile, but didn't feel very convincing.

They all knew their parents weren't dumb. They just weren't sure how long they'd been on the beach.

"Save the small talk, kids. It's time to come clean." Cord said. The children all looked at him and you could almost hear their heartbeats increase collectively.

"Yes, it's time." Heather added. She sounded calm, not at all like an angry parent ready to discipline her children. This confused the four of them and they all had subtle, puzzled looks on their faces.

"Time for what?" Tillie asked, trying to sound innocent and play dumb at the same time.

This tactic worked many times for her in the past. Being one of the younger Lundgrens, she was used to this working for her.

"Oh c'mon, Till, we all know we've got some secrets floating around this family," Cord said immediately, putting everyone else's thoughts on hold.

The children were both scared and anxious to find out what was going to happen next. Every time one of their parents spoke, it shut them up completely.

It was quiet for a moment, then Liam spoke up, "Look Mom, Dad, we've been wanting to talk to you for a while now, most of the summer in fact."

"Be quiet now son, we've got some explaining to do." Heather said gently. "We've also been wanting to talk to you all for a while too. This time is upon us...maybe because I've been in denial about how grown my children have become, but we always knew this day would come." Heather trailed off, almost emotional.

The children's faces went from puzzled to empathetic in no time. They hated to see their mother under stress.

"I'm sorry. I told myself I was going to be fine. That I could do this. Hon, maybe you'd better explain first," she directed toward Cord and he gracefully took over.

"Yes, well, it's alright, dear. Can we sit down, kids?" The two parents stood there looking like the ones who needed discipline.

The kids all gestured and Liam said, "Of course, sit."

Everyone made room on the blanket for Heather and Cord. The tension eased a bit as confusion took over. It was quiet. The children waited. The waves lapped at the background that eased the seconds ticking by.

"Well, you see, children," Cord began, "things aren't as they seem with us Lundgrens." He hesitated for a moment and cleared his throat. Heather took his hand in hers. He seemed to gain confidence from it and went on. "We're...well...special you see. Not in the way that parents think their kids are special and as they should. But we're different. I mean really different." He paused again, trying to find the right words.

"We have powers you mean." Adrian said meekly.

"Wha...yes...well...what? How do you know?" Cord became befuddled and looked at Heather.

"I think after tonight dear, we can be sure they've discovered at least something," Heather said confidently. "We saw what happened here tonight, children. It was a beautiful thing. May I?" She looked at Cord for permission to continue. Cord nodded once, relieved.

"I knew it." Adrian interjected. "I knew they were powers."

"Now take it easy Adrian." Heather tried to calm his excitement, but as they all knew, it was pointless. She continued in hopes that it would explain things better.

"Yes, you all have special abilities. Talents if you like. I'm not sure I would call them powers, per se."

"Lyles seems pretty powerful to me," Tillie said shyly, not wanting to interrupt for a change.

"Well, that may be, in fact, she is very powerful. You all are. These abilities you all have, these talents. They are all growing, changing, evolving. You've all discovered something about yourselves and the water, correct?" Heather waited for all of them to answer in some form. All the children nodded.

"Yes. Yes, we've all discovered we can do different things in and with the water." Liam answered for all of them. "What we want to know is, why? We've been trying to get time to talk to you and Dad for most of the summer about this. We want to know what's going on?"

"And you have every right to know, Liam, that's why we came out to find you tonight." Heather replied.

"So it's true." Lyla spoke up. "It's all true. You're from Atlantis. We all are. And you're like two hundred or something crazy and I'm to be inducted soon! Whatever that means!" Lyla felt the panic rise in her throat and had to stop talking.

"See, I told you she heard everything." Heather said quietly to Cord. "I told you there was nothing to worry about. She's a smart, smart girl and she can handle it. They all can. Look at them. Are any of them freaking out?"

"Well, I'm not sure, as they seem to be playing statues." answered Cord. It was unusual for all four children to be so quiet and still at the same time. "You're all right then, Lyle? You did hear the conversation then? Did you hear all of it?" He waited for an answer. He waited what seemed like an eternity. "Lyle honey, you're all right, aren't you? I know this is a lot to digest." he paused at the sight of Lyla's face.

Lyla's face looked hard. Her eyes fluttered and she went back stiff. The wind didn't pick up, but it changed direction quickly. The tide receded, also quickly. Everyone backed away from Lyla, just slightly, waiting. Everyone knew there was nothing they could do. Everyone but Heather.

Clouds rolled in from the shore. It rained. It was a light, steady rain, nothing harmful. No lightening. No thunder.

Heather wasted no time. She took both of Lyla's hands and held them to her chest. "Rub her legs. Get down there and rub her legs downward toward her feet. Do it now." she instructed Tillie. Tillie moved as quickly as she could.

Heather held Lyla's hands firm at her chest. She leaned forward and put her face right in front of Lyla's. "Lyla," she said calmly but firmly without yelling. "It's momma, hon. Please come back. Please wake up." She took both of Lyla's hands into one of hers and used her free hand to pet Lyla's face. She looked back to Tillie. "Keep rubbing. Keep it firm but not hard. Understand? Don't stop." She looked back to Lyla. The next sounds out of Heather's mouth were something that none of the children had ever heard their mother speak before. In almost a whisper Heather said "Lyla, tími til að vakna."

15

Mom, Who Are You?

Lyla's eyes fluttered, then opened. The rain stopped and the wind died down to a gentle breeze again.

"Oh, no. Not again!" Lyla's face went from serene to distorted with worry in a second. "What did I do this time?"

"Nothing, sweetheart. Nothing. Just a little rain is all." Heather answered her. Heather set Lyla's hands back down onto her own body. "It's all right. You just stay here and rest a bit. It's been a very busy night for you my dear." She looked to Tillie to tell her she could stop rubbing, but Tillie was sitting very still, staring at her mother.

"Are you all right, Tillie sweetheart? It's all right, see? Lyla is fine. A little rest, now. That's what she needs." Heather turned back toward Lyla.

"Umm, mom...what was that?" Adrian asked.

"What was what?" asked Lyla. "I did do something awful, didn't I?" she questioned.

"No Lyles, not you. Mom." Adrian put her at ease a smidgen with his answer. "What did you say to Lyla, Mom?"

"Oh, that. Well, it was all I could think that would reach her in her...state. It is my language; my people's language. And it worked. I knew it would." Heather finished and directed her attention back on Lyla. She petted Lyla's head more. She looked back up at her other children. When she saw they looked so concerned, she continued. "I haven't spoken that language for, well, a very long time. Now that you are all growing up, I have a lot to teach you."

"Well you can start with, who the heck are we?" Tillie asked, a fire behind her words. "And are you really two hundred years old then? 'Cause you look like any normal mom, age wise. How does that work? Mom, Dad, we have so many questions and so many things to share with you. I don't see how we're going to have the time." Tillie finished with a huff.

Cord answered Tillie. "We know, we know, you all. You must be so frustrated. We are here tonight to help settle at least some of that. If it takes all night, we want to be here to answer your questions, worries and help you in any way we can. But let's get back to the house. Lyla is going to need some sustenance after the ordeal she's had tonight. That kind of power is tiring."

"See, I told you. *Power.*" Adrian said victoriously.

They stood and Heather helped Lyla to her feet. She didn't leave Lyla's side for a second and no one dared try to ask her to do so. The three other siblings put their clothes on. The boys gathered the blankets and towels into the beach bag and Liam carried it back to Sigrun. They knew it was going to be a long night. The talking began as they walked back home.

The Lundgrens talked until they noticed the sun coming up. Lyla was barely able to stay awake. They gave her some food and that helped. She was so eager to hear what was being said, she managed to stay awake. She did stretch out on the sofa to rest her body, however.

The children explained their abilities to Heather and Cord. They explained how they discovered them. Heather and Cord confessed to suspecting things with each one of them. The parents apologized to their children for neglecting to tell them these important things about their lives. How they, as parents, got caught up in raising their children and didn't realize that they were at this point already in their lives.

They explained things to the children further. Heather told them a bit about her life.

"I am from what is known today as Atlantis. It's not some legend. It is real. It is not just one place under one ocean. It's a people. There are many of us all over the world living among everyone else. We look and act just like humans because we are, but we are an advanced people who live among the others to help them."

"You sound like guardian angels," Tillie said at this description.

"Well, you might say that," Heather replied. "But it's more like living in harmony. We benefit from each other, not just one side helping the other, but living together helping each other."

"What do humans do for you," Adrian asked most suspiciously. "Humans? Is that right? I mean, are we *super* human or something?"

"We have learned much from manna," replied Heather politely. "They have taught us about our emotions. How to feel and control what we feel. Manna are very good at harnessing their emotions and we have learned how to control ours from them."

"Manna?" Adrian looked like he was calculating something.

"Yes. Manna is human," Heather replied.

"So what does that make us then," Lyla asked timidly. Not completely sure she wanted to know the answer, but it popped out of her mouth before she could decide.

"It's not that we are super human Adrian, Lyla," Heather continued, "we are just a bit more advanced. Our sciences from the early days were very much ahead of their time. Contrary to legends, our world was not destroyed and did not sink to the bottom of the ocean. Our people continued and learned and developed many things. We've lived among other people since the beginning. We learned from them and, in turn, we taught them what we could. Over many, many years these things have made us the different beings we are today."

"For example; we live longer because we have a different strain of DNA from long, long ago. Back in the early days of people, advances were made with natural medicines that gave longer life to our ancestors and permanently changed our DNA to last longer. We refer to ourselves as 'lifsnauðsynleg manna', or 'vital human'. And no, we do not think of ourselves as better or more important than manna. We are different. We use the term 'lifsnauðsynleg', or 'vital' to differ ourselves from others with different DNA. That is all." Heather paused there.

She looked out the window and was reminded of how late it was. She suddenly felt parental.

"Look, I know there is so much more to discuss and dad and I plan on telling you much more. It is already morning and you should all try and get at least a little rest before your day begins. Let's all talk again tomorrow, well, today after closing, all right? I promise dad and I will answer any questions you have then. We do need to get Lyla ready after all."

Everyone looked over to Lyla who was already asleep and everyone else agreed and made their way silently to their rooms, with Lyla on the couch. There was still a little time before they had to get up for work. Hopefully it would give them enough rest.

The next weeks brought on many conversations between the Lundgrens and their children. There were many late nights of talking and discovering who they were and what that meant. At the same time, they had to keep it all a secret from their every day lives, just as Heather and Cord had been doing all these years. There were so many questions between the parents and their children and not all of them could be answered or explained.

"I still don't get it," Adrian bugged Tillie again for the umpteenth time on their way to school. "I just don't see why we have to hide our abilities! I mean, yes, I can see that we shouldn't just let it all out there, but can't we at least enjoy a little bit of it? I mean, just staying under water long enough to show off with my friends, impress a girl, ya know? I mean, these are the things guys my age live for and I can't tell anyone!"

Tillie rolled her eyes. "For the one millionth time Ade, we just can't! It's not our secret to share, even though it is our ability. These things have been given to us by God, for what purpose, that is yet for us to find out. Maybe I've already fulfilled mine when I saved Tim, I don't know. Maybe it's just using our abilities throughout our lives when we can, to help manna. You just have to be patient little brother. And believe me, if I can do this, then so can you!" She finished as they arrived at school and Adrian knew she was right, so there was nothing more he could say. He knew it wouldn't change anything.

Then he added anyway, "I know, I know! I just get so frustrated sometimes! I just need to sound off every now and then and since we can't do that with our friends, then you are my sounding board now, 'kay? Well, you and Liam when I'm at work."

"Gee, thanks, we're the lucky ones, huh," Tillie replied rolling her eyes slightly again with a smile this time. They both walked into school, which ended any further conversation on the topic.

Back at Sigrun, Lyla and Liam were basically in charge this time of year. It was slow at Sigrun right before the holidays and then they closed for the harsh winter weeks, only opening on the weekends to serve hot drinks to the local holiday shoppers. This was always the time the Lundgrens took to not only enjoy being on a break from their every day schedule, but to clean and repair their restaurant and come up with new menu ideas for the new year. Although the actual restaurant was technically closed for a time, they were still busy working.

Until this year. This year would be different from any other that the children could remember. This year they would close and actually not work on the restaurant, but work on Lyla's induction to the Atlantean mores.

"Why do I have to be inducted?" Lyla remembered one of her many questions during the late night talks of the previous weeks. She sat a family at a table for dinner and couldn't help but think back on all of the new information she'd received. It still swirled in her head and every free chance her brain had she would review it.

She remembered her mother's answer. "Well, it's like a coming of age party, a quinceanera or sweet 16 party. Remember being confirmed in Church? It's like that as well. It's all of those things and lets all Atlanteans know that you are ready."

"Ready for what?" was the automatic next question, but from Adrian, not Lyla. Always quick with the questions, Adrian. Lyla paused in her thoughts for a moment to take the table's order. Polite and quick, she was back into her mind.

"Ready to handle the knowledge. Ready to understand and learn," her mother replied.

This was Lyla's favorite part of the weeks' conversations; learning and knowledge. After her initial shock wore off, she was excited to know that there was so much more to know out there. That she will be privileged to learn it and know things she hadn't dreamt of before. It made college look like elementary school to her and she knew she was ready. She just had to figure out what came next.

They were all waiting for the next phone call from one of the officials of the induction. The children all learned there was a council and judging to be inducted. It wasn't just a ceremony. There were many steps involved and Lyla was eager to get to them. They hadn't heard back from the council yet and she was starting to get antsy, despite her parents' words, "Don't worry, there's plenty of time, relax." She really didn't know why she couldn't relax about it. After all, they knew way more than she did about the timing of it all and they seemed confident in her being able to do everything well. So she should have faith in that, right?

Not really. It was around this time where she could feel the adrenalin pump through her making her a tad shaky, which she hated, especially when she worked. Lyla served a couple more tables and then went back into the kitchen.

"I'm taking 5," she told Liam and walked out the back door without even a pause in her step. Liam smiled at her as reassuringly as he could, but didn't say a word. Lyla needed to take lots of breaks these days and Liam never argued about it with her. When Anna or Danny would ask questions, he would try to come up with a quip and blow it off to seem like nothing. He couldn't tell them that she had to go outside to relax before a hurricane came up on Sigrun. This always made him smile to himself, the thought of Lyla bringing a hurricane to Sigrun. The smile was brief, however, because then the thought was oh too real and was no longer funny. Back to chopping.

The phone rang. Liam was quick to answer even though he usually cared less about the phone. But these days all the Lundgrens seemed particularly interested in the phone at work.

"Hello, Sigrun, how may I help you," Liam looked over to Anna and gave his best handsome boy smile to throw off her suspicious look. It must have worked because she went back to her tables. "Hello? Is this today's call from no one?" he asked loudly, then went toward the office door where he turned his back on the main room. "Hello? Is this the council?" he said in almost a whisper. "We are waiting to hear from anyone there." When there was no answer, just silence on the other end, he came back to the kitchen and hung up the phone. He went back to work as if nothing happened, hoping the whole thing went unnoticed.

Danny came over behind the counter, in front of Liam and hung up a couple orders. "So, having private conversations with no one now," he joked with Liam.

"What? What did you just say?" Liam asked as he held his chopping knife up toward Danny at the same time. He looked quite menacing.

"Whoa! Whoa Liam, take it easy man! I was just joking! I don't know who you were talking to or anything bro! I mean it, relax!" Danny backed away from the counter slowly with his hands slightly raised. He looked like he was being held at gunpoint.

"What are you talking about?" Liam's look suddenly changed from menacing to confused. Then he noticed his hand with the knife and dropped both down immediately. "Oh dude! Sorry! I'm...I...I didn't mean that bro, for sure! You know me, sometimes I just get really into my work! I would never...I didn't mean it to be..." he stuttered, which was unusual for Liam to do.

He finally collected himself and said, "I'm sorry Danny. I was into a thought and I really didn't hear what you said. So when you looked at me scared like that, I was confused. I'm really sorry. I didn't mean to do that whole...with the knife and everything...you just caught me off guard. Are you all right?" Liam had come around to the area behind the counter as he was explaining himself and was standing closer to Danny now.

Danny dropped his hands as well. "Phew! Man bro, you had me freaked out there for a second! Sheesh!" He let out a nervous but genuine laugh and patted Liam on the shoulder. "I was just trying to make a joke with you."

"Hahaha...yeah, a joke...about what, the phone or something," Liam looked back at the phone behind him.

"Yeah, you know, you went into the other room for our daily call from no one," Danny replied with a small laugh. "So I was just..."

"Look Dan, Danny, bro," Liam moved close to Danny now, with his hand upon Danny's shoulder. "That call was from a girl I like. I just made it look like a call from no one so nobody here would notice me go into the office and talk, 'kay?" He smiled at Danny and shook his shoulder slightly. Guy code for chick talk.

Danny was confused for a split second, then as if the light bulb came on, he looked at Liam with a big grin, "Oh! Oh yeah, I get it bro! Hey look, no worries here man," he said as he backed away a step or two, "sorry to step on your mo jo.

Won't happen again man," Danny finished and went back to the tables.

Liam shot his smile back at Danny. "Thanks bro. I knew I could count on you." Then he went back into the kitchen and the smile disappeared as he went back to work.

Damn, thought Liam to himself. *When are we going to hear from them? Why haven't they called yet? When are we going to get on with this?* These questions haunted him the rest of the work day. Being in the kitchen, Liam had more time to himself than Lyla to ponder over things. It got to him more because of that.

The nights after work and school, when all of the Lundgrens were home, were still filled with conversations regarding Lyla's induction. All day long each of the children thought of more questions to ask their parents at the end of the day. Sometimes Tillie and Adrian would insist on being able to tell things to "just certain friends," their hot headedness getting the better of them that day. Heather would take on these commands, being more patient than Cord at the end of the day and used to calming her children down. She would again explain the importance of secrecy in their new lives.

"At least for now," she would always finish. This made Adrian and Tillie feel better, knowing that someday they could share all of this with someone else, so the waiting wouldn't be forever.

16

The Phone Call From Someone

November rolled around, cold up in Maine this time of year. Only locals came to Sigrun and fewer in numbers. Mostly for breakfast and coffee, lots of coffee. This time of year drinks of tea, coffee and chocolate at Sigrun kept the town going.

This month was the beginning of the holidays. It always felt like once Thanksgiving came, what was left of the year slid by even faster. The Lundgrens were no exception to this holiday phenomenon. They stayed open full time at Sigrun through the Thanksgiving weekend and then they opened only on weekends to serve hot drinks to the shoppers in town during the holiday season. Usually the Lundgrens were in good spirits this time of year because they didn't worry about getting all their work done through the holidays. Instead they concentrated on their customers and did their best to put them at ease through the pre-holiday rush. They were seen by the locals with smiles on their faces and ease about them, never rushing.

They encouraged their friends and patrons with positive reinforcement. They were sincere and genuine and people loved them for it. Especially this time of year, when everything and everyone else was so hurried, rude and harsh. The Lundgrens made it their special holiday mission to the town to give them a place where they could come to get away from all of that, if just for a little while.

The phone rang on a not so special, mid-November afternoon, when the restaurant was practically empty after a not very busy lunch hour. It sounded particularly loud and made Anna jump a little on the way to get her coat to go home for the day. She turned to answer the phone, but Liam beat her to it.

"Sorry Anna, expecting a call sometime today." He lied. Not entirely, as he was expecting a call sometime every day these days. Liam picked up the phone and said, "Hello?" Forgetting to add the rest of the restaurant's greeting. This time of year they rarely, if ever, had business phone calls, so it was easy to forget.

"Hello? Hello?" A funny, small voice answered, "Is this the Lundgren residence?"

"Yes. Well, this is Sigrun, the restaurant owned by them." Liam looked around the restaurant and suddenly felt a zing of excitement go through him at the question on the other end of the phone.

He gave Lyla a look, which she didn't have to question for a second and both of them went into the office quickly and shut the door behind them. Liam looked like he was about to burst he was so on edge.

"Can I help you with something?" Liam tried to sound casual, but asked his question too fast.

"What? Oh! What did you say?" The voice on the other end sounded flustered, like he had trouble hearing.

"I'm sorry." Liam collected himself with a big breath. "This is Liam Lundgren. Can I help you today?" He waited. A few seconds passed. He wondered if there was still anyone there, but waited longer.

"Yes my dear boy!" The man on the other side of the phone sounded like he won a prize in a raffle. He was very enthusiastic. He had an accent that Liam was not familiar with. "Liam! How nice to finally hear your voice! I...that is to say, we, the Council have been trying to reach you all for months! It seems we have somewhat of a bad connection from where we are calling from and it's tricky, so we don't always get through!"

Before Liam had a chance to say anything in return, the man continued. "So let me make this brief and to the point my lad. Your sister Lyla and you are to be inducted to the Atlantean mores. Is she there?"

Liam blinked a few times, a bit shocked and looked toward Lyla sitting across from him at the desk. He answered quickly, remembering what the man said about their connection. "Yes sir. She's right here."

Liam had no time to ask about the mention of himself, the man directed him. "Okay, can you both get on the line so I don't have to repeat myself? That way I can be as brief as possible if we get disconnected or something."

"Yes." Liam answered. He waved Lyla over to the phone and they both shared the ear piece. "Okay, she's on now."

"Good. Hello Lyla, my dear." The man stated, but did not wait for her to reply. "My name is Bard Dagsson. I am so pleased to be able to talk to you both today." He suddenly sounded like he was reading off something. Like when you answer the phone only to have someone try and sell you something, but more quickly. "As a High Honor Council member, it is my pleasure to inform you that you both, Lyla and Liam Lundgren, have been found to be of age to be inducted into the Atlantean mores. We, the Council, invite you for your test on December 27th, of this year. No studying will be accepted beforehand, as you will learn everything you need to know for the test when you arrive. You shall arrive for the test no later than December 20th and expect to stay indefinitely until you meet all requirements."

There was silence.

Then Bard popped in with, "Hello? Hello? Am I still there? I mean, are you still there? Do you have any questions for me before I go?" He had finished his speech.

Lyla and Liam both sat there for a moment looking frozen in time. *Both* of them are being inducted? Since when was this decided? The two of them had so many questions going through their brains simultaneously, they didn't know how to answer. You could almost see the ideas swirling and mixing over both of their heads. They both raised their eyebrows at one another asking the other to answer. Lyla shrugged her shoulders and her eyes went back onto the phone. Liam huffed and was the first to speak.

"Umm...Mr. Dagsson, sir? Umm...yeah...I mean, yes, we are still here. We are just a little confused. We thought it was just Lyla being inducted. Why is it now both of us?" He looked at Lyla asking if that was an alright response with his eyes. She nodded back. They both listened for the answer.

"Well Liam, when you qualify, you qualify. We have no control over that. We just know when you do. You and your sister Lyla have both been found to be at the age of maturity we are looking for. Therefore, you both qualify." There was some static after that sentence. Lyla and Liam both backed their ears away from the phone a bit.

"Mr. Dagsson, we are both honored to be ready for this." Lyla stated. "Even though we aren't completely sure what all this is about, we accept your offer to have us for the test."

There was more static.

"Is our whole family invited, or just Liam and myself?"

More static.

"Oh, the whole family of course will be expected. We don't induct people without their families here to support them fully."

"Do you need to talk to our parents for instructions on how to reach you and how to get there? We don't know how to find you." Lyla was confident that her reply was thorough and respectful.

"Oh yes, yes, that will be fine. Don't worry children, your parents know how to reach us. I must be going now. Our time for talking today has come to an end. I, that is, we look forward to meeting you very soon." There was a loud burst of static and then all they heard was the dial tone.

Both Lyla and Liam looked very confused, then, as it all sunk in, they smiled at each other. Liam put the phone down and grabbed his sister into a bear hug. Lyla's eyes opened wide at first and then she hugged him right back.

"Holy cow Lyles, this is amazing! The two of us! Inducted into Atlantis!" Liam said the last word in a whisper, then released his hold on his sister. "We're going to have a lot to talk about tonight!"

"For sure! I am so excited that you get to join me, Li! I was feeling so nervous that I'd have to go through all of this by myself. Should we tell Mom and Dad right now?"

"No, no, we can't talk now. There's too many people around."

The two of them walked out of the office and Liam hung the phone back on the wall. Lyla looked around the restaurant. There were no customers to be seen.

"Too many people, huh?" She looked at Liam.

"Oh hush. There's still Danny." Liam said in a hushed voice, shooting his glance over toward Danny, who was completely clueless of their conversation.

"Oh, well, okay. I'll let that slide, this time." Lyla said with a smile, grabbed a rag and went to wipe tables. Liam went automatically to the kitchen.

"Everything all right, son?" Cord finished washing dishes at the sink when Liam came into the kitchen.

Liam looked around. Danny chatted with Anna across the restaurant. Liam caught Lyla's eye and she nodded, so he went ahead.

"Yeah Dad, things are great, actually." He tried not to sound too excited to draw attention to himself, but he couldn't help a little bit of it showing. He tried to keep his voice down. He sounded like an excited librarian.

"Apparently, I am also ready to be inducted." He stepped next to his dad and started drying the dishes. He had a huge grin on his face.

"Really?" Cord was loud, even louder than a normal voice, which of course drew some attention from Anna and

Danny for a moment. Once they realized it was Cord's voice however, they went back to their own conversation. They're used to Cord's loud outbursts.

"Oh son, that's fantastic." He said in a more normal tone. "It really is! Your mother and I were hoping, but we didn't want to say anything, in case it didn't happen this time. But we knew it had to be you and your sister. Congratulations!" Cord dried his hands and patted Liam on the back roughly. Liam beamed even more and let out one laugh, sounding almost like a guffaw.

"You can give us the details tonight, okay son? We don't need to talk further here." He grabbed Liam's hand, shook it firmly and went out back.

Liam looked over to Lyla who came over to the counters to wipe them down. His smile said it all and Lyla couldn't help but smile back. They both felt a tie to each other that they hadn't felt before. It was like being in a special club that no one else can be in but the two of them. It was even better than that, so much more important. They suddenly felt the giddy excitement take them over for this unknown adventure. They finished the rest of the night with an extra spring in their step and smiles on their faces. It spread to everyone around them.

Later that night, upstairs at home, Liam and Lyla sat down with the family to tell them of the phone conversation and Liam's readiness as well.

"That is so exciting!" Tillie almost screamed. They loved it when they could talk openly about everything and not have to hold back. There many nights' conversations filled with loud outbursts.

"Sweet, bro!" Adrian exclaimed. He shot Liam a high five over the heads of the rest of the family. Again, always with the questions, "So, what does this mean? This 'test'. What's it all about?" He waited for the answer.

"Well, first may I say, this is all so very exciting!" Heather almost sounded like Tillie, which is something none of them heard very often. They all looked a little shocked for a moment. She looked at Cord. "I am so thrilled that two of our children will be inducted! This is more than we were hoping for!"

She paused to gain her composure. She still had a big smile on her face.

"So, Adrian, the test. Yes. There is some testing done before the pomp and circumstance. Now, don't get nervous. When I say 'testing', I mean more of a preparation, a passing through steps to reach the goal, okay? There are four stages of testing."

"Four?" Liam almost shouted as well.

Emotions ran high in the Lundgren house tonight.

Lyla shot questions. "Are you sure we are going to have enough time? What about Sigrun? Are we going to be back in time to open?"

Everyone asked more questions all at once and also very loudly.

"Settle down now, kids." Cord interjected. "Now look. We know you are all very excited, as are we. Eeup! Quiet, Tillie." Cord caught Tillie as her mouth opened to say something. "But your mother and I know what we are doing, okay? You have to trust us now like never before. It is ultra important that you take this seriously. Liam, we will have plenty of time to get back in time to open Sigrun. Your mom and I have had this planned for years. Why do you think we close shop every year? Won't look suspicious to anyone, will it?" He looked to Heather.

"Yes. Your father is right kids." Heather started to say.

"As usual." Tillie got her two cents in, then sat herself up a bit more to listen.

"Thank you, Tillie dear." Heather continued. "We know how this goes guys. And we know you can do this, Liam and Lyles. We are so excited for you two. You have no idea what awaits you in our world."

"Wait, *our* world?" Liam stood up and looked at his father with accusation on his face. "I thought this was Mom's thing. Care to explain? Man! What we don't know is starting to scare me!" Liam huffed, sat back down and waited. It seemed they'd all been doing a lot of waiting lately and it got very frustrating.

"Now, take it easy son." Cord said with a pat on Liam's shoulder. "Yes, I am part of your mother's world. Only because we chose to spend our lives with each other. I am not Atlantean. Well, not mostly anyway. There is some Viking heritage apparently, but that isn't the focus right now. What your mother is trying to say, is that it is our world because what was once ours as individuals is ours together. Got it?"

Adrian chimed in with his hands around his throat pretending he was going to be sick. "Gag, Dad. That sounds so gushy."

"As 'gushy' as it may sound, it is the utmost truth. It sounds 'gushy' Ade because people today only talk about spending their lives with someone as a romantic gesture. Something you see in the movies. 'And they lived happily ever after.' Well let me tell you something, kids, happily ever after is a long time and there is a lot more to it than just sitting back and living happily. The commitment your mother and I have toward each other goes even beyond love and way beyond the romantic notion of love. There is nothing gushy about that. We just live in a time where people don't have that very often, so when they see someone who does, it makes them feel uncomfortable. Hence the gushy, Ade." Cord looked at Adrian who nodded. There was a short pause in the chatter.

"So, back to these, 'tests'." Heather continued, back on track. "There are four stages, like I said. The first you both have already passed. You have been found to be of age. Now, this isn't a number age, obviously, as you both are different ages in years. This is a level of maturity, of readiness. It is determined by a period of observation from the Council. They will spend a period of time, unbeknownst to the family or candidate, observing you in your every-day habitat."

The children thought Heather sounded like a teacher, reciting instructions before the big tests in school. Familiar with this tone, they continued to pay attention.

"Now...what, no questions?" Heather asked, surprised. There were none. "Okay then. So, someone has been watching you, Lyla, Liam." she nodded to each of them as she said their name. "Watching you for the past weeks, possibly months, we can't be sure. They are very discreet."

Lyla's face looked tortured for a moment. Heather was quick to put her at ease.

"And no, to answer the look on your face, Lyles honey, they do not take your water incidents into account. They realize that these abilities are out of your control, for right now. That they are untouched, if you will and need to be harnessed. They take your abilities into account, but only that you have them and not what you have done with them so far."

"Darn, so much for my heroic actions last summer." Tillie said quietly, almost under her breath. Unfortunately, because it was so quiet in the room, everyone heard her.

"Oh, Tillie sweetheart, no! No, your actions were quite clear on that occasion!" Heather kept her voice stern, but gentle and sincere. "It wasn't your talent by itself that saved Tim that day, but your choices as well. And that my dear, will count immensely."

She smiled at Tillie and Tillie smiled back.

"But we weren't talking about you and Adrian. Not this time." She finished just as gently.

Tillie was confused for a moment, then the look on her face said she was back on track.

17

Feels Like a Lifetime Ago

"Now your father and I noticed there were weird things happening, starting around the end of school last year. Funny strangers around town we've never seen before."

"OH!" Cord shouted and made everyone jump practically out of their seats. "Oh the guy! With the coffee! On the fourth! Jeez, hon, why didn't you say anything to me at the time?"

"Well, I figured you would have figured it out. Although, I am more used to their telltale signs. Sorry I didn't think to say something."

"Ah, no worries. Good to know what that was about though." Cord finished as he scratched his head. "So, the phone calls from no one kids. Those were the Council. The green lights then too, huh?" He looked at Heather.

As he finished his question, all four Lundgren children sat bolt upright. Their eyes all opened wide. "Green lights!" They said at once.

"They were real!"

"Yes!"

"Oh, my gosh!"

"What do you know about the green lights?" Heather asked her children, curious to hear their answers.

"We saw them!" Tillie blurted out. "And we tried to figure out what they were and we couldn't for the life of us do it!"

"So what *are* they?" Adrian interrupted Tillie's series of sentences.

"Transport." Heather answered.

"The lights you see are the portals opened to travel between long distances quickly. What travels within them are kúla, or bubbles that transport a person or persons to where they need to go."

"There were quite a few of them in July," Cord said, thinking back.

"Yes, I thought there might be, after we saw the coffee gentleman. He was the first I believe and then others from the Council come to confirm it. Now here we are, with both of you ready!" Heather smiled big and excited again.

"Sorry, we're getting so distracted tonight." Heather said and continued, "The second stage."

"Well, we just learned about that today, didn't we?" Lyla asked, almost as a statement.

"Yes, dear, you did." Heather replied. "So as you know, we will be going to an outpost of Atlantis soon for your brief history test. There you will have many days to learn a summarized history of Atlantis and its people. On December 29th, you will have a written exam to test what you have learned. Now I am sure that it won't be a problem for either of you. You've always done well in school and this will be much like that format. I'm sure there will be trues and falses and multiple choices. You will figure it out, I know it. It's kind of like when you get your permit for your driver's license. It's a first step to reaching your goal."

"Yeah, the easy step." Adrian bemoaned. He was still working on the license part of driving and was not always happy about it.

"Precisely," Heather agreed. "It is meant to bring you into the world in a crash-course kind of way. It will open your eyes children! I am very, very excited for you. Okay, now down to the nitty-gritty. Stage three. This can get very tricky and will hardly seem like a test at all."

There were moments of silence before she continued.

"You must complete a quest." Heather sat there looking excited and serious at the same time. "Now what this quest will be, none of us know. But it will be important. There are requirements that need to be met during the quest. One; you will have to go on your own. This will not be something you can work on together. Two; you will be required to travel. This quest will bring you to new places and you will discover new things about the world, about Atlantis and about yourselves! Very exciting stuff!" Heather clapped her hands like a little girl getting a puppy on her birthday.

The children smiled and kind of laughed, but kept listening, not wanting to interrupt this fountain of information. This definitely wasn't going to be any ordinary family vacation. As their first family vacation, this will be hard to top.

"So, that brings us to the final stage; proof. You will bring proof of what you have learned on your quest to the Council for verification. This will be done in the form of a presentation. In any form of your choice, I believe. The details will depend on your quest of course, so I cannot help you further on that. Then, the Council will decide if you have completed all the tasks to their liking. Then you will be inducted!"

Once again, the big smile. Heather seemed so thrilled and confident about it all, that it made the children happy too.

Tillie was the first to voice it. "Oh, man, this is a trip! I mean, wow!" She stood up and jumped up and down like she did when she was little and excited. "Can you believe this, guys?"

"Yeah, wow is right. Here I am worrying about getting a driver's license. That's nothing, huh?" Adrian looked at Liam and grinned.

Lyla and Liam both sat and smiled back. Almost like robots, they did not look natural or comfortable. They sat, quietly smiling like that for a good minute.

"Hey, you okay, you two?" Adrian looked back and forth at both of them.

"Sure." Lyla blinked. "I think it's just a lot for us to take in, seeing as we're the ones who are about to actually go through it. So we just need some time to process it, right, Li?" She looked at Liam.

"Oh yeah, time to process for sure, bro." Liam looked at Adrian. "This is a lot of stuff to think about, I mean, what the heck! It's tons of excitement too. I'll get there, I just need a minute."

He high fived Adrian again, but this time not as enthusiastic, then sat back into the couch looking inquisitive.

Their silence left Tillie and Adrian holding their excitement to themselves for the time being. They looked at each other for a moment.

"Well Ade, want to leave these two alone with their serious, life changing thoughts?" Tillie stood up and offered Adrian her arm.

"Why I don't mind if I do Till." He replied as he stood and grabbed her arm. "Perhaps we should go for a swim and mull things over." He said in jest. They knew it was far too cold for that.

They both walked to the bedroom area arm in arm. Tillie was heard mumbling something about a card game in the boys' room.

Already Lyla's mind was racing a thousand miles a minute. So many questions were popping out that she didn't even have time to form them. It all felt like one giant swirl of chaos. She knew what that brought on if she wasn't careful. She felt the adrenaline building.

"Uh...mom...what do I do with all of this?" She asked hesitantly, afraid to move from her current position. She looked over her head, letting everyone else know what she was talking about. Then her eyes rolled back in her head and no one needed any hints on what that meant.

They were on top of it. Heather placed herself directly in front of Lyla. She stared at her and started to rub her arms from top to bottom, squeezing her hands as she got to them.

"Róa. Róa. Róa." She repeated slowly again and again, until she could see Lyla's breathing calm down. "You are all right, Lyla. You are all right." She continued to rub her arms lightly.

Lyla blinked and saw her mother in front of her.

"This is why I worry!" She said still sounding scared. "How can I go off on some quest by myself if at the drop of worry I bring on fits of weather!" She got hysterical this time and fast.

Heather rubbed more firmly and looked to Cord. He started to calm chant.

"Róa. Róa. Róa." He kept going for as long as it took for Lyla to calm down again.

It was several minutes this time. Heather and Cord's teamwork was like a machine. They would not slow or stop until they had Lyla back to them.

Liam looked out the windows for any signs, but all he saw was the wind pick up a bit.

"Looks all right." He said quietly. He moved closer to Lyla and whispered in her ear, "It's all right, Lyles. We're all here for you. We always will be, no matter what."

Lyla blinked several times. With eyes wide, she said, "Thanks Li. I know you are and I am counting on it." She sat back on her chair, tired from that bit of ordeal.

"Well, that's it then." Cord said with finality. "Time for bed I'd say. You have both had a lot of information tonight and it's time to get some rest with it all. Come to terms with it tonight while you sleep, kay?" He stood up and helped Lyla do the same. He hugged her close and gently.

"We know you can handle this, darlin'. We have every confidence in you. You just need to have it in yourself." He let her go and said, "Now sweet dreams, yah hear?"

He flashed his brilliant, fatherly smile and helped her face her bedroom.

Lyla walked away saying, "Thanks everyone. I know I just need to find that place where I feel good about all of this. I'll do it. It'll just take me a little time." She smiled as she reached her bedroom door and walked into her room.

Heather looked at Cord and hugged him around the waist with one arm. "C'mon. It's time for bed for you too." She kissed him.

"Goodnight Liam." Cord said. "Don't mind breaking up the card game to get some z's, okay?"

"Yeah, okay, Dad." Liam said, but stayed sitting on the couch, rubbing the back of his head in a half stretch. "I think I'm gonna watch a spot of TV, just to veg out for a bit first." He grabbed the remote control from the coffee table and turned on the television. He sat back and zoned out.

"Goodnight guys."

Heather bent down and kissed Liam on the forehead.

"Goodnight, love. We are so very proud of you."

One more kiss and she and Cord were off to bed.

Liam sat back and a small smile came across his face. *Funny,* he thought, *how you can be all grown up and a compliment from your mom or dad can make you smile.* He mindlessly flicked through channels until he passed out on the couch.

The waves rolled fiercely now. They grew bigger with every hit to the ship. Were they going to make it? The sails were tattered and whipping through the wind and water. The ship took on water fast! A wave washed over Liam and all he could feel was the panic and fear of not having air to breathe.

Next thing Liam knew, it was morning. He didn't remember the dream. He didn't remember falling asleep on the sofa either.

"Morning, sleepy-head." Tillie said happily. She went into the kitchen with pep in her step.

"Morning," was all Liam managed to say before she was out of his sight. He sat up and rubbed the back of his head. Then he stood up and went to his room.

The next few weeks were spent preparing Sigrun to close early and probably open again without the Lundgrens. Heather and Cord knew that they would be gone for weeks, maybe up to two months with the induction. They wanted to be sure that their restaurant would open at its usual time in the New Year. They trusted Anna, Marcus and Danny for the task. The three of them were put in charge to find a few more temporary employees to work at Sigrun until the Lundgrens returned.

Tillie and Adrian were put to work at school. They spent the last two weeks before Christmas vacation talking to their teachers and getting any assignments they could that they would need to get done in January. They made arrangements with their teachers as well to send them work through email that they would complete and send back to them.

The Lundgrens told everyone they needed to that they were going on an extended family vacation overseas and they weren't sure of when they would return. Everything was coming into place.

The morning of their flight to Chicago arrived. The girls had been packing for days and chatted about their trip frequently with one another. The boys found themselves packing the night before and frequently laughed at the girls and their excitement. They were all happy to celebrate Lyla's birthday in a new city.

Tillie couldn't stop talking about every detail. "So, we have to take two planes to get to Chicago? I've never been on any plane before and now I get to go on two. Are we celebrating Lyla's birthday right when we get there, or waiting for her actual birthday?"

Adrian tried to cut her off and change the subject. "Hey. I got my English report back yesterday. I got a B minus."

"That's very good, dear." Heather replied. "As for Lyla's birthday, let's just wait and see."

Lyla nodded in agreement. She was much more nervous about the induction than turning twenty-one.

They piled into the taxi that was waiting for them outside their home and drove away.

It was almost 4 hours later that they were on their first flight. They were to fly into Philadelphia and change planes before they arrived in Chicago.

Waves kept coming, washing over him. He gasped for air in between, but they were too fast. He couldn't find where to swim. Where was the surface?

"Hey. Wake up." Adrian shook Liam by the shoulders and pretty hard at that. "Hey, Liam. Wake up. We're here."

Liam inhaled quickly and loudly, catching his breath.

"Whoa! Whoa!" Liam opened his eyes, grabbing Adrian's arms like they were lifesavers.

He just sat there, eyes wide, looking at Adrian.

"Where are we? Did we make it?" He sounded way more panicked than the occasion called for.

"Yeah, of course we made it, Li. We're here, in Chicago. We just landed." Adrian pried Liam's arms off his shirt and tried not to look like Liam just went crazy.

"Oh." Liam sat back, relaxed, blinking. "Sorry, bro. I was having a wild dream! Think I was drowning or something. Weird, huh? Not like that would happen."

He patted Adrian's shoulder and stood up to get his bag in the overhead carrier. Adrian just kept staring at him. He noticed Liam's forehead was wet with sweat.

"Chicago!" Tillie exclaimed. "The farthest I've ever been from home now." She looked at her family with the biggest grin. "Well, isn't that exciting for anyone else?"

She stood there and watched everyone else gather their things.

"Yes, Til, of course we're all excited." Lyla replied. "It's just that we all want to get off this plane, okay?" She, of course, had all her things in hand, ready to deplane. She felt the adrenaline and tried hard to contain it, which was difficult in such a small place. She never noticed before how uncomfortable she was in confined spaces.

Great. Add claustrophobia to the list of my problems, she thought.

They came into Chicago on a most sunny day for December. It made quite the impression with all four children. The city-scape looked modern and sleek. There were so many tall buildings. More than any of them had seen in their lives. Glass. Glass was everywhere, on every building, the main building material in Chicago. It was shining, reflecting and sparkling in the December sun. Against the blue sky, it looked like they were entering a new world. They all felt the irony and were even more excited by it.

"Gee, it certainly is a gorgeous day for Chicago in December." Heather exclaimed.

She couldn't take the grin off of her face. It had been there since they got on the plane in Maine.

"It does feel good to be back." She looked out of the large, mini-van cab window.

"Huh?" several of the children said at once.

"So, you've been here before? How come you never told us about it?" Tillie asked.

"Well children, there are lots and lots of things your father and I have never talked about with you. It's simply a matter of the life we had before you were born. It always feels like a lifetime ago."

Heather looked at the cab driver, then back to her children. They got the hint to keep things quiet for now.

Cord sat in the front seat next to the driver. He looked over at him and said, "Yeah, you know how those years before kids seem like a whole other life." He let out a guffaw.

The driver didn't find it as funny, but he smiled back politely.

It wasn't long before they arrived at their hotel in the heart of the city. The streets were decorated up for the holiday season. Despite the sun being out, the city streets were shaded by the tall buildings. The holiday lights everywhere still shone bright in the shade and looked very festive. Everyone unloaded the cab. The children couldn't help but to look up around them. Everything was so new to them. They looked like small children discovering Christmas morning.

"Gee, I almost forgot about it being Christmastime." Adrian said with his head up. "What are we doing for Christmas? Will we be celebrating it this year?" He asked to his dad quietly so the cab driver didn't hear.

"Oh, sure, son, no worries there. We'll have time to celebrate everything." Cord answered with a smile toward Lyla, then went over to the driver and paid the fare.

They all entered the grand looking hotel. Tillie let out a tiny squeal of joy. They all contagiously smiled back at her. They too were excited. Just as they all got inside, a large gust of wind pushed the door closed and pushed Liam's bag at his legs.

"Whoa! Lyles!" Liam accused as he grabbed his bag more firmly and regained his balance.

"Hey! I had nothing to do with that Li." Lyla responded in an annoyed but hushed voice.

"They don't call it 'the windy city' for nothing." Heather said softly as she looked behind her at all of them.

"Heh, yeah, I forgot." Liam said with an awkward grin.

"You wait over here. I'll check us in." Cord said and walked over to the desk.

18

Cold Hands, Warm Heart

Everyone sat in silence looking around the hotel lobby. It was large, clean and bright with regular and Christmas lights. There were several small evergreens with white lights and each tree had a set of colored ribbons on them. It gave a wonderful rainbow effect on the whole lobby, as well as made it feel warm and inviting. The furniture there was soft, very modern and simple. There was a large staircase in the center with brass and iron railings on each side that were decked out in evergreen garland and little white lights. There were little colored ribbons made into tiny bows on the garland going up the stairs that brought the whole rainbow Christmas theme together. The stairs split to the left and right then disappeared upward. They were carpeted in a red and gold filigree pattern and suited the holiday decorations.

Tillie decided to voice her opinion on it all.

"Well, not that I've been in many hotel lobbies before, but I think this is the most beautiful one I've ever seen!"

"Til, you have never been in a hotel lobby." Liam teased her.

"I know, I know." Tillie pushed Liam's arm.

He laughed.

"Well, this is a very good first impression." Heather said nodding with her approval.

"We have a suite." Cord said as he got back over to them and grabbed a large suitcase from the bunch. "C'mon gang, let's check it out!"

"A suite? Oh they shouldn't have." Heather said modestly.

"Who shouldn't have?" Adrian asked.

"The Council, dear." Heather answered him quietly.

Moments later they opened double doors to their suite, where they would be spending the next several days, possibly more. It was quite a sight for the children to take in. The first thing that caught their eye was the large gift basket with the big green bow on it perched on the entry table.

"Ooh!" Tillie ran over to it immediately, putting her bags down in the middle of the foyer. "Who's it from?"

"The Council." Both boys answered at the same time, then laughed at each other.

They continued past Tillie into the living room area.

"Look at this place!" Lyla exclaimed as she followed the boys further into the living room. "It's really terrific. I think it might be bigger than our house." She looked behind herself, looking sheepish. "Not that I don't love our house. I'm just observing here." She smiled.

"So, where's our rooms then?" Liam asked, holding up the many bags he was carrying.

"Well, not sure. Let's see..." Cord looked around.

The living area was much like their home. A big, open studio space with the living room centered. The wall opposite of them when they walked in was full of windows with sheer curtains closed over them and heavier ones on the sides in a rich golden fabric. There was a dining table on the side of the large room and a kitchen area off of that. From there Cord could see there were even more rooms off to the sides.

"Looks like there are two sets of rooms. So I say pick your room kids and I claim the biggest one for your mother and me!" Cord ran to the largest room, with Liam just behind him going to the one next to it, both of them laughing.

"You mean we each get our *own* room?" Tillie looked like she just won the lottery. "There's no rush to get home, right?" She winked and spun herself in the other direction to the second set of rooms.

"Looks that way." Heather said, almost to no one. She took her bags and followed Cord.

"Well, then I guess I'll take the last room, as always." Adrian said to himself, as there was no one left to hear him.

Time felt as if it went by differently in a hotel suite, much faster than usual. It was like mere moments before Heather went around to everyone to tell them it was time to get ready for dinner.

"I hope you've all had time to get settled. I'd like everyone to dress for dinner. We'll be meeting some members of the Council tonight."

"The Council? Tonight? Already?" Lyla shouted the questions and everyone responded to her concern.

All of the Lundgrens were sensitive to her feelings these days.

"Gosh, Lyles, don't worry. We're only meeting them, right Mom?" Tillie tried her best to sound nonchalant, even though the thought made her a little nervous as well. She had thought about it on the plane. How she wanted to make a good first impression, even though they have probably seen her before. But she didn't want anyone to know that she had thought about it.

"Yes, Tillie. Yes. It's just an informal dinner meeting, to get over the nerves you may have, etcetera. It doesn't weigh on your testing or anything, Lyles. So don't worry." Heather finished and went into her room to dress.

"Easy for her to say." Lyla said to herself. She closed her bedroom door and sat on the bed. It was a queen size bed which felt so luxurious. She'd never slept in a bed so big before. The room was about the same size as hers at home, but not having to share it felt odd. It was lonely, yet comfortable at the same time.

Lyla took a moment to calm her nerves. She felt that if she were going to have to go on a quest by herself soon, she might as well learn to calm herself. She'd done some research on the internet and gotten a few self-help books about meditation. She'd learned some basic things to calm her nerves. She sat in the middle of the bed and found a comfortable position. She took a cleansing breath; breathing in as deep as she could, then thrust it out. She closed her eyes and continued to breathe steadily and more calmly each time.

The next thing Lyla knew, they were being seated at a table in a most lovely and dressy restaurant. There was only time to be escorted to their table, when none other than Mr. Dagsson from the phone was introduced by the waiter, along with a Mrs. Zohra and a Ms. Idasdotter. Mr. Dagsson was a dapper, older gentleman with kind, light-brown eyes. He was a bit on the short side, dressed very well, if a little out of his time period, but it fit the restaurant.

Ms. Idasdotter was a petite, younger woman looking to be around Lyla's age. But they all knew by now that these looks could be deceiving. She dressed sophisticated for her age (or age she appeared to be), in a comfortable skirt suit with a brightly colored scarf. Her hair was dark and her eyes were light, light blue. She paled a bit in comparison to their third companion.

Mrs. Zohra was a tall, thin woman, dressed in a silk gown from top to toe. The colors were bold, vibrant blue, purple, red, green, with some orange and yellow peeking out here and there. There was a design in black outlining the different colors, creating a very stunning pattern across her body, along with gathers of silk at her waist. Her sleeves were long, bell shaped and draped beautifully, ending in gold bangles on her wrists. Her neck was adorned with multiple strands of gold and beads, from short to very long. They clanged when she moved, making a most wonderful sound. She was very tidy and her hair was perfect shiny ebony with blue highlights, which were all too familiar with the Lundgrens. She wore makeup, not too much, but a bold, deep, red lipstick. It enhanced her face perfectly. The children couldn't help but to zone in on her and stare. Mrs. Zohra came right up to Heather.

"Hello, Rialtea darling. We've missed you so."

Her accent was slight and confusing to the children. They'd never heard one quite like it before. She hugged Heather and kissed her on the cheek.

"I've been looking forward to this for months and am so glad I could be one of the Council to meet with you all tonight! I finally get to meet my long lost nieces and nephews!" She opened her arms out to all of them at the table and gestured and smiled largely.

Heather let out a little laugh and said, "Yes, Firouza, these are they! Aren't they just wonderful? Well, of course, I may be biased." Heather let out another uncomfortable laugh.

There was an awkward silence as the new table guests sat down. The children rearranged themselves in their seats.

"So. Lots of new and interesting developments here." Adrian began. "Let's start with Aunt Fir…"

"Firouza, darling." Firouza finished Adrian's sentence for him. She gave another large smile.

"Yes, Firouza. *Aunt* Firouza. We've never heard anything about you, so forgive us if we seem…well…a bit shocked."

"Oh, not at all, dear…Adrian? Yes, of course you are. Not at all, Adrian darling. Of course your mother and father couldn't tell you about me, or any of us for that matter. And there are so many, aren't there, dear Ri?"

She looked over to Heather and touched her on the arm with another large smile. This new aunt of theirs certainly was a happy person. Many eyes met each other across the table, then back to their new aunt.

"So many of you too, huh?" Adrian continued. "So, we have more relatives? Not that I mind and now that we know just the little bit we know, I'm sure you've had your reasons, Mom and Dad. But wasn't there a time, any time at all, where you could have at least told us we had other family? Wait," he said toward his father as Cord started to answer his question. "Now I'm sure you have a good reason and it's all going to make sense when you explain it to us, but I must continue with our newfound information so far, before my head explodes. Now, Aunt Fir..ouza...what did you call my mother, whose name we know is, Heather?" This time he was silent and waited for an answer.

"My, Ri, you certainly were right about your little Adrian here. Quite the inquisitive one." Firouza said and took a sip of water.

The whole table was riveted on the conversation.

"You don't miss a beat, do you? And so adorable. I haven't seen pictures of any of you since you were wee little things, but you all look so grown up now. It's wonderful! Yes, to get back to your question, Adrian," she continued more seriously now, "you know your mother by the name Heather, you say? We have always known her by her rightful name, Rialtea (Ree-*all*-tee-ah). That is her given name. She chose the name Heather when she came to this country to live with your father and to raise you all."

"But why would she have to change her name?" Tillie asked. "Rialtea is so totally beautiful. Mom, you should really change it back." She looked at her mother and could see Mr. Dagsson looking at her out of the corner of her eye. She suddenly, awkwardly, tried to look demure and shy, despite her outburst.

"Well how could she keep it?" Firouza went on, interrupting any hope for Heather to answer. "She had to come and live here, in this...well...shall we say...young country. This not-so-sophisticated place. Not that I dislike it," she answered their insulted looks promptly, "on the contrary, I love it here. But it is a young place and people would be asking all sorts of questions about her exotic name, where it came from and the like and that would lead to all kinds of other questions. They couldn't have that while they were trying to raise you all, now could they?"

She looked at them as if the decision was obvious and took another drink of water, signaling to the waiter. The table was silent as the waiter came over and Firouza placed a wine order for the whole party. Everyone nodded at her in agreement. The Lundgren children had met this woman only minutes ago and already they trusted her with part of their dinner selection.

Firouza hardly stopped talking the whole time they waited for their meal. Everyone else at the table was enthralled by her grand gestures and her loud, but not overpowering voice. The children were shocked to meet a relative after believing they never had any their whole lives. Firouza went on and on as the table placed their dinner orders, about her day to day life, which she said was very mundane and boring. But the rest of the table couldn't take their eyes off of her. The children immediately thought she was one of the most wonderful people they'd ever met. It was a bonus that she was also related to them.

Dinner came and Firouza quieted down enough and let the meal have the spotlight for the time being. Everyone dug right into their meals and conversations started to pop up about how good their choices were. The conversations became a nice, quiet din while everyone ate.

After dinner was cleared and coffees were brought around for those who'd asked for them, Mr. Dagsson cleared his throat.

"Eh hem. Yes well, that was a most delightful meal. I hate to end such a marvel on business, but we haven't yet had a chance to set up our appointment for tomorrow with Lyla and Liam." He looked over graciously to them and continued. "We will be meeting you tomorrow, as I said. There, we will discuss more about your induction. There is a process you see. It will be explained more then and you will also be given study materials for the written exam."

"Yes," Ms. Idasdotter added. "I will be giving you the materials tomorrow. We've set up your appointments for ten and ten-thirty am."

She sipped her black coffee.

"Where are we supposed to meet you?" Lyla asked timidly.

Whenever they talked about the induction, Lyla found herself feeling like a child, so unsure of herself.

"Our building, floor seven. Meeting room one hundred twelve." Ms. Idasdotter replied.

Silent looks went back and forth from children to parents.

"Well sillies," Firouza sang with her perfectly pitched voice. "Your mom and dad will know where that is, I can assure you. Don't you worry your pretty little heads about tomorrow. It's a piece of cake." She took Lyla's hand in hers.

Lyla noticed how cold she was, but didn't react. It did seem strange though, the restaurant was perfectly warm. Her hand was very soft and smooth too. Lyla tried not to shy away, so she sat as still as she could until Firouza gave her hand back with a gentle pat.

"Just formalities. Just formalities, my little dears."

Firouza sipped the rest of her coffee, full of lots of sugar and a smidgen of cream. She delicately and most perfectly wiped her mouth and smiled. Her smile made everything feel perfect. Her stillness made everyone feel calm and happy.

Just a second or so passed, when Mr. Dagsson spoke.

"Yes, yes, children. Your aunt is most correct. Very informative tomorrow will be for you two and it won't take long, so you can have the rest of your day to do what you like." He finished with his friendly smile.

The children could see why these three were all members of the Council. They were most personable and knew how to handle the situation.

"Wonderful." Cord finally spoke up. He was waiting in his gentlemanly way for an opening in the conversation all night. He wasn't used to being the quiet one. "I was hoping to take the kids on a tour of the city. We'll be celebrating Lyla's birthday."

Heather nodded at him in agreement.

"It's their first time out of Mount Desert Island. Well, besides Bar Harbor." He corrected as he saw a few scolding looks come his way. "But you know what I mean, the area in Maine where they grew up. This is the biggest city we've ever taken them to. And I for one am glad that we were all able to come here together. So what do you say kids? Tomorrow, after the formalities, let's see some sights for Lyla's twenty-first."

The table broke out in agreement and the children started to list things they wanted to see simultaneously. Ms. Idasdotter let out a small giggle which got lost in the other noises.

"Fabulous!" The whole table went silent. Once again, Firouza had command of the entire group. "Well, darling Ri, I do hope I can come along? You know, it's been so very long and I would love to catch up with you and Cord." She nodded to both of them. "And it's been years since you've been here. I would love to be your tour guide. Oh, we'll do the museum, Broadway in Chicago...oh there's just so much. Can I, Ri? I would love to celebrate Lyla with you all."

She waited with her perfect smile for Heather to answer.

A few seconds passed, building slight tension. Heather had an excellent poker face. No one could tell what she might say.

She looked at Cord for a split second and then said, "Well of course, my dear sister. Give us the grand tour."

She smiled and Firouza actually got up from the table and went over to her sister and gave her a big hug while she was sitting. It was a bit awkward looking, but Firouza was so thrilled, she couldn't help herself.

"Oh, Ri! This will be so much fun. I am going to get started right away on the list. I'll meet you all tomorrow after the meeting then."

She went over to her seat and picked up her purse. She sat down on the edge of her chair and took a small item out of her bag. It looked like a small, black notebook, but it didn't open. Firouza looked like she was typing something on it. She was quick and placed the object back into her purse. She stood up.

"Yes, I just hate to eat and run, Ri, Cord, children, you're all just so lovely. I wish we could just stay up all night catching up. But we have tomorrow now and I will have to prepare. No, no, don't stand up, please." She indicated to the men about to rise, except Adrian, who was a little slow to it.

"Thank you, Mr. Dagsson, Ms. Idasdotter. It was lovely to see you both again as well. I will see you all tomorrow, then. Bless, darlings!"

With that, she swept out of the restaurant.

"Oh, that sister of mine." Heather began. "She certainly does know how to hold an audience, doesn't she?"

Heather smiled at her children.

"She certainly does." Mr. Dagsson was still looking in the general direction Firouza had gone. He shook his head and placed his napkin on the table. "Well, we hate to follow the eating and running, but we have work tomorrow. It was truly a wonderful time tonight. I am so thrilled that we finally got to meet all you Lundgrens in person." Mr. Dagsson stood up and helped Ms. Idasdotter up from her chair. The two said a gracious, "Goodnight." That was the end of dinner.

Everyone was so tired by the time they got to their room, there wasn't much conversation. They decided to resist the temptation of touring any of the city until the following day. Just, "Goodnight" and hugs and everyone went to their rooms to bed. Thoughts drifted together with dreams that night in more than one head. Tillie couldn't wait to meet cousins. Some Atlanteans her age who she could pry for information. She drifted off picturing Aunt Firouza introducing her to cousin after cousin.

Adrian's head was spinning. He had so many questions and people, new and old, going through his mind. His parents and new family were swirling in his head as he fell fast asleep.

Lyla wondered, *how many more relatives do we have?* She nodded off thinking of meeting all of them, what they might look like and where they might meet, here or Atlantis?

Liam entered dreamland almost immediately after his head hit the pillow. He had almost no time for conscious thought.

The waves really raged tonight! The wind howled at his window and the rocking that had almost put him to sleep had become violent and woke him out of his dreams. He stood up and put on a jacket. The ship was going through the storm! Did anyone else know? Where was the crew? He tried to get up on deck, but the winds were so powerful, he couldn't open the hatch. Then, everything went black.

Liam tried to inhale, but couldn't catch his breath. He grabbed the edges of his bed and inhaled hard. He realized where he was, in his hotel room and his breathing was fast and labored. He was able to get control of it within moments and fell back to sleep.

19

Everything Sparkles

The next morning came quickly. December nineteenth, Lyla's birthday. There was not much talk of birthday plans as the Lundgrens went to breakfast downstairs in the hotel. Everyone sensed the nerves of Lyla and Liam.

Heather didn't want to talk about the meeting, so she kept trying to distract them. She was thankful for Lyla's birthday. "Happy birthday, Lyla dear. I'm so happy for you today. So I wonder what Aunt Fi has in store for us today? Oh, yes, Fi. I'm Ri, she's Fi. We've had those nicknames since we were kids." She answered the looks she saw around the table. "It wasn't our idea, it just sort of stuck." She suddenly felt self-conscious and went back to finishing her breakfast.

Getting together with some of her family, Heather found herself thinking of all sorts of things about her past that she hadn't thought of in years. If the nicknames didn't take their minds off of things present, she had lots of other things to mention for their entertainment and distraction.

"Yes, happy birthday, Lyles." Liam added.

"Happy birthday." Adrian and Tillie tagged.

"Thanks everybody." Lyla said quietly. She wasn't sure she felt like celebrating just yet. Her stomach was too full of butterflies about their meeting.

"I don't understand," Liam changed the subject. "Why have you never mentioned any of your relatives before, Mom?"

"That is a very poignant question, Liam." Heather answered him directly. "Your father and I have been together for many, many years. Before you were all born, our lives were...well...very different."

"Yes, kids," Cord added. "The life your mother and I had before you came along was something we didn't know if we could share with you until you were old enough. Along with the secrets of Atlantis, we have things that we felt were of more adult subject matter and we chose not to talk about them with our children just yet."

"Well, until you were grown, which apparently happened when we were busy doing other things, right, hon?"

"Yes. Apparently, you have all grown and your mother and I are still getting used to it all."

"Yah, well, you never thought to mention we might have special water powers either." Adrian looked annoyed.

Heather and Cord were prepared for this moment. They already knew they'd waited too long to talk to their children about Atlantis. They knew that meeting Heather's family in Chicago would lead to more questions. They still hadn't decided how to go about answering them.

"Unfortunately children, we really don't have time to discuss this fully here and now. We really have to get going." Heather finished apologetically.

They finished up their breakfast, went outside and caught a cab.

"Mom, I can't resist. How do you know where this meeting is?" Tillie said quietly next to Heather.

"Well, hon, your father and I lived here many years ago."

"Oh, something else we didn't know. Great." Adrian said bitterly.

Heather and Cord felt the resentment in their children building.

"Seems like lifetimes ago. We're sorry, kids. We knew this time would come and now that it has, we are still unprepared." Cord said quietly.

"Well, lately I'm starting to feel like we hardly know you two, I swear. So many things and places and people. One of these days you guys are going to have to fess it all up."

"Take it easy, Til." Lyla said most calmly. "There's time to learn everything. We are all still young and Mom and Dad were just waiting for us to all be old enough for their stories. Right?" She looked at them both expecting instant agreement.

"Well now, children." Cord began. The cab pulled over in front of a very tall, glass covered building. "We will make time to talk about all of this soon, promise." Cord ended and got out of the cab.

Everyone exited the cab and stared at the intimidating building. Lyla closed her eyes briefly and let out a slow, controlled breath just like she'd been doing all morning. Heather and Cord led the way inside. They went past the large, glass entrance through a marble filled lobby and got to a small hall of elevators.

"Now when we get to the seventh floor, I will take Lyla and Liam where they need to go. The rest of you will stay in the waiting room and I'll meet you back there." Heather finished as they heard a bell ring and the elevator doors opened.

Everyone got inside. Nerves were nearly palpable. The elevator doors slid closed silently and there was a whoosh as they went upward. There were small but bright lights in the ceiling and Tillie caught a ray of light in her eyes as she glance around the small box of a room. She felt like she'd just had her picture taken and the flash left a mark in her vision. She blinked longer than usual for the next several seconds to try and get rid of it.

Ding! The elevator came to a smooth stop and the doors slid open. Across the pristine hall was a sign that read, *Seventh Floor,* with smaller writing below the title listing the offices contained there. Among the many office names, Adrian thought he saw *Atlantean Studies, Manna Studies* and *Test Rooms 1-4.*

Heather was in charge. "Here we are." She pointed to a doorway and waited, gesturing her family to go in first. "This is the waiting room. Make yourselves comfortable and I'll be right back." She smiled her sweetest smile, the one that always made people feel comfortable.

Her youngest children still looked uneasy which made her uneasy, even though she knew there was no reason to feel that way. She looked at Adrian directly for a moment and he smiled back. It looked genuine, so she let out a bit more of her breath than before and looked at Tillie. She didn't need any time to evaluate her face. Heather touched Tillie on the shoulder.

"I promise. Right back." She held her hand steady.

"Okay. Okay. I know. You know how I am." Tillie breathed out sounding a bit like Lyla. She stood up and quickly hugged her sister. "I love you guys. I know you'll do great." She sat down and smiled at both of them, then huffed out some more air.

"Thanks, Tils," Liam said. "And really, don't worry guys. This is the easy part, right, Mom?"

"Yes, well of course." She continued smiling and really did feel better this time. "Of course you will do great.! You're our children after all, right, Cord?"

"Absolutely, guys. No worries here. You two get going and we'll meet you back here for some fun on the town."

He grabbed the nearest magazine and started looking for an article to read. He looked like he was in the waiting room of a doctor's office.

Heather let out a little start of a laugh and headed out into the hall. Lyla and Liam followed. Liam turned around and waved with a smile to Tillie, who was still watching them. Lyla's eyes were closed and she was breathing deep again, but she looked calm. Tillie watched them until they turned the corner and were out of sight.

Many silent moments passed in the waiting room before Heather returned. The silence made her absence feel long, but it really was only a minute or two.

"Hey, so they're off in room three. Yes they can be in the same room for this meeting." She answered Cord's look, which was the first time he'd looked away from the magazine since he'd picked it up. He put it down on the table.

"Well that's great. Isn't this great, kids? Now I know this is all new to you, but I feel like a kid on Christmas morning. Speaking of Christmas, what do you say about visiting Aunt Firouza for the holiday?" Cord grinned widely and Adrian and Tillie knew by his tone that there really wasn't any choice in the matter. Adrian huffed.

"Yes, she's invited us to stay with them Christmas Eve and meet some more of my family." Heather finished eagerly.

"Ooh, really? That sounds totally grand." Tillie stood up and hugged her mom, then her dad, taking them a bit by surprise. "I just know this is going to be the most interesting Christmas the Lundgrens have ever had."

She sat down and though she was on the edge of her seat, grabbed a magazine and tried to look busy flipping through it. She really wasn't even looking at it. She was way too excited to read.

Adrian on the other hand, was not as enthusiastic. Heather looked from Tillie to him and her face indicated that she was waiting for his opinion. He didn't want to sound disappointed, but he also didn't feel the joy that Tillie felt.

He gave a quick scan in his head of what reaction he should give and ended up with, "Yeah. Yeah sure. It would be nice to meet some cousins." He gave the best smile he could muster and it was convincing. His mother smiled back graciously at him and sat down next to Cord.

The next thirty minutes seemed eternal. It was worse than sitting in any other waiting room. Cord and Heather were relaxed in conversation, leaving Tillie and Adrian to find their own entertainment. Tillie tried talking to Adrian about Christmas with Aunt Firouza.

"Won't it be fun this year? I can't believe this year is so awesomely different than any other we've ever had. Aren't you excited, Ade?"

"Well, sure. I mean, not as excited as you. You look like you're ready to explode. Relax already. Jeez. I really am looking forward to meeting cousins, but as for spending any more time than necessary with Aunt Firouza...well...let's say I could do without that."

He sat back in his seat, at the same time pulled out a small notebook from his back pocket. He started to make notes in it quietly.

"What's that? What are you doing?" Tillie tried to stick her nose into Adrian's space to see what he was writing.

Adrian snatched the notebook up to his chest. "Nothing, okay? I'm just writing some thoughts down from this trip. Questions and such that come to my mind for when we get home and can have some private conversation. You don't need to see it now. It's just my chicken scratch and you probably wouldn't even understand it." He turned himself away from Tillie and kept writing.

"Well fine. I can find something to do myself." She quipped, looked around and sat in her seat finally.

She looked and looked around the room. It was quite boring, an ordinary waiting area. Her eyes glanced down at the magazine she had grabbed just before she was talking to Adrian. The title took her by surprise, *Atlantean Life*. She looked over at the table where the other magazines were. There were quite a lot of them there. Tillie went over to the table and noticed the actual titles on the magazines. *The Deep Blue Sea, Atlantean Life, Underwater Cities Today*, were only some of the strange titles she could see floating about the table. She wasn't sure which one to grab first and instead grabbed a handful, not even looking at all of them individually. She straightened them into a neat stack into her lap as she sat back in her chair.

She decided not to even look at their titles. The first one was the *Atlantean Life* magazine. It was set up much like the *Life Magazine* she'd seen in stores and even read many times over the years. She laughed a little to herself and flipped through the pages. She wanted to go through them quickly so she could see them all before her siblings got back. If there was time she'd go back and actually read some of the articles that caught her eye. The appearance on the whole was normal enough. Where were the Atlantean parts? Pictures, there must be pictures, a spread...something.

About the middle of the magazine there was a double paged picture. It looked like a painting, but very detailed. It looked like a distant shot of a city. Upon looking closer, Tillie saw details that made her feel giddy with excitement. This was no ordinary city. This was Atlantis! Or was it? Tillie read the small print on the lower left corner of the right page. Oh, it was Atlantis, or at least a part of it. It was a neighborhood in Atlantis. Tillie stopped reading and looked at the picture very closely, trying to absorb every detail.

The colors in the picture were so bright and cheery. From a distance it looked like an Impressionist painting with dots of blues, greens, pinks, purples. There were many colors and unusual shapes put together. There were squiggly marks and square marks, as well as round bits that just looked like big dots. She was trying to make out what they all were when Heather startled her.

"What did you find here Tillie?" She sat down next to Tillie and looked on the pages. "Oh, Yes. That's a wonderful part of Atlantis. One of my favorite places. *Atmosphera Tritona*, or *Triton's Harbor*, such a beautiful place. Oh, I can hardly wait until the induction!"

Heather clapped softly and looked so childlike, it made both Tillie and Adrian laugh with her. Heather continued on about the picture.

"See here?" She pointed out one of the larger dots. "This is *Gyro tou Tritaia*, or *Triteia's Round*. It's such a beautiful place. It's like a town square, but instead it's round, hence the name. All of these dots are rounds. It's just how Atlantis is, so organic and flowing. Everything here is sparkling and the corals are just breathtaking."

"Don't forget the main reason you like it dear." Cord chimed in and moved closer. He put his arm around Heather.

"Well of course. I was getting to that. It wasn't that long ago that I've forgotten." Heather blushed. Tillie and Adrian gave each other a funny look and then straight to their parents.

"Oh, that's good. For a second there, I thought I'd have to tell them." Cord chuckled.

"Tell us already." Adrian sighed.

"Yes, well, I was going to say...this is also the place where your father and I got married."

Tillie let out a squealing giggle. "Oh, my gosh! Really? You got married in Atlantis? Holy cow! No wonder we've never seen pictures, except up close. Oh, my gosh! Oh, my gosh!" Tillie couldn't contain herself and the other magazines that were on her lap slid onto the floor. "That has to be the coolest thing I've ever heard. Oops!"

She finally noticed the magazines as Adrian made his way to them to pick them up. He was about to put them on the table when Tillie grabbed his arm.

"Don't you dare! Can I take these with us? Can I bring them home? I can't leave all this prime info behind."

"Sorry, hon, the rules are nothing leaves this building but us. Always been that way I'm afraid." Cord reached out and took the magazines from Adrian and put them on the table. "But you can read as much as you can while you're here. You'll have plenty of time in the next few years to learn so much you'll be sick of it before it's over."

"I can't imagine ever being sick of Atlantis." Tillie went right back into a conversation with Heather about the picture map of Atlantis.

Adrian sat in his chair and took out his notes. He wrote furiously.

Cord took another magazine and as he sat down you could hear Tillie say to Heather, "You just have to tell me all about the wedding. I can't believe my parents got married in Atlantis." She giggled as Heather pointed out more things on the picture map and got talking animatedly.

Just as Adrian thought that he couldn't take much more of their wedding talk, Lyla and Liam returned. Lyla came into the room first, followed by Liam smiling broadly.

"Well, that was quick." Heather stood up and went over to Lyla and hugged her. "See, sweetie, I told you it wouldn't be a big deal."

Lyla smiled and for the first time since they'd arrived in Chicago, looked like she had genuinely enjoyed herself.

"You were right, that's for sure." Liam butted into their close conversation. "Piece of cake. I mean really all we had to do was listen, answer a few easy questions about ourselves and then done. Right, Lyles?"

"Yes, pretty much that was it. Oh, I am so relieved. Now we can get down to some studying for the test."

She took out some sort of small, black box that looked like a television remote control. Liam also had one.

"See? They gave us these and showed us how to use them. They are study remotes that will bring up information about Atlantis on any television we wish. Isn't that cool? We'll be studying on TVs."

"Can you study together?" Adrian asked as he stuffed his notebook into his back pocket. He wanted to get a closer look at those devices.

"Yeah sure, why not?" Liam said as he showed Adrian his remote.

"Yes, we can only study together for this first test. After that we were told that we'd have to go through the last stages individually." Lyla let Tillie hold her remote.

"Well how do these work then?" Tillie tried pointing it around, but to no avail, as there was no television in the room. "Dang it, there's no TV in here."

"Well, they're fascinating really. You see, because we are of Atlantean descent, only we can work them. And because Li and I are of age, these have been programmed for just us to use. So sorry sis, but you won't be able to work it, even if there was a TV in here."

"Oh, man." Tillie shoved the remote back to Lyla. "I am missing out on all this fun stuff."

"Well, there's a lot of work too, Tills. It's not all fun-and-games and remotes. This is for studying and we should get to it if we want to get through all the information on here. I want to get started as soon as possible." Lyla placed the remote into her purse.

"But Dad just said nothing leaves the building besides us." Tillie looked a little put out.

"Well yes, Till, I did say that," Cord started, "But these are regulated by The Council and they are safe for Lyla and Liam to take out of the building. No one else will know how to use them and to manna they will just look like television remote controls. Sorry, sweetie. I should have been more specific. We can't take anything unauthorized out of the building." Cord gave Tillie a sympathetic look.

"Humph." Tillie sounded, but didn't say anything back.

"All right. So, let's get out of here and see some sights." Liam said. He let Adrian hold the remote a little longer, as he was still interested in it even though he couldn't use it himself. Boys are always interested in new toys.

"Well, Aunt Fir..." Heather started.

"DARLINGS!" they all heard from the doorway.

They turned most startled. Tillie let out a giggle. Firouza came into the room flamboyantly, arms waving with bracelets clanking together. Today, Aunt Firouza was dressed very differently from last night's dinner. She was conservative last night by comparison. She had on lots of blues and greens today with hints of reds and yellows. Tillie wasn't sure if she was wearing a dress, or a skirt with a separate top. There were so many colorful layers and accessories. Yet it wasn't overdone. It was fabulous.

Tillie couldn't help herself and went over to Firouza and hugged her. She smelled delightful. Like nothing specific that Tillie could pinpoint, but so fresh and almost a hint of some sort of flower.

"Oh, my dear." Firouza reciprocated the hug most enthusiastically. She took Tillie's face into both her hands. "Oh, Tillie darling. If you aren't just the sweetest thing ever." She shot her brilliant smile and made her way to Heather. "Ri, my dearest." She hugged her as well. Then she turned around to the doorway and said, "Well, come in sweeties. Come and meet your cousins."

All eyes turned to the hallway just outside the door. Two young teenagers walked in with smiles.

"Hi, I'm Chloe. I'm so excited to meet you all, finally." She held one hand up and waved.

She was like a mini Aunt Fi upon first glance. There were some obvious differences. Her eyes were a golden amber, where her mother's were a dark blue/gray. Chloe wore no makeup. But her skin was like glowing porcelain. It shone translucently under the lights. Her hair was dark like her mother's, but it was wavy and more out of control. It came down around her shoulders in long, wild waves, looking very exotic. Tillie thought Firouza must have looked exactly like her when she was a teen. Tillie liked the friendly greeting from Chloe and warmed up to her immediately.

"Hey," the boy said.

He had short spiky blond hair looking very much like he'd just come off the beach. His clothes were baggy and his skin tan compared to his sister's. His eyes were a bright, light green, looking like the sea. He had a small, rehearsed smile on his face that the boys knew well. Everyone returned the smile.

"Hey there, cuz." Liam said and held his hand out. "I'm Liam."

He waited a moment for the boy to shake hands. It took a few seconds, but there was finally a firm shake in return.

Adrian patted the boy on the shoulder. "And I'm Adrian, your cuter cousin." He laughed and Liam punched him in the arm and they had a mini fight and laugh.

"Oh, my." Heather went up to the boy. "This must be..."

"Kallias. Yah, that's me. Sorry," the boy said blushing.

"Oh, Fi. They are simply beautiful."

Heather took both children into her arms for a group hug and just held them there for a long moment. When she let go she wiped tears from her eyes.

"Look at me. Oh, I am such a sap." She laughed at herself which helped put everyone else at ease.

"Oh, please, Ri." Firouza responded. "I went home last night simply bawling at how wonderful your family is." She let out a wonderfully high laugh that sounded like a song. A few laughed along with her.

"Kallias here just had a birthday last week, didn't you, darling? So today, if it's alright with you, Lyla, we'll celebrate the both of you? Happy birthday, sweetheart." She hugged Lyla gently.

"Of course." Lyla responded. "It would be fun to share a birthday. Usually mine gets swallowed up by Christmas."

"Well, we won't have any of that. Today shall be for you and Kallias. Shall we off then? I have so much planned for us. I hope we can fit it all in today. If not, we perhaps can take some time after the test. I don't want to take all your study time up, you two." she finished pointing cutely at Lyla and Liam, one with each hand. "What with Christmas just around the corner...you are spending Christmas with us, aren't you?"

This time she actually paused and waited for an answer.

"Oh, yes. Yes of course, Fi." Heather replied quickly. She was getting excited along with Firouza. Her sister had that effect on her.

20

Fashion Statement

"Well marvelous!" She declared as she led them out of the waiting room to the elevators. "Let's get going then."

Outside the Council building, the Lundgrens were surprised to see a stretch limousine waiting for them. Firouza led the way and the driver opened the door for her. The Lundgrens stood back a few steps, in shock.

"Well, come on then." Firouza said as she turned around before getting into the car. "We haven't got time to lollygag." She and her children disappeared into the car.

"Holy cow, my first limo ride!" Tillie exclaimed.

"Yeah and probably your only one." Adrian responded, trying to take a little air out of Tillie's sails.

"Oh, hush up." She said and rushed over to the car and climbed in as fast as she could. She found a seat next to Chloe, across from Firouza.

The rest of the party filed in and found seats promptly. Lyla checked out every detail, enjoying it immensely. She felt so relaxed for the first time on this trip. She couldn't help smiling as she noticed a large sun-roof over the seats farthest in the back. She saw Adrian also looking about the car, but more cautiously.

"Well, Fi, you've outdone yourself this time. My kids are going to be spoiled by the time we get them back to Sigrun." Cord said with a hearty laugh and his family joined him.

"Yah, Dad, can we get one of these for prom this year?" Tillie almost squealed. "I was going to go in on one with Susan and a bunch of others so it won't be too expensive. Please?" Her face was all smiles, which she knew was hard for Cord to resist.

"See that? Already." Cord laughed again and answered Tillie, "We'll have time to look into it later, Tils. Let's not get ahead of ourselves."

"Yes, let's just enjoy this day." Heather added. Her contentment was contagious as she nestled herself back into the soft leather seat. "Where are we off to first, Fi?"

"Well you know me, dear Ri. We can't have a tour of this fabulous city without some glamour, right? I thought the best way to see Chicago all at once would be from the Observatory, of course. We will head there through some wonderful city-scape scenery, all done up for the holidays...oh it's just beautiful! Wait until you see all the lights Tillie. You'll just love them."

There was another little squeal from Tillie. She was so comfortable with her newly met family members. She felt like this was all a dream that she didn't want to wake from. Almost everyone else was busy looking out the windows at building after building full of glass and decorated with lights, so many lights. Tillie turned her attention outside as well. She didn't want to miss a thing.

"We'll have lunch up there of course and afterward I have something quite fun for us." Firouza added with a mysterious smile.

"Well, I hope you haven't gone through any more trouble than this limo." Heather cautioned her sister. "This is beyond extravagant as it is."

"Oh, Ri. You have been gone too long, my dear." Firouza finished with a laugh, almost as hearty as Cord's. "If I'm going to take my long lost family on a tour of my city, it's going to be done right. Now, there won't be any arguing." She gestured toward Cord and Heather. "This is my city now and you are all my guests, my family. I wouldn't treat you any less. I hope this is the best birthday ever for you, Lyla."

"Yes, but, Fi," Heather started, "It's all so much. We just aren't used to this special treatment."

"Oh, you silly, sweet thing, you. Has country life really turned you that soft already? I do hope you can still appreciate the finer things, my dear." Firouza took a compact out from her purse and looked into it, checking her already perfect makeup.

"Oh, Fi." Heather started to laugh, "I guess you're right." She laughed loudly. "I hadn't really thought about how living up in Maine would be so different. But it's different in a most wonderful way, Fi. It's been so fresh and new and back to Earth, you know? Everything there is real and true. And our children are that way as well. I wouldn't have chosen another path for them." She looked over toward Kallias and Chloe. She blushed a little, "Not that I hold it against anyone else who did it differently."

"Oh, pshaw." Firouza replied. "I don't hold anything against your country life, Ri. I know you far better than to think that you would hold anything against how Metrón and I are raising our brood, darling. Don't be so self-conscious. It's me, Fi."

She gleamed with the friendliest smile Tillie had seen yet. Tillie decided right there she loved her new family, even though she hadn't even met all of them yet.

"So, we have an Uncle Met...Met..." Tillie began.

"Metrón, darling. Metrón. Yes, he is your uncle, isn't he? I just love all of this family getting to know one another. Finally." Firouza went on, "And there are so many more. Kallias and Chloe have five other siblings. Don't you, dears?" Both Kallias and Chloe barely nodded.

Chloe spoke up, "Yes, there are our oldest sisters: Dahia and Adonia. They are twenty-six and twenty-four, in that order. Then we have two brothers: Demetrius, twenty-one and Baalhanno, who is twenty."

"My gosh, you're a busy family. That is a lot of new names to remember." Adrian finally joined the conversation.

"Oh and I'm not even finished, Adrian." Chloe went on, "Then there is my barely older sister Lucrezia, she's eighteen. She wanted to come today, but she is working. But you'll meet everyone at Christmas. I'm so excited that you'll be joining us." Her smile reflected her mother's almost exactly.

"No offense, but there is no way I'm going to remember all of those names." Adrian said like there was going to be a test on them later.

"Why don't you write them down?" Tillie suggested and looked toward Adrian's seat.

"Shut up, Tillie," Adrian barked. He looked at her like he was ready for a fight. Not very like Adrian.

"Now, now, what's the big deal?" Cord interjected.

"Well, I don't want to make a big deal about it." Adrian answered.

"Exactly, so what is the big deal then?" Cord repeated himself.

"I have a notebook that I've been writing stuff down in since we got to Chicago. I told Tillie about it earlier and now she's blabbing it to everyone. I don't really want to advertise it. And now I have done just that. Thanks a lot." Adrian sat back and stared out of his window, sulking.

"Well, there's nothing wrong with that, son." Cord said cheerfully. "That's a sign of smart thinking right there. And we all know it's none of our business, right kids?"

"Oh yeah, sure, Dad," Liam answered right away.

"Of course," Lyla said at the same time.

"Well yeah, I know. I was just trying to help." Tillie said feeling put upon.

"Now, now. Let's forget about this nonsense, children. If you look out of the right side right now, you can see Lake Michigan." Everyone but Adrian turned to look.

Adrian sat stubbornly looking out of his window on the left and could see nothing but buildings. He liked it that way. He didn't feel mad exactly, as much as embarrassed. *Like I would really need to write everyone's names down, when everyone else could figure it out on their own.* He thought about not bringing his notebook with him next time they went out. After a minute or two, he decided to look at the lake. After all, it was Lake Michigan; one of the Great Lakes, the biggest fresh water lakes in the country. He'd never seen them before and was curious how big they looked compared to the ocean.

The coloring was definitely the first difference the Lundgrens noticed about the lake. Today was overcast and being December, it looked like it would be getting dark soon. The lake was mimicking the sky and looked greenish gray. The ocean would reflect the sky as well, but always had its true blue somewhere in it. Adrian wondered if it was due to the salt in the water. Perhaps it reflected things differently.

The lake was vast. It felt ocean-like. You could not see the other side of it and there were waves coming to shore. But even from a distance you could see that they weren't as big as the ocean waves they had grown up with.

"This is the Harbor, darlings. We will see more of that after lunch." Firouza said in a most tour-guide fashion. "Isn't the lake wonderful? Even this time of year I still find it so serene and beautiful."

"It's very big." Lyla calculated while she observed. "I wasn't expecting it to be that big."

"Yeah, it's way bigger than Canandaigua Lake I went to with Susan last summer." Tillie couldn't take her eyes off of it. The feelings she had on her vacation with Susan emerged, only this time, she knew things would stay safe. This made it more enjoyable.

"It's great, that's for sure." Liam said as he let out a snicker.

Adrian caught on, "Yeah, really greeeaaat." Both boys laughed at their brilliance.

"Remember that time on the lake, Ri, with Bal and Malia? When we took that old fishing boat out?" The children looked at her puzzled. She explained, "Oh, Baldur and Amalia are your uncle and another aunt, children. You mother has six siblings you know. Has she never mentioned that to you? Well, never mind." She went on, "There are seven of us total. But the time on the old fishing boat with your mother, me, Bal and Malia, oh! We had quite the time, didn't we, Ri?"

"Umm, yes, I remember, Fi. You don't have to tell them the story, do you?" Heather asked reluctantly, knowing full well the answer.

"Of course I do, darling. It's one of our faves. You see children, we were all, what, in our teens would you say, Ri?" Heather nodded in response. "Yes and the four of us decided it would be fun to take this old fishing boat out, even though it looked like a storm was coming. The boat belonged to a friend of Bal's father and the boys used to use it when it was in dock for some recreational fishing. So we took the boat out right into the oncoming storm. We had no fear you see because we all had confidence when it came to the water. Well, you four know what I'm talking about, don't you? We wouldn't be here if you didn't." She let out a high little laugh. "So out we were, about 2 miles off shore, but far away enough not to see the shore anymore with the rain. Yes, the rain was awful! Thick as can be...it was like someone was just pouring buckets over us! Bal had the wheel and we decided it would be fun to anchor and go below for a swim. We loved swimming below a rain storm...oh, it is such fun. I haven't done it in years and years of course, have you, Ri?"

"Gosh, no. I almost forgot about doing it at all." Heather blushed slightly.

"So, there we all were, below in the water. It's quite peaceful you know, once you get under the wave currents. So, we were all just swimming around like we did and Bal decided it would be funny to take off early. He just took the boat! We girls saw it leaving and your mother was the first to get to the surface. Quite the swimmer your mother is, children." Heather smiled and kept listening.

"So, Malia and I followed of course, your mother was determined to get to that boat."

"Mom, you can swim fast, like Li?" Tillie interrupted, not being able to contain herself.

"Well yes, dear, my family and I come from a long line of Atlantean DNA and we are very adept in the water," Heather replied.

"Oh yes, dears!" Firouza exclaimed. "We are all very good when it comes to just about anything having to do with water. Anyway," she got the story back on track, "Your mother reaches Bal and boy was he surprised! She grabbed onto the back of the boat and was trying to slow it down with her legs kicking away. Can you imagine? What a sight. By the time Malia and I caught up to the boat, Bal had turned the engine off, because apparently your mother had done what she'd set out to do. The engine started smoking, so Bal cut it off and went to look at what the problem was. The look on his face when he got to the back of the boat was priceless! There was Ri, gripping the lower stern of the boat with everything she had and holding steady. Malia and I got there just in time to climb in, laughing at the look on Bal's face. When we tried to give your mother a hand,"

"Oh no, here it comes," Heather said softly to herself, but not out of earshot of the children.

"She outright refused. She wouldn't budge from hanging on the back of that boat. We couldn't figure out why. We thought it was because she was trying to prove her point to Bal. Boys can be so thick headed sometimes, no offense of course, boys. But that wasn't it at all, was it, Ri?" Firouza laughed and got into quite a moment with herself.

Heather decided to finish up the story. "No, that wasn't it at all. I can't believe you still find this so funny. Anyway, the reason I couldn't just hop up into the boat was because I'd lost something during the struggle, you see..."

"Oh, my!" Lyla interjected, "You didn't."

"Yes, I'm afraid I did." Heather shook her head back and forth, but smiled at the memory just the same.

"Did what? What'd you lose?" Adrian asked.

"Oh, don't you see children?" Firouza collected herself enough to talk. "She lost her suit!" But then she laughed heartily all over again.

"It was just the bottom of my suit. I was wearing a bikini." Heather corrected and blushed at the same time.

Everyone in the car shared in Firouza's laughter. They knew how modest their mother was and to picture this scene was hilarious to them.

After the laughter died down, Tillie asked, "So what did you do, Mom?"

"Well, I did the only sensible thing. I made a bottom out of what was around."

"And tell them what was around, Ri." Firouza giggled quietly yet again.

"It was a fishing boat, right? So all I could reach was some old torn netting." Heather said as a matter of fact.

"Yes, it was quite the fashion statement." Firouza calmed down again and was flush with laughter. This made her even more radiant. "She was able to cover the necessities and then it just hung down one leg like she'd been snagged in a net like one of the fishes. Even with all that, she was adorable. When we got to shore, we docked the boat. Luckily the engine proved to be fine and no one ever knew, because no one was out during the storm. Oh, but we laughed about it for weeks after that. Maybe months." Firouza went silent with her memories.

"I guess even years." Adrian said in his smart-aleck way.

"Yes, I guess even years," Firouza said quietly.

After that it was fairly quiet as the car drove along the lakeside.

"You'll be able to see the whole city up where we're going, children." Firouza said after many moments.

"And there's our place." Chloe announced and pointed out of the window. "See? That big brown building." They drove on past. "We live on the top floor, facing the lake." Chloe smiled, looking back on her home.

Firouza smiled and took out a small black device from her purse. It looked like the remotes that Lyla and Liam were given, or even a cell phone. She did not use it like a remote or a phone. Instead, she slid it open and typed on it. At first, no one noticed. After a minute however, all the Lundgren children watched her. Adrian even took out his notebook and started writing. It looked very archaic compared to what Firouza was doing.

Firouza finished her typing and went to put the device back into her purse. She saw everyone looking at her. "Oh, this? Children, this is the future. It's a phone. Well, it's a phone and a computer...of sorts."

"What? A phone? That little thing? And a computer? Pshhh..." Adrian noised.

"Oh, I assure you, it is, dear Adrian," Firouza explained. "You see, I can open it, like this. Then type messages to other people instead of talking to them. It saves time when I just have a quick thing to tell someone and it's not terribly rude in front of others. I hate interrupting being with one group of people just to talk to someone else. Just because we have cell phones now, does not mean we can just up and forget our manners." She clicked the phone closed and placed it back in her purse. "See? Work is done and no interruptions. Now, if you look out the windows, just ahead, you'll see where we're going everyone; The John Hancock building."

Everyone peered out and saw one of the tallest buildings they had seen yet. It looked like a very tall, thin, Mayan temple. It was a dark, solid structure with large glass windows and a crisscross pattern going all the way up the sides. It certainly stood out from the surroundings.

"Ooh, I can't wait to get up there." Tillie clapped as they pulled up to the side of the street and parked right in front of the building.

The views from above were magnificent. The children were awe struck. They could look out and see the whole stretch of the city on one side, then the whole end of the lake on the other side. The children went crazy taking pictures of the views and themselves in front of the views.

"I can't wait to show these to Aaron." Tillie told Lyla. "We made plans to get together once I get back home."

"How do you know when that will be?" Lyla asked.

"Well, I don't. I told him that I would let him know when we were on our way home. Then we'd figure out when we could get together from there." Tillie happily took more pictures of her view.

They were having the best time ever. Cord and Heather sat back, enjoying the whole scene, feeling very happy. Christmastime would indeed be something special this year.

Once lunch was finished, Firouza surprised them all with a yacht cruise through the city. It was sunset as they boarded the yacht and the Christmas lights were shining brightly. Firouza told them they were to have a dinner cruise through town and there they would see the best Christmas lights the city had to offer. Everyone was excited, even Adrian, who felt better on a full stomach and got caught up in the moment.

"Happy birthday, dear Lyla. I hope you have enjoyed yourself today." Firouza finished with her most beautiful smile.

"Yes," Lyla said in return. "This has been a most wonderful day. Thank you so much."

The night couldn't have been better. The yacht tour was amazing, full of lights, sights and city sounds. The four Lundgren children were delighted.

After dinner, Firouza brought out a tray with glasses and a couple of green bottles. "A birthday toast! Champagne and sparkling juice! She can have just a little now, can't she?" Firouza looked at Cord and Heather.

"Well yes, if she wants some." Heather replied.

Everyone looked at Lyla. She smiled. Firouza popped the cork and started pouring.

"A toast then, to my wonderful niece, about to be inducted to Atlantis! Happy birthday, darling!" She raised her glass to Lyla, as did everyone else.

"And happy birthday to Kallias as well. We hope you have a wonderful year." Heather added, glass raised. Another set of clinking glasses was heard all around.

"Oh, family is such fun!" Firouza stated and finished her glass of bubbly golden liquid.

After the birthday celebrations, everyone broke into smaller groups. Tillie spent most of the time after dinner talking with Chloe. They found that even though they were raised in very different places, they had a lot in common, including their talents in the water.

"So, you can stay under forever too?" Tillie asked for more detail.

"Well yes, as far as I know," Chloe replied. "I've never stayed in so long that I thought I had to get out, so I guess that means I could stay under forever." The girls spent the rest of the tour together chatting about teenage life.

Kallias, on the other hand, wasn't as friendly as his sister. Being the youngest, he mostly liked to tag along and observe. When Chloe went off with Tillie to talk, he found himself alone and not sure who to talk to. So, he sat quietly and listened to his mother talk to his newly met aunt and uncle. They were reminiscing and the stories were enjoyable.

Adrian and Liam went to the bow of the boat. It was very cold outside and they were the only two who decided to brave it for a better view. They stayed out as long as they could, but had to give in because of the wind being so fiercely cold. When they came back inside, they plunked down near Kallias to strike up some conversation with their new cousin.

Lyla enjoyed the views outside, but found something that fascinated her more inside: a television. She took out her remote. She'd been thinking about it all day and felt like the tour was a waste of her time. She looked back at her parents and aunt talking. They didn't seem to notice her. She tried the remote. It worked. The screen flashed on and was blue.

Then waves and water washed over the blue with the title, *Atlantis* on the screen. There was a little tune too that sounded like shells being blown on a beach. When she heard the sound, Lyla felt very warm. She looked for a volume on her remote, but there was none.

"Studying already, dear?" Heather came up behind Lyla, startling her slightly. "Oh, I'm sorry hon, but I would recognize that music anywhere."

"Music?" Lyla asked.

"Yes. It's the music of Atlantis. How did it make you feel when you heard it?"

"Well, it's weird, but…I felt kind of warm, like the sun just came out," Lyla answered.

"Yes, that's how I feel when I hear it too," Heather replied, "It affects everyone differently, so I was curious. Well, better to it then. I know how you've been eager to get started with your studying. Happy birthday, sweetheart." She hugged Lyla's shoulders from behind and went back and sat down next to Cord who was laughing at something Firouza said.

Lyla turned back to the tv. She found a comfortable chair, pulled it a bit closer and sat down. She watched the screen. She was told to only press the *next* button on the remote after each chapter. She was excited with curiosity. The screen lit up with images. Things Lyla never saw before flashed by so quickly, she hardly had time to see them at all. She tried pressing buttons on the remote to slow it down, or pause it, but nothing worked. She stared at the screen and tried to take on the challenge of seeing all of the images. The music played in the background and the warm feeling turned to excitement, like an adrenalin rush.

Lyla was riveted. The images were going by so fast now, but she didn't care. She was taking them all in, dozens of them, flying by. No words, just the music and images.

Then, just as suddenly as they started, they stopped. "End of Chapter 1," came up on the blue, wavy screen. Lyla blinked a few times. She looked down at the remote to press the *next* button. Suddenly her head snapped up and she took a loud breath inward. Her eyes grew bigger and her breathing stopped momentarily.

"Whoa!" she said finally. "What was that?"

"What was what?" Liam noticed the screen was on and came over to see what it was. He looked at Lyla. "Hey. You okay, sis?" He pulled up a chair next to her and grabbed her hand.

"Oh, yeah. I'm really okay." Lyla said and caught her breath. "If that's just chapter one, I can't wait to see the rest. This is amazing, Li. I don't know what just happened, but I now know a bunch of places in Atlantis. It's not just one city. It's everywhere." Lyla looked into the distance. Her mind was clearly somewhere else.

"Wow, guess I should have checked it out with you. I'll catch up tomorrow though. I'm an early riser, remember? You're okay then?" Lyla nodded in a trance like way. "Good, don't tell me anymore, I want to find out for myself, kay? Happy birthday, sis." Liam stood up and walked back to the table where everyone else gathered.

Lyla found the *stop* button and decided that was probably enough for tonight. At this pace though, she could see finishing up the studies before Christmas day. This put her at ease and she went and enjoyed the rest of the night with everyone.

The cruise ended what felt like all too soon. The four Lundgren children felt they could have stayed up and talked all night with their new family.

21

City Meets Country

For the next few day the Lundgrens were busy getting ready for Christmas with the Zohros (Firouza, Metrón and their seven children). They busily shopped for gifts for Heather's family. It was so long since they spent Christmas with any of them, they wanted to make their gifts special. They had brought some things from home and wanted to combine them with things from Chicago to make nice, meaningful gifts for their nieces and nephews.

Lyla and Liam stayed busy with their studies. Both found it very easy and wonderful at the same time. They would talk about what they'd just learned and found it an amazing way to absorb information.

"If only we had gone through school like this." Liam said one afternoon.

"I know. Imagine the time we would've saved." Lyla replied with a smile. She was truly enjoying herself. The two of them were so confident that they would pass the written exam, they planned on taking a few days off after Christmas to enjoy themselves.

Christmas Eve morning came, quick as a flash. The Lundgrens packed their overnight bags. They were going to stay with the Zohros for Christmas so they could share all of Christmas day together. Overall everyone was happy about the mini excursion for Christmas.

Christmas for the Lundgrens was usually very small and simple. They went to Church every year. Now that they were older, they went to midnight mass. They all loved the singing and candlelight and special feel to the Christmas vigil. This would be the first time they'd miss it.

"I can't believe we're missing mass this year. It feels so weird." Lyla said to Liam in the living room. They were waiting for everyone else to gather.

"Yeah, I felt the same thing Lyles." Liam replied, "I wonder if we could get any time to fit Church in. Maybe we can go tomorrow morning somewhere. There's got to be a lot of churches in a city this big. There must be one near their place." Liam placed some last items in his duffle bag and zipped it closed.

"You kids all set?" Cord said as he walked into the room with a bag in each hand. He sat down next to Lyla on the sofa.

"Yes. Well, we were just wondering..." Lyla sputtered.

"Dad, are any of mom's family Catholic? We were just talking about how strange it feels that we're not going to Church this year. So we were wondering if we could go tomorrow, somewhere?" He looked at Lyla.

"Well son, I thought we told you! We're going in the morning this year, with the Zohros! Gee, yeah, I guess there's a lot about your mom's family that you don't know. I forget the amount really." Cord looked down into his lap, his face full of reminiscence.

Just then Tillie bounced in the room. "All set. I am so excited! Christmas with relatives." She came to the middle of the room and waited to hear what they had to say about it. There was silence. "Well? Aren't you all excited? Where's the happy?" She placed herself on the arm of the sofa next to Cord.

"I was just telling these two," Cord started, "That we'll be going to Church tomorrow morning. They were under the impression that just because we're not home, there would be no Church."

"Oh." Tillie smiled. "Is that all? I could see how you would think that," she smirked.

"What's that mean?" Liam looked his standard confused.

"Well, when I was talking to Chloe the other night, she was telling me what they do for Christmas. One of the things was go to Church, of course." Tillie loved being on the knowing side before her siblings.

"Yes, so as I said, we'll be going in the morning." Cord tried to thwart the oncoming sibling battle. "You have another aunt we'll be meeting there as well. Aunt Haseena. She's a deacon in the Church we'll be going to and you'll get to see her in mass, then meet her afterward."

"Oh, great." Adrian announced from the bedroom hallway. "Another relative to remember. Thank heavens we're not going to be quizzed on these later at home, are we?" He came into the hall with a similar looking duffle bag to Liam's.

Cord laughed jovially. "Not at all, Ade. It took me years to remember all Mom's family."

Heather came into the room and everyone stood up. "What's this about my family?" She smiled. "Oh, I know. They're huge." She laughed and for the first time all her children noticed how much she sounded like her sister. Of course they'd never had a chance to notice something like that before, this was something new. They looked at each other and smiled briefly.

In less than half-an-hour later, the Lundgrens arrived at the tall, brown building they were to spend Christmas in for the first time. They each had a look of excitement, anticipation, anxiety, relief, wonder and familiarity at once as they got their things out of the car and looked up at the new space they would live in for the next couple of days.

Tillie was so overwhelmed with excitement, she just kept squealing with each new sight, sound and thing. "Ooh! This is just too rich! I can't wait to tell everyone back home about this Christmas." Another squeal as the elevator doors closed.

The doors opened and Firouza and Metrón were waiting to greet them. "Hello darlings! Merry Christmas, my sweeties!" Firouza grabbed Tillie's face and hugged her quickly, then went onto everyone else. Not even Adrian escaped her holiday greeting.

Metrón stayed quiet, greeted everyone with a smile and a, "Hello," and helped grab some of the luggage. Firouza saved introductions for when they were inside their apartment. She swooped Tillie up and entered their domicile first.

"Here we are, everyone!" Firouza announced. "Please, come in, come in. Make yourselves completely comfortable. We are so thrilled to have Ri and her family here for Christmas this year." She looked to her husband, then she remembered introductions. "Oh yes and intros, intros. This is my adoring husband, Metrón, children. That makes him your uncle. I can't imagine what you all must be going through meeting all of us at once like this. My head would be spinning just trying to remember all the names, not to mention how they were related to me." Her laugh was short, but made some of them smile anyway. "But how I adore family! I hope you do too."

Metrón went on to shake hands with all of the children, getting their names as he went. Finally, he shook hands with a one armed hug for Cord and a warm hug with a kiss on the cheek for Heather.

"Welcome to you all." Metrón finally said with a warm smile. "Our home is open to you. Make it yours as you wish." He finished with a slight bow of his head. Except for his complexion, hair and beard being dark, he had a Santa Claus quality about him that made everyone feel comfortable. "Boys, come and meet your cousins. They will show you where to sleep." He gestured to Adrian and Liam. They stepped forward and followed Metrón down through the apartment and out of sight.

"Your apartment, if that's what this is...is absolutely beautiful, Aunt Fi." Tillie finally looked around and was mesmerized.

The entrance had a white marble floor with an oval Oriental rug in rich reds, gold and blues. The furniture looked like something out of a magazine to Tillie, as that's the only place she'd ever seen things that nice before.

Everyone stepped down two steps the width of the foyer, into the living room. The design was open. The living room was on the left, with a small wall dividing the large kitchen on the right. Each room had a back wall of windows which looked out onto the lake. They were all uncovered and the living room windows had reams of chocolate burnout velvet billowing to the floor, held with brass tie backs every few windows. They looked so lavish. The living room furniture was mostly modern, but was mixed with old details. The overall feeling was comfort with interesting things to look at all around.

Firouza told Tillie about a piece of art on the wall as Chloe came out of the back hallway, presumably the bedroom area. "Hi, Tillie. Hi, everyone. Merry Christmas eve!" Everyone greeted her back. "Hey Tillie, Lyla, come with me. I'll show you where you'll be staying. I hope you don't mind sharing space."

The two girls looked at each other and smiled broadly. "Not at all," Lyla replied. They followed Chloe into the back hallway, out of sight.

"Oh, this is just going to be too fun, Ri. I can't believe you are here at last!" Firouza hugged her sister once more. She grabbed Heather's bags from her and led her and Cord out of the room.

After everyone had a chance to get settled and more names were exchanged, it was time for Christmas Eve dinner. Chloe and Kallias introduced the Lundgren children to their siblings; Dahia, Adonia, Baalhanno and Lucrezia. Then there were the families of Dahia and Adonia; Their husbands Christian and Quentin, respectively and their children, who were still practically babies. Dahia and Christian had two children, Sella, who was three and Roland, who was just one. Adonia and Quentin had the youngest, Kai, who was nine months old. The two families were able to fit at the dining table, with all of the leaves on it. It accommodated everyone quite nicely.

The table was lavishly set. None of the children remembered ever having a dinner this fancy before. The food came and went quite quickly. The Zohros had help in the kitchen. Tillie wondered if it was just for Christmastime, to impress them, or if they had them every day. She couldn't help but ask quietly to Chloe. "So, do you always have...*servants*...for dinner time?"

"Well, yes. I mean, they're not servants, they're paid." Chloe corrected Tillie's train of thought, taking a sip of her drink. "They've been here as long as I can remember. Don't you have help around the house?"

Tillie let out a hysterical giggle that caught the attention of her end of the table. She looked around and blushed. She paused and waited for everyone to go back to their previous conversations, then answered Chloe.

"Gosh, no, Chloe. See, we own Sigrun. We run it ourselves. Well, I mean, we have help, other employees, but we work there as much as we all can." Tillie paused when she saw the confused look on Chloe's face. "Sigrun. It's our restaurant that my parents own."

"Oh, yes, right. Mom told me they owned a restaurant. They just neglected to tell me that they *worked* there too. I pictured more owning like they walk in every so often, greet people, check on their staff, then leave sort of thing." Chloe quipped then took another bite of her gourmet looking meal.

Tillie was put off by her statement. The Lundgrens took pride in owning and running their family business. Chloe's statement made it sound like they were slaves or peasants. She explained further. "You see, Lyles and Liam work there full time since they finished school. Ade and I work there part time during the school year and full time in the summers." She took a bite of feathery mashed potatoes. They were so light and airy, yet buttery and smooth, she couldn't go very long without eating this meal.

"You mean, you *want* to work there?" Chloe asked genuinely.

Tillie answered, "Well, yes, most of the time. I mean, I do get a bit sick of it now and then, when I would rather hang out with friends and such. But we manage to work it out. And tips are great spending money for when we do get to go out." Tillie tried to smile and sound chipper. She really was proud of her job and her family. She continued. "Our home is above Sigrun. When we are there, which sometimes feels like never, there's no one else but us. I've never even known anyone before who had help in the house. I thought that was mostly in movies." Tillie finished with a small laugh. She took another bite of succulent roast beef.

"Well, I wouldn't want to be a waitress." Chloe went on with her food in her mouth, but remained graceful. She resembled her mother from their first dinner gathering. "I mean, no offense, Tillie, but that's like the help, isn't it? I don't mean anything by it, really. It's just not something that's ever appealed to me." She tried to expand on her statement when she saw the look Tillie gave her. "I mean, I guess since your family owns it and runs it, that's different, yah know? I guess, in a way, it's cool. Working with your family all the time could be cool." She paused for another sip of her drink in a beautiful red goblet with gold trim. Then she smiled at Tillie and hoped that made up for any insult she may have caused.

"Yes. It is cool. It's just what I've known my whole life, so I never saw it as a lesser thing to be, Chloe," Tillie said gently. She knew Chloe was still young and she could remember feeling similar when she was Chloe's age. She wanted Chloe to understand a different view of the work they did. Her view.

Tillie took a bite of her dinner and saw, with a little dismay, that her plate was clean. She felt shy to ask for more, so she continued her conversation with Chloe quietly at the end of the table. The two came to an understanding and the chatting went on past Sigrun, restaurants and working.

Soon everyone gathered in the living room, feeling full and listening to Heather and Firouza reminisce about their childhood Christmases. Lots of laughter and awkward stories made the Lundgren children feel more endeared to their mother than ever before. All four of them learned so much about her family and her past and every now and then, Atlantis. According to Firouza, Atlantis was a part of their lives always. They didn't know any differently.

"Kind of like you said earlier, Til." Chloe pointed out, "About working at the restaurant. We've just always had Atlantis in our lives."

"It's just so thrilling to us." Tillie replied with a wide smile. She sipped on some hot cocoa. "Not as thrilling as the restaurant business to you though, huh, Chloe?" Tillie and Chloe laughed.

Metrón came in from the back hallway. He was followed by his two oldest daughters who'd just put their children down to sleep. "Well, my lovelies, it is time for our presents." He carried one large present into the room and placed it on the coffee table. It was bright, shiny red with a green ribbon all the way around with a giant bow on top. All the Lundgrens couldn't help but smile at Metrón as he set it down and gestured to his wife to join him.

"As this is our first Christmas with the Lundgren family, we would like to hand out their gifts first." He said as Firouza opened the lid of the giant gift and reached inside. Chloe clapped her hands together along with her siblings. The Lundgrens felt eager to see what came next.

Firouza pulled out a small present and read the tag. "Ri, darling. This one's for you, of course." She handed the present down to the closest person and they passed it on until it reached Heather. As it reached Heather's hands, Firouza added, "Now you must wait, dear, until all the presents are handed out." She smiled at her sister and Heather reflected one back to her.

Firouza kept handing out gifts until everyone in the room had one, including herself and Metrón. The two sat down, Firouza in the nearest chair and Metrón on the floor by her side. The Lundgrens looked around at the Zohros for cues of what to do next.

"Well, everyone, Merry Christmas!" Firouza gestured to let everyone know to open their gifts.

At first there was quiet, timid opening, but the boys, in both families, tore into theirs as boys do. All of the children found they had the same looking gift. The adults had another similar looking one, but larger. The Lundgrens were stumped as to what they were, except Heather.

She smiled and simply asked, "Tonight, Fi?"

"Well yes, my dears. We're going to have such fun."

22

Collaboration Eve

"What's tonight?" Adrian asked looking over his new present. It was round and it almost looked like a girl's make up compact. It was gold with a black circle in the center. And there was a crystal looking thing right in the middle of the black circle. Adrian kept turning it around, looking for some sort of button to push, or seam to open, but to no avail. He looked to the adults for some answers.

"Yeah, what is this thing?" Liam got to the point.

"We get them every year." Answered Lucrezia. "They are our light show for Christmas Eve. What is the actual name again, Mommy?"

Tillie made a funny face at Lucrezia for calling her mother, "Mommy". She hadn't called her mother that in years, but it was kind of adorable the way she just said it in conversation. Tillie's face changed to a smile almost immediately.

"This, my dears, is an Ostend Glass. It's a temporary light that works with water. We'll show you. You are going to help us make our Christmas Eve show more spectacular than ever this year. Come children." Firouza rose from her chair and Metrón joined her.

Heather and Cord stood up, Heather smiled, looking childlike.

"You do this every Christmas? That's great." Cord said as they headed to the balcony. "I haven't seen this in years. Kids." He called. Everyone went into the foyer to put on coats, gloves and such. "You are just going to love this. Now, listen to Aunt Fi for directions and I'm sure the others can help too. This is a real treat." The other children who were familiar with the device were already nodding their heads and pairing up with a Lundgren child.

"Now," started Firouza, "All of our children have paired up with one of you because of your ability with water. You may be confused by all of this, but really, it's not too hard once we get going. We need you to think about your ability, even if it is new for you. Come, let's gather onto the balcony." Firouza led them all outside after they were bundled.

The balcony was vast. The Lundgrens expected everyone to have to crowd together. That was not the case. This was more like a patio, large enough for a party, which is just what the two families added up to. There was furniture placed around that made it look like a living room. Metrón went to the center and started a fire in the fireplace. Apparently it was a gas fireplace, as the fire started almost immediately and sent its warm glow out all around the area.

They were all covered in the orange glow of the fire, which looked warm compared to the blue gray darkness surrounding them outside. The Lundgren children found themselves settled into seats with their cousin partners for whatever was about to come. Still confused, they sat and listened to the instructions they were individually given.

Lyla sat with Kallias and Adonia. Adonia was dark, like her father and her long hair flowed out of her fur hat gracefully. Her light-brown eyes caught the glow of the fire and looked as if they were dancing as she talked. Her voice was controlled, Lyla thought and it helped ease her anxiety to listen to it.

"We are excited to have you with us this year, as Mom said. Kall and I are so anxious to see what you have to offer with us." Kallias smiled back.

"Yeah, Mom says your powers are like, awesome." he added.

"Yes, awesome. Well, they do scare the crud out of me. If that's awesome, then so be it." Lyla added. "You're not expecting me to use that tonight, here, now, are you?" She asked.

"Well, yes. And no." Adonia answered. "We will work together. You see, Kallias and I have similar powers. We can both manipulate the weather, sort of like you. But mother said that your power is extensive. She thinks because Kall and I work together that we haven't fully developed ours, so it's not as strong as yours." She noticed the look of fear rising in Lyla's face. All too familiar with Kallias, when his powers started, she continued to try to put Lyla at ease. "There's no need to worry. I've seen that look before." She looked at Kallias. "We will simply think lightly. Working together our powers won't be as strong as individually. They join and coordinate and organize in a gentler way. You'll see. Now, what we'll be doing is to help control the atmosphere. We need to bring in a fog off the lake. This time of year can be tricky with the cold, but tonight doesn't feel so frozen, so it shouldn't be too hard. Then we bring snow. No wind, just snow. As big and bold as you want to make it. You can play with it if you want to, but we are working for cover here. We don't want to give away what we are doing to raise suspicion with anyone nearby."

"Snow is the best cover. It hides the lights, the water, everything." Kallias added. His smile would have been contagious if it weren't for the sick feeling in the pit of Lyla's stomach.

"Look, I know you're nervous. Mom told us you were very new to all of this. But we need you relaxed. It's supposed to be fun, enjoyable even. Trust Kall and me. We won't let you get out of control. Just think about the weather we mentioned. The fog, the snow...and we'll take care of the rest, okay?" Adonia smiled and took Lyla's hand. Lyla felt a spark, like an electric shock, but didn't pull away. It felt good.

"See, you're starting already." Kallias said and joined hands with the two girls. They sat quietly.

The fog rolled in gently, coming off the lake slowly. It looked very festive and peaceful under the street lights. As the rest of the Lundgren children noticed it coming onto the balcony, Tillie looked over at Lyla. She stood up to go to her, but Heather and Firouza stopped her.

"But, Mom. Lyles." Tillie tried to explain.

"It's all right, darling. She is in the best of hands with my Adonia and Kallias. Trust me." Firouza took Tillie by the hand and waited for her to sit with Chloe. Firouza joined the girls and explained what their jobs were when the time came. "Now, when it starts snowing, Chloe, you know what to do. Tillie, just follow her lead and you'll do fine, honey." Firouza sat quietly with them, holding hands in a circle formation.

"Is everyone settled? Are we good?" Metrón inquired. His family nodded back to him, ready. The rest of his family was gathered around him. "Bring on the cover!" Metrón raised his arms into the air. As he did, the fog lifted up over their heads. It spread to all the neighboring windows and formed a wall around the outside of the balcony. It was like being inside a box made of fog. Snow fell. It was hard to see nearly your own arm's reach.

Adrian and Baalhanno joined Chloe, Firouza and Tillie, looking up at the snow. "Ready?" Baalhanno asked Adrian. They moved to the center of the girls' circle.

"I think so," he answered. He faced Baalhanno, they grabbed each other's arms and looked up at the snow. The girls joined hands around the boys. From the center of the boys' arms, a spout of clear air shot out. The fog and snow from around them cleared and made a dome around the whole balcony. Adrian looked almost as surprised as Liam when they saw it happen.

"Ah, perfect." announced Metrón. He clapped loudly once. Adonia and Kallias opened their eyes and smiled. The cover was indeed perfect as well as beautiful.

Lyla still had her eyes closed and concentrated very hard on not losing it. She felt a peace inside her tonight, however, that she had not felt before. She knew it was the other two helping her stay calm. She was happy. She felt a tap on her shoulder and opened her eyes. Adonia was grinning at her.

"You did it." Adonia said to her quietly.

Lyla blinked and looked up at the sky. Well, where the sky was supposed to be. What she saw instead was a glorious dome of lacy-looking snow and misty fog that was breathtaking.

"We did it." She said to the other two and took their hands once more. "How is it staying up there?"

"Our brothers. They're good." Kallias answered and pointed over to the two boys still looking up at their dome. "They need a bit more time to solidify it. It's so thin, it takes a bit more time."

"Oh, my gosh." Lyla breathed.

It was such a beautiful sight and she and Liam were partly responsible. It was glorious.

"Once they are ready, we will begin the show." Metrón announced once more. He nodded at his children. They all took out their Ostend Glasses and held them, ready in their laps. The Lundgren children followed. The adults stood up and lined up behind the children. They held their devices in front of them with both hands at their waists.

After a few seconds more, Baalhanno looked over to his father. "It is ready."

Liam blinked rapidly a few times, they released hands and found seats. They got their devices ready.

"Fabulous! Darlings, we wish you all much love and beauty this Christmas." Firouza exclaimed. "May this night's show be just a sample of it for you for the whole year."

Her children clapped and the adults started their devices. They pressed the crystal in the middle and it popped up. A bright light started up, each adult with a different color in the center of their device. The light shot through the crystals. They each took turns turning the crystal in the center and the show began.

Colors of the rainbow shot around the dome above. The children couldn't help but clap. Then the Lundgren children saw the Zohro children start their Ostend Glass, each taking their turn. Theirs were brighter, golden white lights in the middle, different shades of gold, yellow and white. Their lights danced smaller shapes over the colors onto the dome. It was such a magical sight. The snowflakes didn't pile up onto the dome, but slid around it, dancing in the lights.

"Oohs," and "Ahs," were heard all around. Clapping sounded when a light danced with a snowflake. The fog was a misty veil, moving in and around the snowy dome. It truly was a special Christmas Eve!

The show felt like it went on for only a few minutes when, just as quickly as it started, it was over. The lights went out and the crystals shattered into a snowy powder and fell to the ground. The discs now looked like ashtrays, with a few burnt edges and felt hollow. The Zohros went over to the fireplace and threw their discs onto the fire. As the dome faded, the snowflakes made their way down to faces with chilly tingling touches. The Lundgrens were beckoned over to the fireplace and gestured to do the same with their Ostend Glass.

"Hurry now children, before the cover is gone." Firouza encouraged them.

As the last disc was placed on the fire, sparks flew up from the fireplace and a rainbow of colorful sparklers shot up through the chimney in one last flaming dance.

Then it was over. The fire looked just as it had before. The snow fall lightened and the fog rolled away gently as it fell to their feet. The balcony took on its previous, plain appearance.

Suddenly they all felt the cold of the outside. They hurried inside and took off their outdoor clothing. Everyone gathered in the living room. There was a tray of what looked like champagne on the table. Everyone took a glass, Tillie looking to her parents for permission.

"Of course, darling. It's only sparkling juice." Firouza explained.

Metrón made a most humble and sincere toast and they drank their bubbly down easily. Everyone hugged and wished each other a Merry Christmas. It was way past midnight by this time, to the surprise of many. The light show lasted over an hour. That's when everyone said, "Goodnight" to each other. Most went to bed, letting the peace of the light show take them to dreamland.

The Lundgren children were far too excited to go straight to bed. They said goodnight to their parents and the Zohros and sat in the living room trying to comprehend the evening, feeling blissful. The orange glow still danced outside from the fireplace, hypnotizing whoever looked at it. The children felt so tired and so happy at the same time, no one needed to talk.

Soon there was fire and smoke everywhere. Liam was coughing, trying to find everyone and help them out. The floor felt like it was rocking and water was coming in from somewhere. It was getting hard to breathe. Where was everyone? Why couldn't he find them? He had to get out! He was having trouble keeping his balance. The floor rocked hard and he fell into a puddle.

"Ow!" Liam shouted. He looked up and everything was dark. He sat up quickly, coughing and catching his breath. He looked around for the fire and smoke. There was none. It was dark and he couldn't remember where he was. Wasn't there just a fire? Wait. It was just a dream. He stood up and realized he was in the Zohros' living room. Everyone else had gone to bed. He must have dozed off and they decided to leave him there. *Nice*, he thought. Liam sauntered off to bed, bumping things here and there, being unfamiliar with this home in the dark.

The next morning came too soon for the Lundgrens. They were used to sleeping in a bit, now that everyone was older, before opening gifts and starting their Christmas day. The sound of crying babies was startling. Lyla and Tillie awoke looking for the problem. When they learned it was just the little ones having their morning diaper changes, they were a little weary. Everyone started to filter into the living room, but were stopped by Firouza. She was in a Christmas colored caftan, billowing at the doorway.

"Sorry, chickadees. We have to wait for everyone." She said loudly. Then, more quietly to the Lundgrens, "We don't want to ruin it for the little ones, dears."

Soon the littlest in the family were ready. They made their way to the front of the line and were let go to find their stockings by the fireplace. Their excitement was contagious. Tillie handed out stockings to their owners and the present opening frenzy began.

It was a pleasure to watch the little ones learning how to open their gifts. There were so many people. So much wrapping paper flew about, it almost looked like snow indoors.

The morning present festivities were over within the hour. The children received things they loved and the Lundgren children put theirs into a pile belonging to each of them. It was already time to get ready for Church. They all went to get dressed.

There were two cars outside waiting for the families. "Gee, do you guys always travel by limos?" Adrian asked with slight sarcasm.

"Well, no, silly." Firouza answered him with a hug as well. She felt very festive and having her sister's family with them made her bubble over with love. "But we thought it would be such fun to travel this way for the holidays with you all. Isn't it grand, the holidays?" She swept her lace shawl over her beautiful winter coat and leapt into the first limo. Within moments, they drove away.

The Church was huge compared to any the Lundgren children had seen in their lives. It was gray stone and the steeple rivaled the taller buildings around it. It had a gothic look to it. Lyla thought this was a fitting look for a Church. She thought every Church should look this way.

They went in and sat one pew from the front. They took up three rows easily and the little children tried to get settled. Their parents brought things to help keep them busy, but the baby was being fussy. Her father took her out the back of the Church for a few minutes before the mass began.

The mass was beautiful. There was a choir and a harp playing the Christmas music. Flowers covered the altar along with white and gold streaming fabric. It was quite a production. The Lundgrens were used to their quiet, country Church. This was like watching mass on television. The altar was large and the people serving mass wore microphones. Tillie looked around for cameras.

There were so many people at the altar, the Lundgren children couldn't tell who their other aunt was. There was a lot of whispering and guesses. Then a woman approached the pulpit for a reading. She was shorter than both Heather and Firouza, her hair was sandy and sleek. Her olive skin was smooth and she wore little or no makeup. Her eyes were dark brown and drew you to them. She wore a white robe with a beautifully embroidered gold stole on her left shoulder, signaling that she is a deacon in the Church. As soon as she spoke, the children knew it was her; Aunt Haseena. Her voice, both in sound and intonation, was much like their own mother's. They felt comfortable with her immediately.

After mass was ended, the families filed out of the back of the Church, where everyone greeted the priests and deacons. The Lundgren children automatically lined up to say hello to their aunt. When they reached her, she took one look at Tillie, who was first in line and a big smile came across her face.

"Tillie, right? Why you look just as Fi described." Haseena finished as she grabbed Tillie into a big hug. She then reached out to the others and hugged them too. "I'm your Aunt Haseena children. I'm so very pleased to see you on this fine Christmas morning. I'll be joining you later at Fi's house. We'll have more time to chat then. It's so good to see you here this morning. God bless." With that, Haseena corralled the children off down the steps and out of Church.

They were pleased to meet another family member, but confused by the hurried introduction. Heather explained to them that her sister, the deacon, loved the social aspects of her job and wanted to make sure she had time to greet everyone coming out of the Church.

The rest of the day went on quietly, as the aftermath of Christmas usually does. Hours passed like minutes. The children did get to know Aunt Haseena a bit better when she came back to the Zohros home later in the day.

The dinner table tonight was even fancier than the night before. The settings were completely different, with many colors, bold and bright. The silverware was, well, silver. Tillie looked closely at each one, looking like her little cousins gazing at their new Christmas gifts.

"This is actual silver then?"

"Yes, it was my great, great grandmother's. I think." Chloe answered quietly as they started their prayer before the meal. Their heads bowed.

Tillie couldn't get over the gleaming shine of silver everywhere on the table; the candlesticks, platters, plates and serving pieces. The shine stood out from the vibrant colors of the table cloth and the plates in front of them. The centerpiece was so fancy and elaborate, she found herself staring at it, instead of engaging in conversation, while she ate. There were flowers, yes, at first glance. Looking at it further, she saw greenery that complimented the flowers and the container was an amazing shell shape. It looked like the inside of a shell, iridescent and shiny. She even found tiny Christmas ornaments of all kinds sprinkled throughout the arrangement. So many things to look at, she was preoccupied through most of the meal.

The children listened to Haseena talk with her sisters throughout dinner. They heard even more stories of their mother's childhood and were amazed that there were so many. Aunt Haseena congratulated Lyla and Liam once more before she had to make her early exit.

The night came to an end and everyone felt full and happy. Even Adrian, with all his skepticism and questions, felt content for the night. He thought he would like meals like this more often.

As people trickled off to bed, Liam asked Lyla, "So should we get back to studying tomorrow?" Half joking, he thought they'd agreed it would be a piece of cake from here on out.

"Gee no," Lyla surprised him with her response. "I'm not worried about that test anymore." She stretched, yawned and told everyone who was still awake, "Goodnight," and was off to bed.

Liam shrugged his shoulders and went to bed as well. He thought he'd better put himself there earlier than later after what happened the previous night.

Another Christmas had come to an end. Lots of new people, things and traditions were learned by the Lundgrens. None of them would be forgotten.

23

Tillie's Detour

The next morning the Lundgrens were packed and ready to go back to the hotel. Despite Firouza's pleads for them to stay, Heather and Cord agreed that they just couldn't put the Zohros out any more. Dahia, Adonia and their families left first thing in the morning and Firouza insisted there was more than enough room for the Lundgrens to stay, but they wouldn't hear of it.

Firouza just kept saying, "Oh, darlings! You are just too polite for words. Impose! Impose!"

Before they left, Tillie asked if she could go out with Chloe to get some coffee. Chloe told her about the little coffee shop she and her friends hung out in after school. Tillie thought she could quickly check it out before they left. She asked if anyone else was interested, but there were no takers. So she and Chloe threw on their outer vestments and were out the door.

"It's just down here." Chloe pointed up ahead as they exited the warm building for the brisk city street.

"Good, because I am already freezing." Tillie crossed her arms and hugged her coat and scarf in closer. The girls walked faster.

Just a few doors down, they came to a building with glass front doors. Tillie saw they were already at the coffee shop. She was glad to see it wasn't a fancy big name, but one she'd never heard of before. It was full, but not crowded, which put a smile on her face. She was eager to see their menu. She loved ordering new coffees, as well as seeing what a big city had to offer compared to back home. *Maybe there is something here we could adapt and offer next winter.*

Waiting in line, the girls warmed up and chatted about how much fun they had on their Christmas day. Before too long they were at the order counter. Tillie took her time to read what ingredients these fancy names offered. It all sounded so good, but she was trying to figure out what she was in the mood for. Chloe ordered her "Usual," and made a couple of recommendations for Tillie. She finally decided on a choco-mint latte macchiato. Christmas always put Tillie in the mood for peppermint.

As they got to the cashier, both girls reached into their purses for their wallets.

"Put that away dear cousin," Chloe said to Tillie.

"Oh no. I'll get it. It was my idea," Tillie rebutted.

It was no good. "No way. You are my guest here and this is my joint. I will not have you shelling out your money here today." Chloe insisted with such a charming smile, Tillie almost laughed.

"Okay, but when you come to visit me, it will be my treat," Tillie replied.

"Deal." Chloe turned to the cashier to complete her transaction.

Tillie looked out the windows and watched the people pass by. She was surprised how many there were on the street the day after Christmas. Back home the streets were practically empty for a couple of days after the holiday.

Just then, she spotted someone she thought looked familiar. Just a glimpse as they went around the corner. At first she thought it was her imagination, just having thought about home and all. Tillie went to the door to see if she could get a better look. She saw the little woman in the fabulous pink hat just crossing the street. She swore it was Anna.

So caught up in the moment, Tillie found herself going out the door, her hands wrapped around her hot latte. Her gray wool coat was undone from being in the shop, her purple hat was still on and the matching scarf was untied flopping around in the city gusts. She tried to walk as fast as she could to catch the woman, even get a look at her face, just to be sure, but the latte slowed her down. She missed the light to cross the street. The instant flow of traffic had Tillie lose sight of the woman within seconds. She waited for the light. She looked back at the coffee shop, wondering if Chloe saw her leave. *She'll figure it out*, she thought to herself, justifying her instant quest.

That's how she felt. Like she was suddenly on a quest to find this person. She wasn't sure why she felt it so necessary to find her, to know whether or not it was Anna.

The *Don't Walk* light turned to *Walk* and Tillie started to walk. Just then, Chloe came out of the coffee shop. She looked both ways for Tillie. She saw her and called out to her. It was too late. Tillie didn't hear her and crossed the street. Chloe shrugged and walked back toward her home. She thought a little bit of exploration on her own would be fun for Tillie in a new place.

After Tillie moved past some people, she saw the bright pink flash she'd seen before and got a look from behind at who was wearing that great hat. It could be Anna. She was short and built like her. She walked like her too. Again the question in her head screamed, *What would she be doing here?*

Tillie didn't hesitate to follow the pink hat. She had the advantage of a larger stride and caught up halfway to this mystery lady. Whoever she was, she moved through the crowd with great ease. Where Tillie kept dodging around people, the woman seemed to flow through them. Tillie started to second guess herself. Perhaps she was wrong about this person being Anna. *Anna isn't a city girl. She doesn't have much, if any, experience in any big city besides Bar Harbor, as far as I know.* At this point however, Tillie knew that of all the things she thought she knew, there was even more she did not know. This kept her following the pink hat.

She shouted out to get the woman's attention, but the traffic was too loud for her voice to be heard.

Tillie followed, trying not to be obvious, second guessing calling out to her before. The woman stopped at a news stand. Tillie immediately stopped in her tracks and scooted over by a phone booth, nearly hiding behind it. She watched and sipped her steaming coffee. The woman bought a paper and moved on, quickly crossing the street ahead.

By now, Tillie decided it was time to get rid of the latte so she could catch up to this woman before the light changed. She tossed it into the garbage can closest to her and made a run for the light. The *Walk* sign flashed orange-red as Tillie reached the curb. She went quickly and made it just before the stream of noisy traffic continued.

Tillie became bold in following, as she noticed the woman had no idea anyone was behind her. She faced forward, walking determined to her destination, wherever that may be. Tillie found herself only a few people away from the woman when suddenly she looked back, directly at Tillie and just as quickly she ducked off to the right, disappearing into, what at first, Tillie thought was a library.

"How odd," Tillie thought aloud, pausing to read the many small signs on the building.

The woman, Tillie saw, wasn't Anna, but she definitely looked like her. *Did Anna have a sister here in Chicago?* Tillie couldn't remember her ever mentioning it. *Why wouldn't Anna say something about a sister here, knowing that we would be here too? And why did she look right at me?* Tillie thought.

The building Tillie found herself in front of was dark, with the front all open to the sidewalk, with pillars of concrete in place for support. The door, set back about twenty feet, was old fashioned; dark wood, with individual window panes and brass fittings. A large window, with smaller framed panes, was just to the left of the door. The whole scene looked very old, compared to the coffee shop. There was a small tarnished sign next to the door in one of the panes that read,

Official Members Only. There was another sign above that that read, *Official Association Members.* She thought these two signs together were odd.

Under the large window were rectangular wooden tables with all sorts of piles of papers on them. Upon a closer look, Tillie saw they were brochures and flyers of all sorts. *The International Flyers Association* and *Map Collectors of America* were among the ones that stood out to her. She perused the tables some more, trying to get a look inside the window. *Oceanography; a Hobby* lay in front of Tillie as she glanced into the window. She couldn't see anything at first, her eyes still used to the daylight. Then she saw round lights at the top of the window. She looked down at the tables again when someone reached next to her for a paper. *Be a Weather Finder for a Day* was the headline on that pile. Quickly Tillie looked back into the window. This time she was disappointed to see that curtains hung across the bottom half. They were puce and blended into the darkness at first. They hung on a brass rod, which she noticed gleamed just dimmer than the light orbs above.

The door swung out and caught Tillie's eye. She looked over, the door swung in, out and quickly came to a tight close. Tillie made her way over to the door and looked around to make sure no one noticed her. She pushed on the door. It opened inward, Tillie let go quickly and stepped back. She turned around to the table closest by and waited. Nothing happened. The door closed tightly once more. Tillie took another survey of the people around her. There were a couple of teenagers near one of the pillars. One older woman was at the other end of the tables looking at brochures. No one looked at her. In fact, no one seemed to take any notice of her at all. Anyone else in the area was just walking past and quickly at that.

Tillie took the opportunity and walked through the door like that's where she planned on going all along. At first everything looked hazy and Tillie thought it was smoky. Then she took a small breath in through her nose to test the air and smelled a sweet fire. It smelled so good that Tillie found herself breathing deep because she didn't want it to end. She looked around hesitantly, realizing she was in the way and stepped slowly forward as people walked toward the door to get out. She wondered if she would get in trouble for being in there, but no one looked as though they cared. She couldn't really believe what she was doing. She could hear Lyla's voice in her head warning her to go back to her family. She decided to ignore it for once and do something adventurous on her own.

The room was covered all in mahogany wood; dark, warm and cozy. Straight ahead of Tillie was a large counter. It looked to her like a mix between a bar and a hotel lobby counter. There weren't any stools or chairs near it, but people lingered with cups of coffee and tea. There were two people behind the counter; a tall thin man and a smaller fair-haired woman. Tillie couldn't tell what their job was exactly, but they were both engaged in conversation with a couple of people on the opposite side of the counter.

When no one approached her, as she thought someone might, Tillie walked further on to the left. She removed her hat, scarf and gloves and placed them in her bag. She saw a series of square wooden tables and chairs set up in this area. This was where the globe-like lights hung over the tables. They were much bigger than they looked from outside. Even though they were large, the lights emitted just a soft, warm glow, enough to gently light the high ceiling, but not too bright on the eyes.

This table area was about half full of people sitting, scattered about the room. Tillie noticed that some people sat, some stood at a table talking to the ones sitting and funniest of all, most of them wore turban like hats. All different colors, but definitely the same size. The turbans almost mimicked the lights overhead. This made Tillie quietly snicker. *I feel like Alice in wonderland*, she thought to herself as she took in this odd scene.

234

Just then, a small woman walked up to her and said, "There you are, dearie. Come right this way. We've been waiting for you to come in out of that nasty cold."

She took Tillie by the hand and led her past the tables, behind the counter, underneath to a staircase. Tillie tried to object, tried to tell the woman she must be mistaking her with someone else, but the woman kept right ahead of her and Tillie couldn't get the words out. She finally gave up and found herself walking down a long hallway with this little person.

"Umm...I'm Tillie," she said as if she was unsure that was true.

"Oh, yes, dear, we know, we know." The woman said with a little chuckle. "Clara told us you followed her here and we've been so very eager to meet you."

"Uh...Clara? Is that the woman with the pink..." she thought about it and finished, "turban?"

"Yes, dear, that's Clara alright. You know, she's Anna's older sister. I'm sure you know that already."

"Um, no. I didn't know. I didn't know Anna had an older sister, or that I was supposed to follow her in here."

"Oh, yes, yes. Well we seem to be keeping everything very hush-hush around here, don't we?" The woman kept ahead of Tillie by a few steps, so she turned her head back to talk to her every time.

"Well...yes." Tillie exclaimed, "Yes you are!" She finished with a hint of annoyance in her voice.

The hall was long and wide. As they walked slowly down, Tillie could see there were doors every so often on both sides. They were all closed except for the one at the very end, on the left. This one had light emitting from it and Tillie guessed that was where they were headed. She noticed they walked unusually slow and Tillie took a closer look at this woman she so blindly followed. She was very small, shorter than Anna and even her sister Clara. This woman looked to Tillie like a half a person. She didn't know how else to think of her. She was proportioned perfectly, about the size of a ten year old, but with the figure of an adult woman. She had on black, sensible shoes, black stockings and a gray dress suit. The skirt, Tillie noticed, was so tight, it would also explain the small steps she took down the hallway. The woman's hair was a chestnut brown and pulled tightly back into a bun at the nape of her neck. The bun looked like a shell.

"Here we are. I'm sorry about everything seeming so strange, dear. We just can't take chances." She looked back behind Tillie and said, "Out there." She stood at the edge of the doorway and gestured Tillie into the room.

Tillie stopped in front of her and said, "If you need to be so careful, why do you leave the front door open? Anyone could just walk right in."

The little woman smiled coyly. "The door is locked, dear. Only those with DNA such as yours can open it."

"Oh," said Tillie in reply. "OH," she said again fully understanding exactly to what DNA they were referring. Now her mind spun. She thought they definitely had the wrong person, the wrong sister. She blurted out, "Oh, gosh. You must want my sister, Lyla then. What is this all about? I'm not the one being inducted. I'm not Lyla."

"Here you are now, dearie. Relax. We know who you are and we've brought you here on purpose. Mind your steps down now." The woman took Tillie by the shoulder and led her through the doorway.

The light Tillie saw coming into the hallway came from torch lights on either side of the stairway which led down five steps. The steps widened with each one, down into a small, but cozy room. As Tillie reached the bottom of the steps timidly, she realized it was a foyer. Columns stood on the opposite side of the anteroom marking the entrance to the larger room behind it, which was a half circle with smooth walls.

Huge tanks were embedded in the walls on either side of the room with the most glorious aquatic setups in them Tillie ever saw. The soft glowing blue green light in each tank grew slightly brighter when Tillie walked slowly into the room.

It made Tillie notice the beautiful underwater city mural scene on the curved wall between the tanks.

"Atlantis," Tillie said softly.

It was like nothing she ever imagined and far more beautiful than the pictures she saw in the magazines back at the Council waiting room.

"Holy...cow," her thoughts just spilled out of her mouth.

The mural was a fresco, looking shiny and new. It looked like an overview to the underwater city. The city that Tillie, only recently, knew truly existed.

"Wow." Tillie looked closely at the fresco, swooning over all the details.

As she reached the center of the room, furniture appeared. A soft white loveseat and two aqua chairs on either side.

"Oh." Tillie was startled by the furniture's sudden appearance. She stepped back and a coffee table appeared where she had just stood. Tea and a tray of desserts were on the table.

"My word. I really could change my name to Alice."

Tillie caught her balance and went over to the loveseat. She leaned down and touched the cushion to make sure it was really there.

"Well, so it is," she answered herself out loud.

She sat on the edge of the loveseat. She took off her coat and set both it and her bag down next to her. Then, something caught her eye, to the right, from the fish tank. A flash of orangey-red. Tillie looked over, but saw only shades of blue and purple in the tank. There was some pink coral, but it was not moving, as Tillie thought she saw. She wasn't sure what she saw, or what she was even doing here. She put both hands up to her face and rubbed her eyes with her palms. She felt frustrated, put her hands on her lap and sat back into the seat.

"Ugh. Maybe I'll just try to relax a little. I've gone this far, I might as well ride it out." She closed her eyes and set her head back with the memories of Christmas still fresh in her mind.

Just then the door, back up the steps, opened. Tillie jumped to a straight seated position.

"C'mon now, dear, don't be shy. Everything is going to be all right now," she heard the little woman say at the top of the stairs. "Someone is waiting to meet you down there. Her name is Tillie. Now enough shyness. It's time to go."

The door closed and Tillie waited to see who was coming. She was anxious, but not worried, as someone that shy couldn't mean any harm. Her imagination ran wild by this time.

Literally on the edge of her seat, Tillie heard whoever it was sniffle, then a little whimper. She thought right then it must be a child.

This couldn't get any stranger, she thought. Then she saw two small feet. One more step down and it was confirmed, the sniffle came from a small child.

A little boy, no more than five or six from the looks of him. Beautiful blond hair; fine and straight. He looked very sad indeed and his cheeks were wet. He wiped his nose with the sleeve of his shirt. Tillie felt immediately sorry for this little fellow and tried to think of something she could say to comfort him. She didn't want to scare him, so she thought she'd better start off by introducing herself. The boy walked past the columns and was almost to the coffee table.

"Hi there," Tillie said gently but brightly. "My name is Tillie. But I guess you were already told that, weren't you? What's your name?"

The boy did not answer. He continued to sniffle, wiped his eyes once again and looked at Tillie. He stopped at the table and grabbed a cookie. Still looking at Tillie, he sat down in a chair next to her bag on the loveseat.

"You like cookies, huh? Me too," Tillie said trying to sound cheerful.

The boy nodded his head and kept eating.

"So what is your name?" Tillie asked again.

"Dorn," said the boy, after he swallowed a bite of the cookie.

"Dorn? That's a very unusual name. Where does it come from? Do you know?" Tillie thought that was a strange question for such a little child to know the answer to, but she really wanted to know.

"My mom...my mommy and daddy gave it to me," the boy said plainly. Tears started to well up in his eyes again. He sniffled once more.

"Why are you so sad?" Tillie asked and looked for a tissue in her bag. She handed one to Dorn.

Dorn took the tissue and wiped his face.

"I m...m...miss my mommy...and daddy." He blew his nose into the tissue and balled it up into his hand.

"Where are they?" Tillie asked, increasing concern on her face.

"Home."

"Where is home?" she asked, but had a feeling she knew the answer.

Dorn pointed to the mural behind Tillie. She turned to look at it, then back to Dorn.

"Well, can't you go see them?" she asked.

"Y...yes. We are going to see them."

Tillie looked confused. "What?"

The boy stood up. He placed the tissues and rest of his cookie on the table. The table disappeared. He crossed over to Tillie.

"We are going to see them," he said again. He sounded sure of himself this time. He took her hand ever so gently and waited.

Tillie stood up. Just as she did the furniture disappeared, taking her bag and coat with them. The room emptied except for the two of them and the aquatic tanks. She looked at the boy. He looked so innocent and adorable. It put her at ease for a moment. She knew something was about to happen. Something big. Her heart pounded a bit faster, even though Dorn's face looked so calm.

Then she saw the red color she thought she saw before in the tanks. This time Tillie looked back and forth at both tanks. The red glow grew inside of them. She looked down at Dorn. He looked up at her, with a last wipe of his nose on his sleeve. He smiled at her.

"I'm sorry we had to do things this way, but you needed to trust me," he said to her as he let go of her hand.

"Trust you? What for?" Tillie felt very uncomfortable suddenly. The glow on the tanks was now bright red, like a red traffic light gone haywire.

"You'll see, but you have to stay with me. Promise you'll stay with me until we get to Mommy and Daddy. That's what they said, okay?" Dorn looked excited. He took two items from a pocket. They were small and Tillie thought they were guitar picks. She looked at him and them, very puzzled.

"Here. Put this in your mouth." Dorn instructed Tillie as he did the same.

"What is it? What is happening Dorn?" Even at these questions, she did what he said and put the disc in her mouth.

At the same moment they both closed their mouths around the discs, the tanks flew open and water flooded into the room. Tillie looked terrified. She looked for a way out. The stairs were already covered and in a matter of seconds, they were both under water. She looked for Dorn. She was scared. Not for herself, as she knew she could stay under water if she had to. For Dorn. He was so little and she worried that he would drown. Thoughts of Timmy flooded into her mind with the raging water. Her heart jumped and pounded. She swam with the disc still in her mouth. She looked for Dorn, but couldn't see well in the turbulent water.

Suddenly something grabbed her shirt from behind. She started and turned as fast as she could in the water to see Dorn. He looked happy and not at all like someone drowning. She looked at him for what to do next.

"Hold on to me." Tillie heard like a speaker in her head. Dorn's lips barely moved.

"Did you just say that in my head?" Tillie tried to say, but couldn't move her lips with the disc in her mouth. So, she thought it in her head and saw Dorn nod his head.

Tillie let out a gasp of bubbly air into the water at the surprise of sharing thoughts with Dorn. Dorn turned around and indicated for Tillie to hold his waist. She grabbed him and they both were suddenly pulled forward toward the fresco on the wall.

At first Tillie objected, but then she saw how it looked and was intrigued. She let Dorn lead them onward. They swam forward into the life-like painting, then it turned solid. The water drained out of the room. The glass tanks came back together and filled more gently with the water and fish they had in them before. The room was empty now. Except for Tillie's bag.

24

Darkness Came

The door opened and closed quickly. Chloe held her coffee with both hands to keep warm.

"That was quick. The day after Christmas and all," Kallias said to her. "Where's Tillie?" He looked past Chloe.

"Oh, she went on a little adventure of her own apparently." She placed her coffee on a table and proceeded to remove her winter gear. She grabbed her coffee and went into the living room.

"What do you mean she went on an adventure on her own?" Liam was in the living room with Lyla watching television. The two overheard the conversation in the hallway.

"Well, as I was paying for our drinks, Tillie took it upon herself to leave the shop without me." Chloe sounded a bit put off, but continued in a more mild tone. "So when I went outside to find her, she was crossing the street. I tried calling after her, but the traffic was too loud. She seemed very determined in her walk, wherever she was headed, so I just let her go. She'll be back soon I'm sure. She probably saw some Christmas lights up the street that she wanted to get a closer look at or something. She does seem to love those." Chloe sipped her steaming drink. She relaxed back onto the sofa.

"So, you let Tillie go walking the streets of Chicago, *by herself?*" Lyla rose to her feet.

Liam added, "Yeah, I don't know if that was such a good idea. Tillie's never been in a big city before and she's not exactly known for her navigation skills."

"Oh I'm sure she'll be fine, relax," Chloe replied.

"That's easy for you to say Chloe, your sister didn't just go off and get lost in Chicago." Lyla raised her voice. Thunder cracked in the distance.

"What's all the fuss about? Lyles, dear, what's the matter?" Heather came into the room from the bedrooms. She heard the thunder, as did Liam. Both moved toward Lyla calmly.

Lyla answered, "Oh I'm fine mom, I'm great. Chloe here, lost Tillie, is all." She plopped back onto the chair. Another small bit of thunder boomed.

"What? What does she mean, Chloe?" Heather sat down next to Lyla.

"I didn't lose her. She went for a walk. She left me in the coffee shop and when I went to see where she was going, she had already walked up the street. She couldn't hear me and I couldn't catch her because the light had changed. It's no biggie, she knows where this building is. I'm sure she'll be back any minute now." Chloe looked over at the front door nervously. She sipped on her drink again.

"Oh. Is that all?" Heather sat back in her seat. "Yes. Tillie will find her way back," Heather said very confidently.

"*That's all?*" Lyla repeated. "Mom, this is Tillie we're talking about. How many times has Tillie gotten lost, just on the island? We should really go out and find her. It's a big city out there."

Thunder cracked louder this time. Chloe looked up.

"Sweetie, please don't get yourself all worked up. We really don't need a storm for Tillie to find her way through, do we?" Heather rubbed Lyla's arm gently.

"Oh gosh, you're right, Mom. I'm sorry." Lyla stood up, but slowly and more calmly than before. "I'm going to meditate. Maybe that will keep things calm enough outside for her to find her way back." Lyla walked back to the bedrooms.

"Mom, do you really have that much confidence in Tillie?" Liam asked quietly.

"Yes, I do. I know this city well, Liam and it's a good place. She'll be fine, you'll see. Let's just give her some time to explore and have fun in her Tillie way, okay?"

After a little while, Adrian came in with his bag, ready to leave.

"Where is everybody? Are we leaving yet?" He placed his bag on the floor and headed to the kitchen area.

Heather answered him, trying to sound cheery. "Well, your sister decided to have a little adventure on her own and we're waiting for her to come back."

"Oh great." Adrian said as his hand went up in the air. "Another Tillie adventure. Gosh knows what she's going to get herself into this time." He opened the refrigerator and buried himself inside of it.

"Don't worry bro," Liam yelled over to the kitchen. "If she's not back soon, you and I will go out looking. Then we get to have our own time out on the city...just us guys." Liam finished with a guffaw.

Adrian emerged from the refrigerator with an armful of food and drink and headed to the counter to prepare some breakfast for himself. "Yeah, okay, sure." Adrian replied.

Liam looked up and noticed no thunder. A small smile crept over his lips. "She's getting better, huh. Lyles, I mean," he said quietly to his mother.

"Yes. She always was a fast learner," Heather replied.

Chloe finished her drink and went into the kitchen. "What are you making?" she asked Adrian. Kallias followed her into the room as well, also curious.

"Oh, I dunno," answered Adrian. "It looks like I grabbed stuff for a mean omelet. You guys want some?" He was already chopping some peppers. There were other veggies, eggs and some cream on the counter as well.

Kallias' eyes grew big, "You know how to make an omelet? That's cool." He placed himself on a stool at the counter to watch Adrian at work. "I totally want some of this." He grinned at Adrian.

"Sure, cuz. Chloe, you in?" Adrian heated a pan on the stove.

"Umm, no thanks, Adrian. That latte filled me up. But, enjoy." Chloe smiled at the boys and went to her room.

It was almost an hour later, when Liam said, "Okay, that's enough for me. Ade, let's go get Tillie."

"Alright, I've been waiting the last half hour for you to say so." Adrian replied, ready and headed to the door.

"Hold on there you two," Cord interrupted. "Haven't you the slightest confidence in your sister?"

The two boys stopped in their tracks. They looked at each other for a second. They turned back to their father and answered him in unison, "No." They continued to the door and put on their coats.

"Ha. You two. Well, don't go out there and get yourselves lost now." Cord laughed.

"Do you want Chloe to come along with you, dears? She was the last one with Tillie. She can show you where she started." Firouza breezed into the kitchen, closer to the entrance hall.

"Sure, if she wants," Liam replied. "Tell her to hurry. I'm sick of just sitting around here."

"Yes. Yes of course." Firouza hurried out to get Chloe. Just a few seconds later, they both emerged from the back hallway.

Chloe headed toward the door. "You guys want me to go with you?"

"Yah, will you show us which street you saw Tillie heading down? Then you can come back here if you like." Adrian handed her coat to her.

"Thanks. Yeah, well, we'll see how cold I get." She said in her upbeat way.

All three scurried out the door.

Liam looked back into the living room. "We'll be back before you know it."

Out on the street, Chloe led the boys down toward the coffee shop. She directed them toward Tillie's earlier path.

"There. She crossed the street here and headed over that way." Chloe pointed in the direction she last saw Tillie. "But I don't know how you expect to find her now. She could be anywhere." Chloe had a tinge of worry in her voice.

"We have our ways," Adrian smiled at her.

"Now go back home, Chloe. You look like you're freezing to death." Liam directed her.

Chloe's clattering teeth gave her away. She knew she couldn't argue, even though she felt bad that Tillie hadn't returned yet. She wanted to help if she could. She tried to grin and bear it, but it was no use. Before she could even say anything, both boys shook their heads at her, shooting down whatever attempt she might have.

"All right. But I just want you two to know...I'm sorry." Chloe finished with her lips fluttering like shutters in a wind storm.

"Aww, cuz...don't worry." Liam placed his arm on her shoulder and hugged her, partly to reassure her, partly to warm her up. "We're going to find her, promise."

"Yah, we've gone through similar situations before, don't worry, 'kay?" Adrian looked at Liam and his look back made Adrian feel confident.

Chloe turned to both boys and grabbed them into a big hug. Adrian looked a bit startled, but Liam just grabbed back.

"Okay. I trust you guys. And thanks for being so...so...awesome. Yeah, I said it." she smiled at them both and headed back to the apartment. "Good luck!" she shouted back.

They didn't necessarily hear her, but they waved at her anyway with smiles. The boys crossed the street at the next light.

"All right, no b s-ing bro...are we going to find her? And how?" Adrian looked serious, as worry made its way to the conversation.

"Yes, Ade, we're going to find her. You know why? Because we are the ones who can." Liam answered him in a similar tone.

Both boys walked down the next block in silence.

The morning lost to the afternoon. Everyone back at the apartment was worried, some more than others, but all had concern to a degree. Firouza buzzed around to everyone trying to keep the mood cheery and lighthearted. She even made some hors d'oeuvres, chatting all the while.

Haseena came over in the afternoon for a visit. She was glad she did when she heard the news of Tillie. She changed her evening plans and stayed for the rest of the day. Haseena had many words of comfort and reassurance. Her ministry skills came in very useful at these times. Heather and Cord felt much more at ease with her there.

Metrón went into the office. He usually didn't work the day after Christmas, but he received a call in, for some reason. He wasn't very happy about it. Everyone else tried to keep their minds occupied with things other than the three who had not come home.

The afternoon dragged on for what seemed an eternity. There were some board games played, some cards and lots of TV. Everyone stayed silent about Tillie, Liam and Adrian. No one wanted to express how the worry grew as the hours went by. It could be felt all over the apartment.

Darkness came in hues of purple, blue and a spark of pink. Heather watched the sunset from her chair in the living room. She spaced out on it and was feeling very tired, like she'd been drugged. She knew it was the worrying that made her feel that way. She gave into it like a defeated soldier in battle as she watched the sun sink into the horizon. Her thoughts of her three children still not returned made a knot in her stomach. She jumped up out of her chair. "All right.

That's it. I can't take it anymore. *Where are they?*" She demanded from everyone in the room.

Chloe and Kallias looked up from their game. Lyla played solitaire across from them.

"Oh dear, Ri." Firouza stood up immediately and came over to her sister. "Now, now, sweet sister...don't despair! You know your boys won't stop until they find her. That's why they haven't come back, you'll see. It's all going to be all right." She tried to hug her sister, but Heather bucked out of it.

"I know. I know, you're right. If I had to trust anyone to find her, it would be those two and you, Lyles honey." She looked to her only child left in the room. "It's just that I can only wait so long before I need to hear something. I feel so helpless here! Why haven't they at least called us or checked in or *something?*" She grabbed her sister's hands, pleading at her.

"Oh, darling!" Firouza's emotions fed off of others, especially her family's. She grabbed Heather into a quick embrace. "It will be all right." She looked her sister in the eyes and they locked on each other for a few seconds.

Heather calmed a little after several minutes. "I'm going to get something to eat. Anyone else?" Heather walked into the kitchen.

"Oh, let me, dear," Firouza said gently. Both ladies walked into the kitchen talking quietly to one another.

Just then the front door opened. Everyone jumped, Lyla even stood. Her nerves felt so tender and on edge, it was an instinct. Metrón walked into the entrance hall and everyone sagged like an old balloon with a slow leak.

He looked at Firouza in the kitchen with Heather. "Sorry, everybody. No news yet?"

"No, darling. No one is back yet," She gave him a quick smirk of a smile, trying to remain cheery.

"Well, there's no question." Metrón started as he walked into the living area. "You will stay here tonight and as long as it takes. I will go out tomorrow if they are not back…but I have faith that they will return." He walked up to Cord, shook his hand and hugged him briefly.

"Thank you Metrón. We are truly grateful for your kindness. Thank you." Cord said as he sat back down and tuned out to the television.

Chloe stood up. She moved into the center of the room. "I just wanted to say to you all here now," she began in a slightly louder than normal voice, "That I am wholeheartedly sorry for the trouble I have caused here today." Her last word was followed by whimpers and she started to cry.

Heather and Cord immediately went up to her and hugged her.

"Oh, sweetie. You sweet, sweet girl." Heather said with tears welling up in her eyes. "It wasn't your fault. I know you and Tillie have just met, but believe me, when she goes after something, there's no stopping her. This wasn't you at all, hon." Heather wiped Chloe's face with a tissue and tried to get her to calm down. Firouza and Metrón stood close to them as well.

"Thank you, both of you," Metrón said. "We know you are worried. We know how you love your children as we do ours and this is very hard for you. We will find the finish line to this, you will see." He patted Cord on the back.

"I just wanted to let you know that I didn't mean anything by leaving Tillie alone. I walk around here all the time by myself, so I didn't think anything of it. I am so very sorry." Chloe wiped her nose with the tissue.

"Thank you, Chloe. But like Heather said, when Tillie goes after something, there's really no stopping her." Cord repeated Heather's words and found a seat.

"Wait," Lyla said. "What did you say about Tillie?"

Cord tried to remember the words that just left his mouth. "What?"

"You said…about Tillie…and Mom said…" Lyla tried to get the words right before she said them. "You said, 'when Tillie goes after something, there's no stopping her', right?"

"Yeah, yeah, that's what I said. You know how she is." Cord was still unsure where Lyla was going.

"Well maybe she was doing just that," Lyla explained, feeling slightly excited and hopeful. "Maybe she was *going after something*...and that's what she's still doing." Lyla almost jumped where she stood, she felt so excited. She suddenly felt light and calm at the same time. She sat back down feeling like a feather.

"What are you saying? That everything is suddenly fine because Tillie was going after something?" Heather asked Lyla accusingly.

"Or someone," Lyla said almost to herself. "Yes. Basically. That's what I'm saying." Lyla suddenly felt her appetite return and helped herself to the snacks on the table.

Heather sat silently for a moment. She took Lyla's words into her brain and it felt like they swirled around in there looking for a place to land. Her head felt dizzy. She collapsed back into her chair. Cord and Lyla rushed to her side immediately.

"Oh, my gosh, Mom!" Lyla said. She grabbed Heather's hand.

"Heather, are you all right?" Cord wiped her hair out of her face.

Heather took a deep breath and collected herself. "Yes. Yes I'm fine." She looked at Lyla. "I'm okay. I think the stress of the day finally caught up to me."

"That and you've hardly eaten a bite." Firouza brought her a glass of juice. "Here, you can start with this."

"Thank you Fi," Heather replied. She took a sip of juice. The cold liquid felt good going down to her stomach. "You do have a point about Tillie. I hadn't thought of it that way. I was too busy worrying to really think about any other possibilities. Thank you, sweetie."

Lyla sat down near her mother. "Yes. Well, I am the logical one in the family, aren't I?" Lyla smiled.

"Thank goodness." Heather replied tiredly.

"Speaking of logical, the other thing that's been on my mind today is the test tomorrow. Do Li and I still have to take it if we haven't found Tillie yet?"

"Yes, I'm afraid you do." Metrón answered the question floating in the air like a speech bubble. "That was one of the things discussed today at the office. When I told my secretary about Tillie, the Council called me to let me know that, under no circumstances, are you and Liam to miss the test, or you will forfeit your opportunity to be inducted."

Kallias chimed in, "Man, that's harsh." He stayed quiet all day, but those few words said it all.

"Yes it is. But I am afraid that once these steps are put into motion, there is no stopping them." Metrón explained empathetically.

"Oh, wow. I was going to study all day today. Li and I were going to, I mean. I totally forgot. I hope he gets back soon. Should I wait for him? No. I'll just get going and then maybe I can catch him up when he gets here." Lyla said. She left the room to study.

The sun had set hours before. Dinner came and went. No word from Liam, Adrian or Tillie. Someone at dinner mentioned that maybe they all met up and are just having a grand 'ole time in the city. They all clung to that notion, maybe a bit too hard.

The door burst open and in almost fell Liam and Adrian. They startled everyone who was still awake. Looking bedraggled, the boys took their coats off and dragged themselves into the living room. They proceeded to tell everyone about their day. The most anyone remembered was, no Tillie.

The boys finished talking long enough to eat something. Heather and Cord explained to Liam about the test. At first he was angry, but was also very tired from the day's events, or lack thereof, so he didn't really argue about it. He felt that if he didn't pass, then he wouldn't care. Right now he only cared about finding his sister. Even after hearing

Lyla's point of view, the boys still felt they had to find her, sooner rather than later.

Liam and Lyla stayed up very late that night, studying as much as they could. They hadn't realized that there was so much to go through and were grateful that they could do it with such speed. Everyone else went to bed, but not everyone slept. Everyone felt some degree of worry, wonder and helplessness. This made for a restless night.

The next morning came as if the night sped up time. Lyla and Liam's test was at one o'clock, after lunch. Originally they all planned on doing lunch at one of the Zohros' favorite places, but now, all plans except for the test were off in case Tillie came back. They planned to stay in the apartment until the test, when Heather and Cord would take their children, while the rest of them stayed behind. Metrón had to go into the office, of course, so it was decided that he would take Heather, Cord and the children in early. Firouza promised to call Heather if she heard any news.

"Good luck, my dears. Try not to worry." Firouza bid to her niece and nephew. She remained positive for her sister's family.

Up on the seventh floor, Lyla and Liam studied like mad, while Heather and Cord paid a visit to Amalia, who was in the office with Metrón for some business. Before long, it was noon. Lyla and Liam got a quick introduction to their Aunt Amalia. They insisted they just have take-out for lunch, as they didn't want to waste a moment away from studying. Heather and Cord went out to get lunch for their students.

"Well, it was good running into Amalia, yes?" Cord said as they walked down the street.

"Yes. Yes it's so good to see all of my family here. Such a surprise from Amalia." Heather finished with a smile.

There was a lightness about their steps as they entered a deli nearby.

With their thoughts so full, next thing they knew, Heather and Cord were waiting for their two oldest children to take their first step to be inducted into Atlantis. They appeared patient, reading magazines, when Haseena came into the room. The three chatted and there was even laughter. It didn't look like a room of people worried about a missing teenager.

Two hours later, Lyla and Liam emerged. They looked as hopeful as they could, sat down quietly and greeted their family.

"We're to wait here until the tests are graded. Apparently it won't take long." Lyla said drearily.

"And they were right." Heather smiled at them and nodded her head toward the doorway.

The two children had barely sat down and already they were going to find out if they passed or failed. Lyla's hands started to sweat. Liam already gave up before he went into the test and felt edgy, ready to go look for Tillie. He didn't really care how he did and at the same time was grateful for the quick end to this obstacle in the way of finding his sister.

A severe looking woman came into the room.

"You have both passed." She declared. "Next you will be sent to find your sister, Tillie."

"Yes, thank you. We appreciate your understanding of us wanting to find our sister." Liam replied as he stood up and went to shake the woman's hand. He turned around and faced his family. "Now let's go get Tillie."

25

Quests

The woman proceeded, "I'm afraid you don't understand Liam. You will find Tillie. This is part two of your test. We know she has been missing since yesterday. We know where and when she went missing. We know everything."

Liam didn't hesitate, but got right up in the woman's face. "What do you mean? What is going on here?" He demanded quite forcefully. Cord grabbed his shoulder but he shook it off. He waited, panting as his blood pressure rose.

"Explain yourself, Miss." Lyla asked, more gently, but still very much concerned.

"Yes. Yes well..." the woman stepped back a bit and readjusted her glasses. "You see, you have now begun step two of your induction. We waste no time here for our inductees. This is your quest; to find Tillie, your sister."

She sniffed and adjusted her suit coat. Her shiny black hair was still tight and controlled which was more than anyone could say for the rest of her. Liam was very intimidating.

Liam backed away apologetically, "So, she's safe? You know that Tillie is safe?" He stood there like a statue, solid and unwavering.

"Yes, sir. She is most safe, of that you can be assured. This is your quest..."

Lyla interrupted, "Yes, you said that already." She stood up and rescued the woman from Liam. They both turned and everyone sat down.

Relief spread to the two test takers. They looked at their parents, learning that by now they always knew more than their children.

"Did you know about this then?" Liam asked more gently than his previous questions.

"Well, no. Not until today. You see, we just learned about it when you went in for your tests." Heather explained. "Amalia told us."

"Anyway, you guys are missing the point, aren't you? *Your sister is safe.*" Cord finished slowly, hoping that would help it to sink in.

There were a few seconds of silence then the woman cleared her throat and sat down. She proceeded to go over the rules of the quest. Apparently there were rules. With their heads spinning from the stress of the last eighteen or so hours, it was almost hard to hear what the woman said.

Luckily, when she finished with the technicalities, she handed both Liam and Lyla a notebook.

"The rules are written here, so as to not forget them. Do not lose this, or else memorize them first. You have until New Year's Day before midnight to find Tillie. The one clue we can give you both, is that she disappeared in the vicinity of the city. Once you leave this room, you will no longer be able to talk to one another about the quest, or anything else. You will be separated. Your rooms have already been arranged. Are there any questions?" Her pointy face looked bird-like.

"Not now, at least," Lyla stated. She figured if she couldn't think of any, then Liam probably didn't have any either.

"Yah, I have a question." Liam began, "What the..."

"Liam!" Heather cut him off. It made the woman jump a little bit. Liam breathed out an almost laugh.

"Well then," the woman concluded, "You know where to reach us if you think of anything to ask us. That information is also in the notebook. Take care of those."

With that, the woman stood up and said, "Good luck to you both, from the Council." She turned and exited as quietly as she had entered.

There was silence in the room and a lot of puzzled looks at each other. Lyla and Liam quietly looked over their notebooks for a few moments, then someone else came into the room.

"Mr. Liam Lundgren?"

Liam looked up in acknowledgement.

"Please come with me, sir." The young, dark haired man requested politely.

Liam stood up to follow the man. Heather and Cord grabbed him, hugged him, wished him luck and said goodbye.

Moments after Liam exited the room, an older woman came in and asked for Lyla. More goodbyes and hugs and the quests were underway.

The two were taken in separate elevators down to the lobby. Lyla saw Liam getting into a limousine as she came out to the main door from the elevator. She also saw one waiting for her.

Lyla suddenly felt very alone. For the first time in her life, she was without her family behind her to help her do what she had to do. *Tillie! Where oh where can she be? What would have possessed her to up and walk away from Chloe in a strange city?* The questions rose and flowed like the tide. Lyla got a pang in her chest. She suddenly missed home.

After only fifteen minutes, or so, the limo pulled up to a high-rise hotel. The car ride was quiet, even though the old woman sat with Lyla. Lyla was so wrapped up in her thoughts, she hadn't noticed whether or not the woman spoke since they got into the car.

"We're here," the woman said brightly. "My name is Bertha Jorken, by the way. I am your assistant for your quest." She held out her hand.

Lyla shook her hand and was directed to exit the car.

"I will be your right hand. If you need anything, you just let me know. We're staying in the suite here and we will each have our own room." Bertha finished as they entered the building.

"But my things," Lyla began, "I never packed anything."

"Oh, don't you worry about that, Lyla. Your parents were told to pack before you came to the test this morning. Everything is taken care of. Your things are already here."

"Oh," Lyla said faintly but surprised. They went into the elevator and up to the top floor.

Liam entered his bedroom at another hotel suite. He thought about Tillie as he unpacked. His head spun from all that happened in such a short time. He wondered if he had time for a nap.

His assistant knocked on the open door. "Excuse me, sir. I was wondering when you will want to get going? Oh and I'm sorry, my name is Brian Barrison." He held out his hand to shake Liam's. His hazel eyes looked full of excitement and very young. Liam wondered how someone so young got such a job as this.

Liam grabbed his hand, a bit too strongly, then shook it more gently.

"Hi, Brian. So, you're going to be here with me then, right?"

"Yes, sir." Brian replied.

"You do what I say and if I need anything, you'll do your best to get it for me, right?"

"That's right, sir."

"Okay, first off, stop calling me sir. I can hardly be older than you, so," Liam got cut off.

"If you'll excuse me, sir, I cannot bring myself to not give you the respect you deserve as an inductee. I could never mistreat you that way." Brian rubbed his hand slightly and blushed.

"Oh. Well then," Liam rethought his harsh mood and tried to calm himself with a large breath. "I'm feeling exhausted from all this testing and questing. I know it sounds awful, me wanting to rest and my sister missing and all, but I've just got to catch a couple of winks."

Brian looked at Liam, puzzled.

"What I'm saying, Brian, is that I need a nap. I think better on a rested head. So, feel free to do what you like while I sleep, but wake me up in one hour. Don't let me sleep longer than that, or I get all groggy. You think you can handle that for our first line of business?" Liam finished putting the last of his packed clothes in the closet.

"Yes, sir, absolutely. One hour. I will wake you then. Have a good rest then, sir." Brian backed out of the doorway, closing the door with him.

Ugh. Sir. Eesh, thought Liam. He put his shoes and empty bag into the closet. He went over and sat down on the bed. He put his head into his hands and heaved a sigh. "Tillie," was all he said before he passed out on the bed before even turning down the bedspread.

Liam awoke coughing, choking. There was smoke everywhere. He couldn't see the way out. He could barely breathe. He grabbed the bed covers, ripped a piece and tied it around his mouth and nose. Catching his breath a bit, he dropped off the bed. There was water all over the floor. He dipped his face into the water to wet the cloth. He crawled toward the doorway. Down on the floor he saw where the door was and headed in its direction. He pulled it open. A huge explosion of fire and smoke burst through and pushed him back to the bed. Coughing...coughing...

"Sir! Sir! Liam!" Brian shouted, shaking Liam awake.

"Get out! Save yourself!" Liam shouted, although he wasn't even awake yet. He grabbed Brian's arm and threw it off. "*Go!*"

"Sir! Please wake up! Are you all right?" Brian reached for him again.

Liam sat up and grabbed Brian's arms hard. His eyes opened wide. He coughed and sputtered, trying to figure out where he was.

Brian looked shocked. He kept pleading for Liam to come to his senses and tried to free himself.

"Sir. Liam. Please wake up. It's all right. You're all right. *Wake up!*" Brian yelled. That brought Liam back to reality.

"Wha...What's going on?" Liam blinked furiously, trying to focus. He released Brian's arms and saw Brian scurry into the corner of the room.

"Jesus!" Brian exclaimed, catching his breath. "Are you okay?" He rubbed his arms, but kept his distance.

"Oh, jeez," Liam started, still feeling out of breath. He was sweating as well, which he had just noticed and wiped his brow. He sat up and Brian backed up more. Then Liam just sat there, breathing heavy. He put his head in his hands and shook it side to side. "Oh man, oh man," he repeated several times. He looked up to find Brian just as scared as a deer in headlights. "Brian man, I'm sorry, so sorry. Did I hurt you? What did I do?" He reached out to Brian, but Brian stood firm in his place.

"I'm...I'm okay," he stuttered. "I'm all right. Are we to go somewhere now? When you get yourself together, I mean?" He straightened himself up and awaited orders, appearing more back to normal.

"Oh, crap, I hurt you, didn't I?" Liam stood up and started to cross over to Brian. But Brian went to the doorway. "Look man, I didn't mean it. It's these dreams. These freaking dreams are driving me nuts." He huffed and turned around so as not to scare Brian out of the room.

"But you have to tell me what I did, or I'll go crazy thinking about it instead of Tillie. Please," he said as gently as he could muster. "What did I do?"

"You grabbed my arms. Hard. I know you didn't mean to. You were right out of your mind with sleep, I could see it on your face. I'm all right though, so you needn't worry about it. Can I get you something to drink? Maybe that will calm your nerves." There were a few moments of silence, which both welcomed after the turmoil.

"Yes. Yes, that would be fine. I don't care what it is, as long as it's not coffee. I don't think we need to be any jumpier than this today."

Brian turned to leave and Liam asked, "Did I say anything?"

"You told me to go." Brian answered, turning back around. "To save myself. Then you yelled for me to go. That's when you grabbed my arms." There was silence as Liam looked tortured. "I'm sorry I had to yell at you, sir, but I thought it was the only way to reach you." Brian turned back and left the room.

Liam paced and thought about the dream. *What did it mean? These dreams are so strong and intense. Look what I did to Brian. Will it get worse? And where the hell was I in this fire? Did it have something to do with Tillie?* His pacing grew faster as the thought of Tillie in such danger made him practically manic.

Tillie. Got to think of where she is. Get on task. He figured Lyla had it all planned out by now and all he had done so far was sleep. Not even very well at that.

Brian came back with a tall glass with some liquid and ice in it.

"Pomegranate juice, sir." Brian held it out for Liam. "It's about all I could find in the refrigerator."

"Thanks man." Liam took the glass gently and gulped down a nice swig. The cold liquid felt numbing on the body as well as the mind. Liam set the drink down. He sat on the bed.

"Look, Brian," he began, "I know you think it's respectful to call me, 'sir' and I do appreciate it." He wiped his brow again. "But can you please just stick to Liam for now? The sir throws me off and I really need to think of where my sister might be. I can't have these verbal distractions, okay?"

"Yes, sir." Brian answered, then smirked. "I mean, okay, Liam. I will try."

"Good. Also, I will never have you wake me again. I'll use the alarm clock. Deal?" Liam stood up and offered his hand.

Brian accepted and smiled back. "Deal for sure," he said.

Liam apologized once more. "Again, I'm really sorry about the arms thing. I don't know what gets into me with these dreams lately. I can't figure out what they mean, if anything." He took another gulp of his drink. He felt more calm.

"Maybe it's a past life trying to work itself out," Brian offered.

"A past life? You believe in that stuff, do you, Brian?"

So full of his own thoughts, this idea intrigued Liam and he tuned in more finely to the conversation.

"Oh, sure," Brian answered. "Atlantis teaches us that our dreams are very important things to listen to. Ones as strong as yours must be trying to tell you something. Oftentimes our past lives can remain in our subconscious. They come out in dreams if there are unresolved issues."

"That, or I'm just nuts, huh?" Liam said with a laugh and another sip of juice.

"No, sir, I mean, Liam. Sorry. I don't think you're nuts. Dreams that powerful deserve to be looked at. If it's not a past life, perhaps you are linked to someone else's. That can happen when you share a strong Atlantean gene bond with someone else. But no matter what it is, you shouldn't ignore them. You should talk about it with someone. Someone who knows about dreams. I'm sure I could find someone for you if you like, back at the Council. You just let me know whenever you wish. I'm not here to evaluate, that's just my simple advice. You can, of course, do whatever you like."

"Well, Brian, I appreciate that, thanks. But right now, we have to get on task. I feel like we've already fallen behind and we haven't even started to look for my sister."

"Yes, well," Brian began, but was cut short.

"Well nothing, Brian. Look. Are you familiar with this city? You from here, grow up here, lived here a while?"

"Yes. I've been working here at the Council for almost eight years now." Brian's young face made the almost eight years hard to believe.

"How old are you, man? If you don't mind me asking." Liam finally managed to use some manners.

"I'm thirty-eight, why?" Brian answered with a question.

"Wow. Thirty-eight? You don't look a day over twenty. That's terrific. Good for you."

"Well, thanks to my Atlantean heritage, I will look young for a very long time. I don't mind, it has its advantages." Brian smiled.

"Huh. I wonder if I'll be the same way then." Liam said more quietly, mostly to himself.

"Oh, most likely si--," Brian stopped himself. "Most likely, Liam. With your mother being one hundred percent Atlantean and your father being such a good percentage as well, there's no way you're going to age like manna."

"Really? Wait...my dad is a good percentage Atlantean? How do you know that?"

"Well, we assistants have been briefed on our clients and their backgrounds, so we can be of the utmost help to them during the quests. I had to study up on you while you studied for the first test."

"So, do my parents know about their heritage? I mean, do they each know that my dad is also somewhat Atlantean?" This thought rose Liam's curiosity to a new level of head spinning.

"Well yes, I would think so. They are the ones who supplied the information about themselves. Of course we follow up with background checks, but in your family's case, the Council already knows so many of them, it was hardly necessary."

"Damn," Liam slipped. "This day just keeps getting better and better, doesn't it?"

"I'm not sure what you mean, but we should probably get going with the task, don't you think?" Brian stood looking like an impatient butler.

Liam had so many questions flying around in his head, he couldn't think where to begin. He shut the mental doors of all the topics that didn't have to do with Tillie and the quest for now. He had to concentrate.

"Yes. That's exactly what we have to do," Liam answered. "So, you know the city, right?"

"Yes," Brian got down to business too.

"Good. I need a map of the part of the city where my aunt Firouza lives. I'll show you where Tillie was last seen."

"Sounds good. I have a map in my room. I'll go get it for you." Brian left the room.

26

Pass or Fail

Two days passed. Lyla didn't feel any closer to finding her sister than when she found out it was her quest. Time was going by quickly; they were halfway through the week. She felt so frustrated. She'd gone over and over the mapped out area where Tillie went missing. She and Bertha walked those streets for the last two days. They were both drained.

Lyla was in her room meditating, hoping for something to come to her. Something that she'd missed. *There must be some little detail that I overlooked. There has to be a clue out there!*

Nothing. Nothing came to mind at all. She stayed in meditation for a bit longer, letting her mind relax and wander.

She thought about how they'd asked the people in the streets if they'd seen Tillie. Lyla had a picture of Tillie in her wallet and showed it to everyone in the coffee shop for the last two days. Bertha took it around yesterday to the street vendors in the area, while Lyla scoped the coffee shop for suspicious characters. Nothing. For two days.

Lyla got very good at meditating and although some of her sessions would last over an hour, they gave her a clarity that she didn't have before. She felt much more comfortable in her own skin and also with her newfound skill of controlling the weather. Most of the time, right after a meditation, Lyla found learning new things to be of great ease. She tried to use this new technique to find clues to her sister. She also tried to calm her nerves about her sister being alone for so long for the first time in her life.

Being the big sister, Lyla sometimes had those bad dreams parents have about their own children, about her siblings. She felt very responsible for them and worried for them, much like their mother, when they were in trouble. She couldn't remember a time in her life where she didn't feel she was partly responsible for them. Even though her parents never made her feel that way, it was something just born in her. She never complained about it, or felt burdened by it. It was just the way she was. Most of the time, she was grateful for having her siblings in her life. Being so shy in her youth, she always had them around her for company. Even through the little fights or arguments, Lyla was the one they all turned to, to solve their problems. She was good at it and it made her feel loved and important in the family.

There was one time she could remember Tillie and she were on the beach, Tillie was about five. They'd spent a lot of time there, so it was nearly mundane to them. Sometimes they got bored and whiny. The day Lyla remembered was a hot, sunny day and Tillie was throwing a tantrum because she wanted to be home, not at the beach. Their mother tried her best to calm her down and distract her, but Tillie wasn't falling for it. With tears in her eyes and almost a Rumplestiltskin stomp from Tillie, Lyla saw what was coming next. She felt instant compassion with her mother and went over to Tillie.

"Hey there, Tillie." She said as cheerfully as she could muster, with Tillie's screams drowning out most of her voice. "Want to build a crab castle with me?"

"A what?" Tillie sniffled and wiped at her face, blowing the oncoming fit away.

"A crab castle. We can build a castle and put the crabs in it. After all, they need a place to stay on such a hot day on the beach." Lyla smiled and looked excited to be with Tillie.

This made Tillie turn almost one hundred eighty degrees. She went from tantrum to playful happy in mere seconds.

"Crabs! Yeah! Let's do it." She stood up, grabbed Lyla by the hand and dragged her off to build a castle.

Lyla looked back at her mom, who lipped a "Thank you" to her and blew her a kiss. She smiled and ran off to build their first crab castle.

Lyla smiled in her meditation. She wondered where that memory came from. She hadn't thought about Tillie's temper tantrums in so long. Things were so different now that they were all older. A melancholy nostalgia came over her. She held onto the meditation, concentrating on her breathing. As she did, images flashed in her mind. They were fast, like the lessons on Atlantis. Lyla's eyelids fluttered furiously, like she was having a vivid dream. These images were confusing; there was nothing she could recognize. Everything turned into hues of rainbow colors flashing before her.

She suddenly felt like she was swimming, like she was underwater. She didn't feel panicked for herself, but for someone else. There was someone there. Who was it? There were air bubbles all around. She couldn't see anything else. Something grabbed her back and she turned quickly. There he was, just a boy. He couldn't have been older than five. Beautiful blond hair floating around his head and the most innocent blue eyes she'd ever seen.

Lyla's eyes popped open in surprise. She blinked a few times, catching her breath. *What was that? Was it a dream?* She checked around, she was in the center of the bed, but was still sitting up, so it couldn't have been a dream. Still out of breath, she got up, went to the window and threw the curtains open. *Was the weather all right?* She felt revved up enough to have caused something. There was nothing but sunshine and calmness out there.

Lyla looked puzzled. She was still blinking, taking some deep breaths to calm herself. Still trying to figure out what exactly she saw.

Just then, Bertha came into the room. "Are you all right, Miss? I called you, but you didn't answer. I know you don't like to be disturbed while you are meditating, but there was a phone call for you. Are you all right?" She asked again. "You look like you just saw a ghost or something. Let me get you something to drink. You've been in here for quite a while now." Bertha finished and left the room before Lyla could reply.

"Thank you." Lyla called out after her. A few more deep breaths and Lyla felt like she'd come back to earth. Everything felt solid again. She felt awake and clear. That face, that innocent, adorable face was bright and stark in her mind as well.

"Well, it has to be a clue then." Bertha offered her opinion after Lyla told her what happened. "That must be important. We'll have to keep it in mind while we search."

"Yes. Yes I agree." Lyla added as she sipped the chamomile and honey tea Bertha brought in for her. "It obviously is important, I felt everything so vividly. Do you think it was a connection to Tillie? Is it possible that I might feel what she's feeling if I concentrate on her enough?"

"Well, I don't know about that," Bertha replied. "I do know that your family is close and that your heritage being what it is...I suppose it might be possible."

"What do you mean, my 'heritage being what it is'? Are we special for some reason?" Lyla finished her tea and placed the cup and saucer on the bedside table.

The two ladies walked into the living room and sat down. Bertha looked nervous from Lyla's question, but Lyla was steadfast and waited eagerly to hear more about her family.

"Well, I'm not sure it's my place to say, Miss," Bertha started, "But you do have a long line in Atlantis. That is common knowledge to most of us there."

"Really?" Lyla asked surprised. "So, what are we, like...famous or something?" She finished with a guffaw at her own words.

"Well, yes, I guess you could say you are," explained Bertha. "I mean, you're not celebrities like people up here, manna style, if you will. But you're family has been around so long, everyone simply knows you or knows of you. It's more like...well...up here the closest thing I could compare it to would be royalty. Yes. Like the royals in England and all that? That's your family in Atlantis."

"Whoa," Lyla breathed. "Royalty? Really? Us? Wow. It's gonna take some time to wrap my head around that one." She stood up to go back to her bedroom.

"Wh..where are you going? Shouldn't we be going out to search?" Bertha stood up as well.

"Well yes, we'll need to search again this afternoon." Lyla focused back on reality. She turned back toward Bertha. "Get your things ready, I need to sketch up this face. I can't get it out of my mind and it might help if we can show a picture of this boy to some people too. Give me ten minutes...well, maybe twenty." Lyla turned and went into the bedroom.

Bertha scurried away and rounded up a pad of paper and pencil for Lyla. She knew she wouldn't have anything to sketch with. She brought them in the room as quickly as she could. She found Lyla searching semi-frantically through drawers.

"Here you are, Miss." Bertha handed her the pad and pencil.

"You know, sometimes you're like a dream come true, Bertha. Thank you." She took them both in hand and got right to drawing.

Bertha left her in silence and went to pack things they'd been using the last couple of days. Lyla was not an artist by any means. She didn't draw on a regular basis, other than simple art classes through school, which now felt like a lifetime ago. She looked at this blank paper and wondered how she was going to do this.

Lyla closed her eyes. The boy came to her like he was standing right in front of her. His image was so clear, she just knew she would be able to draw enough of his face to be able to use it today. She had made lines on the paper before she'd even opened her eyes.

It wasn't much longer than twenty minutes before she emerged from the room, happy with her sketch. She showed it to Bertha and asked what she thought of the rendering. She wanted to make sure it looked like a person and not some creature or modern art.

Bertha was more than pleased. She was thrilled. "Oh, my. Oh, my, Lyla. That is really very good." She sat down almost in shock.

"What is it? What's wrong?" Lyla went over to her, setting the drawing down on the table.

"Nothing, my dear, nothing, I'm fine. It's just that I think I know who that is and I'm not sure I'm allowed to say any more."

"Oh, jeez, oh!" Lyla started, "Well, that's all right Bertha, don't worry. If you recognized him, then maybe others will too. That's actually good. We're taking this with us then today, let's go."

The two ladies hustled out of the apartment, down, once again, onto the streets searching for Tillie, with a little more hope than they had yesterday.

Back at Liam's apartment, things were going just about as slowly as they could. Liam sat on the sofa, vegging out in front of the television. It had been four days of searching and nothing. Liam's nightmares got worse by the day as well. It seemed every night there was a fire, or a flood, or both. He woke up so much during the night, he felt groggy all day. Sitting in front of the television was the only way he could relax and think.

Brian was at the dining table going over the map, tracing and retracing their steps, marking where they'd been so as not to backtrack unless they wanted to.

"We've covered this whole area." he said in frustration.

"I know, I know." Liam said halfheartedly, staring at the screen. "I don't know what else to do." He said feeling defeated. "I hope Lyles is having better luck. I mean, someone should be inducted after all this." He finished to himself. Feeling like he failed made him feel sleepy. Of course, the nightmares didn't help either.

"I know, I wish I could be more of help to you Liam." Brian tried to make him feel better when he could. It was the least he felt he could do for Liam. It had been a futile few days and both of them were so tired.

"Let's go over it again." Liam began. He sat upright on the couch. "We questioned people at the coffee shop, three times. We hit every news stand and street vendor in a twelve block area. No one seems to know or remember seeing her. We've been up every street around the coffee shop...I don't know...a dozen times? We're obviously missing something here." He laid back down in defeat.

"I know, I know." Brian added. He had much more energy and his frustration showed. "But what did we miss? How can these clues to your sister be so obscure? What out there would have caught her attention so?" He went back to perusing the map.

"What did you say there, Bri?" Liam sat up again. He actually stood up this time and walked over to the map. He sat next to Brian.

"What? What did I say?" Brian said, confused.

"You said something about catching Tillie's attention?"

"Yes. Well, what reason would she have for leaving your cousin at the coffee shop to begin with? We've gone over and over this, Liam, but we still don't really know."

"Yah. Yah you're right. We really need to think of what she might have seen that could bring her to leave by herself. Let's think...like Tillie. Oh, God, this isn't gonna work." Liam put his head in his hands once again.

"Wait now, just wait a minute. I know she's a teenage girl and all, but she's your sister too. You've been connected your whole lives. There must be some way of tuning into that.

What would catch her eye in this big city?" Brian looked at the map again, hoping to see a building or marker around the coffee shop that would trigger something.

"What would catch Tillie's eye?" Liam said in thought and really tried to put himself in her shoes for a moment. Of course he'd been trying to do this for the last four days, but had no luck. He closed his eyes and stayed quiet for a minute.

The rocking shook him awake. It was violent on the sea and everyone ran around in panic trying to control the ship...

"Liam!" Brian shouted, shaking Liam at the same time. "Jeez man, I know you haven't been sleeping well, but damn! Can you concentrate on your sister here? I know I'm here to help, but I can't very well do that if you just keep falling asleep."

"Oh, crap, man, I'm sorry! I did it again! I've really gotta try and get some rest tonight. These dreams are really messing with my head. Hey! Do you think they have anything to do with Tillie and where she might be?" Liam felt he was suddenly onto something.

"Well, you said you started having these dreams when you came to Chicago, right?"

"Yeah," Liam replied.

"Well, how can they be about Tillie then, when she didn't go missing until four days ago? Sorry to burst your bubble Liam, but I don't think they have to do with Tillie. You might want to concentrate a little harder on her and a little less on those dreams for now." Brian stood up and went over to the kitchen.

"Tillie...Tillie...where are you girl?" Liam said quietly, this time keeping his eyes open. He looked down at the map, but didn't focus, just let his stare lead the way.

"What would make you leave Chloe?" He asked quietly. "Something, or someone caught your eye." He said aloud.

"Someone." Brian said as he came back to the table. "It must have been some *one* caught her eye. Maybe a friend of hers was here and she didn't know it and saw them out the window." Brian was so eager, it often made Liam feel better about this whole quest thing.

"Well yes, I suppose that could have happened." Liam began, his thoughts still in progress. "But why would that person she knew lead her somewhere off into an Atlantean quest?"

"Maybe the Council contacted them to help with her kidnapping?" Brian tried to sound cheerful, but the word kidnapping never sounded like a good thing.

"That seems a bit odd, doesn't it? I mean what are the odds that she'd even have a friend coming here for the holidays or whatever at the same time as her and she didn't know about it?"

"Maybe it was all set up by the Council to begin with?" Brian offered.

"Maybe, but maybe they just used someone to look like someone she knew." Liam drifted off into thought.

There was silence, then it broke.

"Yes! That's got to be it. She thought she saw someone she knew, so she left the coffee shop and followed them to say hello." Liam stood up and his fist came down onto the table.

"That sounds good Liam, keep going." Brian sounded like a cheerleader.

"Well, that's all really, but I think that definitely would have been the thing to make her leave Chloe at the coffee shop. She's the social one in the family, you know. She knows someone wherever we go. So, it stands to reason that she saw someone and either she knew them, or thought she knew them enough to follow them."

"Yes and if they were a member of the Council, or someone working for them..."

"Then they'd lead her right where they wanted her." Liam finished Brian's thought.

They both gave each other a high five. Brian had set lunch on the table and they both sat and ate. Liam had a whole new eagerness to his day and ate like there was a race.

"So after we finish lunch, I want to see pictures of the Council. I want to know the names of all the people involved in inductions." He kept talking, over Brian's incoming protest. "I don't care if it takes the rest of the week, Brian, I want names."

"Yes, Liam, I know, but I don't think I can give you that information. I don't even know how to find out who they all are." Brian said timidly. In just the few days he'd been working with Liam, he knew Liam didn't like being contradicted.

"Damn! It's always something in the way." Liam startled Brian. "Why can't you just disclose whatever information I need?"

"Well, I can, except for the information I can't get. You see, I don't know everyone on the Council. My job isn't that high up. I'm sorry, Liam." Brian tried to think quickly of how to resolve this and continue on the clue they had. "But maybe we don't need to know who she was following, just that she followed someone and they lead her somewhere." Brian added feeling proud of his deduction.

Liam sat quiet for a moment, then agreed. "Yes. I guess that's true. Good thinking, Bri." He was back on nickname terms with Brian. That was a good thing. "So where was she lead to?"

Both of them went back to looking at the map underneath their plates. It was back to looking at every building, this time with a bit more purpose.

Meanwhile, Lyla's search for Tillie and the boy continued. She and Bertha went back to all the places they'd been, showing the sketch to everyone they could. No one could identify him. Except, of course, Bertha. Lyla kept asking her from time to time who he was. She even tried to trick Bertha into answering the question mixed into some other ones. She didn't fall for it.

"Can't you just check with the Council if it would be alright if you told me?" Lyla asked at the end of day five. "I mean, you didn't tell me about him, I saw him on my own.

Bertha, you're the only one who can help me with this." Lyla looked at Bertha imploringly.

"Oh, I know you're right." Bertha exclaimed. "I'll call them first thing in the morning. I just hope that's not against the rules." Bertha finished to herself as she went off to bed.

After Lyla's first vision, she decided to make time at least once a day to meditate. She felt she was onto something with it and hoped the visions continued. There wasn't much time left to find Tillie. She wondered how Liam was doing. *Had he already found her? Would I be notified?* Tired, after such a long day of inquisition, Lyla headed off for a bedtime meditation. Maybe it would clear her head enough to figure out tomorrow's plan.

Meditation was particularly short, as the bed felt too comfortable to sit up for too long. Lyla's head reached the pillow just in time for sleep to take over.

Morning of day six came with a bright outlook for Lyla. She felt clear and hopeful for some reason. She sat up in bed and started a morning meditation, as she couldn't remember meditating before going to bed. She remembered that she had dreams the night before, but couldn't quite remember what they were. They were fading fast, so she felt it a good time to clear her head from the night's activity.

Sitting in the middle of the bed, Lyla took three deep breaths with her eyes closed. As she exhaled her third breath, a red-orange light flashed in her face. Her eyes popped open, as she felt the light was in her room. There was nothing out of the ordinary there. She closed her eyes immediately upon another breath. She tried to keep it slow and steady. The red light flashed again. This time she held her eyes shut and pushed her breath out a bit harder for some cleansing. Suddenly, among the flashing red-orange glow, a picture came into view. Lyla didn't know what it was and this time she could feel her eyelids flashing. She held them closed, as she didn't want to lose what she saw.

The picture came into focus and she saw it was a book or a pamphlet or something like that. It had the words,

Oceanography, a Hobby, with a photograph of a boat on the ocean, with people diving into the water. Just as Lyla made out the words on the pamphlet, it was gone. There was nothing now and her eyes fluttered open.

"Yes!" Lyla shouted as she got out of bed and ran to find Bertha.

Bertha was already in the kitchen making breakfast for the two of them. She was confused by Lyla's excitement, but listened intently over biscuits, fresh fruit and tea. She heard Lyla mention the pamphlet and exclaimed, "Oh! Oh, really?"

"Yes, that's what it said. *Oceanography, a Hobby* on the front with..." she was interrupted.

"Yes, I know what you are talking about dear." Bertha suddenly sounded in charge. "I know just the place. We've been past it probably a dozen times. I always thought it was odd to have papers out on a table in the winter. But I didn't think to stop there, no one ever does. It's a basic tourist trap."

"Oh, gosh! I think I know where you're talking about. I didn't even think to look at what was on the table there, because yeah, there were so many touristy people and I was too busy to bother. Well, I should have known, Tillie is a tourist, Bertha. We've got to get going." Lyla finished another bite of biscuit, drank the rest of her tea and went off to get dressed. "This is it, Bertha. I can feel it." The door closed behind her.

Bertha took out what looked like the same device as Firouza had when they were on the boat tour. She opened it and typed furiously. She finished her tea as well, closed the device and went to get dressed. A smile was stuck to her face like someone slapped it there.

Before too long, the two were back on the street, this time with direction and purpose. They were going straight to the table with the papers on it and Lyla felt it all the way to her toes that this was where she'd find Tillie. They jumped into a cab and were on their way.

"Hey, you know what's funny?" Liam asked Brian as they walked down the street from the coffee shop where Tillie was last seen.

"No, I don't. Not at this point." Brian answered.

"Well, we've been out on these streets every day. You would think I would have run into Lyla by now, you know? I mean, she must be doing the same thing as us, right? Combing the streets, looking for Tillie." Liam went silent.

"Gee, I guess you're right." Brian said. His hand went into his pocket and he gripped a device nervously. "Let's try down this way Liam." Brian suggested. He looked behind them and led Liam down another block. He saw Lyla and Bertha crossing the street down about a block. He and Bertha had to keep in touch about their whereabouts, so as not to come in contact with each other. It was of the utmost importance, they were both told when they were put on assignment, that the two Lundgrens not come in contact with each other during the quest.

"Anything familiar here?" Liam asked, pulling Brian back to the task at hand.

"What? Well, yeah sure, everything. We've been here like a dozen times, Liam, so what are you talking about?"

"Exactly, Brian. So, why did you pull me this way when we've already been here and found nothing?" Liam stopped walking, facing Brian for an answer.

"What? Oh. Well I thought..."

"You thought nothing." Liam cut him off. "What the hell is going on here? Are you trying to make me fail or something? Is that it?" Liam's voice got louder and some passersby looked at them.

Brian got nervous. He really didn't know how hot Liam's temper might get and he also couldn't tell him about what he was just thinking. He had to cover up and quick. "No, Liam, no. Not at all. Look, calm down..."

"Don't tell me to calm down! My sister is out here somewhere and you are supposed to be helping me. You know what? I don't even care." His voice went down to a more normal level. "You're not helping, so go back to the apartment. I'll meet you back there when I'm done out here."

Brian looked like someone who just got dumped. He was afraid that if he left Liam alone on the street he would find Lyla for sure. He tried to make amends.

"Liam. Look man, I wasn't trying to kill your efforts, honest. I got turned around and picked the wrong street to turn down. That's all. Don't be mad. It was an honest mistake. I'm really sorry. Let me help you."

Liam walked, Brian followed. "Fine." He said gruffly. "But from now on, I say where we go, got it?"

"Yes, got it. Absolutely." Brian answered most obediently. He shuffled off after Liam's fast pace, glad to still be on the job.

Meanwhile, Lyla and Bertha came up to the building with the table full of papers in the winter.

"What is this place anyway?" Lyla asked as they approached the tables.

There were so many people, it was hard to get in to see anything on the tables. The ladies just stood back, awaiting their turn. Lyla looked all around the place to see if anything would trigger a vision or something.

"It's just a tourist place, like I said earlier." Bertha answered. "I wouldn't have thought of it as somewhere Tillie would go, as what you've told me, she's not the hobby/book type."

"No, that's true." Lyla said with a smile.

They saw an opening in the crowd around one of the tables. They took their chance and made their way in. There were pamphlets scattered all about, looking like a go-fish card pile. Lyla hardly knew where to look first.

Bertha shuffled through papers. "Oceanography...oceanography..." she said as she flipped through piles of pamphlets.

Lyla closed her eyes for a moment and breathed out. She pictured the pamphlet she saw earlier back in the room. It was clear. She kept her eyes closed and felt through the papers on the table. She could almost tell what they looked like by how they felt. The picture in her head was so clear, she could tell the ones in her hands weren't the one in her mind. She opened her eyes and looked around the table. She saw nothing like the one in her mind.

"This has to be the place though, right?" She asked Bertha hopefully.

"Well, my dear, let's just keep looking. There are lots of papers here." Bertha said cheerfully.

Lyla walked to the next table. There was hardly anything on this one and it looked very picked over. She felt a heavy feeling in her chest. She felt sad.

"Nothing. Nothing. Day six and still nothing." She said, defeated once again.

Bertha kept shuffling through papers and pamphlets.

Suddenly the red flash Lyla saw earlier in the morning came to her. Her eyes were open, yet all she could see was the red-orange light. She stood still; looked, waited, hoped. A bright white globe of light came into the center and the red-orange light diminished, leaving the orb of white light hanging there.

"Lyla. Lyla dear, are you all right?" Bertha grabbed hold of her arm.

"What?" Lyla blinked, trying to focus her eyes. The white light in the center of her vision didn't go away. She saw that the white orb was in fact a light inside the building. Her eyes came into focus on the inside of the building and she saw many globes of light hanging over tables.

"Bertha, can we go inside?" Lyla asked going toward the door.

"Well, I don't know." Bertha answered, "I don't see why not."

"There's no handle." Lyla said, still trying to look inside.

"Well then push the door, dear." Bertha suggested.

"Oh. Right. Push." Lyla said as she did push the door and it opened. She turned to Bertha and smiled.

The two went inside, looking around like children in wonder. Lyla saw two people at the front desk and went up to them. She took the sketch out of her pocket.

"Hello there. My name is Lyla. I am looking for my sister. I believe, well, we believe that she was last seen with this little boy. I think they might have been here. Possibly." She showed the sketch to the two people and waited patient, but hopeful.

"Your sister you say? What was your name again? Lilly?" the woman across the counter asked.

"Lyla, Lyla Lundgren. My sister is Tillie. She has sandy blond curly hair, she's hard to miss." Lyla described Tillie.

"Lundgren you say?" The slender, tall man across the counter asked, more interested in the situation now. "Well, we haven't seen a Lundgren in these parts in a very long time, have we, Gina?"

"No, I daresay, we haven't." the woman replied.

It was like the two of them forgot Lyla was there. Apparently dropping the name Lundgren had this effect on people. The fact that they reacted so to the name, led Lyla to understand that they must know about Atlantis in some way. She knew she was on the right track. She persisted.

"Eh-hem," she started. "Yes, well, like I said, my sister, Tillie *Lundgren* is missing. Perhaps you saw her come in here, oh, say, six days or so ago?"

"Oh, a Lundgren, in here, six days ago you say?" The woman said and tilted her head up as if in thought. She looked at the man next to her, then back to them. "No, I don't seem to recall anyone of that name or description coming in here six days ago."

"Were you working here at that time?" Bertha added.

"What time was it?" the man inquired.

"It was in the morning, December twenty-sixth, before eleven a.m." Lyla answered.

"Were we in that day, dear?" the man asked his co-worker.

"Well yes. Remember I was so hung over that morning? You had to take most of our customers." She finished with a laugh and he joined in.

"Oh, how could I forget. You were a mess." The two continued laughing.

"I see." Lyla interrupted their reminiscing. "Well, can you tell me, does everyone who comes in here have to go through you here at the desk?"

"Well no, sweetie, we're information, not security." the woman smiled at her, then laughed some more with her partner.

Lyla could see that would be all the help they would get from those two.

"C'mon," she said to Bertha. The two of them walked into the room with the globes of light, leaving the giggling behind them.

Their eyes adjusted to the indoor lighting and they could see many people around at the tables, chatting, studying, they weren't quite sure what was happening. Many of them had funny hats on their heads. Lyla smirked at the colorful array of them. She thought, *It's no wonder Tillie followed these if she saw them.*

The two ladies made it to the back of the room. Nothing clued them into Tillie. Lyla got no vibe as she kept herself open to them. When they reached the back of the room, they turned around and surveyed the entire area.

"Should we start asking people if they've seen her?" Lyla thought out loud.

"I suppose we could. The picture too?" Bertha added.

"Yes." Lyla took the picture out again.

They walked back through the room, slowly. Lyla tried to decide who to ask first. She didn't want to interrupt or bother anyone, so she quickly rehearsed in her head how to ask what she needed to know.

Just then, out of the corner of her eye, a red flash appeared. She stopped in her steps, Bertha looked at her. She focused on the place the flash came from. It was a dark spot behind the counter where they had come in. She focused again and could see a hallway.

27

Trials and Errors

"Down there, let's go." Lyla said quietly. She noticed some people staring at her.

"But aren't we going to ask anybody..."

"No, not just yet." Lyla answered Bertha's unfinished question.

The two made their way to the hallway. They walked down slowly. Lyla wasn't sure where the flash came from as there were many doors in this hall. Most of them were closed. The ones that were open were easy to see before they even got to them, their light cut through the hallway shadows. But none of them had the orange-red light coming out of them. Until one of them did.

A flash, quick, but both ladies saw it, all the way at the end of the hall. They almost ran down to the doorway. They stopped, just for a moment, before descending the stairs. Lyla knew they were on the right track. She felt the heat of excitement running through her along with the adrenalin and she couldn't help but rush down into the room. She didn't care what or who was down there, she knew this was where she was supposed to be.

"I can feel her. I can feel her!" Lyla shouted as they entered the room.

It was quite stark, but Lyla didn't care. She saw the sofa. Then she noticed the fish tanks on either side. They were glowing blue-purple. They took her attention for a few moments as she slowly made her way over to sit down. She noticed the pink coral and the beautiful fish swimming so gracefully. The glow was soft and had a warmth about it even though it was shades of blue.

When she sat on the sofa, she saw the mural. She tilted her head in thought. It looked familiar. She knew automatically where it was; Atlantis. She knew it like she knew her own skin. Like she'd been there her whole life. Everything else became unimportant. Everything else melted away from her mind. It was here. Here, where she should be. It was *home*.

Bertha hardly knew what to do. Lyla wouldn't respond, wouldn't say anything to her. She just stared at the mural. She decided to give her a few moments alone. She went over to the stairs and sat quietly. *Would be a shame to get this close, then not make it*, she thought to herself.

Lyla felt like she entered a dream land. Looking at the mural, she swore she saw it move more than once. She just kept looking at it longingly, wondering. She blinked, trying to wake herself up, but to no avail. This picture had a hold on her. Something about it was drawing her to it. It really was a beautiful fresco, like none she'd ever seen before. Suddenly she felt pulled to it. She stood up. She felt herself walking over to it. She couldn't help it and she didn't want to stop. She came right up to it. She could see details now. Such details. There was what looked like a whole village in this scene and she could see every part of it. Like it was really in front of her. But it wasn't photograph real, it was watery, like waves washed over it from time to time. Perplexed by this, Lyla reached her hand out to touch it.

"No! You mustn't!"

Lyla turned, startled. She saw Bertha coming into the room, waving her hands in the air.

"You aren't supposed to touch it!" She yelled as she approached Lyla.

Lyla took a couple steps back from the mural. Bertha looked like she had run a mile. She was breathing heavy, shaking a bit.

"Are you all right, Bertha? What's wrong? Did I do something wrong?" Lyla asked, not even sure what she was doing in front of the mural in the first place.

"Oh, my dear, you just shouldn't be touching art work you know." Bertha tried to sound calm, realizing what she must have looked like to Lyla. "I mean, the artists. They get so touchy, don't they?" Bertha let out a big breath.

"Oh, you're right. I'm sorry. Of course." Lyla finished and turned to sit back down on the couch. "Let's sit down, you look exhausted." She said taking notice of Bertha's shaky condition.

The two of them turned around and Lyla saw it. Just sitting on the couch like it had just been left there; Tillie's bag.

"Oh, my gosh." Lyla said as she ran over to the bag. She picked it up, sat down and went into it to be sure. "I can't believe it. Look! It's hers. It's Tillie's bag. Oh Bertha, we've found her. She must be here somewhere!"

Lyla stood up and looked around.

"Tillie!" She shouted "Tillie, are you here? It's me, Lyles. Tillie, where are you?" A smile shot onto Lyla's face as she hugged the bag close to her. "She's here, right? You can tell me now. It's over, right?" Lyla looked at Bertha, then saw the look on Bertha's face. Suddenly she didn't feel so excited. She sat back down.

"I don't know, dear." Bertha began. "I really don't know. I really can't say, Lyla. I was told you had to find Tillie, not her bag."

"Well, she wouldn't have left this behind, I just know it. She has to be in this building somewhere. We can search here, it shouldn't take long." Lyla said full of hope.

The two ladies stood up. Lyla looked around the room to see if there were any doors or other places to go from here. Perhaps she was in a room just off this room. Lyla couldn't help but feel excited. As her excitement grew, the lights in the tank changed. The glow got brighter and brighter and turned red-orange.

"I knew it." Lyla said almost jumping up and down. "I knew this was where she was."

"Hold this." Bertha said handing her a small disc.

"What is this for?" Lyla asked, still clutching Tillie's bag.

"Put the bag down on the couch and put the disc in your mouth."

Lyla stood there, doing nothing.

"Now, child! Do it!" Bertha placed their bags on the couch as well and threw another disc into her mouth. The furniture disappeared.

Just as Bertha placed the disc into her mouth, Lyla saw the mural swirl furiously. Bertha grabbed her hand and put it to her mouth. Lyla put the disc in her mouth. The tanks broke open and the room filled with water in seconds. Lyla found herself under water in no time, with Bertha holding tight on her arm.

"We need to get to the village." Lyla heard Bertha's voice in her head. "If you need to say something to me, just think it in your mind and I will hear you. Are you all right under water for long?"

Lyla's eyes bulged out for a moment, trying to adjust to these strange circumstances. "Think what I want to say to Bertha? And I don't know...can I stay underwater like my siblings?"

"Well don't worry about it, dear." Bertha's voice came into her head again. "With your genes, you'll do fine. We'll be to the village in just a moment." She finished as she tugged Lyla's arm and they both glided forward.

Lyla held fast to Bertha's arm. She was part scared, part excited, part confused. The village, that was once a picture on the wall, came closer to them. Or rather, they got closer to it. She had so many questions arising in her head and she forgot that Bertha could hear them all.

"Slow down, child, one thing at a time." Bertha said like a scolding parent.

Lyla tried to organize her thoughts better. "Do you hear everything I'm thinking?" she thought to Bertha.

"No, just what you direct to me." Bertha answered.

"How are we moving?" Lyla wasted no time getting to the next question.

"You just think of where you need to be here and off you go." Bertha turned and smiled at her reassuringly.

"Oh, my God." Lyla replied unintentionally.

"Yes, I guess it's quite different from what you are used to. Sometimes I forget what it must be like for you and Liam, having grown up on land with manna." Bertha looked forward again. "Here we are, dear. This is Yitri Village. It's a little outpost really, a small place that a few people live in to keep in touch with Atlantis from this part of the world."

Lyla looked around. Everything was very neat and pretty at the same time. The little homes looked like they were made out of coral and were vibrant shades of pink and orange together. They were tucked into each other, looking a bit crowded, but there were no people around to tell whether it was a busy place. It was as if they grew out of the reef that way. There were plants and flowering things flowing in the water that Lyla had never seen before. Purples, pinks, orange and yellows were floating delicately in what Lyla guessed to be yards. Lyla was in awe.

She noticed now that she indeed was not having trouble being under water for this long. She wondered, *how long they would be here?*

"Well, as long as you want to." Bertha's voice came into her head again. "We are here because you wanted to be."

"Oh, right. I forgot again. Sorry. I'll try to keep my thoughts straight." Lyla apologized. "Wait...what did you say? We're here because of me?"

Bertha nodded her head. "Yes. You thought it so hard, mixed with your excitement to see your sister and here we are." Bertha smiled and gestured toward the middle of the town. "Shall we, to the square?" Bertha placed a necklace around Lyla and then one around herself. "We will wear these for oxygen. Even though you don't have trouble being under water I see, these replace the oxygen into our bodies for us. It takes the oxygen from the water and helps absorb it into your lungs. Put it inside your shirt like this." Bertha tucked hers under her layers of clothes. "So that it lies on your chest."

"Thank you." Lyla thought. Then trying to keep her thoughts undirected at Bertha, she remembered Tillie. She knew she was here somewhere. "What's in the square?"

"Well, it's the center of the village, so I thought it might be a good place to start for you. Do you know where you want to go?"

"No, not really. I didn't expect to be here at all. Is there anyone we could talk to? To see if maybe they've seen her or the boy?"

"We should see people in the square, just around this path."

There were paved paths, even though they weren't technically walking on them, but Lyla found it easier to follow it with her thoughts. Just around the bend they came to an opening paved with different shaped and colored stones. There was a mosaic in the center. It was of a large shell in the middle, then smaller ones all around. It took Lyla's attention immediately.

"It's made of shells and precious stones." Bertha answered her before she even thought of the question.

"Oh," Lyla breathed her thought. Bubbles rose up her face, tickling her nose. She thought that was funny.

There were many people in the square. It made the whole place suddenly come to life.

"Oh, no. My picture, Bertha. I left it back..."

"Don't worry. Remember, think it." Bertha assured her.

"To anyone?"

"Yes. If they're looking at you, they will see what you send them."

Lyla looked around. She thought it was a strange sight for these people to be milling around the square under water like it was something that happened every day. She also thought there were too many people to be asking each one individually. They didn't have time for that. She walked to the large shell in the mosaic. She put both hands up in the air, or water, as the case was, then back down. She closed her eyes. The water swirled like a large breeze around each person in the square. They all stopped what they were doing at looked at Lyla.

"Lyla, what are you doing?" Bertha asked. There were now many other voices asking what was going on as well.

"I've got this, Bertha, don't worry." Lyla decided.

She pictured the boy. He came into her mind clear as day. She pictured Tillie, also as clear. "Has anyone seen either of these people? It is important that I find them." She kept their faces clear in her mind.

The people in the square looked at each other, then gathered to one side. Lyla thought that was strange and wasn't sure if they all heard her, but then there was a collaborative, "Yes."

The crowd parted, out came Tillie and the boy, holding hands. The crowd started to clap and even though they were under water, it made a noise in Lyla's head of cheering and clapping. *Thoughts. Such funny things.*

"Tillie!" Lyla tried to scream out loud, but only more bubbles came out. She thought again very loudly, "Till!" The crowd grabbed their heads and started to disperse. "Sorry." she thought.

She looked back at Tillie, then she zoomed right to her. They hugged. Tillie smiled. She looked wonderful. "Are you all right?"

"Yes, I'm fine. Lyles, I'm so proud of you!" They hugged again.

The boy tugged at Tillie's leg.

"Oh, let me introduce you two." Tillie said. "Lyla, this is Dorn, our cousin."

"Our...cousin?" Lyla replied looking down at Dorn. There he was in the flesh. The beautiful boy she'd had in her mind the last two days. She grabbed him up into a hug too.

"Hello, Dorn. I'm Lyla. I saw you the other day in my mind. It is so good to meet you at last." She hugged him again.

Then she heard in her head, "Hi Lyla. It's nice to meet you too, but you're squishing me."

"Oh, sorry." Lyla let Dorn go.

"So, your name is Dorn? How old are you?" Lyla hugged Tillie close to her again.

"I am six. And that is big." Dorn smiled and looked even more adorable.

"You're right, Dorn, that is big." Tillie said and grabbed him up into a group hug with Lyla. "Oh, Lyles! I'm so happy for you. I knew you would figure it out, I just knew you would. Now we just have to wait for Liam. I imagine he should be along any minute." Tillie said with a big smile.

Lyla hugged her again. "I just am so happy to find you. I hardly could think about it as winning something. I got here first then? I thought for sure Liam would be here already."

"Yes. You are here first. But it wasn't a race." Bertha chimed in. "It doesn't matter who's first. It's the quest that matters."

"Yes, of course." Lyla said, almost forgetting about Bertha and being under water and everything except for Tillie. "Oh, I am so relieved." She let go of her sister and twirled around and around. Tillie clapped and squealed with delight.

"You have one more day for Liam. If he does not show up, we go back without him. We'll see him at the verification with the Council regardless. There you will both present your reports. You may start on yours whenever you wish, Lyla." finished Bertha in her official tone.

"Right," Lyla replied. "Umm...how do you write under water?" Both girls giggled and bubbles came out of their mouths, making them giggle a little bit longer.

"I'll show you to the computer." Tillie lead the way down a path, out of the square.

Tillie spent the next hour or so showing Lyla around. She showed her where they would be spending the night and then to the computer, which Lyla thought didn't look anything like a computer. She said she wanted to start working on her presentation as soon as possible.

Meanwhile, back on dry land, Liam looked like a lion pacing in his den. His furrowed brow added to the appearance. Brian was very quiet and let Liam do most or all of the talking. Most of it was muttering and thinking out loud to himself anyway, so Brian thought it best to stay out of it.

"I don't get it, I just don't get it." mumbled Liam for the third or so dozenth time. "I know I'm missing something. Let's go back to that corner where that building was, you know, that one with all the Christmas lights."

Brian nodded and followed obediently. He pushed his hands deeper into his pockets and his shoulders went up to push his coat collar around his ears. The sun was setting and it was getting cold fast.

Liam knew he had until midnight to find his sister. The two young men lingered around on the corner with the Christmas lights for as long as they could stand, with Liam trying to figure out any type of clue.

Ironically, this corner was right next to the building with the tables outside full of pamphlets. The two of them must have passed by this building at least half a dozen times and didn't even think to look at anything on the tables. Pamphlets didn't hold much interest for Liam.

For some reason though, Liam felt compelled to come to this spot to look, over and over again. He felt this pull and decided that it must be instinct pulling him toward Tillie. He felt it, yet he couldn't tell where to go next. They circled around and around the four cornered intersection for almost an hour, with Brian staying quiet, getting colder. Finally, when Brian couldn't keep his teeth from chattering, he had to say something.

"Liam, couldn't we stop in and get a warm drink at one of the restaurants for just a minute? I'm not trying to distract you, but perhaps frost bite is not the best way to find your sister." He added hesitantly, "If we warm up a bit, maybe that will help you think of something you haven't before?"

Liam stopped in his tracks, turned and looked Brian right in the eyes. Brian shivered uncontrollably from the cold and the look. Liam's look softened a tad just then and he nodded his head curtly.

"You're right, Brian. A warm drink sounds like heaven right now. Let's be quick." He patted Brian on the shoulder and they went into the first restaurant they saw.

"Too bad I can't legally drink yet." Liam turned and said to Brian as they entered the restaurant. There was a bar on one side, a few tables and a line of booths on the other. It was dark, but very warm, with a fireplace in between the bar and the seats. The décor was dark wood and brass. It felt very sophisticated, but comfortable as well. "I feel like I could go for a nice shot of whiskey to really warm my bones. At least, that's what I hear it does." He added quickly.

Brian smiled back as both of them passed by the bar to be seated.

The two men ordered hot chocolate and some appetizers. They figured they might as well eat since they were there. Liam knew it was important to keep hunger at bay if he wanted to think clearly. He didn't realize how cold he was until he sat down in the cozy booth. A chill ran up his spine, making him shiver head to foot.

"Sorry I kept us out there so long, bro." Liam said as he blew hot breath onto his hands. "I just can't give up. Not ever, yah know?" He sipped the water that was already on their table.

"I know, Liam. I'm sorry that the conditions aren't the best for this quest for you. But I suppose that is part of it, isn't it? I mean, quests aren't supposed to be easy." Brian finished with a shiver. He kept his coat on a little bit longer.

The steaming chocolates and appetizers came quickly.

"That's the one great thing I do love about this city." Liam said with a grin. "Service is fast."

Brian took his coat off finally, still feeling a bit chilled. They dug right into the food and nearly inhaled it.

It felt good to Liam to get off the path they were going around on outside for a bit. He felt like he was in a trap and couldn't figure his way out of it. Puzzles were never a strong point with him.

Taking his last slurp of hot cocoa, Liam said, "I never have been very good at problem solving." He smiled, feeling the warmth of the food and drink spread over his body. "I bet Lyla's got it all figured out by now."

"Don't worry, Liam." Brian started, but wasn't even sure what he was trying to say. He just wanted to make Liam feel better. "Things have a way of working themselves out." *Yep. That sounded good.* He held his hands around the warm mug.

Less than half-an-hour passed before Liam waved down the waitress for the check. They left the restaurant just as they were both feeling warmed. Liam with a smile and Brian with concern and extra bundling of his coat.

"I know this time we'll find something." Liam said sounding more positive in his voice than Brian heard all day.

"It's 7:58, Liam." Brian said almost robotically.

"Yes, thanks, bro." Liam replied. "Four hours. I can do this." They walked into the intersection they'd been around all day.

Lyla worked away on the computer for what seemed like hours. Tillie tried to distract her with her questions and knew-found knowledge of underwater life.

"C'mon, Lyles, don't you want to go out for a little while? You have plenty of time to finish that when we get back topside."

"I know, sis." Lyla replied politely, still so happy to be reunited with Tillie. "But I want to get everything down while it's fresh in my head. I shouldn't be much longer."

"You said that an hour ago." Tillie said with disappointment in her voice.

Inside, they were no longer under water. Somehow, unbeknownst to them, they were able to have homes under water. Tillie told Lyla it was like living in a submarine, at least that's what she had been told. The girls didn't question it more than that for now.

Lyla couldn't help but smile as she worked, thinking that things were like this when they were little; Tillie always trying to get Lyla to play with her.

"We only have just over an hour before we have to go back." Tillie almost buzzed.

"Oh. I didn't realize it was already that late." Lyla looked out the window. It was hard to tell the time of day by the lighting outside here. "I thought Liam would be back by now. You don't think he's cutting it close for dramatic effect, do you?"

"Well, that would be like him, wouldn't it?" Tillie thought. "Oh c'mon Lyles, let's go!"

Lyla knew that Tillie would persist until she got her way. "Oh, all right. Show me the sights, sis." She saved her work and the two floated off outside.

The night lights were bright in the city. Liam wasn't really used to such electricity. The brightness bothered him as he tried to think of what to do next. He was almost out of time and he knew that if he didn't find her, he would fail. He wondered if anyone in his mother's family ever failed a quest. He thought surely some must have. *It must happen from time to time, right?* He started to slip into thoughts of not finding Tillie and what would happen afterward.

Minutes slipped out from under him. His hands passed over pamphlets on a table outside. He briefly thought how strange it was to have these out at night, but that maybe it was some city thing. Something else in this big place that he hadn't seen before.

"I'm sorry, Liam," was all Brian could offer. He knew he didn't have to remind him what time it was.

"Well, it happens, right?" Liam shrugged his shoulders and started back to their hotel.

Brian felt awful for him. He hadn't been at this job very long. He still felt bad for any hard times he couldn't help with. He wondered if it would ever get any easier. "I'm sure it does, Liam."

"Yeah," Liam replied. They caught a taxi and headed back to their suite.

In the car, Brian had to finish up his job, hating the timing. "I have to tell you, Liam, you still have to write up your presentation for tomorrow. It is due by 4 pm at the meeting with the Council."

"I know, I know. Do you have to talk about it now?" Liam was tired. It showed in his face and his defeated, round shoulders.

"Yes, I'm afraid I do, Liam and I'm sorry. I can help you in any way..."

"Yes, yes, help. You've been so much of that lately." Liam huffed. He sighed. "Sorry, man. I know you're here to help. I just don't feel like doing anything right now. Let's just get back and get some rest. I promise I'll start it first thing in the morning, kay?" He looked out the window at lights blurring past. "I'm not sure how I'm supposed to present that I failed, but I guess I'll figure it out. I can at least make sure I get that part done right." He finished more to himself.

"We'll go over things in the morning then, sir." Brian stopped. "Sorry."

"Oh, don't worry about it, man, who cares now?" Liam replied dazed and tired. Sleep had been interrupted so many times with dreams of suffocating, of fire. Liam suspected that they meant his failure was imminent and now he was sure of it.

The rest of the ride was silent. The two made it back to their room and to bed without any more conversation. There was nothing more to be said.

"SIR! SIR! GET OUT NOW SIR!" Liam heard through the smoke. Coughing, coughing, he made his way to his feet and stepped slowly forward. He found the doorway and went

through. He followed the smoke, knowing it would lead him out.

"Sir! Follow my voice! We are here sir! Follow us!"

He came to the stairway and went up as fast as he could. Suddenly there was a jarring shake and everything collapsed. Everything went black.

Morning came fast for the Lundgrens. Heather and Cord woke up knowing they would see all of their children today. Heather felt so anxious, she hardly slept at all. She felt like a child on Christmas morning. Even Adrian felt excited and was extra helpful and polite this morning. Being an only child may have been a dream of his once or twice, but in reality, he found he didn't like it at all.

Lyla and Tillie woke up almost at the same time, happy to be going back topside right in time for breakfast. The food selection down here wasn't exactly up to Lyla's standards. A lot of the food was preserved to last a while down there and she found it a bit flavorless.

Liam dragged himself out of bed and over to the alarm clock. He felt like he had been hit by a truck. "Probably a good thing I don't drink." He said to himself.

He met Brian in the kitchen, who had set up a nice breakfast for Liam.

"Wow, Bri, you outdid yourself, man. This is really great, thanks." Liam sat down and loaded a plate right away.

"Well, I am here to help, even though…"

"You definitely have helped me, bro." Liam started. "I won't ever say otherwise again. That was my own defeat talking. After we eat, you can show me how to get this presentation done." He shot his famous smile to Brian.

"Thank you, Liam. We'll start right after breakfast." Brian sat down, setting a pitcher of pomegranate juice in the middle of the table.

28

And the Winner Is...

The morning flew by for everyone. Lyla and Tillie made it back to Chicago without incident. They brought Dorn back with them, excited to introduce him to the rest of the family. Dorn could not stop talking. He talked about everything that came into his head, as only a six year old can do. The girls found him so cute and his chattering made him even more so.

Liam finished up his presentation just in time for lunch. "Glad I got an early start on this, now I can relax until four," he said. He went into the kitchen and offered to make lunch, explaining to Brian how that was his job back home and to thank him for all his help.

Lyla felt a bit anxious about seeing Liam. She knew he didn't come back in time, but she wasn't sure what that meant for him. Did he fail? Even Bertha didn't have a clear cut answer for her. She missed her whole family, but when she thought of Liam, she got butterflies in her stomach.

Four o'clock came finally. The meeting was about to begin. The room was split into two sides in front of one Council panel. There were ten people sitting at the front of a long curved table. Lyla and Liam were directed to each of the two desks opposite the Council. The rest of the Lundgrens were sitting behind each desk; Adrian, Heather and Cord behind Liam. Tillie and Dorn behind Lyla. Brian and Bertha sat with their assigned inductees. It looked and felt like a courtroom. It was very quiet.

Amalia came in and sat next to Tillie and Dorn. Dorn cried out, "Mommy!"

Everyone looked, some smiled and even laughed. Lyla and Liam welcomed the broken tension, even if it was just for a moment.

Amalia took Dorn into her arms. "Sorry I'm late, darling." She said quietly to him, returning the smiles to some of the others. She caught Heather's eye in particular. "Sorry I'm late." She mouthed to Tillie and Lyla. She looked at the Council and nodded, settling into her seat with Dorn.

Tillie looked up at the Council. She saw Ms. Idasdotter and Mr. Dagsson from the dinner that felt oh so long ago on their first night in Chicago. There were also seven others whose faces Tillie did not recognize. Both men and women, some older in appearance, some younger. She wondered, *How old do you have to be to get on the Council?* Then there was Aunt Fi, who looked very serious compared to her usual self, dressing totally unlike her daily colorful flare. Her suit was dark grey and blouse white. Her hair pulled back with no fasteners showing. Her jewelry was minimal, in fact, Tillie had never seen her wear so little since she met her. She was all business. Tillie felt the seriousness of the meeting at once and settled quietly into her chair.

The man in the middle of the Council group stood up. He looked to be a middle aged gentleman who was not very tall and fairly hefty. He was cleanly shaven and had grey hair on his temples. He wore a black robe and an iridescent navy blue hat that all the Lundgren children thought looked ridiculously inappropriate for such an occasion. It looked like a swirled shell was coming off the back of his head. Not really like a hat, but like it was attached to him. They all thought to themselves that this must be some sort of Atlantean thing that maybe they'll ask about later. It went to the back of their minds as soon as he spoke.

"Welcome, ladies, gentlemen and Council members. I am Council Chieftain Naemur Porrson. Today we gather here at Council Seven, Chapter Chicago, to welcome our inductees

Liam and Lyla Lundgren. We will hear their presentations on their quests today." He nodded forward to the two Lundgrens. "We welcome their families as well." He nodded forward once more, to which Heather, Cord and Amalia returned the nod. Then once to the side, to Firouza, who also nodded back once to the Chieftain's small grin.

Suddenly the whole Council broke into applause, along with Heather, Cord and Amalia. Tillie and Adrian didn't hesitate to join them. Lyla felt the blush rise in her cheeks and Liam looked down at the desk.

"We will hear from Ms. Lundgren first today." Naemur finished with a gesture toward Lyla, then sat down.

Lyla already felt heated from the applause. She gave herself a cleansing breath. *This would be a really bad time to start a storm*, she thought. She stood up slowly and looked up at the Council. She noticed Firouza and hoped to get a glimpse of a smile from her, but there was none. Lyla's slight grin disappeared. She approached the curved table. The size of the table made her feel like a small child. She carried something small and black in her hands. She placed it on the table in front of Chieftain Porrson.

"Here is my presentation. I hope it is done correctly. Bertha showed me how to do it." She looked back quickly at Bertha who smiled quickly back. Lyla stood there, not sure what to do next.

"Thank you, my child." Chieftain Porrson said. "You may sit down."

Lyla took a couple steps back, then turned and went back to her seat. She noticed the smiles on her parents' faces and also noticed that Bertha looked pleased as well. She glanced briefly toward Liam, but she couldn't bear to look him in the eye just now. She sat down and waited.

The Chieftain placed the black box in front of himself and grazed his hand over the top. A blue ray of light came out of the device and went up into the air. He pushed the device off the counter and it moved forward. It hovered there while above it a story unfolded. It was Lyla's telling of her quest and what she did and thought throughout the time she was looking for Tillie. Then it showed the time she found her. This was a record of her mind's memory of finding Tillie. Things looked a bit blurry, but through her eyes, everyone could feel the elation of the moment. She felt a bit embarrassed again as she saw how her emotions made the whole scene look. She felt exposed, but justified it by telling herself she was in good company.

The presentation ended and everyone clapped.

"Thank you, Ms. Lundgren. That was most informative." the Chieftain finished, holding out his hand. The device returned to him as if it were called. He held it, waved his hand over it turning it off. He touched a spot on the table in front of him and it slid open. He placed the device inside, hiding the device from sight.

"That was really cool." Tillie whispered to Dorn.

"I like the blue light box." Dorn said a bit louder.

Tillie giggled quietly and decided it best if she kept her thoughts to herself until everything was over.

"Next we will see Mr. Lundgren's presentation. Mr. Lundgren did not make it back to his sister in the time allotted." Naemur sat down.

Liam stood up also with the black box. He felt a twinge of hostility as he made his way forward to place the box on the table.

"No, I didn't find Tillie." He stated almost blankly, "But I hope you find this complete." He didn't wait for a response before he walked back to his seat. He didn't meet any of his family's gazes.

The presentation lit up the room in its blue hue. It was shorter in length than Lyla's, but not any less meaningful. Everyone saw plainly that Liam's intent was just as strong as Lyla's in finding his baby sister. His search was true and just. He was very candid and honest. When it ended, the round of applause was joined by a handful of the Council members standing as well. This pleasantly surprised Liam, but then he thought maybe they were just feeling sorry for him and were sending him off with pity praise.

With the presentations over, the Lundgren inductees were dismissed. All of them gathered for some long awaited greetings with lots of hugs. The Council members exited the room to each side and the rest of them stayed for a few minutes more, gathered in the middle of the room.

Even though everyone was extremely happy to be back together, Lyla and Liam still didn't know for sure if they were successful in their presentations. They were told that they would be notified by the end of the day. Among all the phrases of love and missing, there were also the two of them worrying.

"I do hope I did it right." Lyla said hugging her mother, again.

"Oh, Lyles darling, you did..." Heather reassured her.

"OH, PLEASE!" Liam interrupted with explosive force. "YOU CAN'T TELL ME YOU'RE ACTUALLY WORRIED? YOU'RE 'LITTLE MISS PERFECT', AREN'T YOU?"

"Liam," Cord started, but was cut off.

"NO DAD! C'MON! We all know out of the four of us, it's Lyla that always gets it right! I just can't believe she has the nerve to wonder about it out loud right now! I mean, right now? REALLY, LYLES? Because we all know that I'm the one who FAILED!" Liam took his father's hand from his shoulder, threw it aside and stormed out of the room.

Everyone was so shocked, they were still in their embraces, still and silent, as if someone flash froze them into place. It was Bertha who broke the silence.

"That has yet to be determined." She said as a matter of fact. "These things aren't as black and white as they seem. Someone should tell him that." She looked at Brian. With that, she shook hands with the Lundgrens, hugged Lyla and said her goodbyes.

Brian took Bertha's clue and volunteered to go talk to Liam to explain what Bertha said to them.

"Thank you, Brian. I know you have been most helpful all this time to Liam." Heather said.

Lyla was still so shocked, she couldn't bring herself to say anything.

"Oh, don't worry about, Li," Tillie said.

Lyla just looked at her with big, serious eyes. They started to water, she blinked a tear and ran out. Off in the distance, there was a crack of thunder.

"Oh, dear." Heather said quietly. She looked at Cord.

"All right, all right. Enough of this drama. We're all just over excited with everyone being together again, that's all." Cord explained in his most fatherly way. "This'll blow right over, you'll see." He said to Heather and looked at his remaining two children.

"Oh, I know it will," Tillie stated. "Or I will make it." She looked deadly serious, then broke out in her infamous giggle.

"Give the guy a break, Till," Adrian said as he grabbed his sister into a headlock. "Imagine the stress they've both been under this last week. All because of you." He finished with a light noogie on her head, to which she broke free, still laughing. They both stood there, their arms hanging over each other, happy to be together again.

"Well let's get back to the apartment then, we're waiting for an important call after all." Cord finished and led everyone out of the room.

"Lyla." Heather pleaded. "Should we go look for her?"

"I don't think that'll be necessary, Mom." Tillie said, looking out of the windows.

The black clouds were rolling in fast from the west. All of them left the room and went outside as fast as the elevators would allow.

They got onto the street and went immediately in the direction of the clouds. They could see Lyla just walking down the street, holding her coat up around her face.

"I'll get her." Adrian offered and ran ahead. He caught up to her right away, as she wasn't hurrying, just aimlessly walking. He could see her shoulders shuddering and knew it was because she was crying.

"Lyles." He said as he caught up to her and placed both his hands on her shoulders.

She flew around to look at him. Her eyes were glossy from crying, but also looked glazed, like she didn't really see him.

"Oh, God." Adrian said in a breath. "Lyles. Lyles. Lyla!" He screamed, but she just stood there, tears running down her face, her eyes hazy.

Adrian took her shoulders gently, just as the rest of the family reached them. He looked at his mother pleadingly.

"It's okay, Adrian," she started. "We have to get her off the street."

Just then a crack of lightening and almost immediate thunder sounded making almost all of them jump.

"Quickly, get in." A voice came from the street. They all turned and looked. They saw Firouza in a black limo with the back door open, waiting. Amalia was with her. They hadn't even noticed she had gone. They piled into the car, guiding Lyla.

"I went and got Fi as soon as she left." Amalia explained to Heather.

"Thank you, my dear." Heather replied without even a glance to her sister, but nonetheless sincere.

Heather focused all her attention on Lyla. Everyone else backed away as far as the limo would allow from the two of them, except Adrian, who sat next to them.

"Get there as fast as possible." Firouza said to the driver.

"Get her gloves off and her coat too if you can." Heather instructed Adrian.

He did as he was instructed, trying to sooth Lyla quietly the whole time. He noticed Lyla felt stiff and it made it hard to remove her outer clothing. After what felt like many minutes, he managed. Lightning and thunder came every few seconds. Tillie kept checking the direction of the storm with every boom.

Heather knelt down in front of Lyla. She took both her hands into hers, rubbing them. "Lyla," she said sternly, but not angrily. "Lyla, it is time to calm." She said just as sternly, as if she were disciplining one of her children. They all knew the voice too well.

Tears streamed down Lyla's face. There was no response.

"Róa, Lyla, róa." Heather said sternly at first and ended more gently. She kept her voice on the loud side, as she knew Lyla wouldn't hear quiet now. The trance had her full attention and Heather had to break it. She rubbed Lyla's arms, pushing her sleeves up to touch her skin. "Það er kominn tími til að róa," she chanted, all the while, rubbing Lyla's arms.

Heather's sisters began to chant with her. "Róa. Róa. Róa." Quietly, but it filled the car with humming.

Tillie looked at her aunts and was going to join in, but a look from her father told her not to do it. He took her hand and held it to his lap to reassure her. She sat quietly and watched, but thought the chant in her head.

Adrian wasn't sure what to do, but he kept placing hands on Lyla so she would feel his touch. On her arms with his mother, on her face, brushing her hair back. But he remained quiet and let his mother's words permeate the air.

Then there was the biggest crack of thunder yet, followed by sunlight. It was a most strange sensation. They looked out the window and the black clouds dispersed from the sun outward. They disappeared like smoke wisps into the air.

Heather didn't take her eyes off her daughter. She did not stop chanting. She kept her eyes on Lyla's. As soon as the sun shone, Lyla's eyes cleared and she fell back into the seat. She did not blink, but sat still. Too still.

"Oh, my God. Oh, my God." Adrian said with some faster rubs on Lyla's arms, nearly pushing his mother aside.

"Lyla. Oh, my God! Are you there? Are you all right? Lyla!" He was frantic.

"It's okay, Adrian." Heather said, grabbing his hands, placing them gently on his lap. "Give her a minute. She's all right." She looked back to Lyla and kept rubbing, more gently now. Her chant back to simply, "Róa". Amalia and Firouza trailed off their chant and there was a collective sigh of relief.

Lyla blinked. She blinked and blinked until her eyes fluttered for a moment. Her body went limp and her eyes closed. Heather touched Adrian's hands again, stopping their surge forward. She placed herself on the seat next to Lyla and held her in her arms.

Soothing her head and holding her, Heather said, "It's over now. It's all over."

It felt like days had passed rather than hours, so much happened in that small space of time. Everyone was back at the apartment and Lyla was tucked into bed, getting the rest she needed after her ordeal. Brian and Liam returned shortly after everyone else and were filled in as to what happened. Amalia and Dorn stayed to wait with their newly met relatives.

"I know you think you failed," Amalia said to Liam, "But these things aren't so cut and dry as that."

"I know. I feel like such an idiot." Liam got mad at himself all over again as he said it. "I knew what would happen if Lyles got upset and look what I'd gone and done. *Idiot.*"

"It's understandable that there would be emotion at a time such as you had Liam." Amalia began. "Sharing your emotions earlier with the whole room for your presentation makes it even harder to contain the ones we currently have. It's no wonder you exploded. You've never had that kind of feeling going through you before."

"Yeah, thanks." Liam replied. "I know all that stuff felt weird, I just didn't know I would react to it in such a way. I've never gotten that angry at anyone in my family before. I hope I never do it again."

Amalia patted Liam on his knee. "Oh, that was nothing, dear." She said with a smile in her voice. "You should have seen Anwar back in his younger days!"

"Anwar?" Liam questioned. *Was this another relative*?

"Oh, yes, you know, your uncle?" She looked at Liam as inquisitively as he was looking at her. "I keep forgetting you don't know. Sorry. But yes, your Uncle Anwar. He's the youngest in the family and also used to have the hottest temper." She laughed. "Of course I can laugh about it now..." she trailed off.

"Laugh about what?" Firouza came into the room with a tray of snacks and drinks, sitting next to Liam on the sofa. "Lord knows we could all use a good laugh."

Amalia and Firouza continued telling Liam stories about their childhood, particularly about Anwar and his temper.

Meanwhile, Tillie kept Dorn busy after their wonderful dinner. He was tired and a little rambunctious but didn't want to admit it. Tillie was happy to have the distraction of keeping him occupied while she waited.

An hour, maybe two passed. Lyla still slept and Dorn joined her in slumber on Tillie's bed. Everyone else was too jumpy waiting for the phone to ring.

So, everyone actually jumped a bit when the doorbell rang. It was 9:37pm. Firouza and Amalia looked up. Both turned to Heather.

"It couldn't be." Heather said, standing up.

"Well, I beg to differ. It most definitely is." Firouza finished and went over to the door. "Who else could it be?" She opened the door.

Chieftain Porrson stood at the doorway with a smile. "Good evening, Firouza, may I come in?"

"Of course, Naemur, of course." Firouza gestured him into the apartment. They both had smiles stuck on their faces. He still wore the funny blue hat. Tillie sniggered to herself and it reminded her to ask about it later.

"I'm sorry to be calling on you all so late without notice." Naemur began, "But," he snorted, "You knew someone would be getting in touch with you tonight, didn't you?" He chuckled. Firouza took his coat and he went into the living room. He kept his hat on and Tillie found it difficult not to laugh.

Naemur knew he'd have the room's attention, so he began right away. "Good evening everyone. I thought I would make a personal call myself to inform you, Lyla and Liam Lundgren, of the results of your presentations." He looked around the room, met Liam's eyes and kept looking for Lyla's. The question was plain on his face and was answered by Heather.

"She's not awake right now." Heather eased his questioning face.

"Oh, yes, yes, of course. We heard all about Lyla's storm this afternoon, didn't we? Well, we lived it actually. What a doozie." he chuckled again. "Still asleep then? Poor thing. She'll be right as rain in the morning." He clapped his hands together once, bringing everyone to attention.

"Well it pleases me greatly to be able to inform you, Liam Lundgren, that you are to be inducted into Atlantis as soon as possible." He announced with a big smile, looking like a child who was proud of his school work.

Everyone clapped and gathered around Liam, patting and hugging him.

"Yes, we were very impressed with your presentation. Even though you thought you failed because you did not find your sister, your presentation went on to prove that you learned from your quest. You have what it takes to become an official Atlantean." He shook Liam's hand heartily.

"Thank you, sir! Thank you." was all Liam could manage to get out. He was shocked and so relieved all at once.

As everyone patted and congratulated Liam, the Chieftain went on with his speech. "As for Lyla Lundgren," he started most officially, "We congratulate her on finding her sister in the time given to her." He paused dramatically even though he knew everyone knew what was coming next. "It is with pleasure, times two, that I also announce that Lyla Lundgren will also be inducted into Atlantis as soon as possible."

Everyone clapped again and smiles were rampant.

"You, of course, can tell her when she is ready to wake up, I assume?" Naemur finished.

"Yes, of course." Heather said as she shook his hand. "And thank you so very much for coming over here to tell us such wonderful news in person."

"Well yes, my dear." Naemur replied. "It's not every day I get to announce two inductees from the same family at the same time. It's been a wonderful day. Now I really must be going. The wife awaits me at home. Firouza and all." He bowed and Firouza walked him to the door.

He was gone just like that.

"Well, isn't this wonderful?" Heather asked her family. She was so thrilled, she wanted to hug them, all at once, in that moment.

"It most certainly is!" Firouza said with a twirl of her caftan, coming in from the foyer. She looked flushed with excitement. "When do we get to tell Lyla? Do you think she'll wake up soon?"

"I'll tell her." Liam said darkly. He looked at all of them. "I owe it to her."

Cord patted him on the shoulder. "Alright, son." he said, "You tell her. That is a great idea."

29

Red Light Green Light

"Darn." Tillie said to herself. Despite liking to be the bearer of news, she knew it was a good idea for Liam to work things out with Lyla. Then she remembered the funny blue hat. "Hey." Everyone turned to look at her. "Why does the Chieftain wear that funny blue hat everywhere?"

Heather, Amalia and Firouza looked at each other and started to laugh. Tillie's face crinkled. Her siblings also looked to the ladies for an answer.

"I was wondering the same thing." Adrian added. "Why is that funny?"

"Same here." Liam said.

The women composed themselves. Firouza, of course, was the first one to answer. "Well my darlings, Chieftain Porrson is a *Leahzoon.*"

"A what?" Adrian asked.

"A *Leahzoon.*" Amalia repeated.

"A liaison?" Tillie thought she heard that right.

"No sweeties," Heather answered, "A *Leeaaahhhzooooon.*" She stretched the word out to differentiate it from liaison. "They're a people from Atlantis." She looked to her sisters for further explanation.

"Well yes, they are a people, a tribe, a nationality, if you will." Amalia added.

"Yes, they've been in Atlantis since the beginning." Firouza said. "Chieftain Porrson is from one of the original Atlantean tribes."

"How many tribes are there?" Tillie asked, always happy to learn anything she could about Atlantis.

"Seven originally, but there are only four still around today." Liam answered, surprising his siblings. "What? I had to study for the test, remember?" He shrugged his shoulders.

"So, why does he wear that thing on his head?" Tillie was still confused.

"That 'thing' is not a 'thing on his head,'" Firouza started, "It is part of him."

Adrian and Tillie both looked at each other. Then it came to Liam.

"Oh. Oh, the *Leahzoons*. Oh, yeah. I totally didn't realize that's what they would look like." He chuckled.

His siblings didn't share in the same apparent joke.

"So let me get this straight," Adrian started, always having to get it right. "That crazy blue shell thing on his head comes from...his head?"

"Well not exactly," Amalia started.

"He more or less comes from it." Heather finished.

More strange looks were exchanged.

"Weird." Tillie said quietly. It made her so curious about Atlantis. She could hardly wait until she was called for induction.

"Yes well, there aren't many of them left in Atlantis, you see." Firouza tried to put their confusion at ease. "Mr. Porrson's family tree goes back as far as Atlantean history. So naturally he would have a place of power in the Council today."

They continued talking a little while longer about the tribes and what the shells were. It satisfied the Lundgren children for the time being.

It was late by the time the conversation about Leahzoons ended. Amalia took Dorn home and everyone drifted to bed. It didn't look like Lyla was going to wake up that night. But they all took comfort in the Chieftain saying she'd be right as rain in the morning.

"Grab my hand sir!" Liam heard the voice say, but he couldn't see through the smoke. "Just reach!"

Liam felt through the smoke like a blind man looking for a helping hand. He felt a hand grab his and was pulled hard.

THUD.

"Wha? Where am I?" Liam opened his eyes to see the floor. He rubbed his head and looked around. He saw Lyla standing there looking at him quietly in the dark.

"Oh, Jesus, Lyles. What are you doing? Did I wake you up? Sorry." Liam stood up. He stepped closer to her, but she stepped back. He stopped.

"Sorry, Liam." Lyla said in a broken voice and half whisper. "I thought I heard you say something. I was passing by your room on my way to the bathroom and I thought you were talking to me. I'll go now. Sorry to disturb you." She turned around to leave.

"Don't go," he pleaded. "I'm sorry." He said dejectedly. He sat back on the bed.

Lyla stepped into the room.

"Shut the door, will you? We have to talk." Liam instructed his sister gently. He turned on the lamp at the bedside table.

Lyla did as she was asked. She came over to the bed and Liam moved as far to the corner as he could to give her plenty of room to sit down. He didn't blame her for feeling the way she did right now.

"I am so, so very, very sorry, Lyles." Liam began. He dropped his head for a moment, but then looked back up, into her eyes, so she would know that his apology was heartfelt. She looked back at him so tenderly, he felt another pang of guilt for what he had done.

"I don't think I can ever find the words to apologize to you enough for what I did." He said. "There is no excuse for my behavior, for the things I said. I know I can never take them back, but I want you to know," he took one of her hands as softly as he could. "I will do my best to make this up to you. I will never let myself forget what I did and I will make it

310

up to you. I love you, Lyles." He said choking up. "I love this whole family." He broke off.

"Of course you do." Lyla replied softly, no broken voice this time. "We all have a ton of love for each other and we all know it Li." She explained. "And the two of us showed that today, in living blue hues." She said with a soft smile. The light on her face was so pretty. She looked soft and kinder than ever. "Everyone felt the love we both have for Tillie. They *felt* it, they didn't just see it, or hear it explained. The beauty of those boxes was that it captured things we could never have written down on paper or on a regular computer."

"I know. Those things are amazing." Liam added quietly.

"Exactly. They are amazing. Just like Atlantis. Just like us. We are a part of this world now, whether we get inducted or not. Our lives are changed forever."

Liam looked at Lyla and squeezed her hand. "We are inducted. Both of us." He couldn't help but smile at her with those words.

"Are you sure? How do you know? Oh, crap. They called while I was sleeping, didn't they?" Lyla punched the mattress with the strength of a small child.

Liam smiled at her, almost laughing. She smiled back. He continued to explain what happened, how they found out about their inductions. Even Chieftain Porrson's strange hat, even though Lyla figured it out by the end of the presentations.

By the time they were done talking, the sun was coming up and shining into the cracks of the curtains in bedroom window. The two were unaware that they were up most of the night, but enjoyed all of it immensely. They hadn't talked with each other since they got back to Chicago, so they caught up on everything.

Liam shared his dreams with Lyla to see what she thought of them. She wasn't sure, but she thought Liam should talk to their parents about it for certain.

"I know, I know. I will when we get through all this induction stuff." He replied.

"Well, we are through it now, aren't we?" Lyla stated the obvious.

"Right. I need to get used to that." Liam answered shyly. He noticed the sun coming through the curtains. "Oh, crap, Lyles, I've kept you up all night. I hope you get some time to sleep more. I don't know what the plans are for today. If we have to get going right to Atlantis, or what?"

"Oh, I'm fine." Lyla said happily. "I don't care what we do today. We could climb mountains and I think I'd be great." She looked around. "I am kind of hungry though. Should we go eat?" She smiled mischievously.

Liam laughed. It felt good to be back on right terms again with Lyla. They were both so relieved and enjoyed each other's company through the night, they continued right on into breakfast in their aunt and uncle's kitchen.

When they got to the kitchen, they saw they weren't the only ones awake. Adrian was raiding the fridge and Tillie sat at the table with some juice and a magazine.

Lyla said, a bit surprised. "I thought we were the first ones up."

"Yeah, no." Tillie looked up from the latest winter fashions. "Who could sleep with all that giggling going on next door?" She sipped her juice and went back to her magazine.

"Us?" Liam tried to look innocent.

"Umm who else was giggling at five o'clock this morning?" Adrian added.

"Sorry guys." Lyla said, smiling. She couldn't help herself. Here they were, the four of them, together in one room.

"What's the eats?" Liam leaned over Adrian's shoulder, looking in the fridge.

"Have a seat. I've got us some bagels toasting and I'm whipping up some eggs. I already added some for you two. I knew you'd be out when you smelled the bagels." Adrian pushed Liam away from the fridge and shut the door.

"Hey, nice, thanks." Liam replied genuinely. He sat at the table between the girls.

There were glasses and a pitcher of juice waiting for them.

"Thanks, guys." Lyla said pouring herself a glass.

"Don't thank me," Tillie claimed. "Adrian's idea all the way."

"Yeah well, you know, a welcome-home-sibs kind of thing." Adrian answered with a slight blush.

"It's good to be back together." Lyla said plainly.

Everyone else agreed quietly.

"So, what's next?" Tillie asked.

"What do you mean?" Lyla asked in reply.

"Well, are we going to Atlantis today or what?" Tillie got up from her seat. She got plates out of the cupboard and handed them to Adrian.

"Dunno," Liam replied. He gulped down almost a whole glass of juice.

"We don't know." Lyla confirmed. "We're still trying to get used to the idea that we've been accepted." A giggle escaped her lips. She sounded a bit like Tillie.

Adrian placed full plates at the table. The four children sat down to enjoy their first meal together in a long time.

"I know, holy cow!" Tillie's excitement boiled over with her sister's. "I mean, we're all going to go to Atlantis. I'm super happy for you guys, of course." She ran on, "But we all get to go. It's so fantastic! I can't wait to see the main city. The pictures are so fabulous, I can hardly imagine what it will be like in person."

"Yeah, it is pretty cool, I have to say. Even I'm pretty stoked about it." Adrian said as he sat down.

The four of them enjoyed their meal, talking, laughing and sharing. Putting the past few weeks behind them and wondering about the next few. They were just finishing up, taking plates to the sink when others showed up in the kitchen.

Cord came in yawning. "Ah, morning kids." he said cheerfully, but tired. "See you've eaten then?"

"Yeah, we're done in here." Adrian said. "Can we get you guys anything?"

"Oh, no, dear." Heather followed in behind Cord. "You all go enjoy yourselves, we can get our own breakfast. Good morning, kids." She smiled brightly at her wonderful family all together in the kitchen.

"Morning, Mom." All four kids said collectively.

Lyla hugged Heather and Liam kissed her on the cheek.

"That's the stuff I'm talkin' about." She said, hugging them back, one in each arm. "You feeling well, Lyla dear?" She pushed Lyla's hair back out of her face.

"Yes, I feel much better, thanks Mom." Lyla smiled.

"So, what's happening from here?" Liam asked. "When do we go to Atlantis?"

"Well, the instructions were to go as soon as possible, so that's what it will be." Cord answered him.

"Holy jeez." Tillie broke in, "Does that mean we are leaving today?"

"Well now, we can't just up and leave Sigrun, can we?" Heather asked, bringing her logic to the conversation. "We've been making arrangements for Sigrun to, well, run itself, since we came to Chicago." She explained.

"That's right," Cord added. "Anna and Marcus have been getting things under control for the past few weeks. Hiring some new hands and the like. Training and making sure they can trust the new help."

"See kids, when we go to Atlantis, even though it is just as visitors for the induction, we are going to be there for a while." Heather tried to squelch the confused looks on her children's faces. "Just getting used to an underwater world is going to take a little time. We all have to be used to the conditions and ways before the ceremony."

"Well like what conditions?" Tillie asked.

"And how long is 'a while'?" Adrian added.

"Well, I can see it's to be a morning of questions." Cord said with a chortle.

"You could say that again." Tillie said seriously. She was tired of not knowing things about Atlantis. Now that they were ready to answer her questions, she had a bunch lined up for them.

The Lundgrens sat around the kitchen table and chatted. It sounded like a murmur or a drum rolling. They were talking in low tones and every so often an exclamation would spout out, usually from Tillie.

The morning became afternoon. Tillie still wondered how long it would take to actually go to Atlantis. The Lundgrens found they hadn't moved much except taking their conversation into the living room to make room in the kitchen for the others as they came in search of sustenance.

Tillie felt satisfied with most of her questions being answered and the rest of them had ones she hadn't even thought of, for which she was glad. They all received a lot of information on how they would travel to Atlantis, where they would be staying and how things were done in an underwater city. Some explanations were unexpected.

"Well kids, an underwater city is not...well...underwater." Heather began.

"What do you mean, 'not underwater'?" Adrian demanded. "Aren't we going to get to float around like Tillie and Lyla did with those thingies?" He gestured to his chest, referring to the breathers.

Tillie giggled. Adrian gave her a serious look. She cut herself short.

"No, Adrian. That was just an outpost. It wasn't a city. It's just occupied by a few people for short periods of time." Heather looked at her son's disappointment sympathetically. "But we will be passing through the outpost in the kula vessel." She added, hoping that would cheer him up.

"Aw, man," Adrian slurred out. "So I don't get to use a lung thingy." He shrugged his shoulders. "Well, maybe when my induction comes along, I'll get to use one then, huh?" He made a silly face and continued listening.

Heather and Cord continued to explain things to their children about Atlantis. They told them it was about the size of Chicago or even New York, so to expect a great number of people living there.

"Living in Atlantis." Tillie imagined. "How dreamy is that?"

"It's quite crowded, actually." Cord popped her imaginary bubble. She shook her head a bit and looked at him. "Well, it's a city, so it's quite populated. Not like where you kids have grown up. It's part of the reason we raised you where we did."

"That's right." Heather agreed, "We made the decision to raise you somewhere less crowded, but by the water, so you would grow by it and love it and develop your skills in it, without the crowds. We knew we'd be taking you there some day and we wanted you to experience a different kind of living. A manna life first."

"To give you a better perspective on the peoples of our planet." Cord finished.

"We chose to have you raised as manna and then become Atlantean, if that were to be your destiny." Heather summed up. She looked at Adrian and Tillie, encouragingly.

The afternoon quickly turned to dusk and the Lundgren children noticed that Firouza and her family were very scarce.

"Where's Firouza and everybody?" Tillie finally asked.

"They thought it best to give us some family time today." Cord replied. "They'll be back after dinner."

"That was nice of them, since this is their home." Lyla said.

"They're pretty awesome. Nice to be related to awesome people." Adrian spouted his opinion to everyone's surprise. "What? That's right, I like 'em." He laughed and everyone else joined him.

The phone rang. Heather answered it, thinking it would be her sister asking if it was alright that they return. It was Anna. "Cord. It's Anna, for you." She sounded serious. Cord took the phone and went into the kitchen.

"Anna sounded upset. She wouldn't even tell me what was wrong." Heather said more to herself, but not out of earshot of her children.

"Oh, I hope everything's all right." Tillie said, sounding very concerned. "I would hate for this to get in the way of us getting to Atlantis."

"Tillie." Lyla almost yelled. "Our first and foremost concern is for Sigrun to be all right and that includes making sure everything is okay with Anna."

"I know. I didn't mean I didn't care about Anna. Of course I do." Tillie tried to explain herself.

"Let's just wait and see what this is all about." Liam said with the voice of reason.

"Yes. It could be anything. Let's just see what your father says." Heather finished.

Many silent minutes passed. They felt eternal and all the while Cord was very quiet in the kitchen. Lyla felt the silence was a good sign. Her dad was known for his outbursts, so if there were none, then perhaps the situation wasn't as bad as mom thought.

Cord walked into the room. "Well, that's timing for you." He said. "I'll need to head back home in the morning. Anna needs help with the training."

"Why? What happened? She wouldn't even say anything to me." Heather was in a near tizzy.

"Well, she said she didn't want to upset you. You visiting with your family and all. You know how Anna is with family. Anyway, she thought it best to tell me what's going on because she thinks of me as the boss."

"You are the boss, Dad." Adrian said.

"Well yes, I know. So, I'll be leaving in the morning. You might as well all stay here. There's no sense in everyone missing out on family time because of this little problem."

"What is the problem?" Heather stood, she couldn't stand any more suspense.

"Right. Well, Marcus broke his leg." Cord started, but was interrupted immediately.

"What?"

"Oh, dear."

"What happened?"

Cord elucidated, "Well, he was on a hike with some friends. They took a short winter trail that he'd been on many times. Apparently this time though, he lost his footing and fell."

"The fall broke his leg? Does he have weak bones or something?" Adrian couldn't contain his questions.

"Well no. I guess the trail was icy that day, from a slight thaw earlier in the week." They all nodded their heads.

"When he fell, he slid down the trail and then off the edge." Cord continued.

"Oh, my Lord." Heather breathed.

"He fell 'bout twelve feet Anna said. That's what broke his leg. Luckily, he was with friends who were able to get him help immediately. But needless to say, he's hospital bound for the next month or so." He paused. "Anna is broken up about it and she just needs one of us to go back to help her finish the training. I shouldn't be more than a week."

"A week!" Another exclamation from Tillie. "What are we gonna do around here for a week?"

"Jeez, Till." Adrian gave her a look of mild disgust. "Could you be any less sympathetic? Marcus broke his leg on a bad fall. It could have been worse. A lot worse. Don't you have anything better to say than worrying about what you'll do here in Chicago for a week?"

"Aw, crap, my mouth always speaks before my brain, you guys know that." Tillie answered, feeling bashful. "I'm really sorry about Marcus too. He's going to recover though, right?"

"Yes, he's doing well. He's been in the hospital for about a week now. He's in traction and the doctors say that will last four to six weeks. So hopefully he'll have lots of visitors and they will keep his spirits up." Cord looked fidgety, like he was looking for something in his pockets. "What did I do with my wallet?" He stumbled off to the bedroom to look for it.

"I'm going to have flowers sent right away." Heather said and went into the kitchen.

The Lundgren children sat quiet for a moment.

"We don't seem to get a break anymore, you notice?" Adrian observed. "Ever since all this Atlantis stuff came about, it seems like our lives are one crazy thing after another."

The four of them settled into furniture and reminisced for a little while. The rest of the night was spent making travel plans for Cord, enjoying dinner with each other a first and last time for a while and just spending time together. Firouza and her family returned shortly after dinner. They filled her in on Cord's new travel agenda and of course she had just the right thing to say.

"Oh, darlings! I'm so sorry. That is a travesty for sure. And you all just got back together." She looked at all of them with a pout. "But don't you worry, my pets. I will take great care of you whilst your papa is away. We'll go sight-seeing, both in Chicago and under water."

"Will I get to use one of those breathing thingies?" Adrian sounded hopeful.

"Absolutely. If that is what you wish, we shall make it happen. Don't worry children, Aunt Fi is here." She swirled about them kissing the boys on their heads and hugging the girls.

They all smiled back at her, Tillie nearly giggling, as she just loved Firouza's zest for life.

The week flew just as Aunt Fi promised. They went to so many places, both above and below the sea, that they couldn't keep track of them. Even Adrian worked diligently on his journaling to make sure he got all the places correct. Aunt

Fi had given him an upgrade to his paper journal; an electronic one.

"It has fingerprint recognition, darling. You can write whatever you want in here and no one can see it without your permission."

Cord checked in every day with Heather. The training was going well. He was happy with the people Anna and Marcus hired. He commended both of them for being such wonderful employees and friends. He got to visit Marcus twice during the week and said he was in very good spirits. His room was hardly ever empty due to all the female visitors he had. Heather was relieved to hear that and not at all surprised. Cord told them he expected to be back within the next two to three days. They were all excited to get on with their journey.

Cord's flight arrived on time. The whole family met him there with lots of hugs and squeals of delight. He brought back a special gift for the Zohros as a thank you for the extended hospitality; a wind chime made by a local artisan, along with some handmade soaps, also from a local shop. A basket of jams and sauces from their state as well. It was a small gesture of thanks for the huge favor they had given them by opening their home for such an extended period of time.

Plans were set to go to Atlantis. Heather arranged for the family to travel via the kula vessel as soon as they knew when Cord would return. It would pick them up the next afternoon from New York City. Their flight was set to leave first thing in the morning.

As they arrived back at the apartment, Tillie thought out loud, "It's funny. I wish we had time to spend sight-seeing in New York, but at the same time who cares? We finally get to go to Atlantis." She couldn't contain her laughter and was joined by her siblings. Excitement floated around them all.

"Oh, darlings!" Firouza fluttered around her nieces and nephews. "How we're all going to miss you so. Aren't we, Metrón?"

Metrón nodded and announced, "Yes, yes. We have enjoyed having you all in our home. It has been truly wonderful getting to know you all. Thank you." He said with a bow.

Cord and Heather presented their thank you gifts to the Zohros. Heather hugged her sister tight.

"Thank you so much. This has been a great gift to our family. You don't know the importance of our children getting to know you all." She hugged Metrón.

"Oh, my darlings." Firouza exclaimed, "It has been such a great pleasure meeting your wonderful family and watching your two eldest be inducted. We so look forward to seeing you all at the ceremony."

The rest of the evening was planned by Firouza and Metrón. They insisted on taking the Lundgrens out to dinner at their favorite Chicago restaurant as a goodbye. Kallias, Chloe and Lucrezia were able to join them, as well as Haseena, Amalia and Dorn. It was a wonderful way to end their time in Chicago.

The next morning came and all of the Lundgrens were up and packed first thing. Firouza's cook came and made a spectacular breakfast for everyone. At Heather's insistence that she did too much for them, Firouza simply replied, "Too much is never enough, my loves!"

The Lundgrens made their goodbyes and piled into a limousine one last time. It was a cold, crisp morning, but the sun made its way up the sky, which gave a wonderful yellow glow on the top of the city.

They reached the airport with time to spare. The girls went into a shop to pick out some magazines while the boys checked the luggage. Everyone enjoyed just being back together, as it felt like it had been so long since they'd been a family, just them.

Tillie picked out some nail polish at the shop in the airport and offered to paint Lyla's and Heather's nails. They had the time, so they let her dote on them.

Finally, it came time to board. The flight was smooth and fast. Tillie couldn't help but comment how remarkable she thought flying was. Adrian of course, couldn't help tease her a bit for it. He really did miss his sister, but that never stopped him from teasing her before.

New York felt even colder than Chicago, as if that were possible. The winds were strong by the airport. A small bus picked up the Lundgrens there, arranged by the Council and took them to the port, where they would board the kula vessel.

Going through Brooklyn and Manhattan, the bus driver gave them a bit of a city tour. They got to see some things Tillie hoped to see, then went on, to the Port Authority.

"Isn't it kind of a busy time of day for us to be traveling...this way?" Lyla couldn't help but be curious. Even though they already discussed how this works, she felt she had to see it to fully understand it.

"Well, yes it is, but that is the idea." Heather explained again, gently as usual. "You see, the more people who are around, the less we'll be noticed. It's hard to explain, but you'll see very soon." She smiled at Lyla and that satisfied her for the time being.

The bus arrived at the Port Authority with no time to spare. There were no major goodbyes, those being said and done back in Chicago, so the bus pulled away and they made their way to Pier 61. It wasn't far. When they arrived, they saw a small tugboat and nothing else.

"Is this right?" Adrian asked.

"Yep, this is the one." Heather answered smiling.

"All aboard!" Cord shouted and they scurried onto the tugboat.

The driver greeted them and helped with their luggage. "Sorry for the nasty bit of weather," he added.

"Oh, we're from Maine, so we're used to it." Tillie said with her smile so bright, it could be heard in her voice.

The tugboat made its way out to open waters. They went past the Statue of Liberty, where they all stared and stared until she was so small, they couldn't make it out anymore. The wind was cold on all their faces, but they didn't care, they were so excited to be on their journey.

"Not much longer now!" The driver shouted out to them. They all huddled together, trying to keep warm.

A few minutes later a bright, green light appeared to come from underneath the boat. It surrounded the boat and the driver cut the engine. The Lundgren children felt an all too familiar feeling in their guts. This was the same green light they saw all those months ago. Now they got to see it up close and in person. Everyone scrambled to get their things together and ready. Cord and Heather stood on the starboard side. The green light made its way to the same side and bubbles rose from the water. Big bubbles and foam made their way to the surface.

Suddenly a glass-like dome popped out of the water and the green light disappeared. It looked big, for a bubble, but small for a vessel.

"Don't worry kids, we'll be fine!" Cord shouted out to them.

They stood up with their luggage and waited. Adrian and Tillie looked around to make sure there were no people or boats around to see what was happening. It looked clear; an empty winter sea. The top of the bubble opened and made a hissing sound, steam released.

"Okay, kids!" Heather shouted.

They climbed into the bubble, feeling a bit crowded with their bags. They waved to the driver of the tugboat as he drove off, back to the city pier. Tillie and Adrian looked completely frightened.

The lid closed. It made the same hissing noise.

Heather said, "Take your seats, kids."

Bits of the floor opened up and the children saw Cord and Heather placing their bags into the openings, so they did the same. The floor closed. There was a rumbling noise.

Cord repeated, "Take your seats and buckle up."

The children looked around and seats popped up from the floor, almost directly underneath each of them. They sat down, along with Heather and Cord and buckled the seat belts.

As they did so, they noticed they were going underwater. The green light came back, brighter than any of them had seen it yet. There was a jerky movement, the rumbling turned into a buzzing sound. There was a swooshing noise and they were off.

"Here we go!"

The Bandamann Saga

Thank you for reading!

*Please take a moment and give Sigrun a
rating/review on Amazon and/or Goodreads!*

*For more about Sigrun and the Lundgrens, please
visit them on the website:
http://ddzines007.wix.com/sigrun.*